# PRAISE FOR
# +HORROR LIBRARY+

"Excellent stories of the highest caliber."

*—Dread Central*

"Impactful tales that throw the rules of both reality and genre fiction out the window."

*—Fearnet (Chiller TV)*

"Uniformly well-crafted and original."

*—Rue Morgue Magazine*

"A range of material that produces extraordinary results."

*—British Fantasy Society*

" … A mixture of surprising treats: Stark, livid, engaging."

*—SFRreader.com*

"You can't read just one."

*—Monster Librarian*

"…perfect representation of how truly horrifying and intelligent horror fiction can be."

*—Horror Underground*

"*+Horror Library+* is a welcome addition to horror fans' collections."

*—Dark Scribe Magazine*

"+*Horror Library*+ sets a standard by which modern horror collections are measured."

*—Shroud Magazine*

"A diabolical delight."

*—Hellnotes*

"A snapshot of modern literary horror fiction . . . imbued with literary energy and purpose."

*—Daily Dead*

"Nicely varied all-original stories."

*—Baen Books*

"The stories that make horror what it really is."

*—HorrorNews.net*

"Keeping the traditional horror genre alive and well."

*—Bookgasm*

"Outstanding . . . extremely dark stories."

*—Horror World*

"Well-deserved repute for literate horror penned by talented authors."

*—The Haunted Reading Room*

# VOLUME 4

**Fiction Written by Eric J. Guignard**

*Doorways to the Deadeye* (JournalStone, 2019)

*Last Case at a Baggage Auction* (Harper Day Books, 2020)

*That Which Grows Wild: 16 Tales of Dark Fiction* (Cemetery Dance Publications, 2018)

**Anthologies Edited by Eric J. Guignard**

*After Death...* (Dark Moon Books, 2013)

*Dark Tales of Lost Civilizations* (Dark Moon Books, 2012)

*The Five Senses of Horror* (Dark Moon Books, 2018)

*+Horror Library+ Volume 6* (Cutting Block Books/ Dark Moon Books, 2017)

*+Horror Library+ Volume 7* (Dark Moon Books, 2022)

*Pop the Clutch: Thrilling Tales of Rockabilly, Monsters, and Hot Rod Horror* (Dark Moon Books, 2019)

*Professor Charlatan Bardot's Travel Anthology to the Most (Fictional) Haunted Buildings in the Weird, Wild World* (Dark Moon Books, 2022)

*A World of Horror* (Dark Moon Books, 2018)

**Exploring Dark Short Fiction (A Primer Series) Created by Eric J. Guignard**

*#1: A Primer to Steve Rasnic Tem* (Dark Moon Books, 2017)

*#2: A Primer to Kaaron Warren* (Dark Moon Books, 2018)

*#3: A Primer to Nisi Shawl* (Dark Moon Books, 2018)

*#4: A Primer to Jeffrey Ford* (Dark Moon Books, 2019)

*#5: A Primer to Han Song* (Dark Moon Books, 2020)

*#6: A Primer to Ramsey Campbell* (Dark Moon Books, 2021)

*#7: A Primer to Gemma Files* (Dark Moon Books, 2022)

**The Horror Writers Association Presents: Haunted Library of Horror Classics Edited by Eric J. Guignard and Leslie S. Klinger**

*Vol. I: The Phantom of the Opera* by Gaston Leroux (Sourcebooks, 2020)

*Vol. II: The Beetle* by Richard Marsh (Sourcebooks, 2020)

*Vol. III: Vathek* by William Beckford (Sourcebooks, 2020)

*Vol. IV: The House on the Borderland* by William Hope Hodgson (Sourcebooks, 2020)

*Vol. V: Of One Blood: or, The Hidden Self* by Pauline Hopkins (Sourcebooks, 2021)

*Vol. VI: The Parasite and Other Tales of Terror* by Arthur Conan Doyle (Sourcebooks, 2021)

*Vol. VII: The King in Yellow* by Robert W. Chambers (Sourcebooks, 2021)

*Vol. VIII: Ghost Stories of an Antiquary* by M.R. James (Sourcebooks, 2021)

*Vol. IX: Gothic Classics: The Castle of Otranto* by Horace Walpole (Sourcebooks, 2022)

# VOLUME 4

EDITED BY

R.J. CAVENDER
AND BOYD E. HARRIS

DARK MOON BOOKS
Los Angeles, California

**+Horror Library+ Volume 4**

Dark Moon Books edition copyright © 2021 by Eric J. Guignard

Individual works are copyright © 2010 by their respective authors and used by permission.

The stories included in this publication are works of fiction. Names, characters, places, events, and dialogue are either the product of the authors' imaginations or used in a fictitious manner. Any resemblance to actual events, locales, or persons, living or dead, is entirely coincidental and not intended by the author.



Edited by R.J. Cavender and Boyd E. Harris

Interior layout by Eric J. Guignard
www.ericjguignard.com

Cover art by Ania Bibulowicz: *To Know Evil* (2010)
www.deviantart.com/corporalphantom

With additional thanks to original production and reading team:
Michelle Garren Flye (Proofreader), A.J. Brown (Proofreader), Bailey Hunter (Original Layout and Design), Erik Smetana, John Rowlands, Lee Thompson, and Dameion E. Becknell.

First edition by Cutting Block Press published in October, 2010
First edition by Dark Moon Books published in July, 2021

Library of Congress Cataloging-in-Publication Data
+Horror library+ volume 4 /
edited by R.J. Cavender and Boyd E. Harris.

Library of Congress Control Number: 2021936840

ISBN-13: 978-1-949491-63-0 (paperback)
ISBN-13: 978-1-949491-32-6 (e-book)

DARK MOON BOOKS
Los Angeles, California
www.DarkMoonBooks.com

Made in the United States of America
DMB 10 9 8 7 6 5 4 3 2 1

(V061821)

This book is for those authors who have confided in us.
You place your very best work into the care of our
churning wheel—year after year. You are the magicians,
the dreamers of dreams, the perpetuators of the
nightmare. Without you, all would be lost.

R.J. Cavender

# TABLE OF CONTENTS

# INTRODUCTION: A VERY IMPORTANT MESSAGE FOR THOSE PLANNING TO TRAVEL TO COSTA RICA

BY R.J. CAVENDER AND BOYD E. HARRIS

A S THE DAIHATSU TERIOS RUMBLES AND GROWLS TO climb the misshapen road toward Volcan Poas, the rich San Jose street exhaust gives way to the cleaner smell of damp mountain air, and you suck in deep breaths of satisfaction.

The day is bright. While it is cool with patches of fog lingering in the last of Alajuela's side streets, you break into open country, which boasts endless kilometers of rolling hills filled with coffee plantations, one on top of another. The plush rows of trees hug the hills from the edge of the road expanding to both horizons. The sun is rising, and you feel some warmth through the windshield. While it is looking to be a promising day at Volcan Poas, you hope it will hold.

There is no shoulder. You've run the tires over the edge of the narrow road several times to avoid transport trucks and passenger buses rumbling downhill, and there is little room to maneuver, but it doesn't slow you. The higher you climb, the more clouds roll into the plantations and spill into the roads, obstructing your view, and the midday rains begin. The visibility erodes and yet oncoming traffic keeps stampeding past.

Things are tricky, but that doesn't slow you.

Most women wouldn't travel alone in a third world country. "Too many things can happen," your family would tell you. "Who's going to help you when your rental car breaks down?" they might add. Yours gave up that nonsense long ago. You've backpacked Europe, road-biked through Nova

Scotia, hiked Machu Picchu. You usually rent a car in Costa Rica so you can see more of its vast beauty in the time you have. You usually go alone, and that by choice.

You've never been to Poas. You've heard of the plush green landscapes and rainforests that cake the slopes leading to this ancient mid-earth pressure release valve. Unfortunately it won't happen today. About halfway up, heavy rain forces you to search for a place to pull over. You see a restaurant or hotel through the sheets of rain pelting your windshield, and you turn off onto a gravel drive that leads to several empty parking spaces hugging the entrance. A man wearing a white jacket, a common uniform in Central America, rushes out with an umbrella and opens it over your car door.

You step out and almost forget to lock the door but turn back and push the electric button near the inside handle. You recall the Tico Rentals representative at the San Jose airport trying to guide you away from this area, holding a map in front of you. You remember his exact words.

*"Ms. Quincy, it's just that some places up there are not as good as others. We had some problems up there with the cars. We had some thieves breaking in and some cars stolen. May I recommend another volcano for you to visit?"*

You remember his expression, and that along with the misty breeze gives you a chill. There had been more than concern for his rental car on his face, but you had brushed him off, and here you are, almost forgetting to lock up.

The waiter walks you in, directs you through the rustic restaurant and seats you at a front window table. You peer through the ancient, warped glass at the torrential downpour. The sloped streets are under siege with milky-red runoff water colored from the volcanic soil. Through the foggy window there is a sign in the road that reads, "Volcan Poas . . . 13." You remember that you are now dealing with kilometers, and you comfort yourself in the thought that it is not much farther.

After lunch, you decide to rent a cabin behind the restaurant. The nice waiter hands you a key and checks you in from your table.

Later, you go into the bar and order a Cerveza Imperial. They serve it in a glass with a few rocks of ice, a traditional thing here. The bartender seems nice, like everyone else, but your Spanish is rusty, and you are too tired to try conversation.

This is as alone as it gets. No one back home has any idea where you are, and to find you someone would have to know to visit Eduardo at the car rental office, which is one of about eight or nine agencies. And then they would need perfect timing to stop into this particular restaurant when they know you could have gone in five or six directions leading out from San Jose. Being this isolated from your life is very comforting.

Last week you walked away from another relationship. You loved him, but it just wasn't right and both of you knew it. You'd never been the marrying type, and he wanted kids. You are happier sitting alone in this bar around strangers than you will ever be at any point in marriage. It is unsettling, but such is life.

After a while the bar takes on some new guests. A French couple, some Eastern European backpackers, an American banker and his wife that are a little too loud for this quiet place. A clean cut, friendly looking man comes over and sits, poised for conversation. He smiles and says, "Hello, friend. Do you like de beautiful weather we have here en August?"

You chuckle and he grins, the ice broken. Then he introduces himself. "I'm Hector, from Nicaragua".

You say, "Hola, Hector, I'm Joan. The weather is wonderful compared to Houston this time of year."

He nods. "Ah, yes. Houston. Humid like this, but also hot. Are you here for fun? To fiesta. You know, to party?" He holds his palms out and while still sitting, does a little lower body shuffle, and to accent the cutesy Latino flirt, he winks.

He has a charming way about him. He appears to be in his early forties, and he keeps good looks for his age. He's dressed in an ironed, fashionable button-down and sports a pleasant masculine scent.

But there is something not quite right. Maybe it is his unbridled forwardness or lack of patience. But really you can put this one down as simple intuition.

You answer in a more guarded tone, "No, just here for relaxation."

He nods. "This is a good place for that as well." He looks around. "Where do you stay?"

"Here, for the night. Then, who knows?"

"Ah, you like to wander." He moves a little closer and asks, "Do you wanna know of a good place near to the volcano?"

You keep a closed posture, partly facing the bar, preventing him from moving in too close. You say, "I'd like to ride by horseback to the mouth of Poas."

His brows arch. "This is very best place for horseback riding. You should go to the Camino Verde Lodge. Ask for Fernando. He take you to see the Volcan."

"Thank you, Hector. You've been most helpful."

As you stand to leave for your room, he quickly says, "Joan, I know of another bar close to here. It's more relaxing . . ."

You make deliberate eye contact. "No thank you, Hector, but it has been nice to meet you."

After forty-two single years, you've learned to be very choosy with men. You do have a weakness for good-looking, smooth-talking Latinos, and you admire Hector's valiant effort, but he's just trying too hard.

Walking away you hear him say, "It's the Camino Verde Lodge, all the way until you see the park to the volcan. And you should try their caldo soup. It's delicious."

As you leave the room, you feel a need to look back at Hector-from-Nicaragua. You do, and there he is, watching and smiling. You briefly wonder if all Nicaraguans are that different from Costa Ricans. Though cute and friendly, there was something odd with this guy. Beyond the outgoing nature of men from this region. Something a little on the creepy side.


THE SUN IS working its way up over the endless rows of bushy coffee trees. An even blanket of light fog hovers around their bases only a foot or two deep, and as the sun breaks through, you watch it burn off.

After ample servings of *café con leche* in the restaurant and a plate of fresh fruit, you resume your trek to the summit. You find the sign for the Camino Verde Lodge along a cutback in the steep road. Briefly you consider continuing on, but curiosity prevails, and you turn into the ungraded gravel drive. Over a steep hill you pass a *Tico* working on a small building. He waves and a concert of silver teeth beams from his friendly face.

Topping the next hill the lodge becomes visible, and there is only one vehicle in front. It's a Toyota Rav-4 with a Budget Rental sticker on the bumper. Someone else on vacation. You get out and walk around the small rustic building, appreciating an abundance of different colored hydrangeas along the path. From the back patio there is a breathtaking view of a valley rolling off this side of this volcano. Puffy clouds work their way through these hills, and you pause before entering.

Inside it is dark and quiet. You skirt around a couple of heavy handmade wood tables and lean against the kitchen counter. You see no one, though you smell something cooking.

"Hola!" you call into the darkness.

Someone shuffles through a pantry, pots clanking against one another in hollow percussion. A female mumbles something that you don't understand. A large woman with hard features steps into view. A *Tica*, but maybe part German or Eastern European. She smiles.

You say, "Quiere un caballo para viaje a la volcan. Es Fernando aqui?" It's badly broken Spanish at best, but she seems to understand.

She nods and goes outside. She waves at the man you passed on the way to the lodge. He appears to be gathering supplies from a small shed. He stands, waves back, and puts away a few things before walking down to the lodge. The Tica comes in and brews you a cup of coffee. You engage in conversation, keeping your Spanish deliberately slow, and you learn her name is Estrela.

Soon, the man with the silvery smile enters the lodge. His English is poor, but he chooses to practice it on you. He says, "Hallo, I'm Fernando." Then he asks, "You have practice weeth caballos?"

"Yes," you answer. "I would like to ride to the volcano, but by trails." He squints and so you attempt to translate. "Quiero traje el caballos con no usar el sendero."

He smiles, giving you a close-up of the numerous teeth crowned in semi-precious metal. He seems glad that you wish to take the adventurous route. He says, "Los caballos, dey like that." He pinches his right forefinger to his thumb and says, "Un momento." He steps around the building and a moment later he's carrying a saddle.

Something about Fernando is reassuring. He's sweet and soft-spoken, and maybe a little simple, but something just feels like today's ride will be an adventurous one.

On cue with this thought, Hector-from-Nicaragua walks in. He stops at the kitchen counter, and Estrela acknowledges him in mumbled Spanish. She comes out of the pantry and hands him a tightly wrapped black bag.

He glances at you and smiles, then hands it back to her. He tells her something and then she disappears with the bag into the kitchen.

He comes over and sits at a table next to yours. You are happy that he has not come closer. Grinning, he says, "You took my advice. I'm very pleased."

Estrela brings each of you coffee, followed by a bowl of hot soup. It's a cool morning and steam carries off, twisting in the breezeway.

She sits it in front of you and says, "Caldo res," and you recognize it as a brothy soup with meat and vegetables.

You sip and find it to be quite succulent; spicy, heavy in cumin. Under the oily broth, you spoon out chunks of vegetables, slices of corn cob, wedges of cabbage, and tomato. At the bottom, you find big, soft chunks of meat. You wonder if they would share the recipe.

Hector says, "You like." His smile and gaze is a reminder of what bothered you about him last night. You hope he won't join you on the ride today.

Fernando returns and points to the two horses saddled up on the side. You finish your soup and coffee and slip your arms through your backpack.

Outside you prepare to mount your horse, when you notice a machete stuck in the ground between Fernando and the horses, and your back tenses up. You hate any kind of blade. Large knives are to you what spiders and snakes are to other women.

You turn to your horse, run your fingers over the side of his head, brushing them across the top of his nose. His name is Pinto. A beautiful brown horse with black features and a black tail. He takes to you, cocks his head back in appreciation. You mount Pinto and pat him on the side, then tighten your backpack.

Fernando adjusts a dusty baseball cap on his head. He leans way over the edge of his saddle, grabs the machete and holsters it in his saddle. He looks at you and recognizes your concern. "To clear de trail," he says, patting it.

You nod.

"Do you have friends with you in Costa Rica?" he asks.

"I'm up here alone," you answer.

His corrected teeth gleam proud. He pats himself lightly on the chest and says, "Now you have a friend here."

He leads you farther up the road you drove in on, then turns onto a volcanic rock path. The trail degrades with distance. At times, the mud and uneven slopes make it difficult on the horses' hooves. After several hundred meters he turns off the path into what seems like no trail at all and begins a climb through the jungle. It is brutally steep. Because of soft soil, the horses must carefully plant every step. Fernando pulls out his machete and chops at the vines and brush. The growth falls clean, which demonstrates the razor sharpness of his blade. Your trail leads you up several switchbacks, repeatedly crossing over a trickling brook.

Eventually you emerge from the rainforest onto an open meadow. The lodge and the entire valley are visible below. You see that the clouds rolling through the hills are becoming larger and darker, but trust that Fernando is aware of the approaching weather.

Fernando turns and points to a tiny but gushing waterfall, a spring burbling from the side of a massive rock. It is the source of the brook that you've been passing over in the switchbacks.

You continue up the hill and enter more forest, but soon after that another clearing appears. You dismount the horses and climb to the crest by foot.

You reach the top and look down into it. The setting is surreal. The crater is a half mile wide, with sulfuric steam crawling up the banks, leaving egg yolk yellow and green-gray deposits. No vegetation anywhere in this chasm.

Thousands of years ago Poas had been a prototypical volcano, cone-shaped. Then subterranean pressure built up to a point where the top blew off, propelling rock through the air for hundreds of miles and ash into the atmosphere for thousands more. As a result, two craters formed. One became extinct and the other remained active. The extinct crater gave way to a beautiful lake with the green jungle that dropped to the water's edge. In the crater that you stand over, a moonlike surface of gray and yellow ridges drop down to a pool of sulfuric steaming liquid, similar in size and shape to the lake in the extinct one.

Fernando puts his hand on your shoulder and points to a storm cell approaching from the other side of the crater. He says, "No looks good."

He holds his hand there a little too long for your liking. You study his eyes, and for the first time, notice a complexity about him.

Is it fear of the storm you see swimming in there? You don't think so. He studies you as well, though you have no idea why. An odd thought percolates. You wonder if Hector is still in the lodge with Estrela.

Once Fernando takes his hand away, he turns and begins toward the horses, and you follow. The two of you ride back to the spring. Before guiding you down to the lodge he dismounts and walks over to the waterfall. He takes off his cap and tosses it in the direction of his horse. He looks at you, cups his hands and fills them with water. He drinks carefully, then puts his head in the flowing spring to wet his long, dark hair. He stands up and shakes, allowing water to spray in every direction. He grins at you and opens his palm to the spring as though to say, "Your turn."

You have your doubts about drinking from it, but you are here for adventure, so you dismount. You take off your backpack, set it down and move over to the cascade, where Fernando steps aside for you.

You kneel and cup your hands just as he did, and fill your hands. You sip the water. It is cool and clean and delicious. No bottle of spring water in the world could taste this good. On your second sip, you notice a piece of red cloth lying on the side of the small brook. It is shredded, and it has a small button attached to it. You curiously uncup your hands, reach over and pick it up. It is a piece of a shirt collar. The material is not red but light blue with . . . bloodstains?

The discovery sends a chill across your neck and body. You are just about to stand up and turn to show it to Fernando, when you realize that the chill is more of a dull pain. You look down at your chest, and your right side is rapidly soaking up large amounts of blood. You try to turn but you have no control over that side of your body. The stream below is now clouded in red. You can't move and yet for some reason you are turned around.

Fernando stands before you with a firm grip on your scalp by the roots of your hair. A fierce hatred has taken over his face. His silver-capped grin is suddenly foul; his eyes wide, the pupils coal black. In his right hand, he holds the machete high. He swings it with absolute tension running from his neck to his wrist. Your last physical sight is that of your bloody, severed body hitting the ground.

You watch from above in the trees as Fernando methodically finishes his task. The slaying had occurred on the rocks lining the edge of the brook. Fernando lays your body across the periphery and peels the clothes away. He presses the tip of the machete directly into each of your major joints, forcing down with both hands on top of the handle. The cartilage separates more easily than you'd expect, which convinces you that he's done this many times before. He raises the machete and chops down in the same places to cut away cartilage and ligaments. Soon he has twelve leg and arm pieces, a torso and a head all separated.

He takes the thigh of a leg and holds it at an angle on the rocks. He pulls a sharp knife from another holster and begins to slice the meat away from the bone in large fillets. He places the pieces of meat in one black plastic bag and the bones in another. He does this for each of the limb parts and then the torso.

When cutting into the midsection, he doesn't bother with the breast plate and ribs. He cuts around the hips and pulls out the kidneys, liver, and heart. They each are placed into the meat bag. He slices liberal amounts of muscle from the shoulders and waistline. You were a lean person, so he leaves what little fat there is on the meat. When he's done, he drops your head in the meat bag, and you wonder about all of it.

He takes each of the two plastic sacks and double bags them. He walks over to Pinto and drapes them over the horse's saddle, tying the knotted part to the saddle horn. Pinto, the horse who had taken to you earlier, is indifferent. You are no longer a rider, but now cargo.

Fernando walks back to the spring and washes his machete and his knife. Then he splashes water over the rocks, allowing the blood and other tissue to run off. In a few places he uses a piece of your clothing to scrub stains off the stubborn stones. He puts your clothing and boots in a third bag and then lays that over Pinto's saddle. He takes your backpack and pulls his arms through it.

The two horses and the tranquil rancher begin their trip back down the mountain. It rains and Fernando tilts the bill of his cap to keep direct droplets from hitting his eyes. He reaches a place in the thicket of the woods where a rusted shovel leans against a tree. He dismounts and picks it up. There are dozens of mounds of dirt in this hidden place, some fresh and some settled by the frequent rains.

Fernando digs.


ESTRELA STANDS OUTSIDE in the rain, waiting for Fernando.

You find Hector in the lodge making calls on his cellular phone. Apparently he has already lined up a buyer for the Toyota Rav-4 in Nicaragua, but is now securing a purchaser for your Daihatsu Terios. He mentions luggage and personal belongings in his calls. He inspects a bulky black trash bag from the refrigerator, the same one Estrela had shown him earlier, and it contains the fresh remains of a guy named Miguel. In his conversations he mentions a second human. A lean female.

You conclude that the most profitable thing about your death is not the pawning of the vehicle, but rather the sale of your flesh.

There is a reason you haven't moved on to wherever you are supposed to go from here, and you understand it now.

You have found an unwitting medium for your message. A writer in Austin, Texas. He too has traveled alone to Costa Rica, and has visited Volcan Poas in a rental car. He has stopped at the same small lodge near the peak of the mountain, though it is not called the Camino Verde. He has parked next to a rented Daihatsu Terios, and days later he has wondered where the renter might have gone off to.

Inside the lodge he has enjoyed a cup of café con leche and a bowl of hot soup with meat in it. Goat meat, he thinks, but the part-German-looking waitress only calls it *caldo res.*

He has relaxed on the back terrace of this lodge enjoying the beauty of the valley and working up an idea to write a story about this place, and its nice people. And how they might not be so nice.

He has taken the private ride by horseback with a friendly guide carrying the razor-sharp machete, who explains it is to clear the trail. He has sipped from the same cool spring… with the guide standing somewhere behind him.

He's lucky to be home.

He now sits at his computer, has been here since early last night, relentlessly clapping away on the keyboard. It's 4:22 a.m. and his palms and armpits are sweating from the nervous energy that has taken over. The words flow from his fingertips without doubt or hesitation. Never before in his life has he had a surge of creative energy like this. He tells his story in such detail that it frightens even him, and yet he's convinced that this is just a creation of his robust imagination. That the Camino Verde Lodge, though not its true name, is a safe place to visit. He has imposed a paradox upon the reader, and he is damned proud of himself for this. After all, if he doesn't believe it himself, how can it be true? Perhaps he is not really the author. And yet he acknowledges this too, by writing it.

Your message has spread. He has consulted with an editor a thousand miles away in Arizona who likes your message. Together they have big plans for it as an intro for their next anthology.

It's been several years, and though things should have changed in that evil place, you know they haven't. There is a reason for everything. You know that this message will reach someone, at least one person, who plans to visit Costa Rica, and that will be your salvation, as well as theirs.

As the last of your blood spills out through a press onto the opening pages of *+Horror Library+ Volume 4*, you feel the first satisfaction of your afterlife, content that soon peace will finally find you.

And yet there is disappointment, even amidst this final success, because he himself, the man whom you found as your conduit to make this happen, whom you've haunted for all this time, will never seriously consider the fact that you are real, and that this is not at all a work of fiction.

—R.J. Cavender and Boyd E. Harris

# INTO THE AFTER

BY KURT DINAN

---

THE ROOM WAS LITTLE MORE THAN A CEMENT bunker located in the back of an abandoned grocery store. Dad and I had stood third in line underneath the flickering fluorescent lights for an hour. No one could stop staring at the same white sheet that obscured the area near the front wall. Unseen spotlights backlit the makeshift partition, and the oversized silhouette of an empty chair shone through. I rocked back and forth on my heels, certain at any moment my nerves would give out and send me to the exit.

Dad motioned to the manila envelope in my hand and said, "Which one did you bring?"

"Hilton Head."

He smiled at the memory, but it died quickly, and he returned to his thoughts and vigil watching the chair. I'd chosen the picture of Mom in a flowered sundress from a rubber-banded pile hidden away in the basement where Dad wasn't likely to run across it. Most days he still couldn't even say her name; God knows how he'd react to unwillingly discovering her picture.

"*. . . in December of 2000, I took a job with security personnel at One World Trade Center where every day . . .*"

Ethan Stuckey's story played from a Peavey amp sitting on the floor at the front of the screen. His voice had been on a continual loop since we'd arrived, slithering into my ears and sending an uninterrupted chill through my body as if he stood directly behind me. Even after all the waiting, I still didn't know if I believed his story which had brought us all together. Dad accepted it though, and that was all that mattered.

Metallic knocking from behind the partition silenced all talk in the room. Burt, the bearded man who'd frisked us upon entry, stopped on his way around the screen and shut off the CD player wired into the amp. I held a breath to ten, hoping to relax. A deadbolt clanged open, followed by the scraping of metal across cement. Seconds later, the outline of Ethan Stuckey, stooped and hobbling, appeared. He moved in jerky motions toward the chair as if his hips had been broken and set improperly. As he passed the screen, his distorted shadow made it appear he was rising from the earth.

Burt reemerged from behind the sheet and knelt in front of the amp. A low static hum filled the room. Dad drummed his fingers against his legs. He had been anticipating this night ever since he'd transferred a thousand dollars for the two of us through PayPal. The guilt I'd experienced since helping him make the plans flooded through me again. I shut my eyes and swallowed hard, reminding myself that tonight was about saving Dad, not about my fears of a man some labeled a fraud and others called the boogeyman.

On the screen, Ethan's shadow lifted a microphone. When he spoke, his voice had the scratchy quality of an old blues album.

"You've all come tonight hoping for answers, and I can promise those to you," he said. "What I can't promise is that you'll necessarily like what you hear. That doesn't really matter to me. All of you have made a deal to hear the truth. Nothing more. What you do with it is up to you."

He lowered the mic onto his lap. Burt restarted the audio of Ethan's story, then waved forward the woman at the front of the line. I recognized her from a midnight showing of *The Lies of 9-11* that Dad had taken me to at an empty warehouse down by the shore. When she reached the edge of the screen, she paused as if reconsidering. I secretly hoped she would turn back, starting a mass exodus that would shake Dad from his waking coma. Instead, she turned the corner. I followed her outline projecting black on white until she knelt at Ethan's feet.

"I know I said it before, but I appreciate you coming along, Will," Dad said. His eyes were ringed by dark circles like he was looking up from the bottom of a well. "Maybe tonight we'll get some truth."

The irony wasn't lost on me. In the years since 2001, Dad had avoided the truth by turning our Hoboken home into a cave of wall-plastered newspaper articles and building schematics whose relevance only he understood. Even with no remains ever recovered, Mom was officially classified as deceased nine months after that September. For Dad though, no body meant Mom might have somehow survived, possibly suffering amnesia and living life elsewhere. He remained immobile in The Before, existing in a perpetual 2001 where he hibernated with footage of plane crashes, building implosions, and mystery jumpers. Meanwhile, I lived in The After, alone and feeling orphaned as if I had somehow lost both parents on the same day.

*"...a massive rumbling on the street like the ground was opening up. Then I was consumed by dust and ash, and there was nothing but darkness."*

I recognized most of the people in line behind us. There was the wheel-chaired man who'd been removed by Borders' security after initiating a shouting match with the author of *Conspiracies Debunked*. Past him, the woman who kept vigil at Ground Zero with a sandwich board covered with her daughter's picture. Then the blogger whose page *Among the Missing* Dad monitored daily. And the Diane Lane look-alike who brought her young son to the support group meetings. And on and on. Despite our common bond, no one acknowledged each other. Years of attending the same events brought recognition but not friendship, as if suffering alone equated to some sort of valor.

On the screen, the silhouette of the woman with Ethan convulsed as if overcome by a seizure. Then, after letting out a deep sob, she cracked him across the face with her hand. The sound echoed through the room. Burt was around the screen and on top of her in seconds.

I unconsciously stepped behind Dad. He showed no sign of my existence, instead watching with everyone else as Burt carried the woman, slumped and weeping in his arms, off to the man standing guard at the back of the room.

*"...hundreds of shadowy impressions wandered about. No one had bodies or heads, but I could hear everyone talking. Some told what they'd eaten for breakfast, or how the contract language needed to be settled, or about the goal their kid scored..."*

Next up was a man in a business suit. I wondered how his days at the office went. Did he spend work hours searching obscure websites for minutia while management debated how long they had to wait before they replaced him? Or could he sequester away his misery enough to work his job before returning home to ignore his children and resume his real quest? Books tell you there is no one way to grieve. When something terrible happens—something truly horrific—you change. For some it may be for the better, for some the worse, but anyone in horror's path is irrevocably altered.

For me, it had taken years of school suspensions and police run-ins before I moved into The After and accepted the truth that Mom was gone forever. Unlike other kids I knew who lost a parent that day, I never idealized my mom. She did the best she could but regularly missed my games and school functions due to long work hours. To compensate for her absence, she showed her love by celebrating birthdays and academic achievements with manic enthusiasm. As I got older, she even created what she called "our signal"—running her index finger over her earlobe—in order to initiate a form of closeness with me. Sometimes it meant "Your father's silly, isn't he?" or "It's time for you to get to bed" or even simply "I love you." Regardless of its use, the signal was a private secret only we shared. The last time I saw her, she smiled and touched her earlobe while driving past me on her way to the train station. Even though I was surrounded by friends waiting for the bus, I returned the gesture, a small memory that tempered any resurfacing sadness.

"*. . . naturally began separating into two lines. One was clearly more crowded than the other, stretching far into the distance until it blurred. In that line everyone radiated fulfillment. But from the much shorter line I felt a painful darkness . . . *"

His time with Ethan finished, the man in the suit reappeared from behind the screen and trudged toward the exit. His eyes were vacant like he was sleepwalking.

"*. . . later, a nurse told me I'd been dead for over a minute before the EMT brought me back. But I returned with their lives imprinted on me. They're a part of me now.*"

Dad and I were next. My heartbeat pounded in my ear like waves pummeling the beach. From the moment I'd directed Dad to the message board about Stuckey's gatherings I'd regretted my decision, knowing I was entering a game I had no control over. Now that I was about to meet Ethan, I was even more apprehensive. Something about the surroundings, Ethan's shadow, his voice—

"I think we're up."

Dad reached out. At first I thought he was going to take my hand, but instead he took the envelope containing Mom's picture. He held it by the corner with only the tips of two fingers. His face was so pale I thought he might throw up.

"Are you going to be okay?" I said.

"I'm not sure I can do this," he said, looking exhausted. "What if he tells me something horrible?"

The nakedness of his admission almost dropped me. It was the closest thing to honesty I'd heard from him in years. I wanted to hurry him from the room before Ethan could whisper his lies. But deep down, past the thick cord of betrayal wrapped inside like barbed wire, I knew this was what we both needed.

"It'll be okay," I said. "We'll do it together."

Burt gave the nod and we stepped behind the sheet into the bright shine of the spotlights. I held a hand to block out the light and saw the outline of Ethan sitting close. His dark form appeared to swallow the light around him. Without amplification his voice was a breathless wheeze.

"Come on over," he said. "I'm not that scary."

His laugh reminded me of a handsaw ripping through wood, and when my eyes finally adjusted I could see he was only partially telling the truth. Reports put him at thirty-three, but he could have passed for sixty. One side of his head was caved in like a dented fender. Short brown hair covered only half his scalp; the other side was nothing but a roadmap of scar tissue. His face hung slack as if sculpted of warm wax. I dug my fingers into my leg and tried not to stare.

"I'm Hank McCormick," Dad said, reaching out a hand. "This is my son, Will."

Ethan brushed Dad's hand aside.

"Do you have a picture?"

Dad hesitated, then dragged a finger across the top of the envelope. Without glancing at it, he withdrew the photograph of Mom standing on a hotel balcony. If he spotted it, Dad said nothing about the red "X" I'd drawn in Sharpie on the back.

Ethan took the photograph into his twitching hands. I held my breath. I was about to find out if I'd given too much trust to a man I didn't know. He studied Mom's picture for less than three seconds before handing it back. I thought I saw a faint smile cross Ethan's face when his eyes drifted to the mark on the back of the photograph.

He said, "Elaine McCormick worked as an actuary with Hutchison Insurance. On September 11th, she arrived at work at 7:53 wearing a black pantsuit she'd bought at Macy's."

Dad gripped my arm, burrowing his nails into my wrist. When I covered his hand with mine his wedding ring pressed into my palm.

"She was writing an email when the plane hit. The wing tore through her floor, destroying the entire office. The impact was so sudden she had no time to react and died instantly. Burning jet fuel incinerated her in minutes."

Dad's legs gave out and he sagged into me. I wrapped an arm around him and swallowed back the bile traveling up my throat.

"Is there anything else?" Dad said.

"When I saw her," Ethan said, "she was at peace standing in the long line. Elaine knew what awaited."

Dad's voice was a whisper. "Was she thinking of me or Will?"

"The dead don't think of the living," Ethan said. "That part of their life is over."

Tears raced down Dad's face. He exhaled, then wrapped his arms around Ethan, who bristled at the touch.

"Thank you so much," Dad said.

When Dad stood there was a faint light in his eyes, a small ember where I once thought only ashes remained. A brief image of the future, of Dad resuming a normal life and returning as my father, flashed in my head.

"We can go now," Dad said. He put his arm around me as we walked away. I leaned in, aware that a good deal of the weight I'd carried when we'd entered the building had now vanished. I'd done it, and I knew whatever guilt accompanied paying Stuckey two thousand dollars to tell my father exactly what I wished was worth it.

We were to the edge of the screen about to rejoin the others when Ethan called my name. I turned and he beckoned me, his thin hand pulling through the air. I tried to keep walking, but Dad stopped.

"What do you think he wants?"

"Let's just go," I said. "We've heard what we need."

"But maybe he remembered something else."

There was nothing I could do. The two of us started back, but Ethan said, "No, just the boy."

Dad shrugged, then told me he'd wait by the others.

Cold sweat trailed down my back. Ethan gestured for me to kneel. Heat radiated off his skin as if he were deeply fevered.

"Your father seems happy."

Not willing or able to meet his eye, I stared into the darkness over his shoulder.

"You're not the first one, you know," he said. "It's more common than you'd think. We're inclined to protect those we love."

"I can't pay you anything more, if that's what you want."

"It's true what I said before. You accepted certain conditions by coming here, and regardless of your intentions toward your father, I keep my end of the bargain."

I went to leave, but then his voice snaked into my brain, paralyzing me.

"For your fifth birthday, Elaine threw you a ThunderCats-themed party and hired an actor to play Lion-O. On your ninth birthday, she took you and four friends to Coney Island for the day. Your friend Joey ate too much popcorn and threw up off the pier. You all watched the seagulls drop into the water to eat his puke."

My chest heaved, and I tried to slow down my breathing before I hyperventilated. Ethan didn't break his stare, and now he had a deep smile.

"And the last time Elaine ever saw you," he said, "you were at the bus stop as she drove away."

I couldn't move. Everything else faded until there was only his voice. I spoke into the darkness.

"Why are you telling me this?"

"Just keeping my part of the deal," Ethan said. "Elaine wasn't in her office when the plane hit. She was six floors down fucking Craig Hubbard on his desk. They'd been having an affair for over three years. He's the one who first showed her that charming sign you and Elaine shared. They would do the signal across the office when they wanted to meet later to fuck."

My mouth was dust.

"I don't believe you."

"It doesn't matter if you do or not," Ethan said. "When the ceiling collapsed, Elaine's back snapped, pinning her down. She watched the fire grow around her knowing she was going to die. Her last thought before her clothing ignited was how she had wasted her entire life."

Ethan's voice faded as if he were walking away in a dust storm. "When I saw your mother," he concluded, "she was with the others in the short line, radiating a shame and terror known only to those who realize they are damned."

I was still unable to move. The long hours, the overcompensation for her absences—somehow I knew. A light illuminated my memories showing the real events that had lived in shadow. Had she been with Hubbard all those nights she wasn't home? Were there others before him? Did she consider me part of that wasted life? The questions wouldn't stop.

"What am I supposed to do now?"

"Well, at least your father's happy, right?" Ethan said. "Isn't that what you wanted?"

Burt poked his head around the corner and cleared his throat. Ethan looked past me as if I wasn't there.

"Send in the next one."

I turned away and had to concentrate on each step just to walk. I emerged from behind the curtain feeling as if I were entering a new world forever altered. Dad waited for me, his hands out expectantly.

"So what did he say?"

He had wiped the tears away and now had a smile with real life behind it. A row of folding chairs stood between us. Aware of the newly drawn line separating us and weighed down by a burden I knew could never be unloaded, I forced a smile and began my new life in The After.

---

KURT DINAN's work has appeared in +*Horror Library*+ *Volume 3*, *Darkness on the Edge: Stories Inspired by the Songs of Bruce Springsteen*, and twice in *ChiZine*, where he won the 2007 ChiZine Short Story Contest. He lives with his wife and three children in Cincinnati.

# ASH WEDNESDAY

BY LORNE DIXON

EVERYTHING WAS A BLUR, MY VISION FADING AND brightening, until the pulsating colors and trembling shapes slowed their spin. I saw broken glass on asphalt, the swaying blue bristle tree line under the Santa Lucia Mountains, the twisting funnels of black clouds against a starless sky. I heard nothing except the hum of my inflamed eardrums. Rolling, standing up, wobbling, shaking, I turned back toward the fire.

I watched as a fireball ascended off the roof of the sprawling building. A line of flame ran across the *Morro Bay Private Mental Health Center* sign, curling the white paint, chewing down into the carved lettering. I snapped my dangling jaw shut and brushed myself off.

The explosion had caught us by surprise, knocking three teams of fire responders off our feet. Our Ladder's Blitz line—two and a half inches of hose—danced on the parking lot like a snake. It struck a uniformed cop, bowling him over, slamming his unconscious body against the Chief's car. Half a dozen firefighters jumped to their feet and tackled the hose and held on until their combined weight and strength wrestled it under control.

The explosion meant the fire had reached the Sanitarium's boiler room. We'd contained it to the offices and Visitor's Center up until then, but now it would spread fast.

"That's the game, folks." Chief Henderscott shouted.

A Volunteer team member from San Luis Obispo ran to my side. He screamed over the fire's roar, "What's he mean by that?"

I shook my head. Only a few scraggly hairs on his chin, the kid couldn't have been more than twenty. I pulled his ear close. "It means the fire just won. We got nothing that can handle the sumbitch. Building's done."

Confusion crossed his face. "Then what now?"

"This just became a pure rescue mission," I told him, careful to lock his eyes on mine. He needed to understand what my words meant—fully understand. "We have to get in there and get those people out."

Confusion turned to panic. "But they're—"

He didn't say the word *insane* but it hung in the air just beyond his lips, almost audible.

"Yes," I said. "They are."

The same horrible thought fluttered through all of our minds, I'm sure, both the veterans of Ladder Six-Fifteen and the weekend adventurers from the eager volunteer squads that had raced to our town. The building was already partially evacuated. *Partially.* The first responders quit pulling patients out when a hallway ceiling collapsed, crushing three of the firefighters. I arrived just as they were regrouping in the parking lot.

Morro Bay divided its patients into three color-coded wards. Green Ward was made up of the self-committed and the homeless. Yellow ward was low-level criminals with mental health issues who had managed to avoid jail time in exchange for some time on a shrink's chaise. They were already gone, filed out and moved to the state hospital.

The violent psychotic incurables of Red Ward were still inside. A whisper echoed in my ear, an earlier voice warning me that some of the inmates had gotten loose in the confusion and that some of the staff was missing.

The Chief barked out orders, pairing up firemen with local cops. No one hesitated to follow the Chief's commands. The old man had gone to Korea and Vietnam, neither time on vacation, and his voice carried more authority than the stripes he had earned.

"You're with me," a voice said over my shoulder. I turned and saw Leo McNeiss suiting up. I'd known him since grade school, before he'd moved to the city and become a cop, before scandal had sent him back home to be a small town deputy, before the deep lines in both our faces. We had never been what you would call friends. As a kid Leo hadn't quite been a bully, but he wasn't someone you chose as an enemy, either. He pointed to the young Volunteer from San Luis Obispo, "Both of you."

Shaking, the kid said, "My name's Fenley. Arno—"

"I wouldn't fling a link of monkey shit for your name, son," Leo said, strapping on his breathing gear. I doubted that he had ever used an oxygen unit before but he didn't need any instructions. That was just who he was. He handed over a pair of filtration masks. "We go in two minutes."

Fenley raced to a truck for more gear. Leo rolled a copper fire extinguisher over to me. Stepping in, he said, "We have a special task. I'm sure you remember the name Otto Weissmuller?"

I did. Five years ago, Weissmuller had been arrested and tried on seventeen counts of conspiracy to murder. He'd led a cult of drug-addled teens on a rampage through southern California, terrorized the nation, and kept the newspapers in business.

"This hospital has four wings, not three. The fourth is Black Ward. He's their star patient. It's a big secret. They don't want any of his *family* to try to bust him out." Leo cocked his thumb over at Fenley. The boy fumbled with the straps to his oxygen tank. "Don't want to say anything to him. Would spook him."

"He's already spooked," I said.

Leo attached the feed line to his tank. "Then maybe he's smarter than he looks. When we caught Weissmuller, he was an animal, filthy, long unwashed hair, three-inch dirty fingernails—like talons. Barely human. He killed three cops with his bare hands at that roadblock. Bit one patrolman's eye right out of his skull."

"Christ," I muttered.

Fenley shuffled back to us as I jumped into my equipment. Inside our suits it must have been ninety degrees, but the kid was shivering. At that point he probably regretted ever volunteering for the Boy Scouts, let alone firefighting. I wondered if he had caught any of our conversation. No, I decided. He was, after all, still standing.

We dropped the air masks over our faces and joined the procession of firemen and cops heading toward the Sanitarium's open front doors. Plumes of black smoke rolled out of the entrance in bursts. It felt like we were walking on a dragon's tongue toward its open mouth. Leo checked his service revolver and it reminded me that Fenley and I were armed only with fire extinguishers. The kid locked step and stayed close by my side. He did not even glance toward Leo.

A wave of swirling darkness reached out from the doorway and choked off our vision. We huddled together and pushed inside, walking blind, each of us with our free hand clenching the shoulder of the man ahead. The fire's fierce growl rumbled louder as our feet hit tile. Timber crackled and snapped. The building's foundation groaned as it weakened.

A rush of bristling hot air hit us and cleared out the smoke. A faint light crept in—the fire's orange glow seeping between shrinking wall panels—and the group separated into teams. Leo headed past the reception desk, walking fast, hands waving away lingering trails of smoke. Fenley and I hurried to stay close on his coat tails.

A thunderous boom shook down from the hospital's roof and I drew the unsettling image of walking in a cavern deep underground while an earthquake raged in the rock overhead. I jerked my head up quick enough to see a section of the ceiling buckle inward. Grabbing Fenley's collar, I bolted for the hallway. The reception room's ceiling collapsed in a black shower of debris. I heard screams but didn't turn. I kept running, dragging Fenley along, until I caught up with Leo.

Glancing back, the reception room was gone, buried and smoldering. I understood at that moment the terror that miners must feel from inside a cave-in. A dark cloud hurled down the hallway like a fireball, covering us in soot. Fenley and I crouched down and followed Leo.

We passed through a set of double doors, and the smoke thinned out. The fire-lit room flickered evil orange and yellow hues. The nurse's station seemed to sway with the light, the floor and walls suddenly turned to rubber. My stomach turned as I stepped forward. Illusion or not, it felt like walking on a raft, the constant movement under my feet making each step a challenge.

We saw the first body as we made the turn into the disturbed ward. A nurse, stripped naked, stretched across the floor. Someone had wrapped her head in medical gauze, but not enough to mask the red stains over her eyes, flattened nose and mouth. In her blood, her killer had drawn a peace symbol between her exposed breasts.

Fenley took two steps back, pulled off his mask, and vomited.

Leo stepped over the nurse and continued down the hall. The doors on both sides had been forced open, some torn off their hinges. I caught up with him, careful not to look down as I hurdled the nurse's body, and peeked into the first room. An inmate sat on a bench against the far wall, his straight-jacket bloodied. He had been decapitated and his head returned to his neck upside down. The deep frown on his face had been carved into a crimson smile with two bloody thumbprints on his chin for eyes.

Fenley came up behind me, mask still in hand. I turned, blocked his view into the room, and shook my head. I saw his eyes glisten. The kid was close to tears.

I didn't look in the other rooms in that first hallway. Leo took the time to poke his head in each, a swift search, before returning to the hall. His face never gave any hint what he saw in those chambers. I shuddered at the thought that he might have seen worse.

Leo spun on his heels until he faced us, pointed to Fenley with one crooked finger, and barked, "Put the goddamn mask over your face."

Fenley obeyed. He brought the mask up to his mouth with shaking hands and rolled the elastic strap over his head.

Gesturing with the same finger, Leo continued down the hall to a set of double doors. Turning the handles, he found them locked, so he kicked them in. He was a stronger man than he seemed—and no one would have pegged him for a weakling. The doors splintered away from their hinges and collapsed inward. He stepped over the resulting debris into the highest security wing—Black Ward—and, God help us, we trailed along behind him, right down a steep flight of metal stairs.

Even in the dimming light I could see that Black Ward's walls were bare, not decorated with art school dropout oil paintings like the rest of the hospital. The hallways were a cinderblock maze, a dungeon. But then, I thought, where else would they keep monsters?

More of the ceiling collapsed somewhere overhead—a hellish crescendo of splintering lumber, crackling masonry, and the whoosh of fire finding a fresh portal to the night sky. For a moment I feared the whole complex was pancaking down on top of us. I saw the drop ceiling over our heads plummeting down, followed by an avalanche of blackened debris. I raised an arm and ducked down, but the collapse was a trick of light, shadow, and my spinning head conspiring to bring my worst fears into my eyes.

Fenley's hand pushed between my shoulder blades, urging me to keep up with Leo and somehow my feet obliged, picking up speed, wandering into the dark. The last feeble trickle of light dissipated and I was blind. The concrete floor under my feet became a promise that I didn't dare trust—I expected to plunge down into an abyss with each clumsy footfall. I was shaking every bit as much as Fenley's hand on my back. All at once, I felt chills and hot flashes, freezing and burning concurrently.

Something was very wrong with me.

A door opened a dozen feet up the hallway and a flicker of firelight danced over the floor. We ran to Leo, standing in the doorway, gun drawn. As we passed through, I glanced up and saw that the fire had eaten away a corner of the ceiling, giving us that precious tiny light but also bringing the flames closer. I felt waves of blistering heat buffet down and suck the moisture from my pores. I continued to shiver anyway.

We passed a security checkpoint. The desk had been abandoned in a hurry, a cup of coffee and half a donut abandoned in the rush to flee the building.

Leo pointed to a door at the far end of the short hallway. A clipboard hung under a small, wire-latticed window. Even from a few feet away I recognized the photograph that topped the medical charts and medication schedules. It was Otto Weissmuller, a few years older than the pictures in the newspaper photos after his arrest, but unmistakable: dark, wide-set eyes, thin, pointed brows, a receding hairline that rose like devil's horns.

Leo checked his gun, stepped up, and unlatched the door. I inhaled, held the oxygen in my lungs, and shadowed him inside the cell. My feet and legs had gone completely numb. An unsettling detachment flooded my senses and I watched myself move without feeling the floor under my shoes, or the ache of my bum knee, or the weight of the equipment on my back. It was an obscene freedom; it was sickening.

Silence greeted us inside the cell, as if even the noise of a collapsing, burning building refused to share space with the lunatic who lived there.

Otto Weissmuller sat on the corner cot, head down, face curtained by a few scraggly strands of dark hair. He rocked forward and stared at us. "Deputy McNeiss, it's good for you to visit. Could you perhaps ask the ward nurse to kindly turn down the heat?"

Leo straightened his arm. His pistol's aim was locked on Weissmuller's pointed nose.

Fenley stumbled into the cell behind me, wobbling.

"Tell me, Leo," Weissmuller said. "Why exactly are there *two* firemen here?"

Leo lowered his gun and removed his breathing mask. "There was an inconsistency in the police reports. The initial report had you at five-foot-ten. The booking sheet listed six-one."

Weissmuller cackled. "I'm six-one."

Leo nodded, turned, and shot Fenley in the chest twice.

I scampered back toward the door, but my legs buckled and I fell to the floor. I began to reach for my outstretched legs but my arms went rubbery and dropped to my sides. I couldn't even raise my head off the concrete. Inside the mask I screamed—just for a moment, until my vocal cords locked up. I couldn't even blink.

Unable to turn my head or even shift my pupils, I watched Fenley's last breath escape his lips. His chest settled and the twin jets of gushing blood slowed to a trickle.

Leo appeared overhead. He removed my breathing mask, sliding it over my head and letting the elastic tug on my ears before it snapped free. "Sorry, bud. Don't try to move, you can't. I injected Pancuronium Bromide into your oxygen filter. It's a muscle relaxant. The disorientation you've been feeling is normal."

Weissmuller took my legs, and together they dragged me across the cell and propped me against the cot. Leaning down, Leo whispered into my ear, "His people have my daughter. What was I going to do? I help him escape, I get her back. Sorry you got put into play, man, but even as a kid you were an easy mark."

He tore off my clothes, balled them up, and tossed them into the hall.

Leo stood up. Weissmuller grinned. "You should Picasso up his face now, like my family told you. Just in case the fire leaves some flesh on him."

Nodding, Leo pulled back his fist and brought it down. Though paralyzed, I felt the blow, felt warmth spread across my face, felt my skull vibrate, shockwaves fleeing from the epicenter under his knuckles. The second and third blows came just as fast. After that, I lost count, unable to tell when the explosion of pain from one punch ended and the next began. I heard wet slaps. I saw his knuckles glisten with my blood.

He backed away and Weissmuller bent down and forced my mouth open with his thumbs. Reaching inside, he pried free my loosened teeth until my mouth was empty. Then he stood up, rattling them in his fist like pocket change before emptying his hands into the pocket of Leo's fire jacket.

Weissmuller smiled. His mouth was toothless, too. He reached under his pillow, retrieved his own teeth, and forced them into my bloody mouth. Cackling through his words, he said, "Now my dental records are your dental records. Like a gift on your birthday."

I wanted to spit his teeth out. I wanted to vomit. But nothing worked. I was an abandoned marionette dummy, a worthless human husk with severed strings.

As they turned away, Weissmuller pointed to Fenley's body with both index fingers. "Drag that shit into the hall, wouldn't you? Hate to have the clean-up crew think I kept a dirty cell."

Huffing, Leo bent down and wrapped his hands around the young firefighter's ankles. Still hunched over, he dragged the body out through the doorway. Weissmuller turned, flashed me duel peace symbols like Richard Nixon, and ducked out of the cell.

I listened to their footsteps travel down the hall.

A black spot grew on the ceiling as the fire burnt its way down. Grains of ash trickled down like fine black raindrops, building up like an anthill on the tile floor.

Four quick gunshot blasts echoed in the hall, close together—desperate, frightened, wild shots. Then there were screams, like wailing pigs, shrieks of absolute panic.

And then silence.

The anthill of ash grew into a small hill. The cell darkened. At first I thought I was passing out, but no, the padded walls were wilting from the heat.

I lay there waiting for a rain of fire to snake down through the hole in the ceiling and devour my flesh. So strange to panic when your heartbeat cannot quicken.

I heard the clatter of running feet and for a moment feared that Leo and Weissmuller were returning to torment me even more. But there was too much noise, too many feet.

They appeared in the doorway, twitching, heads jerking. Six men dressed in blue shirts and matching pants, each speckled with blood. I saw fear and frenzy in their eyes, but also hate and vengeance. I knew beyond question that these were patients from Red Ward.

Moving like an ape with his arms swinging, one of the men bounced over to me and smiled a wild, uneven grin. He had braces, and bits of red stuck in the metalwork. Reaching down, he picked up my hand and shook it.

Another of the madmen pushed him away and knelt down beside me. He never made eye contact, instead choosing to watch the mountain of ash growing beside us. "I wanted to meet you for a long time, Otto, and here we are, like synchronicity. Looks like they messed up your face real good, *shit*, but we took care of them. Jimmy, m'man, he bashed in that cop's head with a metal chair leg. So he ain't gonna hurt you no more, not with his head bashed in like that."

The room darkened more, but this time it wasn't the walls. It was me.


WHEN I AWOKE we were in a van headed south. I don't remember being carried out of the hospital, but I *do* have a few hazy memories of the Red Ward boys carjacking the van. I don't know where we're headed, but I know that wherever they take me, I'll have to answer to the name Otto Weissmuller. I'd hate to think what they'd do if I told them any different.

---

LORNE DIXON lives and writes off an exit off I-78 in residential New Jersey. He grew up on a diet of yellow-spined paperbacks, black-and-white monster movies, and the thunder-lizard backbeat of rock-n-roll. His short work has appeared in such venues as *+Horror Library+ Volumes 2 & 3* Cutting Block Press, *Darkness on the Edge: Tales Inspired by the Music of Bruce Springsteen* PS Press, *Traps* DarkHart Press, *Potter's Field 3* Sam's Dot Press, *Dead Science* Coscom Entertainment, *Lilith Unbound* Popcorn Press, *Strange Stories of Sand and Sea* Fine Tooth Press, and *Dark Distortions* Scotopia. His novels *Snarl* and *The Lifeless* are available from *Coscom Entertainment*.

# GHOSTS UNDER GLASS

BY TRACIE MCBRIDE

COREY HAD DISCOVERED THE FIRST GHOSTS IN A parked car near the bridge they usually slept under. David had run back to the stash of "treasures" he kept in a pilfered shopping trolley and had returned with a huge glass jar with a screw top lid. It was the kind of jar that looked like it should have a pickled fetus floating in it. "I'm gonna catch me one of those," he had said, patting the jar under his arm, "and keep it as a pet." They soon found more of them, all imprisoned within buildings or vehicles, but David had yet to get brave enough to see what would happen if he opened a door and let one out.

They walked past McDonald's, and Corey imagined he could smell fries cooking. He hesitated at the door. For no apparent reason, David started to laugh.

"What's so funny?" asked Julia, but Corey could tell that she didn't really care what the answer was. She was too busy eyeballing the ghosts tapping on the window.

A couple of the ghosts began to fling themselves against the door with all the strength they could muster, which was completely absent, and Corey took a step back. The ghost of a teenaged boy, his cap on backward, mouthed obscenities at Julia and gave her the finger. Julia reached out her hand and spread her fingertips against the glass. The ghosts flew into a frenzy, swarming across the window in a futile attempt to break through.

"Cool," said Julia. "Like one of those lightning plasma ball thingies." Her eyes shone in the light from the crackling ectoplasm. Corey couldn't stand to look at them for more than a few seconds at a time; they made him feel nauseous. He slapped her hand away.

"Don't tease them," he said.

"Why not?" said David. "We know they can't get out. It's the only thing we do know. That, and the fact that we'd better figure out where we're gonna find some food without having to tangle with those." He nodded in the direction of the ghosts and hefted his jar nervously from side to side.

"There's always vending machines . . ." said Corey.

"Glass," said Julia abruptly. "They're all behind glass. Could be the vending machines are haunted too."

"Nope," said David authoritatively. "I've got it all figured out. Wherever there were people inside last night—and that was just about everybody—they were wasted. Wiped out. Nuked. Ghostified. Whatever you want to call it. We were safe, see, 'cos we were sleeping outside." He nodded, obviously pleased with himself.

Julia leant closer to the window and pressed her swollen belly against it. The ghosts froze for a moment, their phantom eyes stretched improbably wide, then renewed their assault on the glass, moving so fast they turned into a blur. David and Corey simultaneously yelled and pulled her away, one on each arm. The blur slowly resolved back into distinct shapes.

"For fuck's sake, Julia!" said David. "You don't know what effect those things might have on the baby." Julia pouted and looked away. Her gaze stopped on a small stuffed toy left lying in the gutter, and she wandered over to retrieve it, David's reprimand already forgotten. David and Corey looked at each other and sighed. Julia's baby might have been Corey's, or it might have been David's, or for all they knew its father might be floating behind glass somewhere. But they had taken responsibility for her. Julia was special, a genuine, free-spirited innocent, or at least that was how Corey saw her. The way her mind was wired up, she alone needed full-time attention. He didn't want to think about how they would cope with her baby as well. The boys trailed after her. It had started to rain again, and they scuttled between shop awnings.

"Look!" said Julia. "There's somebody else! A live person!"

David looked up, swore, and pulled her into a doorway.

"Shhh!" he whispered, clamping his hand over her mouth. "It's a cop!"

"Yeah, but it's a *live* cop," Corey whispered back. "He's the first real human being we've seen all day. Maybe we should all stick together—you know, safety in numbers and all that."

David gave him a withering look. "If you really believe that, then how come you're not rushing out there to greet him with open arms? Betchya it was some government conspiracy or fucked-up military experiment that did this, anyway."

Corey peeped around the doorway at the cop, silently conceding that David had a point. The cop crept down the street away from them, holding his gun outstretched in shaking hands. As he turned the corner, Corey caught a glimpse of his wide, manic eyes. He ducked back into the doorway until they could no longer hear the cop's footsteps. They stepped out of hiding and headed off in the opposite direction.

"So if we're not going to look for other survivors, what do you suggest we do instead?"

"Maybe we could hotwire a car and head out to the coast," David said. "There's bound to be plenty of those million-dollar beach houses sitting empty in the off season."

"And if they're empty, fuckwit," said Corey, "their pantries will be empty as well."

David scowled and kicked viciously at an empty Coke can.

"Or we could go to my folks' place," said Julia. Corey started; he hadn't thought she was listening.

"They went on holiday in Europe three weeks ago," she continued. She cradled a small purple teddy bear in her arms and stroked it as if it were alive. "They were supposed to be coming home on Sunday . . . anyway, Mum had a Natural Disaster kit, so there'll be plenty of tinned food in that."

David gaped at her. "I thought you said your parents were dead."

"They probably are now," she said, shrugging. "Every now and again they used to track me down. Give me some money, ask me to come home, tell me what's been going on with the family, shit like that." Corey nodded. Now that she mentioned it, he had seen her a few times talking to a well-dressed middle-aged couple, and once or twice seen money change hands, but he'd dismissed them as a couple of Christian do-gooders.

"So let me get this straight," said David. He had wedged his jar between his feet and stood leaning slightly toward Julia, his hands gripped together behind his back as if to stop himself from forming them into fists. "You had parents. Parents who were alive, and who loved you, and who wanted you to come home. And you're eight months pregnant, and living on the streets with a pair of losers like us. Why, Julia? Why didn't you go home?" He spoke gently, but he trembled with the effort. Corey groaned and tensed in readiness, just in case David's volatile temper flared.

Julia smiled sadly. Her hair had gone mousy and lank from the rain, and for a moment all her innocence seemed to drain away from her. She caressed her stomach, and muttered, almost too low for them to hear—

"Daddy's not getting his hands on this one."


THE EMERGENCY KIT at Julia's house proved to be more than amply provisioned, with the added bonus of a well-stocked freezer and a full gas canister on the barbeque. Corey and David finished off their meal with a generous slosh of cognac from the liquor cabinet. Even with the warmth of the alcohol suffusing his body, Corey felt weird sitting there with pictures of Julia as a child gazing down on him from the photos on the wall. It felt equally weird retiring to separate bedrooms to sleep instead of huddling together for warmth like they usually did. Corey sprawled on the bed and stared at the shadows on the ceiling. At some point he must have fallen asleep because the next thing he knew, David was shaking him awake.

"It's Julia," David said. "I think the baby's coming."

Julia's labor matched none of Corey's preconceptions. He had expected it to happen very quickly, and for there to be a lot of screaming. Julia was on her hands and knees on her parents' queen-sized bed, which was soaked with amniotic fluid. She reminded Corey of a cat he'd had as a kid who'd had kittens in his wardrobe. She stared blankly ahead, panting a little, and every now and again she would let out a quiet moan. Corey and David sat with her as the night melded into day. Sometime after noon she got off the bed and began to pace the room. Suddenly she stiffened, grabbed David by the shoulder, gritted her teeth, and yowled like a wounded animal. Blood trickled down her left leg. She drew a deep, shuddering breath and yowled again.

"Do something!" yelled David, wild-eyed with panic.

"What, what?" Corey yelled back. "What should I do?"

"I don't know—go get some towels, or boil some water, or something. Do whatever the fuck they do in the movies."

Corey fled the room. He huddled uselessly in the corner of the lounge and tried to block out the inhuman sounds coming from the bedroom. After one particularly long, loud, heartrending cry, the house fell silent. He crept back to the bedroom, afraid of what he might see.

Julia sat on the floor in the corner of the room with her arms wrapped around her knees. An umbilical cord snaked from between her feet, out across the blood-streaked floor to where it was attached to a tiny naked baby girl. The baby curled unmoving on her side as if still in the womb, her eyes screwed shut tight against the world. David stood with his back against the wall, clutching his jar in front of him like a shield. Before Corey's horrified eyes, the infant seemed to deflate. Its skin stretched tight over its frame, then disintegrated altogether, leaving only a mound of bones. Its rate of decay increased exponentially, until there was nothing left but a pile of fine, pale dust. A small, white cloud rose from the remains and coalesced into the shape of a newborn baby. Corey heard the squeak of metal against glass, and turned his head to see David remove the lid from his jar and launch himself across the room to scoop up the tiny ghost and slam the lid on. Momentarily the specter hovered in the jar, still curled in its fetal position. It raised its head and opened its eyes, glaring at them all through the wall of its glass prison with a malevolent expression of awareness. Julia crept toward David and took the jar from his outstretched arms.

"My baby," she crooned, rocking the jar in her arms. The ghost drew back its lips in a gummy snarl and hissed silently.

Corey smacked David across the ear with his palm. "What did you do that for, dickhead?"

"I couldn't leave it just flying around in here," David retorted. "Who knows what it might have done? Anyway, it's all Julia has. Surely it's better than nothing." He glanced at the dust pile.

Corey looked at Julia, still sitting in the muck of afterbirth, cuddling her macabre offspring.

"No," said Corey, "I think nothing would have been much better than this."


BETWEEN THEM, COREY and David managed to coax Julia into a bath and settle her into bed. She fell asleep almost instantly, still clutching the jar. Sleep came more slowly for Corey, and when it did, it was filled with disjointed dreams. He woke abruptly at 2 a.m. Someone was moving about in the kitchen. He got up and padded down the hallway.

Julia stood at the breakfast table, eating from a can of peaches by candlelight and humming snippets of Rock-a-Bye Baby between mouthfuls. The flickering light on her calm, composed face made her look like an angel. And there sits the devil, Corey thought, glancing uneasily at the ghost baby in her jar on the table.

"You know, Julia," he said, "maybe it's not such a good idea to keep your baby in a jar like that. It's a bit . . . creepy. Maybe you should bury her. It'll make it easier for you to let go."

Julia looked at him with wide, demented eyes. "What are you talking about? What kind of sicko would want to bury a baby alive?" She snatched up the jar and hugged it to her chest. "But you're right about one thing. I shouldn't keep her locked in like this." She put a hand on top of the jar and twisted the lid a quarter turn.

"No!" Corey lunged toward her and made a grab for the jar. For a moment they held it between them, Corey's large tanned hands over Julia's small pale ones, and then the jar slipped and fell, shattering on the kitchen floor.

"My baby!" Julia gasped. She stepped forward, slicing her foot open on a shard of glass, and bent over to pick up the infant ghost that now lay on the floor. A wave of nausea overwhelmed Corey, and he dropped, retching, to his knees. David came rushing through the kitchen door, clad only in grimy boxer shorts.

"What's going on? I heard a crash . . . " He skidded to a halt. The ghost baby slowly rose from its bed of glass until it hovered in the air a few inches above their heads. It turned in a circle, examining each of them, its little face oddly intent. Seeming to come to a decision, it flashed a predatory grin.

Then, the screaming began.

---

TRACIE MCBRIDE is a New Zealander who lives in Melbourne, Australia with her husband and three children. She published her first short story in 2004, and since then her work has appeared or is forthcoming in over 50 print and electronic publications, including *Pulp.Net, Coyote Wild, Abyss and Apex, Space & Time, Sniplits and Electric Velocipede.* She won the Sir Julius Vogel Award for Best New Talent for 2007.

She is a member of the Melbourne-based group of speculative fiction writers SuperNOVA, an associate editor for horror magazine *Dark Moon Digest* and vice president of the writer's co-operative Dark Continents Publishing.

# THE DREAMCATCHER

BY NATE KENYON

JEREMY FOXX STOOD AT THE KITCHEN WINDOW, flicking the edges of the photo he held against his breast. He watched as the sheet of rain swept across the hay field and up the sloping lawn to the house.

Mom always says a glass of milk is *good for the nerves.* The scrawny blond boy in wool socks and long underwear slipped away from the window and put the photo on the counter to pour a cup. The carton shook and a little milk slopped onto the kitchen table. He stared at the spilled milk and tried very hard not to think about what was waiting for him upstairs.

His grandmother had gone with his mother to the hospital. Apparently he was too young to go with them, but old enough to stay by himself for three hours. He was half-inclined to prove them wrong by breaking something. But then he would have to "face the music." That was no big deal for movie tough guys like Bruce Willis, but Bruce Willis had never met Jeremy's grandmother. When she yelled at you it was like sticking your hand in a hornet's nest and holding it there while they did what came naturally.

He took his milk into the living room and plopped down into a chair. Bugs Bunny hit someone over the head with a hammer on the television, and that helped a little. But he couldn't seem to focus on the cartoon. He kept looking at the ceiling above his head.

*It's waiting for me.*

Immediately he stuffed the thought into his handy mental drawer and locked it. Everyone gets jumpy sometimes when they're alone. It was, in the immortal words of his father, *No big deal.*

But adults weren't always right. Some said that the way to beat something like that was to stare it down, but these were undoubtedly the same people still sleeping in a room with an especially strong nightlight.

The thing was, he'd never actually seen the coat tree move. At first he thought his mother was responsible for it. But why she would move the thing two or three feet to the right or left made no sense to him, and when he asked her if she was coming into his room in the middle of the night, she denied it.

He couldn't very well tell his grandmother. He knew exactly what she would say: *Don't you go and upset your mother, not in her condition. It was hard enough when your father left, and now this. She needs her strength.*

The coat tree was really a sculpture that Dad had brought back from a trip to Senegal years ago. It was carved from a rich mahogany and polished to a shine. Two legs and a long tail in back helped it stand up straight; the fat belly of the thing tapered up to a round ball that was much too small for a proper head. Two upraised arms made it look like a football referee signaling a touchdown.

There were really three places to hang things, the two arms and the little head in the middle. But when you put a hat on the head, the coat tree began to look a little too human. And if you hung your jacket around it, that was even worse. Alone and naked, the coat tree gave only the barest suggestion of human form, but with a little help it changed into a potbellied troll squatting in the corner, waiting to pounce.

When he told his friend Maria, she said that it must be possessed. She described a show she had seen on the Discovery Channel about primitive cultures. "You should get someone to come look at it," she said. "An expert could tell you right away if there was a spirit inside."

He didn't know anything about any experts. He tried to recall what his dad had said about the coat tree when he brought it home. But it didn't make any sense.

Jeremy realized he had forgotten his father's photo on the kitchen counter. He jumped up and ran to get it, and a familiar feeling of relief washed over him when he held it in his hands. Flick, flick, his thumb absently moved a corner up and down as he looked into his father's face. He forced himself to concentrate. Then he tucked the photo in the waistband of his long underwear and went back to the living room.

Bugs Bunny had given way to a talk show that featured a fat woman with a microphone and a bunch of bigger, fatter people who yelled at each other. A minute later the channel went to a commercial about a diaper that would make old people feel more secure.

That was when he heard a noise above his head.

A gust of wind shook more drops off the big oak tree near the window. The builders had placed the house right on the edge of a valley. Below the porch the ground fell off at a steep angle, and on clear days, if you looked out the back windows, you could see for miles.

Now he was thinking about different things. For example, theirs was the only house within three miles, and if he needed help, it would take someone at least ten minutes to get to him. That was assuming they knew he was in trouble and came right away.

He padded catlike up the stairs and paused at the top. His bedroom was at the far end of the hall, the door partway open. He couldn't remember if he'd left it that way.

When he tiptoed down the hall and peered through the shadows, the coat tree was standing in the middle of the room, halfway between its accustomed corner and his bed.

Jeremy stared. The coat tree stared back, its bulbous face as smooth and shiny as black ice.

He could feel his heart thudding so hard it shook his scrawny chest. His grandmother had come up to use the bathroom, as she always did before a car trip, and when she was on her way back down she must have moved it.

But why would she do such a thing?

I don't know, but she did, okay? *Because coat trees can't move by themselves.*

Okay. Fine. So he would just go back downstairs and watch TV. After he put it back in the corner, of course. Because if he didn't do that, he would be a big sissy. It was bad enough that all the kids made fun of him because his daddy had run away. Maybe he grew an inch already this year, but that didn't mean much if you couldn't even go into your own room and move a stupid coat rack back where it belonged.

Jeremy stepped through the open door. His window was cracked open. He caught a hint of that metallic smell that came with a summer storm. The sky had darkened outside, deepening the shadows in the corners.

Taking a deep breath, he grabbed the coat tree by the neck and lifted it off the floor. The wood was slippery, but it was just wood.

He was almost to the corner when the coat tree wriggled in his hand.

He dropped it like he'd been scalded and ran back into the hall, slamming the bedroom door shut.

*Oh God, oh God, oh God.* It hadn't really moved. His hands were sweaty, and it had slipped, that was all. Just slipped.

*I'm not going back in there, no way.*

He cracked open the door and pressed his face into the gap. The coat tree leaned against the wall, one of its legs sticking rigidly up into the air. He watched it for a minute, but nothing happened.

Jeremy sighed. His hand went to the photo tucked into his waistband, and the callus on his thumb found the dog-eared corner and flicked it up and down, up and down.

As he made his way back down the hall to the stairs, his mother's voice from this morning popped up in his head. *I have to go to the hospital today so they can run a few more tests. I need Gramma there. You'll be okay, won't you?*

Jeremy imagined a very large, very mean-looking needle sinking into her belly. Hospital tests meant needles and knives and machines that made terrible noises as if they were slowly sucking out your insides. He had seen a picture once of a machine that had a hole in the middle the size of a culvert, and in the picture there was a person stuck halfway into the hole. It looked like it was eating the person from the head down. Gulp, there goes the hair, and the eyes, which must have tasted pretty good to a machine like that, because in the next picture the person had been almost all the way inside. The only things left were the person's legs and feet, sticking out like the wicked witch in The Wizard of Oz when the house fell on her.

He hadn't worried too much this morning. He simply pushed the whole conversation back into his handy mental drawer, slid it shut and threw away the key.

Why had the drawer just slid open again with a bang?

*It's because I touched it!*

The thought floated to the surface as he reached the foot of the stairs. For a moment he almost remembered what his father had said about the coat tree, but it slipped away again and he frowned in frustration. He had a terrible memory. His mother always teased him about it. *You'd forget your head if it wasn't screwed on,* she would say when he was younger, or, *how's my little absentminded professor this morning?* Sometimes she would sneak up and tickle him until he gasped for mercy, and then she would give him a kiss on the forehead and say, *that's to keep all those happy thoughts inside, where they belong.*

HE WATCHED TV for a while. The clock on the wall seemed to be standing still. They had been gone not quite two hours now, though it seemed like ten, and if he could just last a little while longer without thinking about anything, he would be all right.

Wolverine was trying to slice up a bad guy on The X-Men, normally one of his favorite shows. Now he wondered why he had never noticed how ugly Wolverine really was. These were mutants, after all. Mutants were not like real people. They were taken over by something terrible that would either make them into freaks or kill them.

It had started to rain again. He turned on all the downstairs lights and that helped a little. But soon it would be getting really dark. This was when his father used to come home from work, before he had run away. *Blink.* One moment he was there, the next he was gone.

One hand on his father's photo, Jeremy got up to fix himself a TV dinner. This time he clearly heard, over the pattering of raindrops, a sound like a small puppy scrambling through the upstairs bedroom.

The rain began to fall harder as he took the stairs once again and faced the hallway. The wind picked up, rocking the house on its foundation. It was now as dark as night outside.

The door to his bedroom was open wide.

I touched it, he thought again, and shivered. Without warning an old, forgotten memory came back to him; he was not quite six years old, and he and his father stood on the porch looking out over the valley to the lights of town. This was perhaps only a month before his father disappeared. He had asked about the coat tree, and his father had told him, *it's a dream catcher, son. A very wise old man made it for me. It's supposed to catch all those mean little thoughts that only come out when you're sleeping.*

Jeremy thought of a big net catching all his nasty thoughts and letting the nice ones through. Something like that couldn't be bad, could it? He had kept it in his room all these years, and he had hardly dreamed at all. In fact, he couldn't remember the last time he'd had a nightmare.

His throat made a dry clicking sound when he swallowed. The darkness made it almost impossible to make anything out in his bedroom. *It'll be standing right where I left it, leaning against the wall with its stupid ugly leg sticking up in the air like one of those dead animals on the side of the road.*

And it was. When he reached the door he could just make it out through the gloom. He let out a great, shaky sigh, and was alarmed to discover he was close to tears. *Stupid old coat tree.* He stepped into the room and felt for the light switch. *Stupid little sissy . . .*

Standing there in the dark with his hand on the switch, he was struck once again with a memory of his father, in a brown jacket and corduroys (the ones with the patches on the knees), the smell of his pipe drifting away as he stared out over the valley. Jeremy had asked, *does it ever get full? What happens then?*

*It has to find some other place to put them, I suppose.*

Jeremy screwed his eyes shut tight and tried to close the drawer again on the memory, but this time it refused to budge. He opened his eyes and turned on the light, bathing the room in a soft yellow glow.

The dream catcher was looking at him.

Eyes had formed within the swirls. A bump that may have been a nose thrust itself out below the eyes; and then a slit for a mouth like the gills of a fish. The twisted legs had gained the look of flesh, and the arms now hung down at its sides. The eyes gained definition and wetness, the nose grew long and pointed, the cheekbones climbed upward and settled, as the lower part of its face sagged inward around a tiny jaw. The fleshless hole of a mouth lengthened and stretched.

The dream catcher turned its creaking head in the shadows. The little twisted man made of wood flexed his limbs.

A bolt of lightning split the dark sky. Jeremy screamed and staggered backward, hitting the door with his shoulder and slamming it shut, closing himself in. He screamed again, soundlessly this time, screaming for help that would not come, screaming in the face of such an impossible thing.

His father's face.

The dream catcher opened its mouth and darted forward. Two fangs of dark wood slipped out from under fleshless lips.

Jeremy searched frantically for the corner of the photo with his hand and felt it crumble into dust. He pressed back against the closed door, as if trying to force himself through.

There was nowhere left to go.


THE RAIN STOPPED and a car pulled up to the silent house. Two women got out; one of them, the older one with silver hair pulled back in a tight bun, helped the other, pale-faced and thin, out of her seat. They moved together up the walk toward the front door.

At the back of the house, a small, dark shape wriggled out of a half-open window and into the big oak tree. It swung down to the ground and darted across the lawn and over the drop.

The wind picked up and the oak tree shook its thick pelt of leaves. Up in the corners of the lonely bedroom the shadows deepened, layer upon layer, reaching out to where little twelve-year-old Jeremy stood, arms up and outstretched like a football referee signaling a touchdown. He had grown a wooden tail, which helped him stand upright. He was waiting to catch that first bad thought, his mouth frozen in a soundless scream.

**NATE KENYON** grew up in a small town in Maine. He sold his first novel, *Bloodstone*, to Five Star Publishing (Thomson Gale), in 2005. *Bloodstone* was published a year later to critical acclaim, becoming a Five Star bestseller, winning the P&E Horror Novel of the Year, and eventually becoming a Bram Stoker Award finalist in hardcover. Leisure Books published *Bloodstone* in paperback. Kenyon's second novel, *The Reach*, received a starred review from *Publisher's Weekly*. It is currently being developed as a major motion picture. *The Bone Factory* was released in 2009, along with a trade paperback science fiction novella, *Prime*, from Apex Books. His fourth novel, *Sparrow Rock*, was released in May 2010, and is currently under option with Chesapeake Films.

Kenyon's stories have recently appeared in *Shroud Magazine*, Permuted Press's *Monstrous* anthology, *Legends of the Mountain State 2*, *Horror World*, *Deadlines*, and *The Harrow*, among others, and he has several more forthcoming. Four of his stories were featured in the 2010 *Dark Arts* anthology *When the Night Comes Down*. He lives in the Boston area and has recently completed his next novel, *StarCraft Ghost: Spectres*, for Pocket Books and Blizzard Entertainment. Visit him online at www.natekenyon.com.

# JAMMERS

by Bentley Little

---

WHEN HE WAS LITTLE, COLEMAN COULD NOT understand the concept of traffic jams. Each time his family was stuck on the freeway on the way to some destination or another, he would ask his dad why the cars were moving so slowly. His dad would patiently explain that this was a consequence of living in a crowded metropolitan area. Coleman would argue that packed freeways didn't just happen, there had to be a reason. He'd say that there had to be a car or truck at the very front, a vehicle either wrecked or stalled or moving too slowly that was causing the traffic jam.

"There is no 'front'," his dad would tell him. "Sometimes, you're right, there is an accident, but usually there's just too many cars for the size of the freeway and the lanes get congested and that causes the rest of the cars to slow down."

"But the traffic jam doesn't go on forever," Coleman would say. "There has to be a beginning. There has to be a car that's at the front of it."

"There is no front," his dad would repeat.

And Coleman would nod, pretending to understand, though he really didn't.

Now, flying over the Santa Ana Freeway in the station's helicopter, he looked down at the winding snake of traffic that snarled through the city below. Early morning sunlight glinted off thousands of windshields, creating what looked like a sparkling river.

The pilot glanced over at him. "Nervous?"

Coleman shook his head. His palms were a little sweaty, but he wasn't really nervous. This would be his first traffic update for a real radio station, but he'd been doing live broadcasts for the campus station for the past two years, and the prospect of being on the air didn't frighten him a bit.

"Four minutes," the pilot said.

Coleman adjusted his headset and checked his mike. He looked down at the packed freeway below.

At the front of the traffic jam.

He quickly looked over at the pilot. "Do you see that?" Coleman asked, pointing out the copter's window. Four cars, moving in sync, drove forward slowly in an even line across the width of the freeway. In front of the cars, the four lanes were clear, free of traffic. Behind them, vehicles were logjammed for miles.

The pilot glanced down disinterestedly. "Jammers," he said.

"What?" Coleman asked.

"Two minutes to air time." The pilot flipped a series of switches on the panel in front of him. The station's traffic lead-in came over their headsets.

Coleman quickly shuffled his notes, freeway numbers, and jotted down a sentence describing the tangled mess below. He wiped sweaty palms on the legs of his pants. "Traffic blocked on the southbound 605 from the 91 junction to Spring Street," he said into the microphone. And he felt a thrill of excitement pass through him as he realized that many of those car radios on the freeway beneath the chopper were tuned into his voice. "There's a chemical spill in the far right lane of the Golden State Freeway . . ."

"I WISH I'D had a camera," he told Lena that night. "It was the most amazing thing I'd ever seen. Four cars, in a perfect row, moving about five miles an hour and blocking traffic all the way to La Mirada."

"Why didn't you mention it in your report?"

"I don't know," he admitted, surprised that he hadn't thought of it before. He leaned back on the pillow, staring at the ceiling. "Jammers."

Lena looked at him quizzically.

"Jammers. That's what Red called them. Jammers."

"What does that mean?"

Coleman sighed. "I don't know," he said. "I forgot to ask."

TRAFFIC WAS BLOCKED on the southbound San Diego Freeway, and Coleman had the pilot follow the winding ribbon of cars to see how far the traffic jam extended. The helicopter, its front end lowered as it cruised at full speed, passed over Torrance, Long Beach, Seal Beach, and Huntington.

"There it is," Red said, turning in a wide circle over the freeway.

Four cars were moving slowly southward in a straight line, blocking all lanes.

Coleman checked the time. He had fifteen minutes until his first report, and he'd already noted the condition of all necessary freeways. He turned toward Red. "Cruise in a little lower, will you?"

The pilot stared at him as if he'd just asked him to crash the helicopter into the side of a building. "I can't do that."

Coleman frowned. "Why not?"

"The Jammers are down there."

"And just who are these Jammers?"

Red shook his head. "You got a lot to learn, kid." The helicopter swung wide and headed north toward downtown L.A., moving in a straight line instead of following the path of the freeway.

"Where are you going?"

"Back."

"What the hell's going on here?"

The older man said nothing.

"Fine. Then I'll just have to ask Andreas when we get back to the station. He'll tell me."

Red sighed. "I guess I should've warned you ahead of time. I should've laid out the rules of the game. It's my fault, I thought you already knew."

"Knew what?"

"About the Jammers." There was a seriousness to the pilot's tone of voice, a sober, almost grave undercurrent that Coleman had not heard before.

"Who are the Jammers?" Coleman tried to keep his voice firm and steady, but against his wishes it came out sounding hesitant.

"You've seen them. They cause the traffic jams."

"Are they hired by someone?" He was confused. "Do they do this for fun?"

"I don't know who or what they really are. No one does. But they're a fact of life up here. Reporters, pilots, everyone who flies regularly knows about them."

Coleman looked at him. "You're afraid of them, aren't you?"

"You're damn right I am. And you should be, too. They're dangerous. They're . . . " He took a deep breath. "You can't get too close to Jammers, so it's best just to stay away. If you fly too low, if you try to follow them . . . " He left the sentence unfinished. "Just leave it be, huh, kid? Just do your job, give your reports, tell everyone which lanes are blocked on which freeway."

"Come on. You tell me some bizarre story about people you call Jammers, and you don't expect me to be a little bit curious?"

"That's the problem with you reporters," Red said. "You're *too* curious. That was Hawthorne's problem, too."

Clay Hawthorne, Coleman's predecessor, had been killed two weeks earlier in a helicopter crash on the Santa Monica Freeway.

Coleman looked down. They were passing over the 710. Below them, four cars moved in tandem slowly, blocking traffic for miles behind them.


"I DON'T LIKE this," Lena said.

"It is kind of creepy," Coleman admitted.

"What do these cars look like? Are they all black, like hearses or something?"

He shook his head. "They're just average, no specific color, no specific make or model. Generic."

"Maybe this is some kind of joke or something. Or a hazing ritual."

He laughed. "Yeah. My little radio station, in the midst of downsizing and budget cuts, is going to spend thousands of dollars to hire people to drive slowly down different freeways to tie up traffic in order to break me in."

"Well, when you put it that way . . . "

"They can't even afford to provide me with a new helicopter."

That made her sit up. "You mean you're flying around in some beat-up hunk of junk?"

"It's not as bad as all that. Really. It's all right; just a little on the old side."

"You be careful. Make that pilot fly safely. And make sure you stay as far away as possible from those Jammers."

"Don't worry," he told her. "Red wouldn't fly me by them even if I wanted to go."


HE WAS OFF on Saturday and Sunday, and Coleman tried to think of freeways that would be crowded. It was almost summer, the weather warm and pleasant, and he knew that a lot of people would be going to the beach. So he woke up Lena early on Sunday morning and told her that they were going to Corona del Mar for a picnic.

"The beach?" she said. "It'll be packed."

"It'll be fun. Besides, it won't be that crowded if we leave early and get there before the hordes descend. Come on."

The freeway had stopped up before they were even halfway there. Traffic slowed from 65 miles an hour to 40, to 30, then to 10. Soon they were creeping along at a rate even the speedometer wouldn't register, staring at a sea of bright red brake lights before them.

"Let's get off the freeway," Lena suggested. "I think surface streets would be faster."

Coleman shook his head. "It'll clear up in a minute," he said.

The traffic did end a few miles before the beach, disappearing almost as quickly as it had appeared, but though he looked for some sign—any sign— of the Jammers, he saw nothing.

COLEMAN POINTED DOWN at the freeway through the copter's windscreen. "What about those cars directly behind them?" he asked. Those drivers must know what's causing the traffic jam. They have to be able to see that there's only a single line of cars in front of them. They must know that it's clear sailing in front of the Jammers."

"Do you hear any horns?" Red asked.

Coleman shook his head. He didn't, but that wasn't to say there weren't any. He doubted that he could hear a rocket engine over the roar of the chopper blades.

"There *are* no honking horns," Red said. "Either those drivers know and are afraid to honk because of what might happen to them—or they're in on it. Either way, they're accomplices. Or they're Jammers too." He flipped the switches on the panel in front of him. "One minute to air time."

THERE WAS TRAFFIC on his way to work the next day.

And the next.

And the next.

No matter what time he left the house, no matter what route he took, Coleman ended up in a traffic jam, and he grew angry and frustrated as he thought of the Jammers.

It was almost as though they were doing this on purpose, he thought. It was almost as though they were playing with him.

"I SHOULDN'T BE doing this." Red's voice sounded thin and scratchy over the cheap transmitter. "It's wrong."

"Only people from the air get hurt. You've seen the cars on the freeway behind them. Nothing happens. They're fine."

"I don't like it."

Coleman drove aimlessly, not answering. He had called in sick this morning, but had told Red his plan yesterday afternoon. "You're a moron," the pilot had said. "You've only been on the job two weeks and you're a bigger moron than Hawthorne ever was." But after several hours of intense persuasion and several Happy Hour drinks at El Paso Cantina, Red had agreed to help out.

Coleman's heart was pounding in his chest. Half of him was excited, thrilled to the gills with the idea of seeing some of the Jammers up close. Half of him was terrified. The transmitter crackled noisily, but Red's voice was silent.

"I've found them," the pilot said a few moments later. "The 91 freeway just east of Rosecrans, heading west."

"Rate of speed?"

"Ten, maybe. At the most."

Coleman did some quick calculations. Even hitting all the red lights, he could still be on the freeway well before the Jammers reached Torrance. Assuming they didn't disappear before then.

He turned around at an abandoned Exxon station and headed south. "Thanks Red," he said.

"I'm sticking with you," the pilot told him. "I don't want anything on my conscience."

"But aren't you supposed to be—"

"I'm AWOL," he said wryly. "I've already called it in. Engine trouble. They'll get it from downtown for the next half hour."

Coleman drove quickly, feeling more confident than he knew he should. His plan was simple. He would get on the freeway well before the Jammers, pull off to the side, pretend that his car had broken down, and watch as they drove by. Nothing more. He wasn't going to follow them or join them or do anything foolish.

He just wanted to see what they looked like.

Coleman reached the freeway in less than fifteen minutes, pulling onto the on-ramp. The lanes were unnaturally deserted, and only one pickup sped by him as he slowed to a stop on the soft shoulder. He picked up the transmitter mike. "You up there?"

"Right here," Red said.

Coleman crouched down and looked through the windshield up into the sky. High above, he could see the station's helicopter circling the freeway in wide arcs. The sight gave him courage.

"I got you covered," Red said.

"Thanks," Coleman told him.

He sat there, staring out at the empty lanes. The deserted freeway made him nervous. The lack of vehicles was unnatural, a sight he had never seen outside of a movie, and the reality of it made him tense up. His hand muscles hurt from gripping the steering wheel so tightly, and he had to force himself to let go. He rolled down the windows, then turned on the radio, flipping through the dial, but nothing emerged from the speakers save static.

"They're coming," Red announced finally, and even through the crackle, Coleman could hear the fear in his voice.

He glanced in his rearview mirror. A mile or two behind, a line of cars was moving slowly toward him. He tried to swallow but his mouth had suddenly become very dry. His palms were sweaty.

The cars came closer.

This was stupid, he told himself. He could speed away right now, get off at the next exit, lose himself on the surface streets and be safe. There was no reason for him to do this. He had nothing to prove.

But he wanted to see the Jammers.

"I think you'd better go," Red said.

Coleman didn't answer.

"I don't like this. This is a bad idea."

The cars moved closer.

Now they were little more than a mile away, and he could see that the vehicles were not quite as ordinary as they had appeared from the air. They were all mid-sized sedans, but each of their hoods seemed to be customized. One came almost to a point, another was rounded, two were forked. The car in the lane closest to him, a black sedan, had a peculiar looking grill that reminded him of a malevolent smile. As it drew closer, Coleman could see that it was made of mirrored glass rather than chrome and spelled something out in foreign characters he did not recognize.

He could see nothing through any of the windshields except darkness.

The line of cars was now ten yards behind him.

Now seven.

Now five.

As one, the cars braked to a stop, even with his own parked vehicle. He quickly rolled up his window and locked the door.

"Get out of there!" Red screamed over the transmitter.

The door of the closest car opened, and an old man stepped out. A perfectly normal old man. He smiled at Coleman and motioned for him to roll down the window. Coleman sat unmoving, too stunned to react. He had been expecting something different. A hideous monster, perhaps. Or an animated corpse. Or . . . *something*. But not this strangely ordinary old man. His gaze shot skyward for a second. Red's copter was buzzing wildly over the scene.

The old man motioned for him to roll down the window, Coleman opened it a crack. "Are you all right?" the man asked. "We saw that your car had stalled and thought you might need some help. "He took a wobbly step forward. "I can give you a ride if you need it."

"Who are you?"

"Name's Carl Jones." He motioned toward the customized hood and grill of his car and grinned, showing missing teeth. "Nice wheels, huh?"

"What are you doing here?"

The old man looked puzzled. "Our car club patrols this stretch of freeway every day."

*Car club*? Was that possible? Were all these traffic jams really caused by a group of doddering, well-meaning old geezers who just drove too slow?

Honks were sounding from the cars behind them.

"Come on," the old man said. "I'll drop you off at the next gas station."

"That's okay," Coleman told him. I think I just flooded the engine. It'll be alright in a minute."

The old man chuckled. "It doesn't look like you're going anywhere to me." He motioned toward the side of the vehicle facing the freeway, and Coleman noticed for the first time that the left half of his car sat lower than the right. He opened the door, got out, and saw that he had two flat tires.

"I guess you do need a ride, huh?"

"That's okay. I'll just use my cell and call Triple A."

"Won't get a signal here. And there's no call boxes on this section of the freeway."

Was the old man sounding a little too insistent? Was he trying a little too hard to give Coleman a ride?

Red shouted something incomprehensible from the transmitter.

"We can't wait here forever," the old man said. Horns were honking behind them. Several drivers were yelling out their windows for the cars to start moving. He opened the passenger door and gestured for Coleman to get in the car.

Feeling numb, Coleman looked down at his two flat tires then up at the kindly face of the old man. *It'll be okay*, he told himself. *It'll be all right.* He sat down in the front seat of the sedan as the old man walked around to the other side. The seat felt soft. Too soft.

The old man got in the driver's side and both doors closed simultaneously. The inside panels, Coleman saw now, were smooth and featureless, with no door handles.

The old man started the ignition and all four cars began moving forward as one.

Coleman glanced back at the vehicles behind them, the ones whose owners had been yelling loudly only a few minutes before, and saw that they were empty. No drivers sat behind the steering wheels.

Out of the corner of his eye, he saw Red's helicopter plummet to the ground in flames.

"There is no front," the old man said, and his voice sounded like that of Coleman's father.

"What the hell?" He turned frantically toward the old man, panicking, but the driver had already started to morph. The wrinkled skin was running, melting, changing color. Coleman glimpsed beneath the shifting flesh a thing of darkness and emptiness.

Then he was thrown back in his seat as all four cars shot quickly forward.

---

Author, sculptor, musician, philosopher, architect, **BENTLEY LITTLE** is the coolest man on the planet. That is his gift, that is his curse.

# SPORTING THE WATERS OF THE BERMUDA TRIANGLE

BY GREGGARD PENANCE

*SPECULATIVE ZONE, 28.499° N, 67°.583 W*

THERE IS NO SENSE OF TIME OR LOCALE, JUST THE sway of the boat to the ocean's violent fit. The water swells, pushes the craft up and bursts over the port side, then recedes, pulling it back. The shipmates keep their feet apart for balance, grab hold of rails, poles, or equipment until it passes. Between these bursts, they move around, pause, anticipating the next jolt.

The midday sun washes the deck, but clouds tower in the distance to the front and port side. They stretch up from the horizon in deep streaks of charcoal and gray that split the day like the shadowed ridges of a canyon.

Blue light flickers across that blackness and charges the water, leaving a dome-shaped glow. Momentarily it is washed out by an outline of brilliant orange, which is followed by lime green. This bizarre electric storm has been brewing and becoming more pronounced as our boat approaches.

I have a full view of the port side and most of the bow. The captain's helm stands tall atop the bow, obscured from my sight by the edges of the rectangular slit that I've been given to see through. Across the deck stands another crate, I think the same size as mine.

A surge explodes over the rails. Mist roils the breeze and brushes across my viewing hole. My eyes should sting, but there is nothing. In fact, no sensation at all in my entire body, not even a tingle in my arms or legs. Perhaps the blood has constricted and my limbs have gone to sleep. Or worse, they might be dead. I'm confined so tight, it is as though I've been set in concrete to my nose. I'm also deaf. I can pick up their vibrations as the men shout at one another, but cannot hear them. Nor can I hear the storm.

The boat crew, burly men in rubber boots and raincoats, pace, industriously preparing. These are experienced seamen, who move with the boat as it responds to the swells that pound its port side.

During a calm moment, I study the other crate. Many rectangular holes in the side of it, and they are organized in precisely spaced columns and rows. These slits look to be the same as the one I view through, though I can't see what's behind them. The way the sun is positioned, shadows cover whatever might be looking out.

Flashes of blue, green, and orange light trade off overhead, spider webs etching the ridges of the storm and the fierce sea. A skirt of shade overtakes the boat, and stars abruptly pepper the sky. We have passed through a gateway from day to night in an instant. Clouds do not exist inside, yet the electrical storm tears through the heavy air, making for the only light to see by, and the swells grow heavier, rocking the boat still harder.

The ship hands scramble, hurried by the deteriorating conditions. It's unclear what they are setting up, or what for. A powerful wave breaks over the side and one man is knocked over. The crewman gets up quickly and grabs onto a rail to brace for the next surge.

The boat changes direction, heads on into the swells. The men open cases, pull out equipment. It is somewhat recognizable, but I just can't place it. Memory of my own life is not only gone, but any education that would otherwise spur recognition of objects and activities seems to be damaged as well.

A violent flash of orange casts blinding light on the ship and illuminates the other crate. As the boat veers toward the center of the storm, the holes in the crate are angled to catch the light.

A massive swell appears ahead. The nose of the boat rises upward, and the hull rocks from side to side from the force. The men keep their legs apart, each bracing their stance as the surge of sea moves under. My box slides on the deck with the roll of the boat, changing my viewpoint. I can no longer see the bow, but instead the stern, though the other crate remains in my sightline.

The ship glows as orange lightning strikes nearby, and brightness washes over me. Consciousness flutters and something smothers my vision—I swoon.

*Open eyes, vision gone. Brief blackness, then outlines appear. The hazy image like a Polaroid photo developing . . .*

*. . . through a window—no—a rearview mirror, a windshield. Night. Streetlights illuminate parked cars. Coming up on the lot, a building behind it, fluorescent with artificial light beaming up from below; a church with a tall steeple. Recognize the bell tower, the windows, the entrance. Come to an*

*intersection, cannot read the cross street sign but can recall what will be next. Cross the intersection, no more street lights. Narrowing road lined only by trees. The curves wind around in the blackness; can only see two lanes, the broken yellow dashes, and the thick line of trees along the shoulder. A charm dangles from the rearview mirror. It swings along as the car leans one way, then the next. Just enough light from the dash. Can see what's on the charm.*

*A woman and a young boy. Her name, Mindy, his, Stephen.*

*A pickup truck turns out in front, leaves no time to brake. The driver swerves to avoid being rear-ended, but too late. Brakes squeal. Smash into the right fender, bounce off toward the trees. Will hit the trees. A thought burbles up—"too fast". See Mindy and Stephen alone, devastated. Feel the loss, the wrenching . . .*

. . . back. I leave wife and son with no warning; they are alone.

Bright blue light flickers from all around. I wonder if Mindy has any idea what happened to me. Where I am.

The electrical storm has engulfed the boat. The water lights up and unnatural splashes ensue. Giant fish surging along the surface; sea foam burbling in brilliant colors, reflecting the lightning that etches the sky. Soon I see that it is not just in the sky, but the water itself has become charged.

The crate in front of me catches a beam of blue light, and I see what's behind the first slit. Big, frightened eyes. They bulge in the darkness and light up with the storm, and they do not blink. The sky casts a new flash with an orange glow, and the lumen brightens, stretching across a few more slits, then the rest of the crate. Dozens of them, all pairs of eyes, all darting around, a pair for each viewing hole. Something's wrong. There are way too many slits, way too many pairs of eyes. There is no room for the bodies!

While the lightning charges the sky and branches across the sea, the water turns calm, churned only by the swarming fish or whatever sea life moves around just beneath its surface. The swells dissipate, and the boat settles. We are in the eye of the storm.

The deck hatch opens again, and two more men climb up from below, both wearing strange suits. They are covered head to toe with metallic material, and their heads have bubble-shaped helmets. The other men hand them the equipment and climb down through the same hatch.

One of the men picks up a stick. It is a fishing rod, but a massive one, thick and long. Constrained by the stiffness of the suit, he waddles to the stern, and carefully sits in a chair. The chair is bolted to the deck and it swivels as he straps himself in.

The metallic man works his way over to the crate. He shifts funny. It stirs in my memory images from TV of men walking on the moon. He pulls up a lid from the top of the box and reaches in. Just below him a set of eyes turn up. He pulls something out of the crate and lightning flashes, enlightening a glass container that hangs from under his clenched palm and fingers. It looks like a two-gallon pickle jar. Inside it are the eyes, and behind them, the unmistakable contours and clefts of a human brain. The three parts float in a liquid, the eyes attached to the cerebral cortex with hundreds of strands of muscles and nerves. The man in the space suit holds the bottom of the jar with one silver-gloved hand, and the eyes stare up to watch as he twists the cap with the other.

A violent blast of orange light washes to yellow, and again my vision fails. I wait as the profile of a new scene takes shape.

*A hallway. White walls line each side. Move forward, a woman in powder blue pulls the bed. She watches, encourages, "You're gonna be okay," but her voice is not sincere. Two metal doors fly open and she pulls me through. A man looks over the top of me from behind the gurney. "The surgeon is waiting in the operating room," he tells the woman. "It appears that there are no head injuries."*

*The gurney is wheeled through another doorway. Two men standing in the middle of the room, gloves on and masks in place, rush to each side of the gurney and look down. They reach into the abdominal wounds, and one shakes his head. He looks at the other, turns, and studies my eyes.*

*"He's in shock", the man says. He glances at the nurse and orderly who just wheeled me in and says, "That will be all." They nod and exit the room.*

*The other surgeon leans in close to my face, near enough to me that when he speaks, I can feel his breath on my cheeks. I wonder, in this trauma, how a sense so subtle remains possible.*

*"Well, it will all be for the best. The bleeding is terminal, the kidneys ruptured, and his spine severed."*

*"He's got a donor card," the other says.*

*"Good, because we should certainly have use for the eyes. Let's see what else we can save."*

. . . I come to and the man in the silver suit has one knee on the deck in front of the jar. He is now unscrewing the cap.

With the lid removed, he sets the jar down on the deck, reaches in with one hand, and pulls the brain through the large mouth. As it glistens in the flashes of green, there is not enough muscle to support the weight of the eyes, so they dangle, staring down at the man's foot. He stands and walks over to the other man, who is waiting in his swivel chair, and stops at the rod. While still holding the brain in one hand, he gathers a clear line attached to a hook in the other. It is an enormous treble hook, larger than his gloved fist.

He turns the brain over and digs the hook into the stem. The eyeballs shudder, from shock or incredulous pain. The man then takes the bait and turns it up as the seated man reels in the line, leaves approximately two feet between the tip of the fishing pole and the bait. The man who set the bait steps away as the fisherman cranks the pole back and, with a powerful jerk, swings everything forward, sending the brain hurtling, its eyeballs gyrating like protons around an unstable atom. The bait disappears over the stern with a splash. Instantly, the water around it churns, and within seconds the man jerks. The hook is set into something powerful, and the rod rattles as the fight begins. The chair swings left, then right, and he reels hard. He lets up as his quarry turns and runs with the line. The drag on the reel whirs.

The electric storm lights the stage for some time until the man, who is standing, waddles over to the stern. He picks up a pole and turns it over the side. It's got a pointed aluminum gaff on the end, and he leans over the edge, in a prepared stance, holding it so that the hook faces out.

Green light illuminates something large as it rises up from the water, and the man with the hook lunges out at it. The man from the chair stands up, grabs a second gaff, stabs it into the fish from another angle. Both squat and strain to draw it in. The catch smacks the sidewall, its fierce fin or tail thumps three or four times, and a moment later a giant, fleshy creature slides over the rail and plunks onto the deck. It flops and squirms, and in the next flash of blue light, I see that it is not a fish. Nor is it an octopus or a sea lion. I've never seen such a beast. Ten feet long, this creature has smooth skin and blubbery flesh. It wriggles on the floor between two pairs of metallic boots. No fins, no features in the tail, and no face or eyes, it resembles a slug without antennae.

The man who reeled in the creature grabs another tool, a device that looks much like a pitchfork, only without the middle teeth, and he pins the monster, keeping its torso tight against the deck. The other man digs his boot sole flat against its squirming head, while the fisherman holds the midsection firm. He then pulls a two-foot-long pair of pliers from his belt pack. He leans toward the creature's snakelike head, turning about to get a look into the gaping mouth. With no further hesitation, he plunges the pliers deep inside the fleshy creature, past several rows of serrated teeth and wriggling gums. He digs around, causing the gums to flare and the long throat to swell and throb. Its six-foot length of tail recoils, unfurls, slaps the deck violently in an attempt to free its upper end, but the tool seemingly designed specifically to restrict this breed of monster does its job.

Seconds later, and the pliers are retracted. Out pops the brain and treble hook. He flips the bait onto the deck and the hook falls off to its side, a serrated chunk of cerebrum still attached.

He picks up his gaff from the deck and plunges it deep into the blubbery hide. Together, the two men drag the beast back toward the stern. One of them pulls open a hatch and they sling the giant thing so that it slides off into the compartment. The boat rattles again as the creature thumps the floor of the holding tank.

I turn my attention back to the sea-bleached brain as orange flashes from around the boat highlight its frayed and softened features. One milky eyeball lies next to it, a barely visible pupil gazing lifelessly into space. Again, a surge of blue energy engulfs the boat, and the eye twitches, turns up to stare at me a final time. Then it goes blank in an eternal stare.

One of the men produces a push broom and uses it to brush the remains in short, choppy sweeps toward the stern. He shoves them through the scupper into the sea, while the other man washes the debris away with a bucket of seawater.

He hangs the bucket on a rail and ambles over to my crate. The skies rumble and beams of neon green creep in from above, as my roof is lifted. I turn my eyes up, and for the first time I can see the lid of my own jar and the metallic fingers finding their grip around it.

---

GREGGARD PENANCE has spent a good portion of his life as a part-time free-lance writer for travel magazines. With roots in Tennessee and Arkansas, he travels more than not, and cannot remember the last place he called home. While his articles have been published in journals and magazines, he has only one horror fiction credit to note: The novella "The Breach" appearing in *Butcher Shop Quartet II* anthology, published by the fine folks at Cutting Block Press.

To his deficit, Mr. Penance does not subscribe to online self-promotional vehicles, and that mirrors his in-person lack of game. Shy people need love too, but who would notice?

# TO JUDGE THE QUICK

BY HANK SCHWAEBLE

---

EZEKIEL HEARD THEM APPROACHING, AN ANGRY rataplan of hoof-beats, drumming like summer thunder. The vibration followed the sound, thumping the soles and heels of his boots, telling him before he looked up that it was horses and not cattle. Horses being ridden hard, but horses, no doubt. The tremors of a stampede would have been felt right before anything reached his ears, not afterward. He knew that, just as sure as he knew the busy tattoo was too high-pitched to be longhorn, and too discernible as to each hoof to be more than six animals. He conceded the possibility of five, if his hearing had grown duller than he wanted to believe. But six was his best guess.

A twinge of pride passed over him as he straightened to see six riders come into view. Blurry, mere blends of moving color, but he was sure there were six of them. His eyes were strong. Always had been. When asked, he attributed this to not reading by candlelight, but the truth was he only read when necessary. Everyone he had ever known to read for pleasure wore spectacles of some sort. He was thankful to have avoided such a nuisance. Not that he was much for reading, anyway. But he was always quick to show those who questioned him that he could do it. Had learned the alphabet, learned to write several dozen words properly. Probably a hundred, all told. His oldest daughter had taught him. After the war.

The figures sharpened in their relief, and he saw there were not six horsemen, but four. The pride drained out and concern, mixed with mild trepidation, filled its place. A smaller number was no comfort, a lesson absorbed from the harsh instruction of life. He allowed that other lives may have taught differently—lives of men who'd fought on a battlefield, maybe—but in his experience, the larger the number, the smaller the threat. Besides, four horsemen were a bad omen. Everyone knew there were four horsemen of the Apocalypse. And there were usually four horsemen in a patrol toward the end, when the confederacy was in its last days and the only men left to ride were the sadistic outcasts, men living in the scornful wake of those who had bravely gone to war, men with something to prove to themselves, and to everyone with skin darker than theirs. And, at the end, always in fours.

No. He shook away the thought, brought himself back to the present, tried to focus on the here and now, on the world he lived in, not the world that was. He was in Texas, a freedman, no longer a slave in Alabama. Mr. Lincoln had freed him, him and the rest of those like him. He had once attended a gathering where some smarty Negro in a bowler hat and fancy suit coat tried to say that Congress had freed the slaves, not Mr. Lincoln; but that slicker had clearly never worn shackles, never felt the bite of the whip. Only one man ever did anything for people like him, at least as far as he could remember, and he was not going to let some flannel-mouthed snoot pretend otherwise.

The details of the riders' appearance became more noticeable as they drew closer. He tried to place a finger on what was so menacing about them, whether it was the violent angle of their bodies or the militant way they gripped their reins, or the large white hats atop each of their heads. But he soon saw it was none of those things. It was the fact they had shadows for faces, shadows that seemed darker than anything he had ever seen. Or not seen.

And he allowed that maybe it was the direction from which they rode that was spooking him. His mind resisted that one. Those stories caused tingles to grope him in ways he didn't like.

As they closed the distance further, kicking up whirls of dirt and dust and grass behind them, the texture and shape of the shadows showed them to be not shadows at all, but masks. Black hoods beneath white felt brims. He thought of the patrols again, though he was not certain why. Those men had never worn masks, never had a need to hide who they were. Maybe it was the way he recalled them riding onto the plantation, barging in like angry landlords. Wielding rifles and whips, looking for niggers learning from books, eating in the main house, having visitors, holding church. He remembered being scared numb by how the owner was powerless to stop them, scared long after they had come and gone. Mr. Morgan may not have always been the nicest man in the world, but he was not a cruel man, nor an unfair man. And he was *the* man. The patrols were made up of mostly poor whites, always stealing, peddling stuff off the roadways that they took from freed blacks accused of harboring runaways or violating curfew. Ezekiel Adams knew that if the man of the estate, a White man of breeding who owned two dozen slaves and a thousand acres, if that man was helpless in the face of a patrol, then slavery had created a force of nature that threatened everything in its path with mindless destruction. Like a funnel cloud or a tempest. Forces of nature could not be pleaded with, could not be persuaded. They were unmoved by invocations of Jesus or Satan. And Ezekiel remembered fearing that more than slavery itself. Fearing that more than death, even.

Evil was not in the blood, his mother used to tell him. It was passed through the tongue. It's what came out of a man's mouth that spread to others. White or Black, evil was learned, and could be unlearned. She used to say that once it got in the blood, once it didn't need to be learned anymore, that's when mankind would feel God's wrath. At times, Ezekiel wasn't so sure it wasn't already in the blood of some, that maybe Him not doing anything about it was the wrath she meant.

The tingling returned. The direction from which they rode was not good, and he was having a hard time not thinking about it.

He said a small prayer beneath his breath to bless the soul of Mr. Lincoln once more as the horsemen crested the nearest ridge and came within shouting distance. He was determined to maintain some dignity, what his mother used to call a free man's bearing, weighing in his mind that he had every reason to think these men were here to kill him, yet no reason in particular. But something told him he was not going to be killed, a sensation creeping around his gut. It told him the danger wasn't to him. Not at this moment. Try as he might, he could find no relief in the feeling.

The riders came to a stop a dozen yards before they reached him, forming a tight uneven line. They stood that way for an uncomfortable series of moments, appraising him through tiny rips in the black cloths covering their faces, the heads of their horses bobbing and snorting intermittently, before each abruptly reined their animal, half of them to the left, half to the right, as if acting on a silent command. It was then that Ezekiel saw, with a more subdued but still tangible flush of pride, that he had been right. A fifth rider strode through the gap on a black quarter horse, his right hand behind him, leading a fully saddled appaloosa. Once clear of the others, the rider made a tight arc with his horse, moving his trailing arm out wide around him, bringing the appaloosa to a stop between himself and Ezekiel.

Ezekiel reached up and snagged the reins out of the air as the rider tossed them toward him.

The rider had his mount continue circling until he was facing Ezekiel again. He said nothing. The only sounds were the huffs of the horses, the occasional clop of a hoof. Even the birds grew quiet. The relative silence seemed unnatural. It hung around Ezekiel's ears like a weight.

"This here's Mr. Campbell's horse," Ezekiel said, pretending suddenly to notice the brand. The tingling grew to where he felt a trembling in his limbs. He laid his shovel down across the post he was planning to reset and pointed back in the direction they had come. "If you were looking to return it, his spread is over yonder."

None of them replied. Ezekiel knew what he had said was pointless, knew the men understood exactly whose horse they had just passed off, just like he'd known whose horse it was as soon as he'd laid eyes on it. And since there was nothing else in that direction for too many miles to count, he even knew they had just come from Bill Campbell's ranch. But he preferred not to acknowledge any of those things. Knowing wasn't always a good thing. Problem was, not knowing always seemed to be worse. And what he didn't know was exactly what it was these men wanted of him.

Fixing a length of fence was not a crime. The law had been supporting fencers for years now. He couldn't remember the last time he heard of violence breaking out over such a thing, even if every week it seemed another section of his was being torn down. Surely no one, not even that mean and greedy Bill Campbell, was going to send men in masks to stop a man from repairing his own fence on his own land, even a Black man. It had to be something else.

The rumors stirred in his thoughts, demanding to be acknowledged, and he did his best to push them aside. Not thinking of something wasn't so hard, you just had to think of something else. But the cold tickle in his neck and spine that accompanied some thoughts wouldn't go away so easily.

He took in a breath. The breeze had died down, and he inhaled the gritty scents of upturned earth and wet horseflesh.

"Were you men lookin' for water?" he asked, because he felt he needed to ask something. "A place to water your horses, maybe?"

The men said nothing. Ezekiel passed his eyes over each of them, looking for a clue to what they wanted. They were all dressed more or less identically. Each wore a long tan coat and a blue shirt. Each wore brown cotton trousers and brown boots. Each wore a holster on his belt with a sidearm, the leather tied securely to his thigh, protruding along his bent leg through the gap of his open coat. Each wore similar black gloves. And, of course, each wore the black hood beneath an immaculate white hat. The only point of deviation in their uniform seemed to be their bandanas. Each had a different color. The one who had approached him boasted a white one, folded over and forming a curved, sagging triangle around his neck.

Ezekiel didn't know what they wanted, but he did have an idea of what they wanted him to do. A saddled horse with no rider, reins thrown to him—it didn't take an educated mind to figure it out.

But that didn't mean he was eager to do it.

As if sensing his reliance on the ambiguity, the rider with the white bandana abruptly turned his horse and paced it away. The others fell in line next to him. They stopped after a few yards and looked back, one by one, black hoods peering over broad shoulders.

His ability to feign ignorance washed away, Ezekiel mounted the appaloosa and followed as the men spurred their animals to a gallop.

They rode for a good spell before he saw anything. Ezekiel guessed fifteen minutes, but he was never much for measuring time. They crossed the open fields and passed between the thickets of oak and pine and sweet gum, over a gully and through a pasture. He did not know where they were going, but he feared he could guess. What he did know is they were on William Campbell's land, passing William Campbell's cattle as they grazed, and that made him extremely uncomfortable. William Campbell would probably shoot him if he caught Ezekiel trespassing like this, especially if he was caught riding Campbell's horse. But he knew that if there was any shooting to be done today, these men around him would likely be the ones doing it, so that was not his concern.

It was the stories he'd been hearing about Campbell the past few months, how the man had gone mad as a hatter after losing his wife and child to yellow fever. Crazy stories, stories that made no sense. Stories he wanted to dismiss as bosh.

Stories about a woman with skin darker than the bottom of his well, and eyes darker still. A woman who was brought to do the work of the devil.

He stopped pretending there was any doubt as to the destination when he saw Campbell's house. There were three figures near a large oak tree out in front of it, and another standing closer to the porch. One of them near the tree was on horseback. The others were standing beneath its canopy, one on each side of the trunk. Standing on something, it seemed. The one on the horse and the one near the porch each had a white hat and a shadow for a face, though Ezekiel allowed that he might be assuming that last part. Five other horses, saddled and bridled, looked hitched to a rail of fence as they grazed.

They halved the distance before Ezekiel saw the noose, halved it again before he saw that the man whose neck was in it was Bill Campbell. He was blindfolded, rocking stiff-legged on a section of log that was too thin to hold its balance. By the angle of his arms, curving at the elbows and disappearing behind his back, Ezekiel assumed Campbell's wrists were bound to the rear. Then he realized there were two nooses, the other on the far side of the tree around the neck of a tall, skinny negress in a ratty prairie dress and white pinafore. Her skin was blacker than charred wood. Ezekiel wanted badly to turn back, to burst off and keep riding, to be anywhere else but in this field with these men approaching that tree. But he knew that was like wishing a pair of deuces were a pair of queens. *Wish in one hand, crap in the other* he remembered hearing a man who'd lost his legs in the war once say. *See which one fills up first.*

The tree was drawing close now, and he began to worry about what plans—what *difficulties*—these men had in store for him. A lynching of a White man, that was not something a Black man wanted to be around, not in Alabama or Texas or anywhere he could imagine. Ezekiel studied Campbell's face as its details came into view. The man's expression, jowly and ruddy, was pulled as tight in a grimace as the folds of flesh would allow. He was nervous, too. His face was slick, his hair shiny, and his shirt soaked, even in the cool breeze on such a mild day. For that, Ezekiel couldn't blame him.

The woman looked worried, but defiant. They hadn't blindfolded her, and her saucery eyes, white loops around black centers, darted from hat to hat like she was taking names. She held her chin up, full pale lips puffed out, almost pursed. He could tell more than one tear had cut a trail down her face, because her dried ebony skin was a bit white and flaky in spots, except for where the long tails of moisture left their marks. She was sweating, too, like Campbell, her dress pressed flat from the dampness. But she seemed determined to keep herself proper. Dignified.

Damn fool, Ezekiel thought. Even a colored woman dark as her stood a chance of escaping the rope if she just blubbered and begged and did things a woman was expected to do.

But then he remembered the stories, and thought, maybe not.

All the riders except the one with the white bandana gathered near the tree, next to the other members of the group. The April breeze was pushing toward them, rippling through their coats like a series of tiny waves as they turned sideways to it. They lined their horses in a row, perpendicular, facing both Ezekiel and the tree. An audience.

Ezekiel examined the rope around Campbell's neck. It was drawn tight up and over a branch, angling sharply to a stake in the ground near the foot of the horse closest to the tree. There was a squat mason jug next to it, like someone had been snorting homemade liquor. Or was planning to.

The rider with the white bandana pulled a rolled-up piece of parchment from his saddlebag, maneuvered his horse near to hand it over. It was tied around the middle with a small piece of leather. Ezekiel reluctantly took it from him and the man stabbed a finger at it, as if to make sure Ezekiel couldn't play dumb. Ezekiel unfastened the tie and unrolled the sheet, holding it with one hand on top and the other on the bottom.

There were words written on it. Big, blocky letters. Some of them he recognized. Others he had to sound out, mouthing them slowly, piecing out the pronunciation. He lifted his head as he realized what it said. He looked at the tall rider with the white bandana, then at the other men lined up near the tree, then at Campbell. The wind was coming from his back, flapping the parchment in his hands.

He studied the rope again, told himself this had to be some elaborate joke. This was not a hanging. Ezekiel had seen several hangings in his day. It was not that easy to hang a man. The rope and the branch both needed to be strong. And the rope had to be secure. He'd seen several men hit the ground running as a rope came undone or a tree branch snapped. This rope didn't seem all that strong, and he doubted that stake in the ground would ever hold a grown man's weight, even if the branch would.

Ezekiel started to say something to the man with the white bandana, but the man drew his pistol and pointed it at him. Ezekiel got the message. He took a breath and raised the parchment. A sharp fume irritated his nose as the breeze ebbed. He wondered if it was the stench of fear. Then he wondered if it was his or Campbell's.

"William Campbell," he said, his voice shaky. As he spoke the words, one of the riders trotted forward, circling Campbell, and removed the blindfold.

Campbell blinked, angling his head down and squinting into the light. "Adams? Adams, is that you? What do you think you're doing? Who the hell are these—"

The rider with the white bandana turned the pistol toward Campbell and cocked it. Campbell's face flushed, but he held his tongue. Ezekiel wondered for a moment if it was a flush of rage, if maybe the mere presence of a Negro placed a heavy thumb on the scale for anger, balancing it out against fear.

But then he saw how slack the man's jaw had become, how the red had turned pale. The man's heart was under a severe strain and was affecting the flow of his blood.

"I'm sorry, Mr. Campbell . . ."

The door to the front of the house swung open, clattered against its stop. A man in another white hat, black hood and duster rumbled out. He was holding a long, hollow pole with a rope double-threaded through it into a loop. At the end of it flailed a boy in tattered trousers and a few strips of cloth hanging from his shoulders. The loop of the rope was around his neck. The boy hissed and snarled as he clutched at the pole.

Right behind him, another hat and hood with a pole clomped out, this one leading a woman the same way. She made less noise than the boy, but her face, scratched and filthy, matched his ferocity, all bared teeth and wild eyes.

Two other men followed, holstering their revolvers as they stepped onto the porch.

Several of the horses nickered and backed away. Ezekiel felt himself almost slide off his saddle as one of his boots kicked out of a stirrup. His hand was trembling so badly, he found it difficult to grip the horn.

He swallowed dry, unable to find any wetness in his mouth. The men with the poles led the thrashing boy and woman to a clearing next to the tree. Ezekiel knew these people, or knew them well enough. Seen them in town, the woman at the general store, the boy every spring at the fair. Before the fever. He felt himself sway, like he was trying to balance on water. Either the stories he'd heard weren't crazy, or he was.

The man with the pole leading the boy stumbled as he reached the clearing, his boot heel catching something on the ground. He didn't let go of the pole, but did let the rope slip and that was all it took. The boy pulled free and scrabbled in a mad rush toward the man closest to him, the one leading the woman. The child uttered a high-pitched growl, reminding Ezekiel of a bobcat as he lunged and clamped his jaws on the man's arm. Ezekiel knew he'd never forget those eyes, burning with something unnatural, lit with the glow of a branding iron just removed from a flame.

The horses reared and twisted. Ezekiel struggled not to be thrown. He heard a man's scream, then several shots. When the horses finally settled down and Ezekiel could see again, the boy and the woman lay motionless on the ground, soupy matter oozing from large holes in their skulls. Their faces were locked in feral expressions, animal ones, the likes of which Ezekiel had never seen, and prayed he'd never see again.

Campbell was weeping now, and Ezekiel wondered if it was his scream he'd heard. The man mumbled through his sobs, just loud enough for Ezekiel to hear, saying, *"It wasn't done yet . . . She just needed more time . . . They just needed more time . . ."*

Smoke rose from the barrel of the gun wielded by the man with the white bandana as the scene settled down. The man seemed to stare at the bodies for a long time, as if maybe he was trying to make a point, or possibly think of one, then he swung the gun toward Ezekiel and cocked it once more.

Shaking as he was, Ezekiel cleared his throat and fumbled to open the writing again. He found the gun in that man's hand to have a remarkable way of aiding his understanding of what was expected of him.

"William Campbell. You have been … found … guilty … of … the crime … of … nek … necro—*mancy* … "

Ezekiel looked up again, catching a glimpse of the bodies, then back down before white bandana had a chance to react. The bore of that pistol looked huge when he stared into it.

"You … and the n-n-neg-ress Obi have called upon … the p-p-prince of darkness to ease your suffering and vi-vi-" He stopped and coughed, wiping at his eyes. "Vi-olated the laws of Heaven.

"For your crimes … against … nature … and nature's God … you … have been … sen … ten … ced … to burn … in … the … fl-fl-flames … of … Hell.

"May the Lord and S-S-Savior … have mer-mercy … on your soul … when He comes to judge the q-q-quick and the dead … "

Ezekiel raised his eyes. He saw that Campbell's face had drained. There was only resignation there now. But Ezekiel knew there also had to be fear, hidden beneath the flesh. The smell of it, or something like it, seemed to be trying to reach Ezekiel against the breeze. It was then he realized why he'd been brought here, what his purpose was. He wanted to tell the man it would all be okay, that they were just trying to teach him a lesson, but he knew that wasn't true. He didn't know what was about to happen, and not knowing always seemed worse. Still, he clung to the hope they really weren't intent on hanging the man. But he also presumed they viewed killing as wrong, that they feared God's reckoning, and he had little reason to believe that. Not these men. Not the one with the white bandana who rode so tall in the saddle, who carried himself like a gospel sharp on Sunday morning.

White bandana holstered his weapon and gestured with a tilt of his head toward the others. The rider who had taken the blindfold off Campbell held it up, then removed something from a pocket in his coat with his other hand. He'd struck it against his saddle before Ezekiel realized it was a match. Within a moment, fire was creeping up the dangling cloth, licking and clawing skyward.

Campbell screamed. He started saying *no* over and over. His eyes grew impossibly wide. The look of someone suddenly realizing something. Seeing his reaction made Ezekiel realize it, too.

The Obi woman started laughing, a loud, raucous laughter that reached into Ezekiel's body, transformed into icy claws, and squeezed his heart. Then the laughter stopped and she began to speak things he couldn't understand, chanting, almost singing words heavy and melodic with m's and b's.

She twisted her head to see the man the boy had bit. He was favoring his arm, pressing it against his side. She turned back to Ezekiel. Through a wide smile she spoke again, loudly and clearly this time, eyes focused only on him.

"*Judgment has already begun,*" she said. Her voice sent a shiver through him, as if a thousand people had just marched over his grave. He would have sworn had he not known better it was his mother speaking. But he knew that could not be. She'd been dead more than twenty-five years.

The rider tossed the cloth onto the rope near the stake. The fire made the sound of wind pressing against a door as it traveled up the rope, looped over the branch, and plummeted down to the noose. Campbell's hair erupted first, then his shirt. Within a heartbeat, his entire upper body was a torch. Ezekiel could see his open mouth through the flames, watched his body shake and shudder, saw the thin log being knocked to the ground.

The woman's rope caught a second later, another cloth tossed onto it. Unlike Campbell, she made no sound. Her body was still, motionless as the flames ravaged her. An empty shell, delivered into Hell. Where its occupant had gone, he had no clue.

Ezekiel knew he'd been wrong. Even enveloped in flames, the rope was plenty strong. Same for the tree limb. And the stake. He watched Campbell's body jerk and twist, watched the fire consume it. Recognized the smell of kerosene and roasting flesh. He tried to close his eyes, but couldn't get them to shut. He felt compelled to face it, compelled to accept that he'd done nothing to stop it. The fact he couldn't have was no comfort. He imagined the painful sensations in his chest to be his soul sagging under the crush of guilt, found himself wishing for the first time ever that he was a slave again. He wondered what he'd done to be singled out for such a horrible punishment as that, one worse than he just witnessed. He knew now for certain these men would not harm him, though he found himself praying they would, praying for any outcome that would not leave him with these thoughts and nothing else. It was as if God had smote this man in the cruelest way conceivable, simply to prove Ezekiel had been wrong about everything he'd ever believed.

The men waited for the hanging bodies to burn out before dumping what was left of the kerosene over the boy and the woman they'd shot. They lit them on fire, then rode off, whipping their horses into a gallop. The man who'd been bitten was the slowest, trailing behind. Ezekiel realized he was in more pain than he had wanted the others to know.

The sun was setting. Ezekiel supposed he should ride into town, tell the Sheriff. That was what he was there for, he knew. To bear witness, to tell everyone what had happened, and why. To let the world know this was not a crime, not a slaughter, but an act of justice. To send a warning.

He tugged his mount back toward his own land instead, shaking and uncertain, the woman's last words echoing through his head.

*Judgment has already begun.*

His mother's words mixed with those as he glanced one more time in the direction of the departing riders, the last one looking unsteady in the saddle, still hunched over and in pain as he shrunk in the distance. Somehow he knew she'd been right, that somehow, some way, her words were coming to pass. *Once it got in the blood, that's when mankind would feel God's wrath.*

He stared at the ground, then peered a final time in the direction of the riders, saw the last man crest a hill. The straggler, the man still favoring his arm. The man who'd been bit by a creature more animal than child, the glow of the devil in its eyes.

Knowing was better than not knowing, something he'd never doubted, something he'd always been sure of. But in a part of his soul he rarely listened to, the one untouched by things like pride, he wondered if he might have been wrong about that, too.

---

**HANK SCHWAEBLE** is a thriller writer and attorney living in Houston, Texas. Hank's debut novel, *Damnable*, won the Bram Stoker Award for best first novel. The sequel, *Diabolical*, is scheduled for release in the summer of 2011.

A graduate of the University of Florida and Vanderbilt Law School, Hank is also a former Air Force officer and special agent for the Air Force Office of Special Investigations. He was a distinguished graduate from the Air Force Special Investigations Academy, graduated first in his class from the Defense Language Institute's Japanese Language Course, and was an editor of the law review at Vanderbilt where he won several American Jurisprudence Awards.

Hank is an active member of the Horror Writers Association and the International Thriller Writers Association. In addition to reading and writing, Hank enjoys martial arts, keeping in shape, and playing guitar.

# DRIVING DEEP
# INTO THE NIGHT

BY HARRISON HOWE

---

*THE SHADOWS TWITCHED IN THE HALL LEADING to Sherry's room.*

*The room itself, as still as a held breath, as silent as a tear slipped down a pale cheek. Nothing there to speak of Sherry's fight against the sadness that overwhelmed her life. It resided even in her hollow smiles when she greeted those who came to her door. Then, the memory of a breath, stirring the air in the hidden world of Sherry's room.*

*She called out.*

Dev stepped onto the porch and knocked softly. He took a deep breath, like an Olympian diver on the end of the board, hands clenching around the bunched stems of a dozen cellophane-wrapped roses. He knocked again. Then he turned the knob, opened the door and stepped into the small house.

Sherry's breath seemed to stir the air, her scent on his nose hairs. How many times had he drifted down this dark place, knocking on her door, pressing himself into her curves, feeling every pore on her skin and bud on her tongue?

But tonight was different. Tonight it was as if she were calling to him, drawing him to that room. He couldn't recall having intentions to come here tonight; one moment he was on his way home from work, the next he was in the floral shop with just enough cash in his back pocket to cover the cost of twelve long-stemmed roses.

The cellophane crackled between his fingers. Rose petals swirled past his knees. Thorns pricked at his fingers, drawing blood.

She seemed to be here, right in front of him, drawing him through the threshold and down the hall. She oozed from the dark pockets in the corners, lightless patches that appeared to hold the very essence of her. Her voice curled into his ear canal. But not his name. Never his name. She never wanted names.

But tonight he would tell her. He would slip it into her ear while they lay together. Tonight was love.

Heads turned when Dev stepped into the room.

Sherry said:

*There's no names in this room. Only me. I'm Sherry. Sweet like wine. Taste like wine. You'll get drunk on me, but I don't need your name. You keep it. There are no names in my room. I hear names and it's over. You get your money back and you go. I love you when you're here, you love me when you're here, but you go when you're done. And don't touch the pictures in the hall.*

Howard watched the house, dropping cruller crumbs onto the mound of his belly. Sugar sparkled on his lips. His leg jerked, the way it always did when he was nervous, rubbing against the steering wheel. He practiced in the rearview mirror.

"I love you."

"*I* love you."

"I love *you.*"

He sounded lame and desperate, silly and sincere, but he hadn't had much time for practice. He couldn't even recall driving here. It seemed one moment he'd been home, half-asleep in front of the TV, and the next he was in his car.

He looked in the rearview mirror and said, "I *love* you." Maybe she would smile. Maybe she would say she loved him, too. Maybe that was why it felt like she was calling out to him without even knowing his name, just her voice reaching out to him, only him. Was that love? Howard thought it must be.

No one did the things she did to him. You had to love someone to do that.

He was forty-six years old and had never known love. He lived with his mother in his childhood home, slept in the same bed he'd wet as a child, the same bed he'd sprawled on to read comic books, the same bed in the same spot under the window for over four decades. If you moved the bed the paint on the wall behind it would be lighter than the rest of the room; the bed's feet leaving divots in the rug, maybe worn all the way through the carpet to the floorboards beneath. Forty years of water marks that slipped in past the sill and left tracks down to the baseboard.

He finished the cruller and got out of the car before he'd even swallowed it, wiping sticky sugar granules from his fingertips. He was sweating though it was cold.

"*I* love *you.*"

He left his wallet in the console. Tonight there would be no money. Tonight was love.

"My name is Howard," he whispered. "I love you, Sherry."

In the dark, he thought he heard her answer. Bellowing her name, he charged the house.

*Framed faces stared sadly from their places on the hallway walls. Sherry would say these were her "heroes". None of her visitors knew what she meant. Sometimes she smiled when she said it, a wistful twist of the mouth, eyes downcast. No one knew who was in the pictures. In some there were kids; in others, adults. Maybe Sherry had the man's eyes, the woman's slope of forehead. She's on a porch with a young man, arm linked in his. They are happy. A thousand questions, but no one asked. Sometimes Sherry would run her fingers lightly over the photos as she led them to her room. Sometimes she'd be crying.*

"We're sorry, the customer you are trying to reach is not in service. Please—"

Phil snapped his phone shut and tossed it onto the passenger seat, next to the gift box the saleswoman had wrapped for him. He was almost there, anyway. She had her phone disconnected, so what. She would be there. She was always there, in that room at the end of the hall. She'd meet him at the front door and they'd go down the hall—too narrow to walk side-by-side, her in front, reaching behind to lead him by the hand—and into her room. Sherry's room. Blood surged in his veins.

He told Jenny he'd be right back, just going to the store for baby formula, and some part of him seemed to believe that's exactly where he had been headed, but before he knew it he was traveling east, toward Sherry's house.

He couldn't catch a green light along the Boulevard.

The night carried her to him: the smell of her, the sound of her. If she knew his name, he imagined he'd hear it now, his name in her voice. The thought aroused him, and so he pushed harder on the gas pedal.

He strummed his fingertips against the steering wheel, chanting "Fuck fuck fuck" every time a light turned from yellow to red. "Fuck fuck fuck."

She would be there. She was always there.

Tonight she had to be there.

Tonight he was going to make her his. He'd profess; propose, if he had to. The night lay heavy with possibility, almost a tangible thing, like a wool blanket or a thick overcoat. Tonight he'd tell her his name and he'd make her his.

He flipped open his cell, dialed her number.

"We're sorry, the customer you are—"

*Sherry's room is shadows. It holds her in its walls; the feel of her melded into the paint, the trace of her footprints in the rug, the smell of her sex on the sheets, of her blood in the air. Sherry's room is empty, yet it is not still.*

There were a few diamond rings on the dresser, glinting like razors scattered in the sun. Her clothes—expensive gifts, Sherry never had to buy her own clothes—were strewn around the room, draped on the bedposts and along the floor. One middle-aged man with a graying goatee and a thin, sharp nose was holding a sequined shirt in his hands and pressing his face into it, sucking up her scent. Weeping.

"Where is she?" Dev asked. The man who had opened the door for him just stared blankly, a gun dangling in one hand, his eyes red-rimmed.

"Not here," the goateed man said, lifting his face from her garments. His voice was flat. He kept staring at a dark spot on Sherry's wall.

Dev took some wilted flowers out of the vase by her bedside, unwrapped the cellophane from his, and put them inside. Petals lay strewn across the top of the night table. Already his roses looked droopy; they'd be dead by morning.

There was another man, kneeling by the bed as if in prayer, face pressed to bloody sheets.

The goateed man cried out Sherry's name.

Dev spun, snatched the gun from the hand of the man who had let him in, stuck the barrel in his mouth, and blew all thoughts of Sherry out through the top of his head.

Howard wept, pressing cruller-scented fingers to his eyelids. He said, "Why?" over and over again. No one would love him the way she did. No one. He wept until it seemed his eyes would melt. Then he stumbled down the narrow hall, shoulders brushing against Sherry's pictures. They swayed on their hooks.

He found the kitchen. The knife drawer.

He carried what he took from the drawer back to Sherry's room. It seemed right, it seemed just, somehow, that he do it there. He was still crying when he gutted himself on the floor beside her bed.

*A sigh filled Sherry's room; a whisper of satisfaction. Her name caressed the air.*

Phil let his gift, forgotten, tumble from his hands to the floor. The person he had been trying to reach was not here, not anywhere. He stood in her room, ignoring the others who ran their hands over her things, cried for her, stared off into space as if watching her undress once more. His mouth worked but no sound came.

He went to her closet, her clothes hung on misshapen wire hangers. He found a hook with a dozen belts hanging from it. He took them down, strung some together and hung himself from the light over Sherry's bed. He choked and gasped for nearly ten minutes, his shoe soles tangling in bloody sheets, plaster dust drifting down like autumn snow.

*Sherry's room lay empty. Just shadows like the thoughts of her, smeared on the walls. Soft echoes of her memory in the wallboard, the rug, the bedposts. From the bloody razor on her nightstand, to the stains on the worn carpet on either side of the bed, to the dried tears streaked into the pillowcases.*

*Nothing moved. In the hall, her heroes stared down like stern fathers over misbegotten sons, smudges of her trailing fingerprints on the glass.*

*Sherry's voice faded. Rose petals curled like dead spiders atop her dresser. A dozen voices cried out for her, and then the room, satiated, fell silent. For a brief moment, there was only the fading light of Sherry's hidden worlds, and then that, too, was gone.*

---

**HARRISON HOWE** came wailing into the world 45 years ago (and hopes to be much quieter when he leaves it), perhaps intent on having his voice heard right from the start. He is the author of *R.I.P.,* a YA zombie novella published by Coscom Entertainment, 2009, and a dark poetry collection, *The Voice of His Brother's Blood: Crying,* eTreasures Publishing, 2006, which became available in print and to Kindle readers in 2008. He has published numerous short stories and poems in various print and online publications. He is also the editor of *Darkness on the Edge: Tales Inspired by the Songs of Bruce Springsteen,* which was released in early 2010 by PS Publishing.

Harrison currently resides in North Carolina with his incredibly supportive wife, two children, and what could unofficially be the world's oldest living beta fish.

# IN THE RED

BY CHARLES COLYOTT

IT COMES IN FITS AND SPASMS, ERUPTING ACROSS THE pages in droplets and sprays. Points intermingle into lines and curves. Lines and curves intertwine into symbols the mind transforms into sounds. Symbols gather and align, changing from sounds to ideas.

It is a kind of magic, really, when you stop to think about it . . .


EVERYONE WANTS TO know how it started. Well, it began like this—standing at the mail box, I opened the letter and read the short, form response. Sadly, it said, *Forizons Magazine* had to pass on my story.

I thought of the piece and ran through it in my mind; was the magic somehow incomplete? I closed my eyes and saw each word. Each part of the formula was whole—everything was correct and perfect.

It was a simple thing to crumple the paper. I threw it into the ditch by the mailbox and walked away. When someone's job is to pass judgment upon the work of others, they lose their own magic. I don't write for them. Their corporate mindsets and their soulless publications don't produce art. They smother it and kill it and dance around its grave.

They only buy what's safe. I know this. If they'd accepted it, that would only have proved my writing was shit.


I DID NOT tell Maureen. Her broken record nagging was feeble and tiresome long before it ever left her mouth.

There was no art in that woman at all . . . not back then, at least.

She sat there at her table, leaning over her new presentation with a rogue strand of hair in her eyes, her hands stained with smears of paint; I felt nothing but a sort of numb disgust.

Tomorrow she would roll up her clean lines and sanitized colors. She would slip the fruits of her labors in a cardboard tube. In time, it would be the backdrop for some corporate hack's mind control ad program to sell more toothpaste or detergent or—God forbid—feminine hygiene products.

The checks, she said, cashed just the same.

And we're back to that again.

"Why won't you just talk to them?" she'd say.

"With practice you could write reams of ad copy in your sleep," she'd say.

"Ever wonder why they call it 'copy,'" I'd say.

"I am not a copier," I'd say.

"I am a revolutionary. I write from my soul."

"Your soul doesn't pay the bills," she'd say.

And, right on schedule, she'd turn away, maybe knock some of her paint over for emphasis, and stomp off to the bed room.

I don't have to tell you that she slams the door, do I? You hear it in your head even though the words aren't there.

That's part of the magic.


YEARS AGO, ON Maureen's advice, I joined a writer's group. She'd gotten the idea from some marketing book somewhere. Not only was it valuable to share and critique each other's work, she said, but it was a tool for promotion. As if sitting in the café of some chain store, once a month, circle-jerking with these morons was time well spent.

One of the first pearls of wisdom I received from them was "Know your audience." Looking around the group, I knew enough to know that this wasn't it—an obese, pink-haired old nag with a penchant for syrupy romance stories; an ill-kempt professor type with hair jutting out discordantly from his scalp and a shirt tail always just escaping the wooly prison of his giant fuzzy sweater (he wrote shitty, masturbatory poetry, of course); and a large-breasted soccer mom with twin interests in young adult fiction and our rumpled professor's disheveled old cock.

Oh, and then there was Tim.

Tim was alright, I suppose, for a hack. He was the only one with the ability to put words together in ways that made other people care. Unfortunately, he'd used his powers to make a quick buck. It started with an article for a men's magazine—one of the ones where nubile young celebrities strip down to their bras and panties to plug their latest movies—and, after that sale, an agent took an interest in one of Tim's novellas.

I'd read the novella. Typical cookie-cutter genre shit. And of all the genres, it was horror. Such a waste of talent.

He said to me once, "It's all a game—learn the rules and play."

Easy enough for him to say. His game was money. He wrote what other people wanted to read and that's why he was on his way to the supermarket racks.

He'd found his audience, that's all. Never mind that his audience consisted of brain-dead teens, socially inept comic book collectors, and—worst of all—giggling little goth groupies that thought Tim was "a cutie."

I know my audience too, and they are the ones that read my words and understand. If only five people on earth truly ever get what it is that I do, that's four more than I would ever have believed. I don't take the easy way. I don't give people what they want to read. I give them what they need. The creation process is hard and sometimes painful, but that's what birth is all about—agony and terror and tearing yourself open until something of worth comes from it.

That's why I laughed and walked out when Tim said, "I think you just need to maybe put more of yourself into the work, Martin."


UNLIKE SO MANY writers, I do not drink.

Unlike so many writers, I actually write.

I went home that night and wrote as I'd never written before. I sat there, eyes closed and fingers moving, for what seemed like forever. A sheen of sickness covered my body and made my scalp itch and ache. My fingers burned for hours before they finally split.

It was easy to ignore the pounding on the door and the rattle of the knob; they came and went in cycles, like the tides. The sound of the keys clacking droned on, and my mind droned with them.

Periodically, as I stopped to sip water or massage the feeling into my back or legs, I checked my word count.

The first time I stopped to change keyboards, I was at fifteen thousand.

The last time, three keyboards later, five hundred thousand.

Looking back on it, the whole process was amazing, but I couldn't tell you what those words meant. It was gibberish and, in truth, didn't matter at all. It was a fever dream, a Braxton-hicks—a preparation for what was yet to come. In the end, I deleted the file without a second look.

During my normal working life, I was lucky to have one thousand decent words after six weeks of struggle; my short stories were finely honed masterpieces that sometimes took a full nine months to create—

They were shit.

—and here I was spewing out words faster than my hands could move. I commanded that they move faster; I pushed the joints and digits to the breaking point, literally.

The pop must've sounded louder in my head than it did in reality, but it was enough to stop me momentarily.

I looked at my fingers. The flattened pads and tips shone without the small ridges and dips of fingerprints. The knuckles were fat and tight, swollen to the point of bursting, the nails sunken and black from the congealed blood underneath. The cuticles had long since revolted, springing the nails outward like miniature scoops. My hands hummed and quivered as I watched. They sang of the symbols and letters and words and ideas that fought to flow through them.

They ached for more.

With a painful difficulty, I clenched and shook them out. I closed my right hand around my left palm and, like a milkmaid with a cow's teat, pulled and squeezed down the length of my fingers. Each nail unsheathed for perhaps an eighth of an inch before slipping loose from its bed and clattering to the keyboard.

Of course I hurt, but that's what artists do.

The blood which flowed, slow as molasses at first and then bright and smooth as new ink, from the vacant craters in my fingers emerged with strength and intensity that eclipsed the flow of mere words earlier; this was unfettered truth, unbridled expression. Droplets spilled and sprayed the keys; crimson spatters coalesced and intermingled into lines and curves; lines and curves intertwined into symbols that gathered and aligned into pure thought in 12-point New Courier font on my screen.

And as the last gelled globule stained the cracked keys, I saw an end to the new manuscript. Using a stained forearm to operate the mouse, I scrolled back to the top of this new story, writ in blood, and I read. Afterward, I saved the manuscript to three separate disks and printed a hard copy.

Over time, I managed to stand. (The stains on my pants did not embarrass me; I had no connection at all to those processes.) I unlocked my office door and emerged into the house. Maureen was nowhere about so I went to our bathroom, washed up, and changed clothes, throwing the stained items into the trash. The house was empty and quiet, perfect for my work.

My stomach roiled and burned in protest but before I fed it, I fumbled bandages onto my hands and with great care folded the new manuscript, placed it in an envelope, and mailed it to the first publication that came to mind.

Two weeks later, I received a phone call from the editor of *The New Yorker*. They wanted to buy my story. Minutes after the conversation, my fax machine spat out the contract. I read and reread it, searching for any loophole that would allow them to steal my work. When I was confident that they couldn't, I signed it and faxed it back.

When the check arrived, I took it to Maureen where she'd been staying at her mother's house, and she actually leapt into my arms.

The only thing I felt was pride. I was right after all, and now she saw it.

I had not sold out.


THAT FIRST STORY generated an enormous buzz. Maureen handled the phone calls and gave the agents and publishers the information I'd written out for her. Everyone wanted a piece of me, it seemed, but I remembered Tim's words—I knew the game, but I wasn't going to play it by anyone's rules.

They would learn to play by mine.

Contracts came and I signed them.

Wounds healed and I opened them.

Stories emerged and I sent them.

I hear they were quite powerful. I didn't read them. Didn't have to.

Calls came from the *Today Show*, *Oprah*, and *60 Minutes*, among others. I declined their offers. The statement Maureen gave to the producers told them that everything I had to say was in my work.

Offers came to sell movie rights. The short list of names included Hanks and Eastwood, Bertolucci and Coppola, Spielberg and even the kid who did that horrible musical I couldn't stand.

I turned them down too, via Maureen. My medium was the written word, she said, and as the written word it would stay.

All of that only made them want me more. And the more they wanted, the more I obliged. I was not totally unfeeling toward my audience, after all, but they would have to understand that this—these words—was where the magic dwelled. And now I was the fulltime magician, no longer in the red . . .

. . . Not that the money mattered; it didn't. Not to me.

I did not leave my office, not even to sleep. Maureen, finally understanding after all these years, never bothered or interrupted me. She left the meals, bandages, and antibiotics outside the door at six a.m., noon, six p.m., and midnight. When I could pull myself away, I ate; when I couldn't, she took the dishes from me without a complaint. She no longer sold her soul to the marketing jerk-offs; she managed my career instead. Don't think for a moment it was because she was proud of me or loved me . . . she, like everyone else, just wanted to be the first to read whatever I bled next.

When the time came that the stories no longer flowed as they once had, I did not panic. All writers face creative blocks at one time or another. For me the solution was simple—there is always more of one's self to put into the work, if one is willing.

When *The New Yorker* solicited another article, I dragged a dull utility knife across my palm.

An essay for *The Antioch Review*? Snips of the first few millimeters from the tips of my index and middle fingers with Maureen's garden shears did the trick.

A creative non-fiction piece for *Brick*? I slipped my teeth under the edges of my newly re-grown thumb nail and peeled.

. . . All just ways to get the creative juices flowing.

I received Maureen's reports of the daily goings-on, with my breakfast and supplies at six.

She was always after me to clean the keyboard until I let her watch me work; the brown, scabrous thing had evolved, somehow. It barely even had keys anymore; they had sloughed off to make way for the thirsty, puckered mouth which waited anxiously for my next project.

A number of the big publishing houses warred over who would print my first book, even if it was only an anthology of reprinted stories.

I had never attempted a novel, but it seemed the right thing to do for my fans. Reprints would not hold them over, not anymore. It was bad enough that I had to wear earplugs for a month while contractors installed an elaborate security system to prevent them from breaking in to meet their literary savior. Some even sent packages—cardboard boxes with dark, wet stains that I regretfully had to return, unopened; it is never a good idea to accept unsolicited work.

Still, they are my beauties. They understand the magic, right down to their very bones. They deserved something bigger, something better—something with teeth.

I developed a system that Maureen followed strictly. Food and drink would now be brought inside the office, providing that she made no sound and wore a black, shapeless dress to avoid distracting me. Any distraction would be cause for punishment, and punishment meant no more reading, ever.

The system worked, and it was more and more necessary the less mobile I became.

Especially after that first disaster . . .

*PARDON THIS DIGRESSION, but I feel the need to talk shop for a few moments—*

*The place to cut, I discovered through a bit of trial and error, is at the ever-so-slight depression of the anterior talofibular ligament—just below that bony protuberance on the side of the ankle.*

*Note—this is true of all joints. Never go straight in against the bone, this is the mark of an amateur.*

*In this instance, I used a Black and Decker Jigsaw equipped with the metal-cutting blades, but the aspiring writer would do just fine with a standard hacksaw.*

*The secondary cut to the forefoot should take place later, certainly after securing and stapling the posterior flap and bandaging the stump. Broad spectrum antibiotics should be taken orally for 1–4 weeks to insure no loss in productivity. Keep in mind rule number one of writing—writers write.*

*Back to that forefoot—the simplest method I know is to cut between the 2nd and 3rd toes to the midfoot region (i.e. the bones you cannot saw through comfortably) and follow up with a secondary transverse cut between the metatarsals and cuneiforms. At this point, it is a simple thing to remove the bones and set them aside for later. Feel free to delegate this step to the agent or publicist if necessary. The bones may, at a later date, be dried, powdered, and added to the fluid mixture. This could well be the meat of your narrative so do not cast this part aside willy-nilly. The fleshy bits may be blended or juiced, depending upon the equipment at hand, and are then available when needed.*

I WORKED AT the novel without ceasing; composing the next day's work in my mind during the hour or so I allowed the body to sleep. This was necessary. Real art comes from pouring one's heart and soul into the work.

*(One last technical note—do not skimp on your blender. The heart is a very tough and fibrous muscle. This is no place to use that fifteen-dollar wonder you received as a wedding gift. You really do get what you pay for, you know.)*

Maureen's assistance was vital during the creation process. During this time I came to understand and value her a great deal more. She earned her place in the front matter of the book.

With such inspiration, she began to create on her own. Before long, producers no longer bothered her about interviews, but it didn't matter. The audience understood.

Maureen showed me videos and pictures. It was easy to pick out my true fans by the patches and the gauze, by the prostheses and the IVs.

My first and only draft clocked in at just under 120,000 words.

That's roughly 480 pages or so.

Critics have said that my writing, the stories, the essays, everything combined, doesn't amount to very much. This, coming from people who no one will remember a single generation from now. They never learned the secret, but I did.

We did.

I live, even now, in these words.

Through this magic, I am immortal.

And as your eyes scan these words we are absorbed to live inside of you.

All of you.

Forever.

But enough about me.

This was never about me, it was about the art. Your art, now. A great and vast vista lies before you, just waiting to be explored. So head on back to the kitchen, grab that steak knife I caught you eyeballing earlier, and let's get started.

We learn, after all, by doing.

---

Bio(hazard): **CHARLES COLYOTT** is the pseudonym of an interdimensional virus frequently transmitted via unprotected eye-to-text contact. Symptoms include: An irresistible urge to raise alpacas, unprovoked bouts of cursing in Mandarin, and possible weight gain.

Past outbreaks have been quarantined within the pages of *Dark Recesses Press* magazine, *Withersin* magazine, *Read by Dawn II* anthology, *+Horror Library+ Volume 3*. Further instances of contagion have been said to echo throughout the mindless, gibbering void of the internet. And Facebook.

If you fear that you may have become infected, do not be alarmed . . . You have.

# SKIN

BY KIM DESPINS

---

THIS THING WEARING HIS SISTER'S SKIN STANDS AT the foot of Jeremy's bed, just as she has every night since he moved back into his father's house. When Jeremy asked Lisa to help care for their father in his last days, she hung up on him. Instead, this thing visits in her place. She whips the covers from his bed, and Jeremy's skin puckers in the cool rush of air.

He thinks she's changed her mind about helping with their father, but when he touches her, the skin slides over the thing underneath and he knows this can't be his sister. He tries to scream but nothing emerges except a soft moan. He pushes her away, but his hands caress that pale skin while something else pulsates just beneath its surface. His body refuses every command his mind issues. He's come to accept these visits, even enjoys them in some unnatural way. There's always penance.

His entire adult life has been penance. In the Peace Corps he taught English in a tiny cinderblock room to children who asked only the English words for food. After failing to feed anything more than their minds, Jeremy joined the seminary. His room there had a wood floor, plaster walls, and no starving children. As a priest, he enjoyed the overgrown garden behind the rectory. The trees hung low, denying the herbs sun and stunting their growth, but the air tasted fresh.

The priesthood had been his escape. The children, their minds hungrier than their bellies, arrived at Sunday school eager to learn. His parishioners responded to his counseling with appreciation. After almost thirty years of searching, Jeremy finally found a community, a family.

His father's illness has ripped him away from that family, and he aches to return. Jeremy waits for his father to die so he can return to his life in the church. His life with no starving children. His life without this thing wearing his sister's skin, and its unnatural hunger.

Lying rigid on his mattress, Jeremy promises when he returns to the church, he'll trim the trees and feed the herbs with sunlight. He can't confess something this unsavory, but he vows to pray every prayer he knows a dozen times. *Anything*, he pleads with God, *just make this thing go away.*

Every door is bolted, every window shut tight. Yet here she stands wearing the skin of someone he loves. This caricature of a woman is not his sister. Lisa lives thirty minutes away in Boston. Her partner and his religion are two of the many things they never speak about on the rare occasions they talk at all. During those conversations, Jeremy does the talking, and Lisa provides vague answers to his questions. Calling her his sister seems wrong, invasive. He barely knows her.

Would she notice, he wonders, that he replaced the Farrah Fawcett poster from his boyhood with a framed photograph of a pale yellow crocus, opening among the crystals of melting snow? The photo was a gift from a parishioner. Jeremy tried to tell Lisa that he'd burned the cache of dirty magazines he'd found piled in his dresser drawers, forgotten since high school. Her response had been a dial tone.

Jeremy called her three times the first week he spent in his father's house. Twice she hung up on him, and the third time her partner claimed Lisa was out even though he heard her voice in the background.

"Wait," Jeremy said, struggling to remember this woman's name.

"What?"

"Does she still like to catch lightning bugs?"

Lisa's voice came through the background. Jeremy pictured her standing next to her partner, one hand on her shoulder. "Tell him not now. I can't talk to him now."

"Don't call back." The partner hung up the phone.

The thing that looks like his sister unties her robe and lets it fall to the floor. Her skin glows in the moonlight. He wishes for the false safety of blankets, to curl up under the covers and pretend there's not a monster in the room. But his body disagrees. She climbs atop him, pausing to kiss his erection much the way Jeremy hopes to kiss the rings of the pope. Every night is the same, down to the hopes, regrets, and memories as she takes his willing body, and his mind pretends to fight from its cage.


AT 13, JEREMY developed a painful crush on Missy Salinger when she pushed her bathing suit bottom to her knees and showed him *hers* behind the boathouse. Jeremy put his family jewels on display for her, but she gasped and ran away, leaving him alone with his swim trunks around his ankles.

Thinking about the freckles on Missy's pale thighs and where they led,

Jeremy hiked through the woods between his family's vacation house and the Salingers' cottage. Her voice reached his ears before he got to the edge of the woods. Crouched behind a lilac bush, he listened to Missy and Toni Wilson chatter about girl stuff while baking their skin in the sun. He ignored their words and drank Missy in with his eyes.

Her red hair, barely contained in a pony tail, shone in the sun. Jeremy imagined weaving his fingers through those curls. He untied his swim trunks and slipped his hand inside. Jeremy massaged his erection until Toni's words stopped him cold. The flesh in his right hand softened.

"You saw it?" Toni asked. "You really saw it?"

"Yeah, it was all shriveled and gross."

"So it was small? Where did he show you?"

Jeremy's skin burned to the tips of his ears.

"Behind the boathouse. I can't believe he really did it."

"Did you—"

"Ew! Of course not."

Jeremy sucked in deep breaths, but it didn't calm the anger flooding him. The word *liar* rested on the tip of his tongue. He breathed in a mosquito buzzing among the lilacs and coughed it out of his throat.

Both girls sat up on their towels.

"Who's there?" Toni called.

Crouched low, Jeremy ran back into the woods. Behind him, the girls giggled.

Missy's words followed him through the trees. "What a creep."


HE'S FINALLY DYING. A down comforter pins the old man to the bed, his outline faint. The rise and fall of his chest doesn't move the blanket, but the thick gasps tell Jeremy it's not quite over. Jeremy waits in a kitchen chair next to the drug-littered night table. Half-empty beer bottles stand among the prescription containers like trees. Jeremy gave up on taking away his father's vice when he found the Styrofoam cooler lodged between the bed and the wall. Instead he picked a handful of daisies and plunked them into a bottle. Now the flowers bend toward the floor, their white petals ringed in brown. His bags are packed and waiting in the car.

Dressed in his vestments, Jeremy reads his Bible. Matthew chapter five, verse thirty catches his eye. "If thy right hand offend thee, cut it off, and cast it from thee." His father tried that. The cancer started in his testicles. Doctors took those almost a year ago, but surgery came too late. The disease marched through his body to the lymph nodes, the bones, and finally to the major organs. Doctors removed every offending organ they could, but it was never enough.

His father struggles under the covers. Jeremy pulls the blankets off his chest and dabs at his sweaty forehead with a cool cloth while muttering meaningless words, telling his father it'll be all right. The old man grips Jeremy's wrist with the strength of a child.

"Forgive me, Father, for I have sinned." He gasps for breath, his toothless mouth a dark window into his diseased body.

Jeremy picks his father's fingers from his arm and looks away. "There's no need." Some things even a priest can't bear to witness.

The old man collapses onto the mattress, his uneven breath hitching into something that resembles a sob. He looks up at Jeremy, his eyes alert for the first time in days.

"Son?"

"I'm here, Dad."

"Remember when we went to Virginia Beach?"

Jeremy had been nine, Lisa six, Mom healthy. What Jeremy remembered best was that the cooler had been filled with soda instead of beer, and they'd built a sandcastle as a family. Dad drove them home before the tide washed it out to sea.

"I do, but then Mom died."

Jeremy checks his watch. It's just after 11. The thing wearing his sister's skin usually visits around midnight. Part of him would like to be gone by then. Part of him will miss her when he returns to his life of penance. It's the most contact he's had with his little sister in years, even if it is with just her skin.

His father shivers under the sheet. Jeremy gets up to open the window and let in the cool air. When he turns back to his seat, she's at the end of the bed, robe pooled at her feet. Her toenails are painted glitter pink.

She raises one finger in the air and looks at Jeremy. Wait. He wraps his hand around the crucifix dangling from his neck. The cross is big enough to be hung on the wall, but he's always preferred the weight of it around his neck.

The thing that's not his sister pulls the sheet from his father's withered body. Somehow the old man has the strength for an erection. Jeremy tries to close his eyes, but they disobey. Heat gathers in his groin.

His father cracks open his eyes as she takes him in her.

"No more," he wheezes. "I'm sorry."

Jeremy's stomach churns. This thing has taken his father every night just before coming to his own bed. Jeremy tries to turn his head, but it remains fixed, his gaze on the two bodies.

She thrusts against the old man, making his body flop against the dirty sheet. The pungent smell of sex mingles with the odor of medicine and beer. His father coughs, gasps for breath, finds none. Jeremy sees himself shove the thing off his father, but his body makes no move other than to slip one hand into his trousers.

His sister—no, the thing wearing his sister's skin—makes no sound, she bounces against his father's hips, her gaze trained on the water-stained wall above the headboard. Jeremy watches with one hand clasping his crucifix and the other caressing his erection, as his father expels a breath and falls limp. The woman runs her knuckle along the old man's cheek, then slaps him before slipping off of his cooling body. His head rocks to the side, his empty eyes fixed on Jeremy, whose hand is still in his pants.

She kneels in front of Jeremy, looks up at him with his sister's green eyes, and speaks with his sister's voice.

"It never bothered you before."

Jeremy extracts his hand from his trousers. She unzips them and takes him into her mouth.

*Not my sister*, Jeremy thinks. His mind chants the reminder, trying to take control of his body. *Not my sister.*

Jeremy focuses on his father's corpse, one age-spotted arm flung off the side of the bed. The yellowed nails are long because Jeremy forgot to trim them. He finds control of his own arms, they still have life. Jeremy grips the long end of the crucifix in both hands, rips it from the chain. He turns it upside down and thrusts it into the thing knelt before him. It slams into the base of his sister's skull.

*Not my sister.*

She gasps, choking on his member. Jeremy pulls himself from her mouth and brings the up-ended crucifix down again and again. In his hands, the metal cross pulverizes her spine. The sound of it reminds him of the crunch of gravel under his shoes on the rectory garden path. It reminds him of freedom. She falls forward, pushing Jeremy against the window. She curls into the fetal position, the blood darkening the wood floor around her head and matting her blonde hair. *Not my sister.*

Jeremy buttons his pants and starts to clean the mess. His erection refuses to fade until he has the thing wearing his sister's skin hidden away in the parlor closet.

JEREMY TRUDGED THROUGH the house toward his bedroom where there waited a copy of a Victoria's Secret catalog he'd swiped from a neighbor's recycle bin. His father thumped down the stairs as Jeremy waited to go up.

"You been to see that Salinger girl," his father said.

"How do you know?" Jeremy braced himself against the wall as his father grabbed his shoulder to steady his balance.

"You been sniffing around that girl since we got here." He limped to his easy chair, collapsed into the flattened cushions, and exhaled. His father had installed carpet before arthritis settled into his knee, twisting it into a gnarled formation that looked more tree than human and bent about as well as wood. "That girl's nothing but a tease. She has no intention of putting out for you."

"But I don't—"

"Don't argue with me, boy." He dug a beer from the Styrofoam cooler next to the chair. "I was your age once."

"Yes, sir."

"If your mother was here, she'd say you was too young for sex."

Jeremy stared at his feet and nodded.

"She woulda kept both you and me on the straight and narrow like we should be." He twisted the cap off the bottle and threw it at the front door.

Jeremy climbed to the third step.

"But she's dead so you might as well grow up." He pulled the lever on the chair, popping the foot rest into place. "Boy your age needs to recognize that a cock-tease is nothing but a waste of time. Boy your age should be practical."

"Yes, sir."

"It's time to stop beatin' off to something you'll never have." He swigged his beer. "Got what you need practically right under your nose, too."


OLD PEOPLE HE doesn't remember fill the house, cluster around their fallen friend. Jeremy imagines he can hear them praying, "Please, God, not me next." His father had insisted on a traditional wake in his home, even asked Jeremy to clear out the parlor in preparation.

Tired of hearing their stories about when he was "this high," Jeremy skirts the group. More often than not, he finds his back pressed against the closet door, palm on the doorknob, blood rushing to his groin, the smell of her lingering in his nostrils. Incense permeates the room, but barely masks her scent. Each time he compels his hands to grasp the oversized crucifix around his neck. It's bent, but he gathers more comfort from it now than ever. He scans the sea of blue hair for his sister's blonde head, then reminds himself that she refuses to step foot into this house.

Jeremy settles those still living into chairs, begins his father's wake. When it's over, he forces himself to the front porch, where he accepts their condolences to the music of crickets. "You're so brave to preside over your own father's funeral," one bent old man says. Jeremy nods, but doesn't feel that way.

The last car backs away and Jeremy means to follow, but he's left his Bible in the parlor. His father's casket dominates the room, surrounded by empty chairs and bouquets of flowers. His feet carry him past all of this to the closet. Exhausted, he surrenders, relying on the penance he'll do later.

It's inside. Cold and stiff, half standing against the back corner behind his father's fishing jacket. He lifts it, and his sister's skin slides across the body underneath. Jeremy's stomach roils, his member hardens. He lays her body on the carpet alongside the casket, brushes her eyelids closed, strokes her hair. Blood has matted it at the back of her head, but the front is still soft and white-blonde. Leaning forward, he presses his lips to hers. His excitement dwindles at the cold lack of response. His hand wanders between her legs, slips a finger inside. What was once damp like a summer day at the lake is now a dry riverbed. The memory is enough for him. Trembling, he stands and fumbles with his belt.

On the parlor floor, the body is sprawled, its torso stretched upward somewhat from rigor mortis, but legs wide and inviting. Jeremy looks away and opens his father's casket instead. Uncomfortable questions slide through in his mind.

*What if someone finds the body?*

*What if I can never stop violating this thing?*

Jeremy uses the pocket knife on his keychain to slice a V into his sister's skin on the thing's thigh. He fingers the tip of the V wanting to pull it back, but afraid to see what lies beneath his sister's alabaster skin. Afraid to know what has tempted him into such vile acts.

He yanks his hand away and leans over his father's casket, lets his forehead rest on his father's icy hands and sobs. "Holy Father, please forgive me." He repeats the plea until the meaning wanes and it becomes five words.

Lifting his head, Jeremy stares into his father's face. "You." His voice is thick. "It happened because of you." Jeremy slaps his father's wrinkled cheek, but the casket prevents him from hitting with any force. The blow leaves a smudge in the pancake makeup and rocks his father's head.

Jeremy clenches his hands into fists and pummels his father's face. Bones crunch under his punches. He steps back to catch his breath. The old man's lips sink deep into his mouth. Jeremy pries them apart. His dentures are now lodged in his throat. His nose sits at a crooked angle and a stream of embalming liquid drips from one nostril into his open mouth.

Jeremy wipes sweat from his face with his forearm.

He picks up the body, gently lays her on top of his father. The back of her head rests between his father's good shoes. He forces her stiffening arms to cross over her bare chest, and closes the casket.


JEREMY CLIMBED THE stairs, leaving his father alone in the living room with his beer and memories. Pausing at Lisa's door in the hall, he tapped and went in. She scrambled for a towel to cover herself, but he caught a glimpse before she wrapped her body in terrycloth. The cleft between his sister's legs reminded him of Missy. The sun had left a similar spattering of freckles across her thighs.

"What do you want?" she asked.

"Just bored. What are you doing?" He plopped down on her bed and pulled a pillow across his lap to hide the stiffness growing between his legs. A mayonnaise jar sat on her night stand. Despite the holes in the metal lid, a colony of fireflies lay on the bottom, legs in the air.

"I'm getting dressed. What does it look like?"

"Let me see."

"What?"

He tried the same line that had worked with Missy a week earlier. "Show me yours, I show you mine."

Lisa's eyes filled with tears. "Jeremy, no," she whispered.


THE FUNERAL IS over, but Jeremy asks for a few minutes alone to say his goodbyes. The congregation has left and the pallbearers wait outside the closed church door. Jeremy runs his hand along the casket's lid. Now that the corpse is cold and stiff, the thing wearing his sister's skin has no more power.

He opens the casket and looks at her face. So like his sister, down to the scar splitting her right eyebrow. She was five, and Jeremy eight. He had her favorite stuffed bear held high in the air as she giggled and chased him through the house. Jeremy raced through the living room, but Lisa tripped on one of his trucks and fell into the glass coffee table. He runs his finger along the broken eyebrow. There was blood everywhere, splattered on the table, soaked into the carpet. Jeremy gave the bear back, but nothing would console his little sister.

Lisa wasn't in the church that morning. He looked for her face among the elderly, hoping for a glimpse of her, and found nothing but disappointment. No surprise, Jeremy thinks. She's been avoiding their father for years. He leans over the casket to stroke her hair, press his lips to her stiff mouth. She could have at least come to their father's funeral.

Reaching for the casket lid, he pauses. His gaze lingers over that V-shaped cut on her thigh. The point of skin has dried and curled.

Jeremy takes it between his thumb and forefinger. He holds down the leg to be sure he separates the skin from the thing underneath. He peels back the V-shaped tab. Under her skin are the ribbed scales of the evil that possessed his sister, forced her into sinful acts. He blinks and the scales are gone, replaced by strands of muscle and gobbets of fat. The only thing he finds under Lisa's skin is his sister's flesh.

---

**KIM DESPINS** lives in Colorado and has been writing as long as she can remember. Her short fiction has appeared in the +*Horror Library+ Volume 2 and Dark Distortions*. She has a story forthcoming in *Black Ink Horror*.

# DRAIN BAMAGE

BY JEFF STRAND

YES, I DROPPED MY BABY SISTER.

Not on purpose. God, no.

It happened while I was babysitting her. She was six months old, and I'd just turned nine. Too young to be responsible for an infant, but to be fair to my mom, she hadn't gone out for a wild night on the town or anything like that. All she did was ask me to watch Laurie for a few minutes while she went to talk to our next-door neighbor. Laurie was asleep in her crib, so it really shouldn't have been a big deal.

The thing is, when you're nine, you don't necessarily obey all of your mother's instructions. Such as, oh, I don't know, the one about not taking your baby sister out of her crib. I wasn't trying to hurt her. I just wanted to pick her up. She didn't wake up as I lifted her, but she did when I walked around the living room with her—I don't think I was holding her right.

She started to squirm and cry and before I could get her back into the crib, she slipped out of my hands. Laurie hit the ground, head-first.

The floor was carpeted, so it's not like I dropped her onto concrete, but I still let out a gasp of one-hundred-percent absolute horror. I scooped up my sobbing sister and hurriedly put her back in her crib, feeling like I was going to throw up and hyperventilate at the same time.

I checked her head. There was a pink mark, but no blood or skull chips. I watched her for several minutes, stomach acids boiling. She stopped crying and went back to sleep.

As soon as my mom came home, I said, "I'll be in my room!" and ran upstairs. I didn't want her to see me trembling. I closed my bedroom door and sat on my bed, an open comic book in front of me, waiting for the inevitable shout of, "*Oh my God! What did you do to your sister?*"

It never came.

My dad got home from work, and my mom called me down to dinner. We had a nice meal of Hamburger Helper and my mom didn't say a single word about me potentially ruining my sister. Maybe Laurie was okay.

While Mom and Dad did the dishes, I walked over to the crib and peered over the side at her. The pink mark was gone. Laurie looked at me and giggled.

I had an awful dream that night. Laurie, who had the body of a nine-year-old but kept her infant head, stood in front of the blackboard at school. She was trying to do a simple arithmetic problem. There was a huge chunk missing from her skull, and I could see her brain writhing around inside. It crawled out, sliced itself in half on a jagged piece of bone, and splattered onto the floor.

I had the same dream every night that week. Although the arithmetic problem changed each time.


I KNEW I should tell my parents what I'd done so they could take Laurie to the doctor, but I couldn't bring myself to confess. This wasn't like having a messy room or sneaking some red licorice from my dad's private stash—if I had really hurt my sister, they might send me away. Even though I was scared for her, she seemed fine. Mom and Dad would know if something was wrong with her, right?

Of course they would. Parents knew when something was wrong with their kids. They could sense it.

Laurie was fine.


I PRETTY MUCH stopped worrying about it until Laurie's first birthday. It was an outdoor party. She was crawling around on the grass in our backyard, while about a dozen of my relatives chatted and drank. I'd been allowed to invite one friend to the party, so I'd invited Howie Taylor because he had the best comic books.

"You know who's boring?" he asked.

"Who?"

"Your baby sister."

We giggled at this clever, insightful observation.

"You know who else is boring?" he asked.

"Who?"

"Your baby sister."

We giggled some more. Howie was a witty guy, although I still only liked him for his comic books.

Laurie cooed and picked up an earthworm. It was a small one, just over an inch long, and it wrapped itself around her index finger. She smiled, then popped it into her mouth and chewed happily.

Howie burst into hysterical laughter. "Did you see that? Did you see her eat the worm?"

I couldn't even nod. Laurie's birthday cake felt like a chocolate-flavored rock in my stomach. Were babies supposed to eat worms? Was that normal? I had no idea. She was only one year old, so it was entirely possible that her sucking down a raw earthworm was nothing to be concerned about . . . but what if it *wasn't* normal? What if she was brain damaged?

"What's going on?" my mom asked, walking over to join us.

I tried to respond, but my mouth went completely dry. What was I supposed to say? *"Sorry, Mom, I think that my disobedience six months ago has transformed my sister into a worm-chomping freak?"*

"Laurie scarfed a worm!" Howie gleefully announced.

"Oh, yuck." My mom crouched down and poked her finger into Laurie's mouth. She dug out an uneaten piece of worm and flicked it onto the grass, then wiped some drool off Laurie's lips.

"She's going to poop worms tonight," said Howie.

"Behave yourself," my mom warned. She'd never much liked Howie.

"I don't think she ate it on purpose," I said. Yeah, it was a dumb thing to say, but I was scared and sweating and not thinking straight.

Mom scooped Laurie into her arms and stood up. She didn't *seem* too distraught about what my sister had done. Maybe it was just a normal thing for a baby to do. Maybe I'd eaten a bug or two at that age. They probably tasted good, and we simply had that activity socialized out of us.

My mom sat back down with a couple of my aunts. The party atmosphere hadn't been disrupted. Clearly, my sister was not insane.

That evening, while Mom and Dad watched television, I snuck down into the basement to retrieve a dead roach. I'd noticed it laying on a cardboard box a couple of days ago but saw no reason to move it until now. I brought it upstairs and placed it in Laurie's crib, right in front of her.

Would she dine?

Laurie poked at the insect, laughed, and returned to playing with her Sesame Street Grover doll.

She didn't try to eat it. That was good.

What if she just wasn't hungry?

What if she only craved *live* bugs?

I picked up the roach and placed it on Grover's stomach, to give her another chance. Laurie ignored it. Though I wanted to do further study, I also didn't want my parents to see me messing with dead roaches around my baby sister, so I pocketed the bug and watched Laurie play.

She looked normal.

She *was* normal. So what if she ate a worm? I was just being paranoid about the whole thing. If all she ever did was sit in the corner of her crib and drool, then we'd have something to be concerned about.

I'd made a mistake, but no harm had come from it, and it was way past time to forget the whole matter.


OKAY, IT WAS way past time to forget the whole matter . . . after I consulted with an expert.

"Hey, Jacob, how's it going?" I asked, walking over to Jacob Terremy during afternoon recess. He looked at me suspiciously. We were both in the third grade, but he was in Mrs. Hansen's class while I was with Mrs. Raver, and we didn't interact very often. He got beat up a lot.

"Okay."

"Your dad's a shrink, right?"

"Yeah."

"If you drop a baby on its head, you can mess it up, right?"

"Well, duh. Yeah."

"How can you tell?" I asked.

"You mean if you turned it into a retard?"

I shook my head. "I just mean messed up. Doing weird things like eating bugs and stuff."

"Retards eat bugs."

"Really?"

"Yeah. It's cool."

"Can the mom and dad always tell?"

"Nah. Some parents are even worse retards."

"No, I'm being serious. If the mom and dad are normal, can they always tell if the baby is retarded?"

"Naw. They have no idea."

"Oh."

"So when did you get dropped on your head, retard?" Jacob asked this with a grin, although his grin quickly disappeared as he seemed to realize that this was a good way to get beat up.

I thanked him and walked off. I usually favored the swing set for recess, but there were already a couple of people counting. If the three swings were occupied, you'd stand in front of the swing of your choice and count out loud until the current swinger had gone back-and-forth twenty times, at which point he or she was required to vacate the ride. In my current mood, if somebody started counting on me, I'd probably try to kick them in the face. Instead, I walked to the far corner of the fenced-in playground and stood alone, thinking.

*Confess.*

No.

*It's not fair to Laurie to let this go on.*

It's not fair to me to tell what I did. It was an accident. I didn't mean to drop her. Why did she need to squirm so much? I wasn't hurting her.

*They can get her help.*

Yeah, and I'll go to jail.

*You won't go to jail. What kind of stupid idea is that? You really think Mom and Dad would send you to jail? It's not even a crime.*

It's not?

*Well, I'm not sure. If you did it on purpose it would be.*

What if they think I did it on purpose?

*They'd never think that. C'mon, get real.*

They might.

*In what universe?*

I dunno.

*Stop being so dumb. Tell them. They can help Laurie. Take her to a good doctor.*

They'll be mad.

*They'll be grateful.*

No.

I couldn't do it. What I'd done was too bad to confess. Especially six months later. This wasn't like tracking mud in the house and blaming the dog, where the punishment of getting caught faded with time. I had to keep the secret. They'd never know it was me.


I TRIED THE dead roach trick again, and Laurie ignored it. Then, after a very long search, I dug up another earthworm—a much longer one—and dangled it in front of her. She batted at it but didn't try to eat it.

Batting at it was normal. If somebody dangled an earthworm in front of me, I'd probably bat at it, too. Flicking it with your fingers would also be acceptable.

I held it closer to her mouth. She didn't take the bait.

"Open wide, Laurie," I said, trying to use the same vocal inflection that Mom did when she was encouraging my sister to eat something good for her. "I've got a yummy yummy worm for you. Mmmm … good! It's squirmy and tasty!"

I touched it to her lips. She turned her head away.

Thank God.

I squashed the worm in my fist, then washed off its gunk in the bathroom. Laurie wasn't brain damaged. Her head was fine. I'd done all of this worrying for nothing.


STILL, I COULDN'T help but watch her closely.

One time, her eyes crossed for no reason. *Brain damage?*

She laughed at nothing. *Brain damage?*

She babbled all the time. All babies babbled, but sometimes it just sounded weird. *Brain damage?*

My stomach hurt a lot. There were times when I wished that Laurie had simply turned into a drooling mongoloid as soon as I dropped her. At least it would end the constant worrying. Seeing my sister in a catatonic state would be miserable, unbearable, but could it possibly be worse than this constant stress?

Less often, but sometimes, I wished that her head had just splattered on the floor.

Of course, I could end the stress by confessing, but … no.


A COUPLE OF months after her first birthday, Laurie developed a cough and Mom took her to the doctor.

"Is she okay?" I asked, as Mom walked in the front door.

"She's fine," said Mom, setting Laurie in her playpen. "I just wanted to be sure is all. I love you guys too much to let anything happen to you."

"The cough isn't because of anything in her brain, is it?" I asked.

"Of course not. Why would you even ask something like that? It's just a regular baby cough."

This seemed like a good time to ask something along the lines of, "Mom, would you still love me if I did something really bad?" but I just couldn't. I couldn't risk getting sent away, to wherever it was that they sent horrible little boys.

What if Laurie had to live in a cage?

What if *I* had to live in a cage, for what I'd done to her?

I couldn't stop the tears. Mom kept asking what was wrong, but I just couldn't tell her.

"I NEED YOU to watch Laurie for a couple of minutes," Mom said. "I'm going to vacuum out the car."

"Can I help you vacuum?" I asked, suddenly breaking into a cold sweat.

"You can help by watching Laurie. You don't have to do anything—just make sure she stays in her playpen."

"I can keep the cord from getting twisted."

"Sweetie, just keep an eye on your sister, okay? I'll be right outside."

Okay, this was a good thing, right? It had to be. If Mom suspected what I'd done, and there was any actual sign of Laurie being brain damaged, she'd never leave me alone to watch her *again*.

Of course not. That would be insane.

Unless Mom was going to spy on me . . .

No, no, no, no. Laurie was fine, Mom trusted me, the car needed vacuuming, and there was nothing else to it. Basically, the only thing I had to do was shout "Hey, Mom!" if Laurie managed to get out of her playpen—something she'd never been able to do, and a feat she was unlikely to accomplish in the next few minutes. My responsibilities were pretty much just ceremonial.

I dragged a chair from the dining room table across the living room over to her playpen. As I heard Mom turn on the vacuum in the driveway, I sat there and watched Laurie sleep for the full fifteen minutes.

NOT TOO LONG after Laurie started preschool, I heard Dad talking on the phone with her teacher about how Laurie was really smart for her age. That was weird. Had I actually *helped* her? Had I maybe pushed a smarter part of her brain in front of a dumber part?

No, probably not, and I certainly wasn't going to test this theory by dropping her a second time . . . but I hadn't hurt her. Thank God, I hadn't hurt her.

I EVER REALLY forgot about it. I mean, she still occasionally did strange things, like wet the bed or spill things that didn't seem like they should be spilled quite that easily, but overall she was an intelligent, cheerful, friendly little sister. Bratty sometimes, yeah, but I liked that. It meant that she was normal.

When my parents and I sat in the auditorium, watching her graduate from high school, I think I was even more proud than Mom and Dad were. I didn't cry as much as Mom—nobody could—but I don't think I'd ever been happier in my life.


NOW THAT I'M telling you this, I guess it all had a happy ending. I didn't remember it working out like that, but I can't really think of anything bad that happened. I'm not even sure why I'm here.

Oh, yeah. My own child.

I know I checked on the baby this morning.

The blood on my hand proves it.

Don't worry, I didn't hurt the baby. God, no. It's entirely my blood. You see, I have memory problems these days. I used to leave the house and be absolutely miserable all day, not remembering if I'd checked the baby, paranoid about what I might find when I got home. I tried the usual tricks, like tying a string around my finger, but that didn't work because I could never quite convince myself that I hadn't just forgotten to take off the string from the last time I checked.

Writing notes to myself, calling and leaving messages on my voice mail, taking photographs . . . none of it worked.

Pain? That worked.

It's a wonderful idea, jabbing my palm with a knife. I do it hard enough to draw blood and hard enough to make sure it really hurts, but not hard enough to do any permanent damage. *That* is something I didn't forget. Thirty or forty times a day I gasp and suddenly have this horrifying feeling that I've forgotten to peek into her room before I left, but all I have to do is look at the blood on my palm and see that, yes, I had indeed peeked into her room.

After all, I wouldn't stab myself unless I'd genuinely checked on the baby. Right?

And I never forget to disinfect the wound in the evening and apply a bandage. Otherwise I'd get blood on my bedsheets, and I can't risk that. Sure, the blood might wash out, but then so would the scent of Yasmine's perfume. It's faded so much that I almost think it's only in my imagination, but still, I can't bear to lose it.

I didn't hurt the baby. I watched her perfectly.

You know that Yasmine told me I didn't need to watch the baby so closely, right? She said it was creepy to stare at her so much. Can you imagine that? Creepy to watch our own child?

And she kept insisting that it was okay to hold her. It was *not* okay to hold her. When you dodge a bullet, you don't jump back in front of the gun, right? If it were up to Yasmine, we'd be carrying her all over the house. I saw her holding the baby in the kitchen, where there isn't even carpet. I swear I didn't lose my temper. I just had to keep the baby safe.

See, I had a moment where I got worried, just now, but the blood on my hand tells me that everything is okay. She's sleeping soundly.

Yasmine can't watch her very well anymore, but that's fine because I checked on her for both of us.

This blood I *know* is mine. It's how I know that everything's okay. For a while I couldn't remember if it was mine or Yasmine's, but that was a while ago, and now I know it's mine for sure.

When you let me go, I should check on her again, just to be safe.

What's funny is that I feel like somebody dropped *me*.

---

JEFF STRAND used to be best known as the creator of Andrew Mayhem, whose insane adventures appear in such horror/comedy novels as *Graverobbers Wanted (No Experience Necessary)*, *Single White Psychopath Seeks Same, and Casket For Sale (Only Used Once)*. But now he's probably best known for his first "serious" book, *Pressure*, which was a Bram Stoker Award finalist for Best Novel. He's written other comedic books (*Benjamin's Parasite*, *The Sinister Mr. Corpse*) and other serious books (*Dweller*), and a couple that kinda blur the lines (*Wolf Hunt*, *Kutter*).

His second greatest career accomplishment was appearing in *+Horror Library+ Volume 3*, but he knew that he would only be truly happy if he could make the cut for *+Horror Library+ Volume 4*. One bribe later (a couple of tacos with extra sour cream) he is living his dream.

You can visit his Gleefully Macabre website at www.jeffstrand.com.

# GUARDIANS

BY TOM BRENNAN

---

KARL PADDED PAST HIS SON'S ROOM, BOOTS IN HAND, trying not to wake him. A sleep-crumpled face appeared around the edge of the door. "Dad? Where're you going? It's still dark."

"I'm off hunting, Mikey. Back to sleep now."

A wide yawn, then, "You going after deefs?"

Karl smoothed his son's warm hair. "You go back to bed. Don't you worry about a thing."

Downstairs, Karl found Donna pouring coffee into a flask. He slipped his arm around her waist and nuzzled her neck. "You smell good."

Donna didn't turn around. "There's toast and eggs still warm in the top oven. Bacon's almost done."

Karl hesitated, went to speak, and then let go of Donna and sat at the table. A faint pearl glow lightened the sky beyond the windows. Inside the kitchen, a single overhead tube flickered. As Karl ate he watched Donna pack sandwiches into his rucksack along with the flask. When she leaned against the sink with a cup of coffee, Karl said, "You know I've got no choice."

"I know."

"We've been lucky so far: we've had no deefs this far north."

Donna sipped coffee and pulled together the edges of her chenille robe. "God, I hate that word."

"Why? Everybody calls them that."

"Exactly."

Karl shook his head and pushed away his plate. From outside came the crunch of tires on gravel and a harsh blast on the horn. Karl winced.

"The neighbors will love that," Donna said.

Karl grabbed his camo rucksack and reached into the tall cupboard beside the stove. He slid his grandfather's old Winchester shotgun into a carrier and opened a box of shells. He paused at the back door. "I shouldn't be too late. Four or five. I won't let Frank get me drunk."

"Karl, look . . . " Donna set her cup down and crossed the kitchen. She stared into his eyes. "Be careful. Okay?"

"Okay."

Another blast on the horn dragged Karl outside. He saw Frank's bearded face leaning out of the pick-up's window. "Jesus, Frank. Wake the neighbors, why don't you."

Frank grinned, waved at Donna standing on the porch and then positioned his hand over the horn.

"Don't even . . . " Karl threw his rucksack and gun carrier onto the extended cab's ripped back seat and climbed in beside Frank. He sniffed, caught the pick-up's familiar smells of bait, beer, sweat, and motor oil. Cans and discarded shells rattled across the floor as Frank turned out of Karl's yard and drove past sleeping clapboard houses, heading north for Route 109. The sky had turned milky, the clouds hanging low to the horizon.

"You heard?" Frank said.

"Heard what?"

"Couple guys found a nest over by Eastham. Hundreds of deefs. Shot what they could and then vaped the shit out of it. The Guard's over there now."

To Karl, Frank's "hundreds" probably meant a handful of bioanalog defectives; Frank liked exaggeration. "So what?"

Frank aimed the pick-up along the highway and rested his thick arms on the wheel. "So what? So there's bound to be plenty more coming our way. Yes sir, we're gonna get some action today."

Karl stared at the road. He'd hunted birds with Frank, deer and even moose; he'd never gone after defectives. But the posted Federal notices gave him no option: all licensed hunters had a legal obligation, a duty, and they received two hundred bucks for each proven deef kill.

The money didn't matter to Karl—he would have volunteered anyway, just as he had for the local Fire Brigade for eight years running. The Community had to come first.

Frank turned off 109 and followed the narrow side road until it became a rutted track. He pulled into a dirt lot and stopped next to a Parks Service notice board. Another pick-up, bulbous with chrome, stood a few yards away. "Shit. I thought we'd be the first."

"It's not a competition." Karl climbed down and reached for his bags. "Everyone's supposed to cooperate on this. Remember?"

Frank spat into the undergrowth. "Cooperate my ass. I got alimony payments to make."

Karl pulled on his hunters' fatigues, camo and fluorescent orange. He took a deep breath and held it; he liked this moment of calm before the hunt. The odors of grass and wet leaves. Birds scurrying through the branches. Peace.

"I picked these up from the Sheriff's station," Frank said, hauling out a yellow box from the pick-up. Inside, orange plastic sacks with the black horned biohazard symbols just visible. Frank gave a handful of sacks to Karl, then produced a black and yellow plastic cylinder with a trigger and nozzle. "Sheriff said we have to vape the area once we bag 'em."

Karl stared at the spray. "Doesn't look like much."

Frank shook the cylinder. "Whatever's in it is keyed to the deefs, according to the Fed in the Sheriff's office. She said this goo munches on deefs and only the deefs. Harmless for me and you. And animals."

"Here's hoping."

Karl led the way into the forest, following the trampled hunters' trail between trunks of spruce and birch. His boots flattened the grass and collected fresh dew that darkened the toecaps. "You sure they're around here?"

"That's what the Feds reckon," Frank said. He carried his own shotgun angled across the front of his body at Port Arms, looking like the Guardsman he'd once been. "If the deefs come over from Eastham, they'll be heading west, so they'll have to come over the bluff."

Karl nodded and headed east toward Jefferson's Bluff. Karl's father and grandfather had hunted the same woods, and had taken him out as a child. Mike would join him soon if Karl could persuade Donna. A city girl from Albany, she hadn't grown up with the tradition, the sense of nature and the year's rhythm.

As he walked, Karl saw small creatures running for cover: rabbits, squirrels, sudden flashes of dark fur. He knew what the deefs looked like, or most of them, from the TV and netcasts: pale and sickly, with hairless gray or green skin. Could be as big as a full-grown dog, but usually smaller. Multi-limbed. Flesh erupting in random configurations, with chaos as both father and mother.

The stuff of nightmares.

Karl didn't want to see creatures like that slithering up Main Street or making nests in the high school. Who knew what diseases they'd spread? Or what they'd evolve into if people didn't erase them.

"Where the hell did they come from?" Karl asked.

"Take your pick. Original story I heard, they escaped from a lab. Guy I used to know in the Guard over at Burlington said he knew a guy who swore the government let them out deliberately to see how they survive. Scatter patterns. He reckons they're some part of the weapons program. Gray goo, he called 'em."

Karl shook his head. Trust Frank to pick the conspiracy theory. Karl had heard many stories about the deefs: some company had created them for medical research and they'd been released by Animal Rights activists; aliens had dropped them to prepare the way for an invasion. *It was all just so crazy.*

But they'd appeared from somewhere. Back in '07, the TV news had picked up on stories of strange roadkill, things with too many arms and too many heads. Things like meter-long slugs and others like armored, headless cats.

"There!" Frank leveled his shotgun and then dropped it. "Shit."

A dappled brown deer stepped into a shaft of light and then darted away.

"When it's deer season, I don't spot a damn thing," Frank said. "But now I can't bag it . . . "

"It was too small, anyway." Karl concentrated on slowing his heartbeat; Frank's sharp response had kicked off an adrenaline reflex. Karl had almost shot the deer himself. He slapped at flies that were beginning to crowd his neck and face.

As Karl and Frank headed deeper into the forest, they saw two more deer and found tracks of other hunters: fresh imprints of patterned cleats. Karl swapped his camo baseball cap for a fluorescent orange one with the name of a defunct hunting outfitter on the brow. He scanned the forest and listened for sudden footfalls or voices, the click of hammers drawn back. The morning lulled him.

A sudden shotgun blast destroyed the forest's silence. Birds screamed from the trees and into the air. Two more shots thundered out in such close succession that they sounded like one.

Karl crouched down and saw Frank do the same. He waited. After the noise, the forest bustled like a nervous grouse; leaves twitched and trembled. Animals flashed through sunlight. When no more shots came, Karl and Frank followed the track until they saw a trio of hunters in a clearing. "Hey."

The two kneeling hunters looked up but didn't speak. With blue-gloved hands, they continued hauling red chunks off the forest floor and into yellow biohazard bags. The third hunter had a shotgun cracked open over his arm. He grinned. "Hey. How's it going?"

Karl nodded to the bloodied floor. "Looks like you nailed a couple of 'em."

"Two big ones. Just like that."

Frank walked up to the kneeling hunters and watched them bag the remains. "Jesus. What's that?"

One of the kneeling men held up a glistening, wriggling lump. "Looks like tentacles. Maybe feelers, too."

"This one's got flippers," the other hunter said. "And about six eyes, maybe more."

Frank shook his head. "Weird shit."

Back in school, that had been Frank's favorite expression. Karl remembered him using it for everything from music Frank didn't like to drugs he'd experimented with. But this time he'd used exactly the right words; Karl could see miniature arms and feet, fingers, bone and gristle, but all in the wrong order, the wrong scale and configuration. Life through an old carnival's trick mirror.

Karl took another step. The remains didn't look human; no way could you ever call them that. But they didn't look like animals either. Maybe something in-between, like Mikey's experiments with modeling clay. And nothing would look too pretty after a few shotgun blasts.

"Where you headed?" the standing hunter asked.

Before Karl could reply, Frank said, "Down to the river. Bound to be a few down there. 'Specially the ones with flippers."

The hunter nodded. "Maybe we'll head that way too. Plenty for everyone, right?"

Karl and Frank left as the hunters pulled on face masks and began to spray the clearing. Karl led the way toward the bluff and away from the river. He found spoor near the trails, nothing he didn't recognize. As the sun rose, the mist cleared but shadows still hid most of the undergrowth. Karl concentrated on the sights and sounds around him and tried to push away the images of the dead deefs.

He thought about Donna and Mike back home. Parents had enough to worry about, what with drugs, diseases, car accidents, chance acts of violence, random shootings. They didn't need to add anything else to the list. Sometimes, as he watched Mike walk to school or play with the neighbors' kids, Karl couldn't breathe; something gripped his chest and wouldn't let go.

It was about nine when Karl and Frank stopped by a switchback stream. Deerflies hovered above the trickling surface and buzzed around Karl's coffee mug. He waved them away and thought about the deefs back in the clearing. "You figure they can feel things?"

Frank shrugged.

"I mean . . . do they know what's going on?" Karl said. "Can they understand?"

"Not the way I hear it," Frank said. "Didn't you catch that program last month? They had that bald Professor guy—the one that does all the science shit—talk about them. He reckons they're just pieces of meat that got out of control. Way he explained it, they started off with a few cells, a few tiny machines, but then everything went haywire. Like cancer. They're walking cancer, deefs."

Karl poured away the dregs of coffee. "Come on. Time's wasting."

Frank yawned. "Shouldn't have had them beers last night. Or maybe it was the bourbon."

"Usually is."

Another twenty minutes brought them to the foot of the bluff. Gray stone sprouted through the forest floor and led up to the jagged spine of the bluff. Karl found the spoor beside the track. Green pellets the size of golf balls.

"I wouldn't want to eat what it ate," Frank said.

Karl signaled for quiet and pulled back the shotgun's hammers. He chose each step with care, avoiding brittle twigs and dark hollows. His heart raced. Every sound of the forest seemed amplified. He could taste the damp soil and decay.

More droppings. Flies zeroed-in on the waste and then peeled away as if they'd hit a plate glass wall. Karl hesitated, listening, then turned to the left. Something had rustled the arching fronds of a massive fern.

It moved again.

Karl signaled Frank to curve around to the left. He held the gun loose in front, ready to swivel and fire. His eyes caught a brief flash of movement; before he could pull the trigger, Frank's gun ripped apart the undergrowth. The shot left a gaping green hole edged with red.

Then something moved to Karl's right. He stepped forward but didn't shoot. The ferns made a tunnel between the old trees; something scurried along the tunnel, as fast as a small dog. Karl ran alongside and saw pale skin. With a deafening blast, the gun's recoil slammed into his shoulder.

Whatever he had hit screamed. The sound cut right through Karl's skull. He leveled the weapon for the finishing shot but the creature staggered along the tunnel. Karl ran to the edge of the ferns, squatted down and sighted along the barrel.

The deef saw Karl and froze. Two of its five legs ended in bloody stumps. Each of its three arms clutched a small gray bundle. A toothless mouth opened but no sound came out.

Karl felt the warm steel of the trigger. His blood pounded in his throat.

One of the three bundles in the deef's arms turned a puckered face toward Karl and mewled. It had the same hairless gray skin as its parent, the same cluster of eyes. Then the other two offspring opened their mouths and made the same sound. The deef pulled its litter close to its chest and tried to shield them with its deformed body.

A second. Two seconds. Then Karl took his finger from the trigger and dropped the gun's barrel.

The deef's body exploded. The blast of Frank's shotgun spattered the deef and its litter over the nearest tree.

Frank, gun in hand, ran over. "What were you doing, man? You had them right in your fucking sights!"

Karl ignored Frank and stood up, then had to double over and puke all across the forest floor. He emptied himself until there was nothing left.

"Karl? Karl, are you okay?"

Karl walked around Frank and headed back toward the trail.

"Karl? Come on, man; half of this is yours. Karl!"

As the trail joined the main path back to the parking lot, Karl hurled his gun into the undergrowth. His walk turned into a trot, then a run. He ignored the branches whipping his face and arms. He didn't take his eyes from the glimmer of clean sunlight ahead that marked the end of the forest; he was concentrating so hard that the simultaneous boom of the three hunters' guns seemed to come from a great distance. Only when their shots tore into him and spun him around did he realize it was too late. For him, for his family, too late. This was the beginning of the end of humanity.

---

**TOM BRENNAN** lives on the coast in Liverpool, UK with his wife Sylvia and many cats, and works 24/7 taking 911 emergency calls. He enjoys a wide variety of fiction, particularly SF/F, Dark Fiction, and Mystery. His favorite authors are Bloch, Gaiman, Dick, and Hammett. His short stories have appeared in *The Year's Best Fantasy and Horror: Nineteen, Writers of the Future, Dark Recesses, Story House, Indy, Baen's Universe,* and many others. His favorite questions are "What if . . ." and "What are we doing to ourselves?"

# GOD'S WORK

BY MATTHEW LEE BAIN

---

THE ROADKILL WAS STARING AT HER. THE EYEBALLS bulged from its squashed face. It smiled with a wide mouth full of sharp teeth, tongue hanging, exhaling a greasy stench.

The hitcher swallowed, gripped her pack a little tighter, and edged farther down the roadstead. The blacktop smoldered like a grill, filling the air with dizzy waves of heat. She struggled for a full breath, unpent breasts panting beneath a thin, yellow shirt. Aside from the strip of highway, she could make out nothing but sand and scrub brush. Somewhere, far off, behind the waves of heat, there might have been hills or mountains, maybe a city, but . . .

The hitcher stripped her pack from her shoulder and, crouching, began to dig through it. She withdrew a brown thermos, unscrewed the lid, and brought the lip to hers. Not much more than a kiss of liquid. Her tongue was quick to savor the drops from between the dried cracks of skin. Wiping her head, she returned the thermos to her pack and stood. She took a long look down the highway—one way, then the other—which blurred on, out of sight.

"Off the edge of the world—fuck." Her eyes slowly slid around the empty, empty landscape. Slinging the pack over her shoulder, she continued west, away from the roadkill. After a few steps, she heard the growl, far-off, but deep. She squinted over her left shoulder. The growl was growing into a roar. Holding her palm up to shade her face, she widened her eyes. A bright shining spot, like a small silver sun, was coming down the highway in her direction.

"God," she prayed. The small silver sun formed into a tall pickup truck. The hitcher jumped and waved her arms, screaming as loud as her dry throat would allow. The roar grew until the truck slowed to a stop in front of her. She heaved a sigh, on the edge of tears. The driver's door cracked open, and a set of heavy boots hit the ground. She looked up—took a few steps forward—but could not see around the cab. A gloved hand reached over the truck-bed and removed a stain-painted shovel. Her heart jumped. A tool that size might as well be a weapon. She backed up a few paces, feeling the instinct to run. But run where? She'd be as good as dead. A moment later, there was a long grating sound, as the shovel was scraped over the blacktop. The pancaked mammal arced into the air, landing in the truck-bed; the shovel followed after with a dead clatter.

"Hello—", she said, but the driver side door slammed shut. "No, wait!" She ran, jumping onto the side of the truck.

The putrid waves of stench emanating from the truck-bed overtook her. "O, *Ghogd*," she gagged, losing her purchase. She fell, ass-first, into the gravel. Struggling to her feet, she screamed, "Wait!"

The passenger door cracked open like an icebox, and a face, five-days unshaven, peered out.

"Hop up," he said with a droll smile.

"Oh, thank God you came along," she uttered, hopping in and slamming the door.

"You're welcome," he answered.

The silver truck roared down the highway, westward bound.


"WHERE WERE YOU headed?" he said, looking her up and down from the corner of his right eye.

"What's that?" She squinted.

"Where were you headed 'fore I stopped?" he said over the *whirr* of the truck.

"Oh," she laughed, "just out of Bumfuck, Egypt or wherever you call this."

"Bum what?"

"Bumfuck, Egypt."

"Bum-fuck, *E-Gypt*?" His face split open with laughter.

"Well—I haven't seen a pyramid, but I wouldn't be surprised." She smiled.

He puckered his lips and squinted. With a snort, he reached across her to the glove compartment, his grubby fingers popping the door to rifle inside. Withdrawing a half-crushed cigarette pack, he held it up to show a camel-headed mascot in front of a pyramid.

"Found one," he sputtered with laughter. The hitcher smiled, shifting in her seat. Taking the brown, tree-shaped air freshener down from the rear-view, the driver replaced it with the camel and pyramid. She stared at the air freshener with a crooked smile. Wheezing, the man composed himself.

His mouth sidled over to the right side of his face, where it cracked open.

"Hey," he said, his voice deep and serious.

"Huh?"

"Hey," he whispered, poking her arm with his dirty index finger.

"What?"

"Know what?" he continued, leaning in, tilting his head like he had a secret.

"What?"

"My *mummy's* buried here." His mouth became a seizuring mess, spewing laughter.

The hitcher smiled and bit down on her lower lip, tucking her chin up. The driver faced forward, still sniggering—"My *mummy* . . ." She noticed him looking at her breasts from the side of his face. She looked down, herself, to see her nipples pointing down the road—the cab was pleasantly chilled. She crossed her arms over her chest.

From the corner of her eye, she spotted a silver canteen sitting between them on the seat and licked her lips. The driver followed her eyes. He pushed the canteen across the seat until its cool metal touched her leg.

"Thirsty?" He nodded at it.

"Thanks." She half-smiled and took the canteen. The cold liquor burned down her throat. She opened her eyes wide and handed the canteen back. He took a swallow and wrinkled up his rubbery face. Grunting, he wiped his mouth with the back of his hand and screwed the lid back on. "Any water?" she asked.

The driver shook his head, then turned his eyes away, staring out the side window into the distance.

"So . . . how far can you take me?"

"Fields of Peace."

"Is that some kinda town?"

He reached down and flicked open the ash tray. He grubbed around and came up with a stoppered glass phial. It was full of tiny colored hearts.

"How far is it?"

The driver gave the phial a proffering shake. "A good trip." He grinned. Shaking a red and a purple heart into his hand, he placed the red one in his mouth and held the purple out to the hitcher. "Be mine." The hitcher glanced down at the candy-sized heart.

"God, it's been so long." Her small, trembling fingers clasped the purple heart and brought it to her lips.

THE ONLY SOUND in the cab was of the truck's big, black tires rolling down the sticky-hot pavement. The driver and hitcher both squinted from beneath their visors' veils. The sun smoldered dead ahead; every surface between glowed molten gold. Prodigious shadows crept from the occasional Joshua tree or century plant. Somewhere the moon was getting wide and ready to watch.

The driver turned to the hitcher, squinting through one eye, the other wide. Traces of his reflection interrupted her view out the passenger-side window. "Hey," he said. "Hey?"

"What?" she squeaked, startled from the interruption of silence.

"Why wouldn't the jackal give the vulture a ride?"

She arched her shoulders, eyes wide, childish.

"Because the vulture had too much *carri-on*."

She burst into giggles, continuing to stare out the passenger window.

"So . . . what'd you do?" he asked.

She turned to look into the mirror, finding her pupils were the size of peas. Then she faced him. "Who? Me?"

"Yeah." The driver gave a feeble grin.

"I *killed* a vulture once," she said.

"What'd he do?"

"He was picking on me," she answered with a sneer.

The driver yelped with laughter. "That's what vultures do," he stuttered playfully.

"That makes it all right? What they do?" The hitcher glowered at him.

"Something's gotta clean up—after things die." He smiled, staring straight ahead.

Her face turned grave. "Do I look dead to you?"

"You look—good." He leered from the right corner of his mouth.

"You wanna see some more?" Her eyes narrowed.

"Yeah."

"Give me another one of those candies, and I'll show you something." The driver quickly shook another purple heart free from the phial and into the hitcher's hand. She placed it in her mouth and closed her eyes. With a deep breath, she opened them again and said, "Let me show you what vultures do." Pulling down her shirt, she exposed the top half of her left breast and a mouth-sized bite scar, inches left of her heart. The depression of mangled tissue was blush red against the pale of her chest. "They try to eat your heart out, alive."

The driver, no longer watching the road, reached across the cab and placed his index and middle finger into the scar pit. The hitcher opened her mouth, to speak, but nothing came out. Her consciousness fluttered.

*The station wagon was parked on that dark road in the woods. The pines loomed over each side of the car. She felt herself settling down from the sky, like a leaf, onto the roof of the car. Then, into the car. There was a man with a long, hooked nose and protruding chin. He was smiling at a young woman in the passenger seat. "Tomorrow, we'll see the ocean," said the man as he took off his tan coat. "I've always wanted to see the ocean," the girl batted her lashes, eyes twinkling in the darkness. "Oh, you'll see it," chuckled the man, "but, there is what we talked about, first." He raised his eyes, questioning. "I know," she smiled. "Good." He began loosening his tie . . .*

*A light rain sprinkled the car, running brown little trails down the dirty windows. The man was between the girl's legs now—she, completely naked, head pushed against the passenger-side door, he with his button-up shirt still on. He was calling her names, all a part of an agreed game. She was* Dirty— Sick—Whore. *The man was grunting, wrapping his hands around her throat. "Like we talked about," he said. She gasped. "Like we talked about." But the girl was struggling for real. She couldn't breathe. She was clawing, slapping, tapping out. "Good . . . good . . . good." The girl blacked out, head slumped sideways over the seat.*

*When she awoke, the man's head was buried in her chest. At her stirring, he looked up. She screamed and screamed. His face had become that of a deformed vulture, the beak bloody and smiling—eyes, big and glassy in the gray moonlight. She screamed. The creature screamed back. Blood was running down her chest. It returned to choking her. She slid her hand across the floorboards along crumbs, wrappers, and found something under the seat. A glass bottle. She retrieved it and drew it up toward the ceiling. She brought it down, shattering it over the vulture's head, who shrieked. Blood filled up one of its black eyes, but its hands kept choking her. Still holding the glass bottle, she raked it back and forth, across the face. She didn't stop cutting until its shrieks died away, and its grip on her throat grew slack. The mangled pulp of the vulture's face receded into the darkness, and it slumped back in its seat with a gurgle.*

*Tears and blood running down her body, the girl grabbed up her pile of clothes and pack, and ran out of the car, into the woods.*

THE DRIVER REMOVED his hand from the scar pit. "Your piece is missing," he said to the hitcher's wordless gape.

Tears spilled over her face. "I had to . . ." She shook her head. "I had to . . . I had to . . ."

"I see," said the driver. In front of them, on the side of the road, she saw a station wagon. A man was standing outside it, running toward them. He had a vulture's face. "No!" screamed the hitcher. "Nooo!" The vulture's face was flayed and bleeding, pieces missing. As they passed, the vulture man slapped his hand against her door. He ran alongside the car, pounding on it again and again, somehow keeping pace. *Is he flying?* the woman thought, horrified. She hid her face in her hands, pushed tight against her skull. Heaving breaths, she looked into the side mirror. The road was empty: no station wagon, no vulture-faced man. Lowering her head into her hands, she broke into tears. "I'm so fucking tired. He won't let me sleep—not real sleep."

The driver reached over and raked his fingers through her hair. She screamed, and he recoiled. She dug into her backpack and withdrew a knife. She pointed it at him.

The driver held up his hands, steering with his knees.

"Whadda-you-want?" Tears ran down each side of her scowl.

"What-do-*you*-want?" the driver responded, cautiously pointing at the knife tip with his index finger.

"To get clean, to sleep!" she snapped, voice breaking. "How much farther is that place?"

"At the end of the road."

"How *far*?"

"Before dark."

The hitcher traced the outline of the driver's face with the knife. "And what toll would you exact, driver?" She regarded him with mock sympathy.

The driver waved his hands. "I just take care of the dead stuff."

"Bullshit. You're a fucking vulture just like him."

Holding the steering wheel with his knee, the driver made V's with his index and middle fingers, saying, in a jowled inflection, "I'mmm—not a crooked beak!"

"Then what are you?"

"I'm more of a jackal." The driver howled, and then erupted in laughter.

"Yeah?" She smiled, reaching for the canteen. "We're gonna see." Unscrewing the lid, she took a swallow.

THE SUN BURROWED into the highway, forming a fat ellipse.

A large shadow, just up ahead, began to dissociate itself with the background. The hitcher wiped away her tears and squinted beneath the veil of sun visor. A massive black shape lay at the roadside. The truck barreled toward the shape. Closer and closer, the shape defined itself. A large beast.

"What the hell is that?" the hitcher gasped. Its long white fangs and claws glinted in the sunset—a shadow with teeth. As they drew closer, it became clearer. "It's got, something..." There was a second shadow, beneath the beast. *The prey.*

The driver squinted indifferently, nodding his head.

"Oh my God," the hitcher gasped. The prey flailed its legs, pale hooves gleaming. "O my God, O my God, O my God..." The hitcher pulled at the skin of her face, tension mounting in the muscles that connected her lids to her sockets. The beast's long jaws opened like a steel trap and snapped down onto the prey. Thrashing its head this way and that, it ripped and shredded the meat. There was a final kick of hooves as the prey was rent into flying pieces. The truck arrived just in time to be speckled by the kill. The hitcher screamed, subconsciously grabbing the driver's arm. She turned to him, emitting a strain of unintelligible cries. The windshield wipers smeared blood across her view.

He turned to her, leaning in. "Sh-sh-shhh. It's past." Even in the chilled cab, sweat ran over her face. Her brain was throbbing against the inside of her skull, her heartbeat and vision a pulsing blur. And then, darkness took her.


THE HITCHER WOKE to the sound of something flapping in the wind. She stared straight up at a brown, rippling ceiling. Her mouth was parched, though her body felt sticky and wet. She struggled up onto her elbows, naked. She lay on a long wooden table, which was covered with strange instruments. Her eyes swam around the room. A brown tent—its walls billowing in the song of the wind. A hanging lantern swayed from a large shepherd's hook. The light moved back and forth over the interior of the tent. The instruments on the table twinkled in the lantern light. She rolled over the edge of the table and attempted to stand. Her legs buckled like stilts of rubber, her head reeled, and she fell into the sand. Holding onto the edge of the table, she tried to raise herself up. Her nude, sand-covered body wobbled violently to its feet. Then she fell again, harder. Her eyes circled the tent, searching for a way out. A flap fluttered in the wind, glimpses of the moonlit desert beyond.

With a full breath, she crawled forward, each push a surge of nauseousness. The sands whispered consolingly through the tent flap. A delirious grin lit across her face. The flap whipped open violently. No one there. She sighed in relief, and crawled farther. Again, the tent flap opened, washing her path in moonlight. Then, the opening became eclipsed by a dark shape. She gasped, tried to scream, but could only manage a dry cough. The figure stepped through the moon-glow and into the lantern-light. It had the head of a jackal, the body of a man—naked to the waist, where a sort of *apron* covered his trunk: a mass of dried blood-matted animal fur dangling down into hooves that hung just above his feet. Upon his hairy chest, a golden ankh hung from a chain. The beast bent down to the hitcher. She slapped at his hands as he gently scooped her up into brutish arms and laid her back on the table. Bringing a wet sponge up from a bucket, he washed her. Her arms wormed over the table, eyes rolling in their sockets. In slow spirals, he washed the sand from her flesh, dipping and wringing the sponge. "God . . ." she muttered, " . . . save me." Melancholy human eyes stared at her from the static jackal-face.

He delicately retrieved a long, thin instrument with a hook at its end. "Please," she growled. The man put his left palm over her forehead, partially over her eyes, and pushed the back of her head against the table. She gurgled, arms flopping. Through half-closed eyes, she watched the hook's descent. It hovered in the air, poised.

*She saw the condemning eyes of her mother—the empty air where her father might have stood before he left. Her thumb in the air—smelled the sick smell of strangers. Starving on the side of the road, like being gutted—using flesh as a bargain—trapped, scarred—blood, death, and: never the same. A cavalcade of shab rooms—needle parties—sex for drugs—drugs for travel—sex for travel. Begging, begging. Hopeless.* One last pain, she wished, and over, gone.

The hook went in. There was a shellfish-like crack and the tear of soft tissue. A wet suck and release of air. The jackal gasped raggedly, eyes rolling heavenward. The hitcher's eyes flickered, her face spasmed. Her arms shot off the table, rigid in the air. The jackal leaned over, puckered his lips and took a guttural suck of air. His eyes came back into the mask. Squinting, he stirred the hook, pulling it in and out. The hitcher's arms slapped like dead fish onto the table. She felt herself floating upward, a leaf in the wind. The colors of her world bled out, leaving only shades of gray for her new eyes. She spiraled away toward the top of the tent, looking down, without pain, at herself, which stared up at nothing.

She stopped at the ceiling, gliding along like a helium balloon. The man's work was a blur of movement, bent over the corpse: cutting, scooping, plopping piles of innards into animal-headed pottery; stuffing the gaping body with brown packets; stitching the skin back together and, re-sponging the body clean.

When sunlight's first gray crept in the door, the man was lowering the corpse into a pit full of slushy salt. He packed the salt around her, over her, submerging the body. The jackal-faced man stood, breathing heavy, and walked to the opening of the tent.

She floated over the tent ceiling, following him to the entrance. He stood there a long while before stepping out into the goldening light. She followed him into the open air.

The sun poured platinum over the desert, defining a vast, wide-open field of rectangular mounds. Hundreds of them.

*. . . how far can you take me?*

*Fields of Peace.*

---

The **MATTHEW LEE BAIN** ship is slowly but steadily approaching its thirty-second year at sail on this dreary and otherwise uncertain sea of life . . .

Other than that, he writes fiction, studies literature, and practices Tae Kwon Do.

# SLEEPLESS EYES

BY TIM WAGGONER

I T'S 1:38 A.M. ON A THURSDAY NIGHT, AND YOU'RE sitting at a small round table tucked into a dim corner of an all-night coffee shop. A steaming mug of hot liquid sits before you, and you know it'll be at least another fifteen minutes before it cools enough for you to drink. To pass the time you glance around at your fellow late-night caffeine addicts. One of the main reasons you came—besides suffering from insomnia—is that this place, especially at this time of night, is usually a prime spot for people-watching.

The barista at the counter, a raven-haired woman in her early twenties, asks a customer, "Would you like aqueous fluid drizzled on top of your whipped pus?"

The customer nods the middle of his three scaled heads, and the barista leans over his drink and squeezes her right eyeball as if it were a large ocular pimple. Clear fluid spurts out of a fissure in the organ and splatters onto the yellow-white mass floating atop the customer's drink.

You turn to look at the fireplace in the corner opposite from where you're sitting. One of the employees has recently added fresh fuel to the fire, and the severed arms and legs—the small, delicate limbs of children—sizzle and pop as the fat beneath the blackening skin cooks. Sitting in a cushy chair next to the fire, an obscenely fat man—naked, completely bereft of body hair—methodically inserts long sharp needles into his testicles, one after the other, as if his balls are fleshy pin cushions. As he works, he chats with a woman whose entire body, including her face, is covered by tight black leather. Only her mouth is visible through an unzipped slit, and you can see she has no teeth in her swollen, bleeding gums.

Over by the window, a pair of exotically beautiful conjoined twins—Asian, high cheek bones, straight black hair down to the middle of their backs, jade-green mini-dresses sans panties—are masturbating each other with dildos fashioned from metal rods wrapped in steel wool. As the women moan in ecstasy, blood runs down their well-toned legs and pools on the tiled floor beneath their table. An old woman that reminds you of your grandmother, except for the pulsating lesions covering her skin, kneels next

to the twins, her head lowered to the floor as she furiously laps up the twins'
blood-cum with a tongue encrusted in fat, happy ticks.

Your attention is drawn by screams coming from behind the door to the
men's restroom. The screams stop, and a few seconds later a man walks out.
He's probably in his thirties, wearing a white turtleneck and jeans, and he
looks okay, if you don't count his ashen skin and uncomprehending
expression of stark terror. He manages to take three steps before bloodstains
begin to show through his turtleneck. Pieces of his body begin to fall off and
hit the floor with meaty-wet plops. Just a few at first—an ear, a nose, a lip—
but then more and more, until there's a veritable rain of flesh, blood, and bone,
and the core of the man's body collapses into a heap. A cheer goes up from the
crowd and everyone—the barista, the three-headed man, Pincushion-Balls,
Leather-Girl, the Steel-Wool Twins, Grandma Tick-Tongue, and all the
others in the coffee shop—race toward the grisly mound and fall upon it,
grabbing slick handfuls of viscera and jamming them into their mouths.

"Now that's good eatin'!" Grandma Tick-Tongue exclaims around a
mouthful of kidney. Her fellow gourmands grunt their agreement.

But you haven't joined in the feast. Instead you slither over to the
counter and wrap one of your smaller facial tentacles around a to-go cup.
You grab a plastic lid with another tentacle then return to your table, leaving
a glistening trail of slime in your wake. You pour your still-hot spinal fluid
into the cardboard cup, fasten the lid on, and then put the empty mug on
the counter for the barista to collect later. You then lift your coat off the
back of your chair—a coat made from the stomach linings of a dozen
syphilitic nuns—and head for the exit while the bloody revelers continue
gorging themselves.

As you stride out into the night, disappointed, you think to yourself
that you need to find a new late-night hangout. This scene is getting old.

---

**TIM WAGGONER**'s most current novels are the *Nekropolis* series of
urban fantasies and the *Lady Ruin* series for Wizards of the Coast.
In total, he's published over twenty novels and two short story
collections, and his articles on writing have appeared in *Writer's
Digest* and *Writers' Journal,* among others. He teaches creative
writing at Sinclair Community College and in Seton Hill
University's Master of Fine Arts in Writing Popular Fiction
program. Visit him on the web at www.timwaggoner.com and
www.nekropoliscity.com.

# FLICKER

BY LEE THOMAS

ALL THAT KATHY KNEW OF LOVE CAME FROM IMAGES flickering on an old television screen. What came from this screen was fiction, and Kathy had discovered the difference between fiction and reality long ago. Fiction was a house in suburbia, cleaned by a beautiful mother who baked cookies, wore pearls, and prepared delicious meals. Fiction was a father who worked a steady job in the city, declared his daughter's beauty to the world, and fussed over the men who might date her. Fiction didn't show a little girl, bruised and crying, hiding in a filthy basement terrified of the fuckers she called Mom and Dad. But reality did. Reality offered a mother who worked out her boredom with vodka and strange men, and a father who expressed frustration with his fists and his cock. Reality offered Santa Monica Boulevard on Christmas Day, waiting for one of Keith's friends to pick Kathy up so she'd have her fix and a warm place to sleep. The company she kept was irrelevant. In this, reality's blindness was equal to love's.

And what did it matter? This wasn't a career, just a means to an end. She had ambitions. Early in the mornings as Keith snored next to her, Kathy laid awake imagining herself on the screen with Mark Wahlberg or Tom Cruise. The dream had followed her from childhood. Like Angelina Jolie or Sandra Bullock, Kathy wanted to be a star and see posters bearing her likeness hung on walls by adoring fans and see her name on movie theater signs. Her parents had laughed at her aspiration. They had no time for her "craziness." So, she'd gone into her basement and mimicked whatever movie she'd seen that afternoon, losing herself in a fiction that effectively filled a vacant childhood—at least for small periods of time. In her basement she became someone admired and loved, became someone strong and heroic, became anyone but Kathy Windman. She'd even played Frankie in her junior high school's production of *The Member of the Wedding.* Of course, her parents had been too busy to attend any of the shows, but her teachers and even some of the other parents had congratulated her beautiful performance. Such an exciting feeling it had been for her, being recognized as an actress.

Sadly, she'd never done another play. Her boyfriend in junior high, Larry, had said it was all so stupid. She'd temporarily abandoned her dramatic pursuits at his request, exchanged them for pharmaceutical dreams. The void she'd once filled with acting was soon plugged by blow, blunts, and a six-pack of Bud.

At fifteen, after Larry dumped her, Kathy hitchhiked from Seattle to the city where dreams were everything. One night while watching the dollar movies in a run-down theater on Hollywood Boulevard, she'd met Keith. He'd given her a place to stay, a purpose, and a new relationship with new dreams. These dreams offered needles and a cloudy world where pain was not allowed.

Almost a year had passed since they'd met. And now she waited on a corner for Keith's friend. She couldn't remember his name but he was supposed to pick her up.

She was going to make a movie.

The news had disturbed her at first. Although she wanted nothing more than to see her image on a screen, she didn't want to make porn flicks. She knew what happened to actresses who took the easy way out, who jumped at the money and then got the reputation, an inescapable reputation, as a whore. She didn't want that. She wanted to be a star, with all of the praise and respect that accompanied the title.

But Keith wouldn't hurt her. He loved her. He always told her so. He just had a friend who liked to make home movies. The guy was a voyeur. The movie wouldn't be seen by anybody, especially anyone from Hollywood. It was simply a game that this guy played, and besides Kathy wanted to see herself on the screen, even if the screen were nothing more than that of a high-def flat panel Sony.

As she grew concerned that her ride might not show, a gray Lexus pulled to the curb. Behind the wheel, a well-dressed man with silver hair and a fatherly smile leaned across to look her over. "Are you Kathy?" he asked. His teeth were very white and his skin very tanned. Looking in from the tall curb she could see that he wore white pants, which were pressed into sharp creases, and a crisp cobalt blue dress shirt. The sleeves were rolled up along thick forearms.

She nodded, flipping her hair over her shoulder as she stepped off of the curb. The man pushed open the door. She got in the car and as the door closed, the lock engaged.

"You're Keith's friend?" she asked.

"My name," the man said jovially, "is Desmond Silver. And yes, Keith and I have something of a history."

Kathy nodded and stared out the windshield of the sedan as the familiar buildings of her neighborhood pulled behind her. The inside of the car was warm and comfortable after the chill afternoon.

"Merry Christmas," she said uneasily.

"And Merry Christmas to you," he replied.

Light cologne, trapped in the car with them, tickled her nose. It smelled like almonds and reminded her of the movie theater back home. The Marquis, a theater down the street from where she'd lived with her parents, sold really good chocolate covered almonds, and whenever she hadn't spent her lunch money on cigarettes or make-up, she'd bought a box of the candy from the concession stand. They'd been especially good with a Dr. Pepper.

Wrapping a thin coil of blond hair around her finger, she studied the driver from the corner of her eye. He didn't talk much. That made her uncomfortable, but nothing else about the man seemed threatening. He had a pleasant smile on his round face and really pretty eyes. They were so blue. He didn't look anything like Keith's other friends. Some of them were old, but they looked different. They looked like lizards, and when they smiled they looked like *hungry* lizards. Most of Keith's friends were really creepy.

This guy—Silver—seemed nice, though. She just wished he'd say something. She didn't like the silence. It made her wonder if the man was having second thoughts about her. Maybe she wasn't pretty enough to appear in his movie. People told her she was pretty but she didn't always believe it. She thought her hair was too curly and her nose was too big. It wasn't like Barbra Streisand's or anything, but it seemed pretty big. At least she didn't have a weight problem, and she was a natural blonde. A lot of girls were uglier than her—like the one who lived downstairs from Keith. She had terrible skin and stringy black hair.

"So um," she began, trying to cancel the uncomfortable silence. "You . . . uh . . . you like movies?"

"Oh yes. They are the only perfect form of art. What about you?"

"I love them," Kathy said. She was going to mention her ambition of being an actress, but sometimes it sounded stupid when she said it aloud. So she settled for, "Are you going to be my co-star?"

The man burst out laughing. The car came alive with its rich, deep sound. As he laughed, his round face constricted, producing dozens of tiny wrinkles around his eyes and mouth. He looked over at Kathy and managed to say, "No, but I'm flattered you'd ask."

"You just like to watch?"

Silver considered this for a moment and then shook his head. "I like to create. Watching is part of that, I guess. You see, I choose to expend my energies into the creation of art. Honestly, the thought of anyone actually touching me is nauseating, which is not to say that I am a completely asexual creature." He turned the car and remained silent for a moment before continuing. "The guidance and manipulation of an act, the creation of an impossible scenario is very satisfying to me. Creation and *recreation*, fighting over something until it's perfect. That's my passion. I think they call it a God Complex."

*Damn,* Kathy thought. *How could you not like being touched?*

"Do you have dreams?" he asked in a friendly but stern voice. He took his eyes off the road and fixed her with a crystal blue gaze. "Real dreams?"

"Sure," Kathy replied. *Didn't everybody?*

Silver nodded and tapped the steering wheel once with his thick palm. "Well this place, this world, doesn't care much for dreams, despite what the poets tell us. It makes no accommodation for them. Dreams, prayers, they guide the young, but life's random inequities separate those who succeed from those whose dreams have been little more than inexpensive entertainment. I couldn't accept that." He shrugged his large shoulders and turned the car again. "It doesn't seem fair to only get one chance at a dream."

"No," she said, perhaps too eagerly.

He grinned at her exuberance. "If you make something and it breaks, well . . . then you've got two choices. If you've got the right tools or the right glue, you can fix it. Otherwise, it's gone. You have to pitch it away. Up until recently, I didn't have the right adhesive. This maddened me. It was like molding a perfect urn only to have the pieces separate in the kiln. But, recently I found a glue that works. I'm very excited about it."

"You make vases?" Kathy asked, uncertain of what Silver was talking about.

"What?" he asked. Then he let his warm chuckle loose to fill the car again. He rocked in the driver's seat obviously pleased by her naiveté. "No," he chuckled. "I was speaking metaphorically. Well, you'll see what I mean. We're here." He turned the wheel one last time and the car left the street.

The Lexus came to a stop in a dead-end alley. Buildings loomed on either side of the vehicle casting deep shadows over the dull façades. Moisture crept down the weathered brick as if the stones cried for solace. A three-story monstrosity stood ahead of them. Condemned and desolate, the three structures comprised a melancholy union in the midst of office towers and gleaming condominiums. Filthy plywood covered shattered windows. Obscure, woven symbols accompanied curses and effigies of genitalia on the boards and brick.

"Perfect, isn't it?" Silver asked.

Kathy made a sound in her throat that she hoped sounded positive; she didn't want to insult her host, but the alley and the buildings that formed it were eerie. Once, she'd gone with a friend of Keith's to an old shack behind a seedy apartment complex in Reseda. One guy took her to a deserted warehouse. The strangest place she'd ever partied was with a bunch of musicians. They'd broken into a fire-gutted apartment building in North Hollywood. A friend of theirs had overdosed in the room a few months before it had burned, so the place had meant a lot to them. But for the first time, while standing in that dark alley with the kindest looking man she'd ever met, Kathy felt scared.

"It's such a lonely looking place." He sighed. Then his demeanor rapidly changed. He smiled and slapped his hands together before his belly and rubbed them as if to make them warm. "Are you ready?"

Kathy nodded.

Silver set off across the pavement, his feet breaking a path in the litter. Kathy hesitated, put her thumbnail in her mouth, and then took a step forward. She moved slowly, looking around the alley as she crushed trash under her heels. The old man waited by a doorway. At that moment she realized how commanding he was. His frame all but eclipsed the black space beyond.

Kathy moved a little faster until she stood before him on the small cement stoop of the structure. A dull, musky odor poured from the building. Daylight was consumed beyond the threshold. Inside, only three steps were visible climbing away at a steep grade.

"Ladies first," Silver said. He stepped aside and waved his arm toward the stairs. He made the motion so gracefully, so slowly, like a magician offering a miraculous illusion to his audience. For a moment, it seemed the gloomy chamber had dissolved his arm at the elbow, but when the arc completed, the man stood before her, whole and grinning.

As she stepped over the threshold into the strange space, a fetid urban perfume climbed along her nostrils and down the back of her throat where it coiled in her windpipe. Refuse, urine and excrement and an underlying odor, an animal odor, coalesced into a rank phantom, a malevolent spirit unwilling to allow her breath, and Kathy choked audibly trying to regain control of her throat. She hesitated, putting a palm over her mouth. What little of the stairway she could see in the dim glow, stretched far above her. At the top, a sickly yellow light fought against a dark siege. Tiny shafts of gray from cracks in the plywood blinds cut the air like minuscule threads woven in raven cloth. They illuminated little, succumbing to the hunger of the darkness.

She turned. Silver stood behind her. His face remained a mask of joviality. He seemed so pleased. She wondered about him. How did he spend his days? What did he do for a living? She assumed he wasn't married because of what he'd said about being touched, but who was he?

The boards beneath her feet complained under her weight. Kathy clutched the splintered rail tightly as she led Silver toward the jaundiced glow. Low raspy voices glided in the air above. The words seemed visible, swirling in the thin gray shafts of light. One of the voices burst into laughter, and then the chamber went silent.

She neared the top. Her heart beat rapidly. The struggling light came from a dusty bulb in the hall to the right of the staircase illuminating graffiti-raped walls. To her left, there was a brightly lit room at the far end of the hall. Then she saw her co-stars.

They knelt in a circle around a flickering candle, the light of which extended no more than a foot in either direction. Two were busy with a needle, cooking a familiar dish in a blackened sugar spoon. The sight of the brew made her stomach knot.

Keith had told her to wait until she got to the party, and they'd fix her up. Now she felt the craving in her belly growing, gestating like a child. The hunger kicked. It grew into an unbearable ache. Only seconds after seeing the smoking spoon, Kathy's entire body hurt.

The third man, an enormous bald figure with tribal tattoos painting his torso and arms, knelt with his back to the wall. He wore a pair of tattered Levi's and black work boots. He balanced the thin point of a switchblade in his palm. When it dropped, he clutched the handle and retracted the blade. After springing it again, he began to roll the weapon between his fingers as his buddies continued brewing the contents of the spoon.

"Our star has arrived," Desmond Silver announced.

The three men lifted their heads. They regarded Kathy with little interest; their expressions remained flat and bland. The bald man stopped spinning the blade, and it jumped in his hand, landing point down on his palm. His stare caught Kathy's as he executed the move.

"Hi," she said. She tried to smile but it collapsed on her lips. "Is that . . ." she began, "I mean, Keith said. . .Well, he said I could get fixed up . . . I mean, did he tell you? Is that cool?"

"You're the star," Silver said, giving himself a wide berth between himself and the girl as he moved into the hallway. "And a star gets whatever she wants. William, will you accommodate the young lady?"

The thin man holding the spoon over the candle's flame nodded slowly. He had long, shaggy, brown hair that dropped in ringlets over his ears and framed his emaciated face. The black T-shirt covering his torso hung loosely, dangerously close to the flame. On the hand that held the spoon, he wore a leather glove with the fingers removed.

Silver continued down the hall, leaving her in the company of his friends. The man who was not William, placed a needle into the soupy contents of the spoon and filled the rig. Kathy rolled up the sleeve of her blouse.

She noticed Silver's silhouette in the radiant doorway of the room at the end of the hall, but her eyes were constantly teased back by the sight of her approaching treat. (She and Keith always called it lunch.) The man who was not William stood. Distantly she felt the tourniquet applied to her bicep. A finger tapped rhythmically on the crook of her elbow, but she couldn't take her eyes off of the tiny rig floating before her eyes. The bald man chuckled hollowly. The odors of the building receded under the dusty, fungal smell of her treat. William began chuckling along with the bald man, slapping the tattooed shoulder of his friend. The needle penetrated her skin. The garrote loosened. Something fell in the room at the end of the hall and Silver barked his discontent. Kathy hardly noticed.

A warm cascade showered her and the ache of craving retreated under a deluge of pleasure, which touched and then drowned her senses. For all of the familiarity of this sensation, it was a strange high. Her stomach did not cramp. Her flesh did not become clammy. Rather, she slid peacefully into a chemical sanctuary unfettered by ridiculous notions of fear or pain.

Hands grasped her under the arms and lifted, and her mind continued to rise until it felt as if she floated across the ceiling. A soothing current embraced her and then pulled away, only to return a moment later. Fingers touched and tickled, running over her chest and waist. They were undressing her and as each garment was removed, she sighed in pleasure. The tide of euphoria lapped at her neck and her breasts and insinuated itself between her legs, bringing a smile to her lips.

She closed her eyes and then opened them, but the scene before her hardly changed. Soft colors like the melted wax of festive candles pooled and streamed before her, and at their center was an inviting illumination, a thousand-watt heaven to which she was inexplicably drawn. Kathy's mind cleared some, though the rapture remained. Her new friends were carrying her down the bleak corridor, a dismal tunnel that ended in paradise.

They brought her into the welcoming glow. The room was a studio, illuminated by three lights plugged into a low-humming gas generator. Behind the lights, chrome umbrellas reflected harshly over the entire chamber. Dirty, painted walls, like those of the hallway, surrounded her, and she noticed the exceptional darkness of the night beyond the two windows on the north wall. Her clouded and contented mind didn't realize that the panes had been painted black. To her right a video camera stood on three chrome legs and pointed at a stained mattress lying uncovered in the center of the room. Four gleaming eye-bolts were driven into the concrete floor at each corner of the soiled bed. Connected to each of the bolts was a length of chain ending in a cuff-like bracelet. Above the mattress was a flaking iron pipe, and polished silver manacles draped from the rusting tube.

"All right," said Silver as the two men helped Kathy to the mattress. "Let's get started. Kathy, you fine honey?"

"Mmmm?" she mumbled.

"Good," Silver said. He rubbed his hands together quickly and grinned. "Dallas, William, help her into position. Hurry now."

Her body glided across the chamber. This was so much better than her other highs. She'd never felt so wholly removed from the pains and anxieties of the world. She wondered if she had overdosed, but this felt too wonderful to be an overdose. Kathy closed her eyes. She couldn't really focus on anything anyway, so why fight it? Besides, everything looked so much lovelier with her eyes closed. Then, she was lying down. When had that happened? Why were her wrists and ankles suddenly cold? Distantly she heard a thick voice call, "Action."

She drifted in a beautiful stream somewhere between consciousness and Heaven, without a single earthbound concern. Oh, she knew what was happening to her body. Distantly she could feel the weight, could feel the pressure on her, in her, but that was too far away to worry about. She'd found a pleasant fiction to lose herself in, and she wouldn't mind staying there forever. Here she could have a mother that baked cookies and wore pearls, and she could have a father that loved his little girl without shoving his cock in her, and here Keith kept her to himself, protecting her and loving her with all of the sincerity he claimed but never showed. What they did to her body didn't matter, because it was just a shell, a cell of meat and fluid and bone and a repository for agonies great and minor. She didn't need it—didn't want it.

But now, she was returning to the cell of her flesh because someone wanted her to. She struggled against it, because being away felt so much nicer. Someone slapped her, called her name (*Kathy!*), called her something else (*Bitch!*). Ice water drenched her face and pooled against her neck before the dirty mattress drank it away. She forced her lids open.

Above her, the bald man knelt. He still played with his knife.

The studio around them was full of people. Women, some dressed in magnificent gowns while others were clad in shabby denim, gazed at her prone body. Men in a similar range of fashion offered glances of appreciation while others looked bored. Couples made love in the shadows behind the glaring lights, their bodies moving as single silhouettes, completely unconcerned with the audience as they writhed in their dark corners. Desmond Silver grinned at her from behind the camera. It looked like his head was part of the device.

"Are we done?" she mumbled. "Can I see it now?" She tried to rise, but something clutched her wrists, weighed on her ankles. Her hands and feet tingled.

"Not quite," Silver said. "We still need to get a close-up. Dallas, are you ready?"

Discomfort shot along her forearm and Kathy cried out. "Can you take these things off now?"

"The close-up, dear," Silver muttered, leaning close to the viewing screen of his camera. "Must... have... a... close... up." He pressed a button on his camera, shook his head and repeated the gesture. "Dallas?"

"Anytime," the bald man replied.

Suddenly the euphoria retreated. Fear covered her like a blanket of nettles. Dallas knelt beside her, flexing his tattooed arms. Silver continued to fiddle with the video camera. He moved a light closer to the mattress. The audience whispered. Silver returned the light to where it had stood. Kathy saw the blade, opening and closing only inches from her face. It clicked loudly in her ear. William and the other man stopped laughing. Rapt anticipation froze their features. The generator hummed. How odd it seemed that this noise should make her understand the silence in the room.

"If it's a close-up," Kathy whimpered, "you don't..."

"Shhh," Silver hissed.

"But you don't..."

"Shut up!" the director said. "I need to frame this scene."

"Hey," she said. "You can't talk to me like... I mean, you could be nice. You don't have to..."

A dry hand slapped the rest of the words from her mouth.

"Action," Silver called.

The blade flashed open and stayed open. Dallas slid against her on the mattress. He leaned down to Kathy's cheek, and his tongue, like a bloated leech, violated her ear. Hot breath oozed over her face. Kathy struggled against the binds. "I'm going to kill you now," the man whispered. "So let's see some action, star-child."

But he wasn't serious. This was just a movie. He couldn't be serious. Just a plot or something. The blade was a stage knife—made of rubber—that's why he hadn't cut himself with his tricks. Just a plot. It had to be. But she couldn't stop crying. Her throat felt swollen closed. Her body convulsed from fear. She struggled against the manacles and tore the flesh around her wrists and ankles, fighting to get away from the ink-painted man beside her. She was only sixteen. Keith loved her. Just cinema. Just a movie. Just a plot. It had to be.

The blade caressed her cheek. Dallas grabbed a handful of her hair and yanked her head back, deep into the mattress. She tried to scream but her windpipe suddenly pinched. The cold blade slid over her chin like a steel tear. It traced along her throat, caught on something then continued across. Warmth spilled over her neck and chest, and when Kathy realized the heat must surely have been pouring from her own body, panic clamped down.

She screamed, and the sound filled her head. The warmth pulsed along her throat. She couldn't move. The bald man crawled off the mattress. Silver directed quietly from behind the camera. Kathy kept screaming. The sound filled her ears though it never left her opened neck. Above her, she saw the cracked ceiling swelling and contracting like respiration, as her body convulsed. The generator droned; the camera kept rolling.

Then, she fell. Backward and down she fell, away from the noisy room and into her screams. The room washed out, bleached of its filth and its threat. And Kathy thought of Keith, thought of stardom, thought of nothing.


SHE SWAM IN an opalescent pool. Dull gray shapes moved amidst the milky fluid. She recognized each of them despite the fact they had neither feature nor distinct form. Larry was there, telling her she wasn't mature enough for him. Her mother surfaced, screaming and swinging a broom handle, and then sank away as Keith and Desmond Silver drifted by, negotiating her fate. Teachers and friends, lovers and dealers coalesced and dissipated around her. A distant thunder of disco music accompanied the shapes in her head.

Kathy struggled to understand this place, and the more she struggled, the louder the music became. The gray images receded into the pool as its glow intensified.

When she opened her eyes, she stared at the ceiling and wondered where she was. She'd taken a long nap somewhere. A girl about her age knelt over her and smiled. The girl wrung a damp pink cloth into a bucket and reapplied it to Kathy's neck where the cool water bathed a nagging itch, which became apparent only after it had been soothed.

As she thought about her neck, she remembered Desmond Silver and remembered Dallas and his knife. Kathy screamed and rolled away from the girl, thinking that she still lay on the studio mattress. But she'd been moved and Kathy rolled into a wall. She drew her nails across the rough black surface. Screaming and kicking, she tried to escape through an impermeable obstacle. Her nails split and her throat ached.

"Oh don't," the girl said. "Hey. Kathy. Hey. It's all right. Kathy?"

But she kept to her struggle. She had to escape or they'd really kill her the next time. Her body shuddered as she thought of Dallas' blade, and she fought even harder against the wall.

"Honey," the girl said. "Kathy?"

A strong hand touched her shoulder and rolled her back onto the cot. The girl's face, concerned and friendly, hovered inches from hers. A sweet perfume came from the girl, and her eyes were so kind.

"I'm Becky," the girl tried. "I'm from Omaha. Where are you from?"

Kathy's eyes raced in their sockets, fueled by panic and confusion. She couldn't understand what difference it made where she came from? They were going to kill her. But if they wanted her dead, wouldn't she be dead? As she considered this, she also considered the fact that she might have been on a bad trip. Maybe the movie magic had just seemed real. None of it made sense.

"I bet you're from Oregon," the girl said, placing a palm on Kathy's forehead, smoothing back the hair. "Are you?"

"Seattle," Kathy rasped.

"I hear it's beautiful there," Becky said. "I was starting to get worried. You've been asleep a long time. All day and most of the night. I know the first time can be traumatic, but . . . "

"Where am I?" Kathy asked.

"Generally, you're in L.A. Specifically, you're in Desmond's studio."

Becky laughed at this, revealing a dreadful smile of swollen gums and broken and missing teeth. She noticed the disgust on Kathy's face, and a cloud passed over her features. She threw a palm to her mouth, hiding the destruction behind her lips. "Sorry, I did a scene yesterday. They haven't grown back yet."

Kathy sobbed.

Becky's face fell into concern again. She leaned into Kathy and hugged her as best she could. "What's wrong, honey?"

"They're going to kill us," Kathy sobbed. "Aren't they?"

"Probably," Becky said. She considered for a moment and said, "They've killed me, eight times, but I'm just about done. Desmond said that he's almost got the scene perfect. I'm very excited—you know, about the finished product? I can't wait to see it. He thinks it's going to be brilliant."

What was the girl saying? How could someone be killed eight times? How could someone be killed twice?

"Desmond is bril'," Becky said. "A total genius. Film is his medium."

Kathy sat up slowly, her eyes never leaving the young woman's beside her. "Aren't you afraid?"

Becky laughed and grabbed Kathy's shoulders gently. "There's nothing left to be afraid of ... except algebra." Another ghastly smile split the otherwise beautiful face. "Let me give you a tour and I'll try to explain."

Kathy stood. She was naked, a light pink sheen covered her upper torso. "I have to get dressed."

"Suit yourself," Becky said. She led Kathy to a door and opened it to expose a rack of clothing. "Something here should fit you."

As Kathy began to dress, the girl explained, "Desmond has been working in this field for years. They used to call them 'snuff films'. Isn't that a terrible name? I hate it. Desmond prefers the term *Film Mort*. Well, when the form was young, he had a lot of trouble. He couldn't maintain any continuity. After all, once a scene was finished, it was *finished*. No chance for retakes, no chance for artistic expansion. Desmond always likens it to vases."

And he'd said something about glue, Kathy thought, retrieving a beautiful yellow sundress from the costumer's rack.

"That'll go great with your hair," Becky said, nodding at the dress. "Anyhow, Desmond could never glue his vases back together. He could have another brought in, but he couldn't maintain authenticity. Well, a few years ago, he came across a woman that solved his problems. She had the glue he needed. The first couple of shoots were difficult because he didn't know how to explain himself to his models. A few ran. One even went to the police but nothing ever came from it."

The dress fell over Kathy's head, draping comfortably over her body. A mirror gleamed from the back of the closet door, and she examined herself. A ragged line, red and gnarled, ran across her neck from one ear to the other. Her hand went to the wound, felt along the rough edges as the reality of her injury sank in. But there was no pain, no lingering ache. It seemed that the damage was merely skin deep.

"I told you, with your hair . . . " Becky said, again indicating the dress with a nod. She wrapped a friendly arm around Kathy's shoulder. "Just beautiful." She guided the new girl toward the hall. "Before you, I was the newest one to enter the troupe. I guess that's why Desmond asked me to talk to you."

"How long have you known him?"

"Oh, about six months now."

"Don't you ever want to leave?" Kathy wanted to leave. She wanted to get to a doctor so he could look at the gash on her throat before it started bleeding again.

"I will soon," Becky said. "I'm going to miss this place. I don't want to go, but the movie is almost finished now, and I'd just be in the way."

"They're not going to let you leave," Kathy said. How stupid could the girl be?

"I keep forgetting, you're new. People leave all the time. Let's go," Becky said.

The disco music that Kathy associated with her dream pulsed in an adjoining room. She gazed at the door as they passed.

"That's Dallas' room. He loves to dance."

One floor below, Kathy recognized the studio. "Shhh," the pretty girl hissed, holding a finger to her lips. "They're filming."

The two snuck down the hall and into the studio. The setup was similar to Kathy's first visit—the mattress, the lights, the camera—except a tall white cross occupied the center of the room. A young man, maybe twenty years old, hung from it. He was naked, and his arms were bound by thick lengths of hemp. William, with his curly feminine hair, stood at the base of the cross, a cigarette glowing from between his lips. He inhaled deeply, stoking a glowing red ember. Then he applied the searing end to the captive's thigh. The crucified man screamed and rolled his head. Pleading and begging filled the chamber. Another application of the searing cherry. This time the ember disappeared into the soft white flesh of the young man's belly. Then William dropped the butt and crushed it under his heel, before walking behind the cross. When he returned, he held a fireman's ax.

"Oh God," Kathy moaned. She had to help the man. But no, she had to help herself. She stepped back, into Becky's waiting arms. They snaked around her, crossing at her chest.

William lifted the ax and drew the blade slowly across the man's porcelain stomach. It did not pierce the skin, but rather caressed it. Still the prisoner screamed, shouted for help and dropped his head to the side. Desperate, pleading eyes caught Kathy's. Then William pulled the weapon back and swung. The blade dug deeply into the crucified body. Blood erupted in splashes and ropes from the wound, quickly pouring down the ivory abdomen to paint the man's pubic hair and genitals. The handle jutted away from the torso like a perverse appendage.

Kathy screamed. Becky shook her and tried to get a hand around her mouth. But it was too late. Desmond and William stared at the girls in the doorway. Whispers of discontent from the audience in the shadows filled the chamber. Kathy fought against Becky's grip, but she was too strong. Then something incomprehensible happened.

"Great," a high voice cried. The man on the cross looked at Kathy, his expression was dark and angry. She stared incredulously. Her stomach knotted and her mind raced. The young man with the ax in his belly gazed down on her. "The shot's ruined. I don't believe this shit," he huffed. "You try and do your best work and some amateur walks in and ruins the whole thing. Desmond," the boy said, "I cannot work under these conditions." He wriggled his hands loose, undid himself from the binds and hopped off the cross. The ax remained firmly planted in his gut.

"I know, I know," Desmond said, rushing forward. "I'm sorry. You were perfection, as usual." Silver regarded Becky for a moment. "You should have known better than to bring her here," he said before returning his attention to the disgruntled performer. "Sweetie," he cooed. "The lighting wasn't very good anyway. We'll re-shoot next week as soon as you're up to it."

"Next week? This is going to take at least two to heal," the boy said, pulling the heavy weapon from his belly. He dropped it to the floor, where it hit with a clatter. Blood oozed from the wound, and a purple rope of intestine surfaced in the gash. "We finally had it. What if I can't get the inspiration back? What if the part is cold next time?" The young man looked distraught. "It finally felt right."

"It'll be okay," Silver said. "You are never less than perfect." He made to put his arm around the man, and then jerked his hand away. Silver whispered accolades in his ear as the two walked out of the studio.

"THAT WAS BOBBY," Becky said, leading Kathy back to her room. "He's a little temperamental but his style is impeccable. He's been here for about two years now. This is his second film for Desmond. Desmond is a little worried that his clients will feel cheated if they realize he's been featured before, but Bobby used to be blonde, and he really does look different now."

Kathy couldn't speak. The horrible images of that bright room still played in her head.

"Don't worry," the girl said. "It doesn't hurt or anything. That's why we have to act. After a while it's like brushing your hair. It might pull if you catch a tangle, but it doesn't really hurt. You might even get into it." Becky turned to her new friend. The glittering expression that told the world how happy she was to be a part of it had faded. "I do hope you stay. I'd really like somebody to talk to, you know? Somebody to go to the movies with."

The girl smiled at Kathy; the heaviness in her eyes reflected an emotion that Kathy had never been able to define in herself. When Becky left, Kathy felt empty.

Desmond Silver came to her soon after Becky retreated down the hall to study lines for her shoot the following week. His face hung with concern. But it was his eyes, eyes that projected such intense sadness, that captured Kathy. He'd changed clothes, opting for a pair of khaki shorts and a black dress shirt.

Kathy felt exhausted. She hadn't even thought of escape. Girls always tried to run in the movies and something horrible always happened. It was better to just rest until her mind cleared. Then she might think of a plan. Right now, she just wanted to sleep. "Tough day?" Silver asked, sitting on the edge of Kathy's bed. "The first shoot can be rough."

Tears rose in Kathy's eyes. How could he seem so nice? After what she'd seen? After what he'd done to her? How could he seem so kind? Did all monsters have such warm smiles and such fatherly eyes?

"Before," Silver said. "Before all of this, I was a doctor, but I had to give it up. I . . . " He smiled wanly. The corners of his mouth pushed at the tired flesh of his face. "There's a certain attraction for me in the opening of skin. The way it releases under a blade and opens like a waiting kiss, and then the blood comes, constant and warm like affection just waiting to pour over me, and of course in that line of work the beautiful wounds proved distracting. But I saw girls like you every night, trundled through the emergency room because their boyfriends or tricks had gotten tired of them, discarded them after making sure their pretty faces would never land them another man." He shook his head. "They always went back to these men. I used to stay up nights wondering what had become of them. Eventually I had to give up medicine, because of my distraction. Financially comfortable, I went into filmmaking. I tried to justify my early films by telling myself that I was saving children like you from a lifetime of pain. It wasn't very effective. When I found my glue, I found a way of balancing my art with my ideals."

All of Silver's talk about medicine and wounds and glue confused her. He murdered people for movies. He was crazy, and she could care less about hearing the details of his insanity.

"I don't care," Kathy said. "I just want to go home."

"Which home is that? The home with the abusive parents or the home with the boyfriend who sold you for a hundred dollars and a bottle of Jack Daniels?"

"Keith loves me," Kathy said. Her voice cracked as tears filled her eyes.

"He doesn't," Silver said. "Kathy, I'm not a good man, but I am an honest one. If you go back to him he will sell you to someone else, and the next man isn't going to have my glue. Any damage done to you will be permanent. Yes, this place is odd, maybe even a little scary, and you will have to endure some terrifying moments, but you will have the support and protection of everyone here—like a family—and when you leave, you will leave whole and ready to make a new life for yourself."

"Can't I just go?" Kathy pleaded.

"If that's what you want," Silver said. "But you need to stay until your neck heels. The glue's efficacy is limited. I'll send William down to give you another shot. We don't want that wound to open."

Silver stood, casting one last smile at Kathy. "I do hope you'll reconsider. I think our film would be stunning." Then he left the room.

The loneliness entered her like frigid air, filling her body and freezing her lungs. She stood hesitantly and walked to the hall. Stepping forward she gripped the door and rubbed the wood with a palm. All that Silver had told her bustled and wrestled in her mind. Her decision should have been easy. Escape. Get as far away from Silver and his freaks as she could go. Run back to Keith. He'd tell her that he loved her, and he'd apologize and kiss her and make love to her and promise he'd never let anyone hurt her again.

Except he wouldn't. She wanted to believe this fantasy, but fantasy was just another word for fiction.

Kathy pressed her cheek against the door, hugged it.

Outside, a child picked through a dumpster, hoping that his breakfast wouldn't make him sick before it relieved the foggy exhaustion in his head and the ache in his belly. In the adjacent building, a mother gave birth to a child and sawed through the umbilical cord with a broken bottle before abandoning the screaming bundle in a cardboard box and creeping back into the dawn. A good husband and concerned father opened the door to his silver Honda and let a fourteen-year-old boy back onto the corner he'd taken him from. Cars raced by and the city awoke. It was the day after Christmas and the season for giving had come to an end.

---

LEE THOMAS is the Lambda Literary and Bram Stoker Award-winning author of the novels *Stained, Damage,* and *The Dust of Wonderland,* and the critically acclaimed short story collection, *In the Closet, Under the Bed.* Current and forthcoming titles include the novellas *The Black Sun Set, Focus, and Crisis.* His novel, *The German,* will be released in March 2011 from *Lethe Press.*

He has published dozens of short stories and non-fiction articles in print and online publications, in addition to appearing in a number of anthologies, including *A Walk on the Darkside, Darkness on the Edge, Inferno, Unspeakable Horror, Supernatural Noir, Specters in Coal Dust,* and *Wilde Stories: The Year's Best Gay Speculative Fiction.* You can find him online at www.leethomasauthor.com.

# THE FISHING OF DAHLIA

## BY ENNIS DRAKE

---

*"There is no such thing as an insignificant life, only the insignificance of mind that refuses to grasp the implications."*

—Laurence Overmire

"MY NAME IS JOB," HE SAID, SPEAKING THE WORDS AS if they belonged to an arcane language from some lost, dark epoch. He was disconnected and in shock, but driven still by a vestigial inner valor he believed himself to possess. His mind was broken; his memory an ill-fitting puzzle composed, or so it seemed to Job, of second-hand albums filled with a stranger's old photographs.

"My name is Job," he said again—his single anchor of certainty—and throttled the boat.

The sun was cooling molten copper in the west. Cypress and heart pine stood along the north bank of the river like grim sentinels to an alien world. The only sound was the roar of the 225-horse Mercury, the sleek boat skipping across the water as it hurtled toward the river bank.

"My name is Job and it . . . it took her," he said.

Lightning flared in his mind and time spun out. He never felt the impact.

When Job awoke, he was sprawled on the prow of the boat, his lip split and bleeding. Below him, water slunk and gurgled, slow-seeping its way through the shattered hull. He ran his tongue across his teeth, feeling the cracked canine and incisor; touched his lip with a trembling hand. Winced. *But were the wounds from the impact?* Job wondered. He didn't think so.

"She . . . " he began, but trailed off, standing shakily. The boat rocked where he had grounded it and he lurched on the deck. "There was," he continued, licking blood from his swollen lip as he tried to order the few fragments of memory he still possessed, "lightning in the woods. Right *here*," he said, pointing at the river bank that rose before him, images tumbling out of the electric-charged blackness of his amnesia . . .

*The river house. Stripped of most of its furniture. Boxes stacked everywhere. A man was pounding on the door. His son, Michael . . . his oldest. Michael was shouting as the door opened and, too quick to anticipate, he punched Job in the mouth, splitting his lip and cracking two of his teeth.*

*The river house dissolved into the river itself. An osprey lunged into the sky from the water's edge, abandoning its nest atop an ancient cypress. The sun was copper, but not yet molten. Something thrashed and thumped against the deck of the boat. There was a flash of light, like lightning in the tree line . . . a tangle of blonde hair . . . a scream, and . . .* there was blankness . . . *and he was throttling into the river bank.*

Job saw again the twist of blonde hair, and bright pain like the blade of electric fire on an arc welder dug a furrow across the front of his brain, as if invoked by some outside power to purge the memory from him.

"No! You're not going to take that from me!" he screamed in defiance, the lightning-pain threatening to sear his mind to smooth scar tissue, to rob him of memory and self. He hooked his hands through his thinning hair, pounded his temples, but for a terrifying, interminable span of seconds, he lost everything. He was, again, an empty vessel; dispossessed of *who, where, why,* and *how.* His muscles seized and there was familiarity in that. He convulsed and there was familiarity in that, too. He heard, again and again, like a distant echo, thrashing, thumping, and a woman's scream.

"Please, she's out there," he said, voice rasping like decaying machinery. "She's out there, goddamnit! *Ali!*"

He fought his own short-circuiting mind and . . .


JOB REMEMBERED THE bass. He remembered it and held the image in his mind's-eye like a talisman. The way it had thrashed and thumped against the hollow fiberglass deck, blood running from its mouth and gills, the monofilament line disappearing into its throat.

He'd gut-hooked it.

By then, the sun had ridden out the last of its track, an unblemished twilight left in its wake as it fell into the west to die its lazy, phoenix's death. The river had faded from chocolate to an ashen copper that reminded Job of the pennies he used to bury in coffee cans when he was a boy. He was fumbling with the bass, thinking of those pennies, when an osprey, frightened from its nest, lunged skyward from the water's edge. She had said something, then . . .

*What did she say? Was it important?*

. . . and that's when he'd seen it: The strange, stroboscopic light, pulsing like a living sapphire behind the veil of heart pine and palm scrub that piled along the north bank of the river. That's when it had taken . . . when she had . . .

Quicksilver pain slid along the curve of his skull.

"Just remember the bass," Job said, grinding his teeth together painfully to keep hold of himself.

When the pain receded, he moved farther along the prow, watching. Sweat rolled down his sun-baked temples, crowded his high, lined brow. He was waiting for the lightning. The pulse. Whatever it was. He knew it would come—he remembered the hunger in that light.

And, moments later, the sapphirine light raged—as if Job had summoned it—throwing the trees into jeweled relief. He tried to look away, knowing the wyrd light was stealing his capacity to think, understand, and reason; stealing, if not his soul, then the very essence of his identity . . .

. . . but Job found himself climbing the muddy swath that clove the river bank, the grass and weeds worn away by an exceptionally large animal, probably an alligator. He didn't remember dismounting the boat and as he caught himself clawing his way up the slope, he realized he'd taken his Smith & Wesson 9mm from the compartment under the steering wheel.

He looked back at his ruined boat. The current had drawn it away from the bank and it wallowed, half-submerged; the metal-fleck paint twinkled in the last of the day's light, then it was gone, pulled downriver, pulled below.

The light flared, deeper in the trees now, and Job shielded his eyes.

*I'm coming, Ali,* he thought, desperate to think of anything but the image of tangled blonde hair.


## MEMORIA


HE HAD NOT seen the light in some time and more images—memories, Job supposed—had been coming in an intermittent flow. All of them began with the bass (he had learned to use this memory to lead him to the revelations he sought) and from there, the flashes of recollection directed him back through crucial moments of his life.

*Ali. His wife. She was showing him quarterly reports for their business. She was shaking her head, her short black hair bobbing and swaying. It was all red. The numbers were red.*

*There was light . . . no,* color. *It was not blue, nor red, but* pink.

*There was another woman. Her hair was blonde.*

*Lightning. The lightning in the woods. Pain.*

*Ali again, now throwing his clothes out the front door of the home they'd shared for more than twenty years. She was screaming. Crying. Furious. Betrayed.*

Pink. *Blonde hair. Crooked grin. Lips glossed with sex.*

*Lightning and pain.*

*The bass. Thump-thump-thump. Its black eyes stared. Its great mouth puckered open and closed as it suffocated.*

The forest opened before him, black as a charcoal rendering. Twilight had gone and stars scarred the night—crystalline wounds in dark flesh.

Job's legs were burning, the muscles in his calves knotted into fiery, stone claws. His breath came hot and fast, and his heart was knocking like an engine about to throw a rod. He raked at his face with mud-caked hands.

Worse than his aches was the emptiness that sometimes followed the surges of memory. There were moments when, on the verge of a breakthrough, he would blank completely; moments when he thought he didn't know who he was anymore, and he'd have to chant his name just to hold his claim on himself. The pistol in his hand was a constant surprise. The darkness and the forest a recurring stranger.

"I am Job. It took her. She's out there," he reminded, leaning against the scaled hide of a knotty pine.

*But who is* she? Not Ali. Not his wife, as he'd hoped. *No, don't think that. It's Ali. Ali's the only thing that makes sense.*

Pink. Sex. Twist of blonde hair.

Job frowned. There was no night-noise. No opera of insects. Not even the chainsaw buzz of mosquitoes, which were in full breed this time of year. There was no noise at all, save the slow, liquid slink of the river somewhere at his back.

In the distance, the light flared. A beacon.

He'd lost his sandals somewhere, and rotting leaves and fleshy pine needles crumpled beneath his toes. Sticks and cones bit painfully into the soft underbellies of his feet.

More time passed. The quality of the night shifted toward pitch, and Job left the lap-and-murmur of the river far behind—though he had no memory of moving so deep into the forest. Silver radiance played over him and through the crosshatch of pine boughs above, he saw a scimitar moon ascending to its zenith.

He tried again, for the thousandth time, to piece together what had happened. Wondered if he was having a breakdown. Was that possible? Could he be having some kind of stress-induced hallucination?

He heard something moving in the brush. Whatever it was, it was big. And it was coming fast.

*This is it.*

Job gripped the Smith 9mm in both hands. Ran a dry tongue across drier lips, the skin, caked with old blood, rasping like . . . like an osprey's feathers.

A deer broke from the scrub, leaped, and Job cried out. He threw his arms up to ward the animal off, but as its hooves left the ground, something seized it, and the deer was yanked violently through the air, back into the darkness of the trees.

Its taking was instantaneous.

Job fell to the night-damp ground. It all locked into place. He remembered everything.

*The bass had thump-thump-thumped its beat of asphyxiation against the deck. The sun had been going down. And Dahlia . . .* Oh dear God, it was Dahlia . . . *had been painting her toenails pink.*

Job screamed. Long, painful wails that he was powerless to stop.


HE'D BEEN FISHING all damned day, skin burning under the fiery August sun, hands performing the dance that cast the line, reeled the line, and cast the line. Doing it again and again. They say muscles have memory and Job thought that was true, because he hadn't come out to the river to fish; had hardly been aware of the act at all. No, he'd come for the peace he equated with the murky brown waters of the St. John's. He'd grown up here, conspired here in play as a boy, and as a man he returned often, reveling in the connection he felt between himself and these waters.

But there was no peace today. And he couldn't help but think he might never know peace again.

Ali had left him. It'd be three months, tomorrow. His boys—men, now; hell, Michael had a wife and sons of his own—refused to talk to him. His business was a hundred-and-twenty-thousand dollars in the red, and he hated his fucking job on top of it all. Here he was, fifty-eight years old, and still selling carpet. Who wanted to sell carpet, whether you owned the company or not, whether you'd made (and lost) millions, or not? Success was a distant memory. Fuck, success wasn't even a concept he understood anymore. His failures were a mourning-suit. *And I wear 'em, 'cause that's all I've got left.*

And today was just another God-accursed day like all the rest of them. That's what he'd told himself that morning, as he blindly performed the ritual of packing the boat. Except, from the moment he woke in the near-empty river house, Dahlia crumpled silent and still in the bed beside him, something had felt different. The morning had crawled his skin like a current and he'd thought: *Today feels like the culmination of something.*

A strange thing to think.

"I must be going crazy," he'd said and sat up in bed, laughing haggardly. Dahlia had rolled over, asked him what he was laughing about. Then Michael was pounding on the front door and next thing Job knew he was lying on the foyer floor holding his bleeding lip and choking on the fragments of his cracked teeth. After that, after *everything*, what was left but the river?

He'd dressed, avoiding Dahlia, but she had caught him in the den shoving his Smith & Wesson down the front of his khaki shorts. She had regarded him, not with compassion or concern, but with a look of shrewd self-preservation.

"I'm going with you, Job. You shouldn't be alone today," she'd said.

"Yeah, it'd be a shame if something happened to me and you had to go back to waiting tables at Steak 'N' Shake, wouldn't it?" he'd snapped.

But it didn't matter. Dahlia was just protecting her ass and he hated to admit, least of all in that moment, what a fine little ass it was. Lust and self-disgust were a bitter pairing.

They had spent most of the day in silence.

Near sunset, he reeled the bass onto the deck.

"Goddamnit, Job, could you stop rocking the boat?" Dahlia drawled.

In her tiny black thong bikini, Dahlia was all legs and tits, golden skin, and platinum blonde hair. *Twenty-three years old*, Job thought and shook his head. *More than half my age*—younger than Michael, a year younger than Joe, Job's youngest son—*but good-God-Almighty the girl fucks like a machine.*

He hadn't wanted to trade Ali for Dahlia. He'd wanted his proverbial cake and wanted to eat it too. But he hadn't just wanted to *eat* it, he wanted to slow-tongue every last bit of sickly-sweet icing from it in a series of long, emotionless acts of unveiled and unrestrained lust. He had wanted this for no other reason than that it made him feel young; a feeling better than the act itself; better than any drug. He hated himself for it, but it didn't change anything.

He knew Dahlia had only *played* because of his money, that she only *stayed* because she believed he had more.

She didn't know he'd ran his business straight into the shitter. Or maybe she did. Maybe she thought she could draw and tongue a few more drops from his assets—the houses, the cars, the properties—like an ape sucking marrow from a bone.

Looking at her now, Job could honestly say he felt nothing, save the sudden desire to put a bullet between her close-set green eyes and then, after having another dance with the reel and rod, eating a bullet himself.

He kneeled over the gut-hooked fish. Thought it was the one that'd been stealing his bait all day.

"Got greedy, didn't you? Got yourself in a nasty fix. Well, me and you both," he said and cut the line.

He held the bass over the copper-hued water, and as he released it an osprey lunged skyward from the water's edge. It let out a single, shrill cry of alarm; its feathers rasped like fine-grit sandpaper, drawing Job's attention to the bow.

"Job? Are you listening to me? I said, 'Stop rocking the boat'!"

Dahlia was slathering an outrageously pink paint onto one of her perfect little toenails. Diamond light ruptured from the darkening bank at her back. And she flew—violently, instantaneously backward, screaming as she was pulled into the tree line. She was there one moment. Then gone. As if she'd never been there at all.

The bottle of pink nail polish rolled across the deck, emptying its contents.

"Dahlia?" Job asked, his voice breaking, his memory of her, of the event, already beginning to crack apart under the influence of the light.

## <u>FROM DARK VOIDS, AN ANGLER OF MEN</u>

"DAHLIA!" JOB SCREAMED, and pushed to his feet.

He stumbled into the underbrush, bellowing her name, running, he knew, toward the culmination of his destiny.

A host of wildlife streamed from the forest, running away from the source of the flaring light. A raccoon. A family of possums. Squirrels skittered through the trees, chittering in confusion. A herd of deer appeared as if conjured, parting around Job in near-ghostly silence, mouths covered in wild froth, black eyes rolling with fear and madness. But, abruptly as the exodus began, it ceased, the woods stilling momentarily in the wake of the deer. The sudden hush hung from the trees like ornaments of promised violence. Job cocked the Smith & Wesson; mopped sweat from his face that had little to do with the clinging humidity. Saplings snapped like gunshots, like bones breaking, and something massive careened off a pine, shaking its thirty-foot length. Job smelled musty fur and sweat and old shit, and a black bear charged past him, grunting, at an all-out sprint. Job screamed, almost discharged the pistol into his foot, but ran on, as much to find the source of the sapphirine luminance, and Dahlia, as to put distance between himself and the bear.

His heart was not in this any longer, now that he knew the truth of himself and the situation, but he was close. He could feel it.

His sense of self-loathing and what little pride he had left drove him on. *There's still time to do something right.*

By the time he came to the dooryard of the old river shanty, there were no more living animals. But from the trees that bordered the clearing there hung a riot of mutilated remains. The dooryard was soaked with blood, scattered with organs and husked carcasses. Some fresh, most putrid. Oddly, there were no flies.

Tommy the Mullet, a kind of local hermit who Job recognized almost immediately, stood over the corpse of the deer Job had seen taken. Tommy the Mullet was ripping the skeleton free of the hide and flesh with his bare hands. He was naked. Every inch of him mantled in gore.

"Oh . . . " was all Job could manage.

Tommy's head snapped up and he half-flinched; Job had startled him. Tommy opened his mouth as if to speak, and blue light flared from between his cracked lips.

Looking into that horrid brilliance, Job felt as though he'd been struck by lightning. His muscles pulled taught. Tighter, tighter, tighter, until bones threatened to crack. He lost all sense of who he was, what he was doing. He smelled fire and thought it was his brain sizzling, frying in the skillet of his skull like ground beef in a pan. He smelled pink and wondered that he could smell such an outrageous color. His motor functions scrambled and he crumpled to the blood-soaked mud of the clearing. Insensate darkness bore him away and Job wondered no more.


HE WOKE FROM dreams of heat, lightning, and rivers of blood filled with dying fish. He was lying in mud and at first he thought he'd slipped from the boat and knocked himself unconscious. When Job looked at his hand, though, it was caked with soiled red earth.

He was not outside, however, but lying on the dirt floor of the river shanty.

Job took a shallow breath and rolled gracelessly onto his side. Dahlia was lying next to him. She moaned, the lids of her eyes fluttering like moths in the semi-darkness. An alien hand—mottled like old leather—was clamped over the back of her skull and she shuddered, once, violently.

Job flopped onto his back like a fish. It was everything he could do to keep from screaming.

Nothing in his life could have prepared him for what he'd seen this day, least of all this: Tommy the Mullet crouched over Dahlia, but he was no longer strictly a man. Tommy's face lay slack around his shoulders; hung down his back like the hood of a sweatshirt. Teeth and rubbery gums the color of liver stuck to his bare chest. The pink skin that had covered his hands and forearms dangled in opaque shreds from his elbows, revealing the leathery flesh of something inhuman. But the worst thing was Tommy's new face, emerging from the humid darkness like a nightmare escaping the ethereal prison of subconsciousness—an amalgamation of a cock and a turd, littered with hundreds of tiny yellow-gold eyes like brass buttons. It had no real mouth with which to speak, only a wide, greasy slit in the center of its grotesque head, possessed no nose, or ears, just those tiny brass eyes, filled with radiant hunger.

Using his palms and heels, Job scrambled away from it, shoving to his feet in a single motion.

The dappled thing that wore Tommy the Mullet like a sweat suit garbled something utterly alien, but in his mind Job understood it clearly: *Fat with corruption . . . sweet with it, suckling-man . . . you make good sport.*

Job was naked, stripped of his clothes, but this didn't slow him. He thought briefly of his pistol, of Dahlia, but these were obligatory reflections produced by fear and guilt, and they were eclipsed by a baser need. His animal instincts were in full control now. Not bothering to search for a door, Job slammed into the wall of the shanty in a dead sprint, breaking through the slimy wooden boards without concern for injury. Dread without fathom had seized him and he was incapable of anything but pumping his legs; incapable of truly caring for Dahlia, or her fate—that which had carried him to this hell on earth in the first place.

It was only then that he realized Dahlia was screaming. Calling his name.

*Don't, Job! Don't leave her!* he thought. But his legs were still pumping. He was still running.

"Fuck her," he said with each rusting breath.

"Fuck her."

"Fuck her."

He wondered if he'd ever really been a good man, or if it mattered? He wondered at the pointlessness he'd created.

He ran beneath the mutilated, hanging corpses, the crimson mud of the dooryard squishing between his toes. Light flared behind him, his muscles threatened to seize once more, but he snarled and waged past it.

While rational, conscious thought was obliterated by this final flare of light, his subconscious mind was a sudden well. He was sorry for the candy bars he used to steal from Old Pap's Grocery in Astor when he was a kid; he was sorry for asking Annette Stuart out in high school, screwing her, then dumping her; he was sorry he never finished his architectural drafting degree; he was sorry for fucking around on Ali, for betraying her and their children; most of all, though, true to his deepest self, he was sorry for coming out on the river today. He knew it was not Dahlia's fault his marriage was in ruins, that this situation had been created. He knew it was not God's fault he was here, at this place, at this time. But he cursed them both anyway. Despite the shallow sorrows of his superego, or because of them, Job needed to place blame outside himself to keep his legs pumping. He knew he should stop, should turn around, so that Dahlia's death was not one more regret with which to torture himself in moments of later mania, but he could not.

A nearly invisible line of filament lashed at Job. He turned, slapped at it, opened his mouth to scream . . . and the line streamed down his throat, into his bowels. Hot barbed pain transpierced him; stabbed and hooked in his guts. He was pulled from his feet, jerked through the scrub, through soft needles of low hanging pine branches. He grabbed fruitless handfuls of them. Screamed around the strange line that snaked into his bowels. Blood, warm and vital, ran from his mouth, down his neck and chest.

Job realized then, the things you did in this life, good and bad—but mostly the bad things—set off chains of circumstance that would, inevitably and with vicious finality, add up to the sum of your end. And man's only claim to significance was made through those gestures of love, mercy, and high morality he was afforded to act upon each and every day.

Job's culmination was complete. His chance for meaning had passed.

**ENNIS DRAKE** gives witness to the wasting of our souls. He opines for the loss of the best of American sensibilities. He talks to himself about the heat-shimmers that haunt the peripheral of waking life; half-glimpsed antagonists born of a culture of rightful fear; shadows of enemies that become fully realized monsters in his dreams. He sees, regrets, ruminates upon, and carries these swatches of blackness, exorcising them onto the white of the page as often and as fast as he can. But, as fate delights in, dear Reader, the collective fears of a collective consciousness are an unexcisable cancer—

*stop*

**ENNIS DRAKE** lives in Florida, where the sub-tropical climate further exacerbates his psychosis (actually, this is a lie; the beaches are nice, the stiffer drinks come with an umbrella, and the beer is cold). He approves this message, but cautions that it is just a test.

# WHAT WAS ONCE MAN

## BY MICHELE LEE

---

I T'S A MOONLESS NIGHT, AND THREE OF US SIT IN THE dark basement of an abandoned house. Meghan. Rick. And me. We found each other by chance, hiding in a boarded-up grocery store not too far away. We stayed together after that, for what little protection an extra set of eyes on the lookout offered. The stairs were the first thing we destroyed when we found this safe spot. Some structure in the house above had collapsed when we did that, and—whatever it was—made the basement hatch impossible to move.

There are tiny windows set into the stained concrete walls that let in the light during the day. The street lamp outside helped us see at night until something out there broke it. None of us complained, because in a way it's better if you don't have to always see how trapped you are.

It's starting to stink down here. It's been three days, and with no bathroom.

Despite the stench, I'm hungry.


## MEGHAN

MY DAD STARTED touching me when I was eleven. I'm not looking for pity. You said you wanted the brutal truth, so that's where it started: when my dad first touched me.

It went on for years. They train you, you know. To put up with it. They call it "grooming." Other predators can tell when you've been groomed. Around thirteen my uncle started giving me the same looks. On my fourteenth birthday my brother took a long grope while my mom wasn't looking, so I ran away.

I didn't think they'd care. But they did and it only took a few days for them to find me. It was in a public place, but that didn't thwart my father's temper.

A friendly, round woman in scrubs with a hospital ID tag that read "Laura" was buying me a meal at a burger joint, and stayed with me while I ate. I was so hungry I didn't care. I figured she'd want to talk. Maybe she knew somewhere I could go, someplace where they'd understand why I'd left, and give me a way to get off the street.

Laura never got a chance. My mother came in, her keys dangling from one of her fingers. I'd always loved playing with the key chains she collected. Funny that I recognized her keys first. Our eyes met across the room and I begged her, silently, to let me go. *Pretend you didn't see me.*

She ordered a soda, then turned her back on me, going to the machine to fill her cup. I thought I'd made it. I thought, stupid me, that she'd helped me. Less than two minutes later my father walked in the door, eyes fiercely scanning the dining room. He saw my mother, who pointed right at me. Laura was awfully startled when I burst into tears.

"Are you all right?" she asked. She reached out to me. I pulled away. "No—"

And he was on us. His hand circled my arm, fingers tearing into my flesh. He jerked me out of my chair. I couldn't fight back or even land on my feet. He flung me to the floor, my drink and what was left of my burger and condiment-smeared wrapper going down on top of me. I didn't get right back up. Hopelessness welled up in me and I couldn't get my body to do anything but go limp, give up. I wanted to fight, but I'd been groomed.

"Don't you dare lay your hands on her!"

Laura's voice was pure steel. I'll always remember, because I'd never seen anyone talk to my father like that. But Laura stood up, vastly outsized, not caring, her eyes blazing. She must have never experienced the intimidating influence of a fist or garden hose. She couldn't know and still stand there as she did.

"Butt out, you fat bitch. This is between my daughter and me. It's none of your business."

"Someone call the cops," Laura yelled. Her gaze darted to the teens working behind the counter, to the older couple eating two tables over. My father moved toward her like a rolling storm. Fury masked his face. I opened my mouth to scream.

"I am taking my daughter out of here."

I forced myself up, to my knees. "I don't want to go with you."

It should have been a scream. It should have had the force like Laura's open defiance. Instead it spilled out from my lips, weak and palsied. Laura bent over to me, her hand out.

My father stepped forward and kicked me hard. I wasn't looking his way; I was reaching out to Laura. I rolled backward until I hit the metal base of the table. Something gave. For a moment I just thought it was my resolve, crushed under the sheer violence of my father's heart. But it was my spine, right below where it met my skull.

Everything went silent. I was aware of something, I cannot remember what, but I was there, with thoughts and feelings beyond the darkness.

Then I woke up in the basement of my home. I was lying on my side, staring into the worried face of my father while someone else's hands moved up and down my bare back, checking my spine.

"Oh, thank God. You're okay."

"She'll be fine," a rich female voice said behind me. It sounded like hot, sugary coffee, rolling around me and through me, as if I'd swallowed it. "She'll be as good as new."

"Good." He turned to me, concern in his face and voice. "Meghan, I need your help. There's a cop, and you're going to tell him what really happened in the restaurant. How you slipped and fell. You're going to show him how you're all right now."

I found myself nodding. It confused me. I remembered wanting to defy him. I remember the crunch of my neck, the terrifying lack of pain, the darkness.

He helped me stand, allowing me just a moment to glance at the beautiful Black woman, her waist-length hair a nest of perfect braids and a smile on her voluminous lips. She started packing supplies into a duffel bag, pausing only to give me a small nod.

Upstairs he led me to the living room, where a young, handsome man in a police uniform waited just inside the door. "Here she is, officer. I'm not sure how much you'll get from her. She's a little retarded."

"Meghan . . . " the cop started.

I found myself nodding.

"Meghan, can you tell me what happened at the restaurant?"

"My dad came to get me." I looked into the cop's eyes, my body alive with fury. Did he have the same look as Laura, or was that just boredom in his eyes? Did he have the power to get me out of here? Could I tell him the truth and just walk out to some place safe?

"What happened when he got you?"

I opened my mouth to plead for help.

"I fell on the floor. I got all sticky."

I sounded like a three-year-old, all short sentences and simple words.

There was no chance to think, no amount of mental screaming brought out the truth. The cop asked, and the answer my father wanted fell from my mouth.

"Meghan, there was a lady there who said that your father kicked you. Did he kick you?"

"Oh, no." Words vomited themselves up and out of my chest. Foul words. The lie came from somewhere else, certainly not me, no matter how much it sounded like me. "My daddy doesn't kick me. She must be a liar."

My eyes turned to my father, but my head wouldn't. He was relieved. The bastard had successfully saved his own skin, and I hated him for how he pulled these things off.

They put me back into the basement. I was being stored like holiday decorations. They didn't need to feed me. They didn't let me go to school anymore, but they did take me out occasionally. My mother refused to even acknowledge my presence, while my father and brother poked me and laughed about it. Sometimes with more than a finger. And once in a while the dark street doctor would come in to check on me. She'd look me over, shake her head as her fingers traveled across my bruised skin.

Then, one day she took my chin in her hand, she stared right into my eyes. "Are you in there, girl?" she asked in her mocha voice.

Without permission to speak I could only managed a gurgle. It was the first noise I'd made out loud in a week. I could scream in my head, curse and rage and howl, but without permission I was mute.

"If I was in there," the woman whispered, "I'd run."

There was a trace of something, a tingle of magic in her words. She winked at me and moved back. I felt her touch after there was space between us, but I felt her words for longer.

And I ran. It didn't matter where. The farther I got, the better it became.


RICK LOOKS UNCOMFORTABLE. I probably do too. How could someone not get upset, feel helpless at the tone of Meghan's voice? She's haunted, but Rick has shown a similar look and I probably have too. If we're broken, at least we're all broken together. Something drew us together. When we met, we recognized each other in the uneasy night, though we're still working out what exactly that recognition means.

She tenses up, and then I hear it. Shuffling, movement muffled by concrete walls. A shadow passes over the mostly buried basement window, lingering long enough to make us all feel that sick churning in our stomach. Above us, on what used to be the ground floor of an old house that collapsed on itself from a fire, something else moves.

## <u>SEAN</u>

I REMEMBER WHEN I told my mom. She wanted grandkids so badly that when it was apparent I would never bring her any, I expected her to disown me. Instead she smiled, patted my hand, and said, "You've done what you can, son, now have another cookie."

She made the best cookies.

She loved me, and that was always clear. No matter what my flaws or choices were. Some people don't have that unconditional love, and for that much I can call myself lucky.

The first time I brought a boy home I was nineteen. I had met him in college. I could have set off fireworks in the kitchen and done less damage. No one plays passive-aggressive like a gay man, except maybe a sixty-year-old woman. Or maybe I was just lucky that way. They say straight men look for a girl just like their mom. So why can't it be true for gay men?

I could barely get a word in through the catty bickering and half-implied insults. When I finally dragged Jeremy from the house he couldn't shut up about it. He said he wouldn't hold it against me, but we only lasted a month after that. I suppose those are the breaks.

Mother never approved of any of my boyfriends. Not that I blame her. I made some really bad choices. I'd hidden being gay for so long that when I came out, I practically hung a sign around my neck, and so she took her frustrations out on the boyfriends.

Once out of college I settled down some. College isn't that different from high school, except that there's more alcohol. After graduating I landed a job nursing at a decent private hospital. Because of work, I had very little idle time. So my priorities changed, and the more time I spent on my own, the more I mellowed from my college antics.

I met Charles at a class on the nonviolent handling of aggressive patients. He worked first shift in the Psych unit. I worked third in Obstetrics. It's amazing we'd worked under the same roof for so long and never met. Of course neither of us had time for a personal life. Concurrently, we chose to give up the party lifestyle and one-night-stands for a chance at having someone to come home to at night.

He moved in two months after we met, but a little quicker than either of us expected. His cantankerous roommate, an unpredictable maniac, hit the roof one afternoon over God-knows-what and Charles had to get his stuff out before he ended up with a size-fourteen stiletto hole in his backside. He showed up as I was getting ready for work.

Everything wasn't perfect, but our fights were usually over silly things, and easily forgotten. I was absolutely dreading having to introduce him to my mother. But it had to be done, especially when she found out we'd been living together. So we made plans for the traditional Sunday dinner. I had a few hours to sleep before we went, so mother could get home from church and prepare the meal.

There was no reason for me to expect a pleasant Sunday afternoon meal. We brought flowers and a cheese and spinach quiche. But this was my mother and my boyfriend, the two most important people in my life, meeting, and I could expect nothing less than a disaster to ensue.

I don't remember how it started. Their hackles rose as soon as they saw each other, and mutual resentment was evident in their eye contact, as each refused to look away. I gave up any attempt at keeping things civil, purely because this calamity was inevitable. The best I could hope for was for them to wear themselves out. I tried my best to eat, but mostly sat silent with a dumb little vacant stare on my face.

When we finally left I felt like I was on the edge of a canyon. I started planning how I'd rearrange my apartment once Charles moved out. He took a deep breath—we weren't even in the car yet—and I cringed.

"Wow, what a spitfire! If I was ever going to do a woman it would be your mom."

"Thanks, I think," was all I could manage.

"Is she always like that?"

"Not to me, but to other people, yeah."

"You mean to your boyfriends?"

I nodded, still a bit stunned.

"I bet they hated it."

"Don't you?"

"Are you kidding? I love a good argument. Why do you think I work in the psych ward?"

I don't think I had ever loved anyone more than I loved him at that moment.

Then came the accident. I don't remember a lot of it, and the doctor told me that's normal. Besides it happened so fast . . .

We stopped at a red light. It turned green so we moved forward and a big old silver Grand Vic plowed through the intersection and T-boned us at probably more than 50 mph. Our little compact spun. I remember the spinning, spider-webbed glass and the smell of vomit and blood. I remember babbling, but I don't remember what I said. I remember feeling like I was drifting in all the mess. I mean, I remember things I couldn't possibly have seen, like the soft, broken look on the face of the fire and rescue guy who pulled Charles' body from the car. I've been told that I was already on the way to the hospital by that point. I don't remember the ambulance, or the hospital, but the look on that man's face . . .

I was in and out for a while. I have a vague memory of the hospital, but it could have easily been because I worked there. There was a woman . . . I don't really know.

When I regained consciousness I was in the guest room at my mother's house. The television was on. It had been giving me strange dreams for some time, which led to a lot of confusion. I was lying there, struggling to recognize the room, when my mother came in.

Tears welled in her eyes as she smiled. "Oh, thank God." The bed bounced slightly when she settled next to me. "I've been so worried. You've been in and out for a week."

"What . . . ?" My throat was very dry. I could barely croak out one word. Mother gave me a long drink of water and I tried again. "What happened?"

Still it came out as a whisper.

"There was an accident. You were hurt very badly. They released you a few days ago. We brought you here and have been praying for the best."

"Who's we?"

"Uncle Danny and me."

"Where's Charles?" I asked.

"He didn't make it, sweetie. You were hit by a drunk driver. The collision was on Charles' side."

I didn't have enough—anything, moisture, emotion, energy—to cry for my loss. Mom made me drink weak tea with too much honey, then she told me to rest and I fell asleep again.

I should have asked why they discharged me from the hospital. It didn't make sense. But I was lost in my grief and loneliness. The next morning, when I'd found the fuel to cry, my mom came in and held me through my erupting sobs.

"It's okay," she said, running her hands through my hair like she had when I was a kid. "We still have each other. I'll take care of you, and you can take care of me. We don't need anything more than that."

I can't say I was abused after that. And I'm sorry that you were, Meghan, for what it's worth. But it was like being a child again. Powerless. I had no choice over where I lived, or what I did, or even what I ate. And at first I thought I just didn't have the strength to care about those things anymore. But then my apathy to my own state turned on me, and she worked her way in.

My mom was good at it, giving a subtle command disguised as a request or a suggestion. But I never told her *no*. I had no desire to. Yeah, I know, it's obvious that I'd always had a controlling mother, but not like this. Never like this before.

THE ONLY NOISE in the basement is my stomach, grumbling at me. Meghan's answers. Above us there are more sounds of movement. You could sustain yourself on the tension. There's a groaning then a crash. Meghan pales and Rick, wearing a face of stone, watches the hatch.

I wonder how long we have. Things become silent and we stare at each other, waiting, knowing the stillness is only temporary.

## <u>RICK</u>

THEY DON'T JUST make zombies out of people who're not ready to die. Of course you know that by now. Some people request it in their wills. Living wills have a whole new meaning now, don't they?

They released you from the hospital because they can't waste medical time and supplies on a virtual corpse.

And your loved ones don't complain, because they are worn out on it all . . . and because there are other options.

I was shot, straight through the heart and raised again. It was about control, like it was with both of you. But a different kind of control. I was raised again as part of the judge's sentence. And that's pretty much it. You can't reform a violent criminal like me and it's not safe to allow us to live in society. So they give us a quick death, raise us back up and put us under the control of a handler. With a puppeteer in charge of us we can be good, productive members of society. We can be sorry for what we did. We can give back, and all that bullshit.

What do you mean "tell you the truth"? I am telling you the truth. Not the whole truth? Well, what else do you want to know? I was once a man, and now I'm a meat puppet, sitting in a basement with a fag and Daddy's special pet.

I'm sorry, I'm sorry. That was uncalled for. No, really I'm sorry. It's not you I'm angry with. See, I'm not a victim like you, or a nice person with a tragic tale like you. I don't doubt that I deserve to be punished, but this, this isn't punishment. This is Hell.

Yes, I know. I promised to be honest. I just, I was starting to like you guys and if I tell you the truth, well . . .

Yeah, I'll start again. I'm not a good person. I have a disease. I have these . . . impulses.

I don't remember an abusive childhood. I mean it was rough; I had two older brothers and also a sister and brother that were younger. We weren't rich, or even well off. We kept a rain barrel for those times when the water got cut off. It didn't happen often, but enough that we prepared. We didn't get beat, unless we damn well deserved it, like the time Bobby pulled a knife on a kid at school. His hide got tanned real good that night. But they weren't beatings. Dad was useless when he was drunk, too maudlin to take a belt or anything else to us, and Mom never had time to do anything more than care for us. We also had a parade of worthless relatives moving in whenever they ran into their own self-imposed misfortunes, and moving out as our own bills piled up.

Chaotic, poor, and overlooked, yeah, that was me, but not abused.

You should know that I tried not to ever act on my impulses. I tried keeping a relationship with a real woman. I tried therapy, and even, you know, porn. But it was like holding back an avalanche with a teaspoon.

No, of course you're not supposed to feel sorry for me. I screwed up and I got caught. And this was their brilliant solution. They should've just lobotomized me, or left me dead, because I still have those thoughts. I still remember tasting the cake. They didn't stop me from thinking about it, they just made it so I can't do anything *but* remember.

So I ran away. That asshole handler, he could beat the shit out of us, then just heal us up like it never happened. He called them the perks. So I slit his throat and made for the hills before any of the others figured out what was going on.

You wanted my story, that's it. Ain't pretty or tragic, like yours. But that's the truth.


IT'S HARD NOT to notice that Meghan has been scooting closer to me. She won't even look at Rick anymore. He's become invisible to her, like she just removed him from her scope of reality. Except he's not really gone, and I think she is still holding on enough to recognize that.

So what are these noises above? Surely if it was kids playing in the rubble, they would have left by now. They wouldn't be digging through ashes and smoke-stained beams down to the crappy linoleum floor. Could it be our keepers?

But I've been thinking about each of us, and our options.

I love my mother, but I know she can't put herself aside to do what's right for me. Why should she mourn if she doesn't have to?

*Meghan.* Not even death is fair, because even death couldn't save her from being stored away in her father's basement.

And what of Rick? *Yes, Rick.* He thinks he's a victim of his impulses, and of a zero tolerance world. But a part of me—a big part of me—thinks he deserves it. I don't even have to ask Meghan what she thinks. I feel the tension as she takes my hand. I'm glad I'm safe for her. She deserves safe.

Rick is not safe. Not for Meghan. The way he looks at her, leers at her. The uncomfortable way he tries to push at all her emotional wounds. There are times when I think he's purposely being crude, he turns a little when he pisses in a corner so he can see Meghan and she can see all of him.

And last night I woke up to his grunts, a rhythmic moving in his sweat pants, as he inched his way toward Meghan, and she, fear in her eyes, trying to hide from him in the corner.

Meghan squeezes my hand, tight. I don't know what to say, especially with Rick watching us. I can't read what's in his eyes. In part because I don't want to.

And so I carry out the plan that's been brewing for a while. I move so fast it takes both of them by surprise. The sound of wood drawing across wood then clattering farther away covers the small grunt that slips my lips and the hiss that escapes from Rick as the pole that had been sitting next to me pierces his chest. It slides through his ribs smoothly. I drive it all the way into the concrete, as a loud crack reverberates around us. I pin Rick to the sheetrock. I bend the end up as much as I can without breaking the pole from the wall. Meghan only takes a moment to react behind me, picking up part of a concrete block and bringing it down on Rick's head. She sobs as the concrete connects and shakes for a while afterward. I reach out and grab her hand so she knows she's not alone.

Rick slumps motionless on the rod and we both relax, until we realize that the rumbling above us has become hurried. And closer.

Meghan takes out one of the windows, the glass falling around her and sparkling in the sunlight, and the rays catch her face just right. She really is a pretty girl.

Three hard yanks between the two of us liberates the window frame from its mount. I make her go first because if I get caught, well, my mom doesn't mean any real harm. She waits for me, even though standing in the open is dangerous.

Our hands entwine and we run as fast as our feet can hit the ground. We were once human, and after what I just did to Rick, I'm not so sure what's become of us.

We're not what we used to be, alive or otherwise, and we may never be truly free, but as long as we keep running, together, they cannot keep us as their slaves.

---

**MICHELE LEE** writes horror, science fiction and fantasy from the relative safety of her haunted house in the oldest section of Louisville, KY. Her work has appeared in *Cthulhu Sex Magazine*, *Dark Futures*, and *Expanded Horizons*. Her novella *Rot* is available through Skullvines Press.

When she isn't writing, she reviews books of all genres, spends too much time on Twitter and grows monstrous vegetables. She can be visited at www.michelelee.net.

# MOURNING WITH THE BONES OF THE DEAD

## BY GERARD HOUARNER

---

ALBINS LOOKED SMALL IN HIS CLOTHES, AS IF HE'D shrunk in the time between diagnosis and his arrival at the hospice. Flesh had melted from his cheeks, revealing the bone beneath and giving him a stronger resemblance to his father, Bernhard, who paid the taxi as the family got out of the car. The boy looked wrong, too much like a miniature version of his grandfather, who still lived in the old country and supported himself with his little garden and as a guide for foreign tourists and movie location scouts. When he'd been healthy, Albins had looked more like his mother, Gizela, with a cherubic face and thick limbs the bullies at school had learned to respect. Albins looked wrong because he was closer to death than Bernhard's father had ever been.

"Come on, Daddy," Albins said, holding out a hand for his father to grab. Gizela already had the other one. "I don't want to be late for my appointment."

His son's cheerful voice, strong and loud against the car engine's purr, skewered Bernhard. He took a breath, snorted at the engine fumes, straightened his sagging shoulders, paid the driver and joined the rest of his family on the steps to the old townhouse on the block of desolate urban wilderness. Gizela led them quickly into the building, as she was already fading under the harsh summer sun. The loss of children always hit mothers harder, Bernhard thought as he shut the front door behind them. He could spend hours in the heat if he had to, though he was relieved the rumble of buses and trucks, the honking of horns and gunning of engines was behind him. Familiar scents greeted him in the tiny vestibule. His ears pricked to the faint sound of crunching. Candles burned along the banister of a dusty set of stairs ahead of them.

In the gloom, his son's skin still glowed unnaturally from his exposure to daylight; the boy could have stayed outdoors forever.

"Are both of you going to stay with me?" Albins asked as two attendants emerged from opposing open doorways in the hallway that led from the vestibule. They smelled like freshly turned earth.

"Yes, love," Gizela said, cupping her baby's head as the attendants stopped before them. Their teeth chattered, their blind eyes gazed past mother, father, son, through the steel door that had opened for the three after each had whispered the name they found in their mother's womb.

Albins giggled at them, but he wouldn't let go of his parents' hands.

"You have to go with them," Bernhard said, pulling his arm up. "They'll take care of you. We'll see you in a little while."

"No!" Albins cried out, and his voice echoed up the stairwell, through doorways, in rooms with bricked-up windows. Dust rained down on them from the cracked ceiling. "You just want to leave me here and get away and never come back."

"What do *you* want?" Gizela asked, her voice quavering as she ran her fingers through his thin black hair

"Don't leave," Albins answered, with determination.

"We won't," said Bernhard. "There's a place for us to wait?" he asked the attendants.

"Upstairs," a woman's voice croaked in the stillness. Beyond the left hand doorway, a flame came to life in a pool of oil contained in the hollow of an upturned skull on the floor. An old woman in rags leaned into the flickering light, pointed upstairs, grinned toothlessly. "That's where we all end up." She cackled, showing gaps in her rows of teeth.

She reminded Bernhard of his mother, in the madness of her later years.

Albins moaned as if his illness was suddenly too much for him. But the healers had said there'd be no pain. At least, no physical discomfort. Bernhard recognized the sign, and understood. The change was upon the boy. He was reacting to the old woman, to the attendants. He was frightened.

"We'll be close by," Bernhard said, going down on one knee to talk directly to his son. "You can come to us, when you're ready. If you want to."

"You won't leave, like you did before?"

Bernhard opened his mouth to say something, closed it, feeling Gizela move, sensing her warning. Don't argue with the boy. Don't explain. Don't make excuses.

"No."

"You'll stay with Mom?"

"Yes."

"And you'll both be there if I need you?"

"Yes."

Reluctantly, Albins released his grip on Bernhard's and his mother's hands. He went between the attendants, but they did not offer their bony, claw-like appendages and the boy did not take hold of them. When they turned and walked down the hall to the back of the building, Albins followed, a step behind. He never looked back.

"He's so brave," Gizela said.

*And I'm not?* he almost answered. But that was an old argument, from another time and place. He'd left that all behind, proved to himself and her and anyone and anything that cared that he was as strong and brave as any. He had the skulls to prove it, and the gratitude of those who'd needed the blood and meat and bones he'd provided. Of course, Gizela would say something like, too bad you couldn't do all of that for us, when it mattered.

Those were old arguments. Dead ones. He was back for Albins. They were here for Albins. Blood called its children out of the wilderness. And death.

"Yes," he said, at last. "He's a brave one."

They went up creaking stairs to the first floor, flickering candles giving way to strings of naked bulbs hung across the ceiling. A young man in a bloody surgical gown emerged from a doorway, nearly ran into them. His startled expression settled quickly into a professionally neutral demeanor as he nodded his head at them and started moving down the hall.

"Why does it happen?" Gizela asked, taking hold of the man's elbow.

In better days, she would have licked the blood from her fingers.

The man's expression hardened momentarily, a belated predator's reaction to surprise and cornering. Responsibility made him pause, obligation softened his body's bearing.

"It's part of the curse, isn't it?" the young man answered. "Another price for power."

"In my father's day," Bernhard said, "they used to leave newborns in his condition on hilltops, or drown them in rivers. If the change took them later, they'd be dressed up in animal furs and driven in their madness to a village or town, where the citizens would rise up in self-defense and slay the monster." Gizela and the man both looked to him with their lips parted, as if burdened by the need to speak but unable to find words. Tears glistened in Gizela's eyes. "Of course, what we do these days is so much more civilized," Bernhard added hastily, cringing at the last word.

Shame accompanied savage elation at having struck a wound in his mate, and himself. The need to run wild and with the pack tore at each other, and at him. In panic, Bernhard's thoughts fled down unexpected paths, and he found himself wondering, for the first time in his life, how he might have turned out differently if, when the affliction claimed his brother, their father had taken the family to such a hospice for final goodbyes, instead of tossing his oldest son, still living, on his own funeral pyre. What might have been said between brothers, rivals, mirror selves, and others? Would the experience of a gentler passing have changed Bernhard, made him able to stay true to his first mating with Gizela? Might he have stayed with the pack, instead of turning wild and reverting to the savagery of the lone outsider to find what he had lost of himself in this new land and age?

"Some say what goes on here makes us more like prey," the man said, showing his teeth in sympathy for Bernhard. "Others claim our work helps bind the tribes closer together, so we can survive this crowded world," he continued, nodding to Gizela. "Who is to say what is right and wrong? We can do only what our hearts compel us to do." The man slipped out of Gizela's hold and took a step, then half-turned and, with a smile, added, "That is our curse, is it not?"

Alone on the second floor landing, tempted by a slaughterhouse stench, Bernhard and Gizela drifted to the nearest doorway. The old apartment walls and doors had been knocked down, the debris left on the floor. In the rubble lay fresh meat, mostly animal, while an attendant in a corner cleaned the bones of old, rotted cuts with its teeth. Gizela bumped against Bernhard. Her stomach grumbled. She wept. Bernhard thought at first from the pain of losing her son, but after a few moments, and the growl of her stomach, he knew also she was struggling against a part of her nature. He put his arm around her, and she held him, and perhaps for the first time in a long while they understood one another.

Bugs and other vermin infested the room, and the stench of blood and flesh and offal reminded Bernhard of old dens in lost places. It was the smell that had welcomed him downstairs. He was comforted as much by the resonance with those faded memories as he was by the feel of his mate pressed against his ribs.

They moved as one to the next doorway, which led to another destroyed apartment. In this raw space, however, others, mainly couples, in their same age range, waited. Along with them, some elders, largely single, and there were a few isolated males and females off by themselves in a corner, separate but linked, Bernhard guessed, by the shared tragedy of losing a mate.

As Bernhard and Gizela entered, an adolescent and an old woman joined the gathering near another doorway. A few people moved toward the newcomers, while the rest backed away. The old woman was greeted by an elderly man and a young pair, while a middle-aged couple bracketed the adolescent. Bernhard looked away from their intimate moment, as did most others. Gizela stared momentarily, then went back to weeping. After a while, attendants came to take the adolescent and the old woman away.

More came and went. Gizela learned to look away. *How many come here to die?* Bernhard wondered, touched by fear. Surely there couldn't be so many of their kind in the city—were they all dying? Had the old spirit illness become a plague? But a challenging grumble from another male, a hiss from a female pacing back and forth, crystallized what his instincts already knew: the hospice served those from within as well as outside the territory. Focused on his boy, still reeling from the reunion with his old mate, he had not been conscious of all the different clan and tribal scents crowded into the building. But the scent of sorrow joined them all, sublimating feuds and rivalries. All were welcome in this neutral ground, where blood lines were pared, culled, and even ended. The place was like an elephant's graveyard, filled with the bones of brothers, sisters, lovers, offspring, ancestors, where the living and the dead parted ways. It was a new way for them. Strange. But as the man in the bloody coat had said, a necessary trial. With prey transforming the world around them, hunters had to adapt. Or stop hunting.

Their turn came. Albins came out from one of the holes in the outer walls. In the short while away from them, his skin had turned yellow and his eyes bloodshot. Bernhard and Gizela were on him in an instant.

"How are you feeling?" she asked, stroking Albins' face and peering into his eyes.

The boy flinched at her touch, blinked, looked away.

"Don't be afraid," Bernhard said, going down on both knees and holding his son still by the shoulders. "Be brave, be strong. Be true to your blood."

Albins started crying, shook himself free of Bernhard, and refused his mother's embrace. He stood frozen, looking at his feet, whimpering. Bernhard went to the dining hall and brought back some meat, as he had seen others do. Food was reassuring, he reasoned, a necessary ritual that grounded everyone in day-to-day reality. They ate the flesh together, like a family, but when it came down to gnawing at the bones, Albins avoided the marrow, continued to pick at flesh and sinew, then lost interest.

"Take me out of this place," he said, sitting listlessly on rubble and dust.

"We can't," Gizela replied, with barely a hint of a quaver in her voice. Bernhard knew she was forcing herself to be strong, to show him, or perhaps only herself, that she was capable of doing what had to be done.

Albins looked to Bernhard. "Please, take me home." The boy's eyes struck Bernhard like an unexpected reflection. What Bernhard saw of himself made him feel lost.

Bernhard had gone home. Home to his birthplace across the water, then to wilderness, and now back to the cities, to his mate and son. Each journey had felt right, until the need came to go someplace else. What could he tell Albins about leaving, or about coming home, that would do any good? Home was not a place anymore, but a state of mind, a feeling one had from the familiar scent of a den, or a meal shared with family. Home was where you needed to be when there was nowhere else to go, when nothing else was right. This place was home, for Albins. Though not for Bernhard, or Gizela. At least, not yet.

"I can't," Bernhard said, and the words hurt him more than he thought possible. He spared the boy the truth.

"I'm scared," Albins said, tears running from his eyes as he looked down.

"I know," Bernhard offered.

"Just don't go away," Albins said. "Don't leave me."

"You do the same," Bernhard said. His head told him the words were unwise, but the heart, the blood, felt their truth.

They sat together, all three, for many breaths that seemed like one. "Sorry," Albins said, at last, shivering as he stood up, "I have to." His gaze flitted about the room. He was terrified of everyone, everything. Including his mother and father. The attendants came and helped him leave.

Bernhard experienced the same crushing emptiness the boy, and Gizela, must have felt when he'd gone off to answer the call of his heart, to prove what he had to by himself, rather than staying to prove what he had to with his mate and son.

He took hold of Gizela's arm. His claws bit into her flesh, but she barely acknowledged the pain. "I wish we could give him what he wants. I wish we could rescue him."

"I wish he could rescue us," Gizela said.

"Careful," muttered a nearby stranger. "Keep talking like that, and you'll be growing a soul yourselves."

They left the waiting room. Frustration bubbled in Bernhard. Helplessness sapped his strength, his focus. He looked for a sign of disdain from Gizela, for the slightest hint of contempt from a young woman passing by carrying a satchel of clattering objects. Bernhard stopped her, barely registering the bones. "We want to see our son," he said, words rumbling together like a challenge.

The young woman gazed past them into the room they'd just left, then turned away, looked down. "They'll take him upstairs, if you want to see that." She trudged off with her burden, then looked back and said, "Not everyone can deal with what happens." Bernhard and Gizela went upstairs, to the building's top floor.

Along with a few others, including the old, cackling woman they had met downstairs, they waited outside a locked steel door with a pair of attendants at the top of the stairs. The old woman nodded a greeting and said, "I tried, but I couldn't keep away. The mystery wouldn't let me."

Bernhard froze in front of her, studied her face, finding grief and pain and remorse, but also the slightest trace of amusement, as if there was a joke hidden in the whole process. Or perhaps he was the jest. He wondered if his mother was still alive, babbling in a cave beneath the earth, stalking insects and smelling like excrement.

"Who did you lose?" Gizela asked.

The old woman shrugged her shoulders. "We never really have anyone."

Was that a comment directed to him, Bernhard wondered. He bit back an answer. He wasn't here to play games with an old woman, to jostle for position in the pack.

The entire floor was sealed off. More hospice workers came and went, slipping through the door, none stopping to talk to those waiting. Finally, Bernhard stepped in front of one of the workers and asked, "Is my son in there?"

"They're brought in directly from downstairs," the worker replied with deference.

"Why weren't we told?" Gizela asked, showing teeth and anger.

"You go in when you're ready."

The worker started to leave, but Bernhard wouldn't step aside. "Did he ask for us?

"No."

The worker slipped away. Bernhard and Gizela went inside, pushing the door open. The attendants did not try to stop them. None of the others waiting followed, even turning away from the entrance, as if afraid to catch an unwanted glimpse of the Heaven, or Hell, that had captured whoever they had let go on the level below.

The floor was brightly lit with natural light from open windows and skylights. Colorful furniture and toys were strewn about in random fashion. The smell of cleansers made Bernhard's stomach churn, and he sagged against Gizela in shock. She took his weight for a moment, then weakened. He regained his composure and held her up.

Children played with each other, running around with abandon, leaping, jumping, rolling on the floor, throwing balls, moving furniture and toys with fierce, focused energy. Adults walked among the children. Some stayed close to the walls, stunned, taking in the alien environment with apparent disbelief, completely lost. Others, especially the elders, stayed close to the children, joining in their play, or sitting with them and telling stories, bonding, forming new families. Everyone appeared healthy, strong. Healed.

Albins was there, running with two girls a little older than him and some younger boys. His cheeks had filled out, his eyes had cleared, and his laughter was like a bird's calling, joyously announcing the hunger of life. He acted as if he didn't see his parents, didn't sense their nearness. There was a wall between them. The world constructed on this floor, the world of prey, was the wall.

Bernhard wanted to vomit all he had eaten.

The old woman finally came through the door. She stood behind them breathing hoarsely. When her throat had quieted, she said, "You know, there's a school of our kind which believes that in the past some tribes let them live."

"And what happened?" Gizela asked, too quickly.

"Their bloodlines died."

"Oh," Gizela said, crestfallen.

"They believe the bloodlines died because their tribes were redeemed, the curse lifted. The act of mercy saved them."

Bernhard snarled, rage catching on the remains of loss and frustration. "And what does redemption mean?" He waved a hand in dismissal. "Becoming prey? Who would believe such a lie? Who would want it to be true? The threat of the affliction of a soul is only part of the cost of our power, but we pay it. Gladly." His tongue thickened and he avoided Gizela's gaze, not wanting to see how happy she might be with the price she'd paid for the life she had. "Even the prey take our curse onto themselves to become what we are. But none of us, not even your precious *thinking* schools, seek out the souls that turn us from what we are. We call the thing we carry a curse, we revere the chance for redemption, as if some great Hand will scoop us all up at once and deposit us in a paradise we can't even imagine. But what is true is this: What we are sets us above the others. It is our curse that remains desired in the world."

"But the curse may not be the only desire out there," the old woman said. "Perhaps, some might want deliverance from being either hunter or prey." She gave him another near-smile, dangerous in its ambiguity. "What do *you* want?"

Bernhard's face twisted with disgust.

"But where do the souls that grow inside some of us come from, if the curse gives us a name instead of a soul conceived in our mothers' wombs?" Gizela asked, almost pleading.

The old woman's gaze followed a middle-aged man for a moment, and her face sagged, her eyes glistened. She shook her head, looked to Gizela. "Maybe they come from the prey who give up their souls to take on our curse. Discarded, they haunt the world, poisoned spores cast to the winds, until one finds an untended garden to seed: one of us, empty, vulnerable through no fault of our own, our curse turned in on itself through age or the chance of our heritage. The prey would call these wandering souls carcinogens attacking the genetically predisposed to cancer."

Bernhard spat. Gizela said, "We are not prey."

"Of course not," the old woman said quickly. "Maybe, for all our power, it is our hunger for what we lack that makes us grow them, to our destruction. Or perhaps they blossom in those whose emptiness is too great, in a revolt of Nature against the imbalance of the curse. There are even elders who believe the One Who Cursed causes these souls to grow among us, as a test."

"For what?" Gizela asked, in a whisper.

The old woman blinked as if momentarily blinded by a bright light. "Debatable, like everything else. To see if the curse still holds, or if we have grown the capacity for redemption. Perhaps we and the prey are bound in a cycle of punishment, either cursed to be without soul and hunt, or to have one, and be hunted. The One Who Cursed is known for irony, in other circumstances."

Bernhard grunted. The old woman's words filled his head like a herd of droning cattle, choking off further squabbling. Instinct remained. Everything in his body drove him to attack. Not the old woman, or Gizela. The others on the floor. His son.

"All for following our hearts," Gizela said, her voice breaking. She took a deep breath, balled her fists, cutting herself with her own claws. "Why would that be so terrible?"

"It depends on what we find in our hearts."

Bernhard let loose a defiant roar. Gizela staggered to the side, went down on her knees, and joined him in raising her voice and releasing what was inside of her. Attendants appeared. Children screamed, ran behind a circular wall the adults had formed with their bodies. The old woman at their back laughed, her voice cracked by madness. Her laughter sank into guttural growls and barks. The attendants threw themselves on the prey. Bernhard stripped, his clothing chafing his skin. Gizela and the old woman did the same. Prey, caught between their former natures and the burden of their newfound souls, tried to change back to what they had been. They fought, turning on each other, and dragging down attendants. The frenzy of whip-sawing bodies and snapping jaws and flashing talons brought Bernhard, Gizela and the old woman short. Bernhard recognized a force at work greater than he—than the three of them combined—could challenge.

Bernhard, Gizela, and the old woman whined and slunk into a corner, away from the frantic battle, satisfying themselves from random sprays of blood or with the meat from a tossed limb.

The violence, the purity, the nakedness of the curse's power and its cost cleared Bernhard's mind. He reverted to being only a vessel for the curse, its reliquary of flesh. He had seen one or two stricken with souls at the same time, but never so many, and the vigor of what possessed them tempered his sorrow over the loss of so many of his kind. The theater of carnage mocked the old woman's speculation about redemption, about wild things becoming human and dispelling the curse. The scene was a reminder that there was no escape from what they all were.

In this place of dying, broken in the face of what he was and could become, despair found Bernhard. The curse burrowed deeper into his heart.

The fighting subsided, the attendants gained control. They crawled like worms through the afflicted, many still locked in death struggles, ending the last battles, granting mercy to the wounded, chasing down survivors who went for the windows, skylights, and door. None escaped the attendants' distended jaws and razor teeth.

Bernhard never saw who brought down Albins. There was nothing recognizable left of his boy.

The attendants began gathering the remains while other staff entered from discreet and secret passages with cleaning equipment and chemicals. Bernhard, Gizela, and the old woman stayed, laying claim to a small pile of what was left of the dead. The attendants respected their claim and worked around them.

Without words, the three feasted solemnly on the remains. Prey or accursed, it did not matter. They honored what had been lost.

And as they gnawed on bones, Bernhard mourned his son; his brother, from long ago; his father and mother, lost to him in time; the packs he had run with; the promise of his mating with Gizela; the freedom of his wandering days; even Gizela beside him, who kept the wounds he'd given her inside for the sake of their son; even the old woman sitting with them, who could have been his mother for all her madness. All that had been a part of him, living or dead, was lost. Devoured by the curse. He sucked at the marrow but found no solace there, only the taste of emptiness, the bitterness of a fresh wound, a hole carved deeper into him than any other. Deeper than the curse, where at its bottom a soul might find space to nest, to grow like an unwanted tumor, and claim him, and kill him.

Or take him far from the curse he'd known all of his life, to another damnation that would consume him.

Relief surprised Bernhard as a new world opened up to him. He let the bone in his hand fall. Gizela did not notice, but the old woman put a hand on his shoulder, blessing him for a third time with her curious expression.

This time, her eyes opened wider.

Perhaps, he felt from the depths of his emptiness, in wonder.

---

GERARD HOUARNER fell to Earth in the fifties, where he became a product of the NYC school system and the City College of New York. Along the way, the likes of Joseph Heller, Joel Oppenheimer, Terry Bisson, Nancy Kress, and others have tried to pass along a clue or two about what they do. He remains, alas, a questionable reflection of their teaching abilities. He has also accumulated the necessary credentials to work in the mental health field in such places as Hell's Kitchen, on the Lower East Side at the beginning of the AIDS epidemic, and in the Bronx at the start of the crack epidemic before settling into a quiet, contemplative, and genteel career as an uncivil servant at a state psychiatric center.

His publishing career includes three novels and over 260 short stories (some gathered into five collections and the occasional "best of" anthology, 50 earning Honorable Mentions in Ellen Datlow's *The Year's Best Fantasy and Horror/Horror*), as well as editing/co-editing three anthologies and serving as Fiction Editor for *Space and Time* magazine.

He continues to write whenever he can, mostly at night, about the dark.

# FINAL DRAFT

BY MARK W. WORTHEN

---

"HOW DO THOSE BASTARDS MOVE SO QUIETLY?" I wiped at my dripping forehead with a sodden sleeve. Moisture from the muggy air formed on the thick leaves of the dense jungle around us, and the wetness mingled with sweat and dust leaving muddy trails down our faces. Even at dusk, it sopped hair and created dark camo triangles on our backs and chests and sides. My hands were so slick I could barely hold on to my M-16.

"That's the thing, Jared," replied a voice from my left. "The Viet Cong can go anywhere without making noise. It's damn creepy."

And the smell. The constant cloying foulness of the rotting plants made my throat clench, and my A-rations, never quiet, signaled an imminent return, coming up from my half-filled stomach into the swamp. My thighs and ankles ached from hours of trudging through shin-deep muck.

I nodded, holding a little tighter to my slipping weapon. "Like Death himself."

The only response I got was a snicker. We slogged on in silence, or our version of it, though we knew the *suck-thwock* sounds of our boots signaled our presence to VC for miles around. Finally, Poet Williams, a tall Black man, intoned in his drawling southern Georgia basso:

*"Upon his shield came the warrior home*
*His face, transformed by Death's unholy grasp,*
*Become a mask of calm serenity . . . "*

"So who wrote that one, Poet?" A new voice, one I recognized as Andy Tyler's.

"I did," Poet replied.

"It doesn't rhyme."

"So what?" I shook my head in the semidarkness. "Who decided poetry always needs to rhyme?" Surrounded by a squad of hard-ass soldiers, how could I say it was beautiful, that it reflected the heroism I saw in the Army that made me want to join in the first place?

"Nicely metered though," came the voice that had complained about the creepiness of the VC. "Iambic pentameter."

"Thank you, Justin," Poet acknowledged.

That's when I saw it.

I don't know why it caught my eye there in the dark-and-light pattern left by the retreating sun, but it did. The muzzle of a Russian AK-47, North Vietnamese weapon of choice, protruded from leaves in the jungle just ahead. My feet froze. I tried to speak, to shout a warning, but fear closed my throat. I screamed and screamed, but no sound came out.

Looking back, we shouldn't have been talking like that. If the enemy hadn't heard our mucky footsteps, they'd certainly heard our blithe conversation as we passed. Too late; we'd made our mistake.

*Crack*! A single shot, a firecracker sound, and time slowed.

To one side, Andy grabbed his neck and just stood there, suspended like a marionette, fingers dark with blood, all the muscle control seeping out of him. He looked toward me as if to ask for help, but I had none to give.

Puppet strings cut, I watched him fall into the mud.

I bent forward and raised my gunstock to my cheek, wet from tears, humidity, or sweat, and scanned the rest of the foliage for unfriendlies. I could see nothing, only the shadows of trees and bushes. I couldn't even find the AK muzzle I'd seen before. Then, *crack, crack*, two more shots, and then the shattering chaotic staccato of fire from both sides.

I lurched forward and squeezed the trigger.

And I didn't see or hear anything further. My mind focused only on the pain that shot up my right leg, a searing, blue electric streak that blocked everything else. Hallucinogenic lights colored my vision.

Then everything faded.

When consciousness returned and things swam back into focus, I saw a vision of chaos viewed from the ground. All proverbial Hell had broken loose. Nearby, Poet triggered his weapon into the wall of foliage, which answered in kind. Screams. Gunfire. The backbeat rattle of choppers overhead, counterpointed by the booming of grenades all around.

I reached out for my dropped weapon with the thought of adding a few shots to the fray, but a new pain flashed down my side, taking my breath away. Lying on my left, pinning my arm, I couldn't move my free shoulder at all and still continue breathing. I panted, and with each breath, sharper and sharper the flare, as though someone had knifed me.

Lying there in the muck, afraid to move, I closed my eyes. When I opened them, I saw Poet's face.

"Jared. You all right, man?"

"Don't . . . don't know." I had to cough the words out as though they'd lodged in my throat.

"Hang on. We'll get you help." Poet stood up just as shots erupted again from the trees. Along the ground, successive bullets kicked up a path of splattering mud. For a moment Poet watched it, then looked at me and winked.

And stepped into it.

His body shook with the impact. Then the crackling gunfire stopped, and I watched him crumple to the ground.

That trail of spray would have led directly to me.

More noise, more light, blurring in and out, and then everything went quiet.

It was over.

I heard the battle break out again in another area, far to my left. As the choppers moved farther that way, so did the rest of the sounds. The distant firefight was all I could hear; everything around me became silent, as though the jungle itself held its breath.

After a time, even the faraway sounds of warfare vanished, and an unnatural stillness lay on the jungle like fog over the Missouri. I heard only my heartbeat and labored breathing.

I inched my hand down my body, feeling for damage, and the pain sharpened as I did, making it hard to breathe again. If someone left a bayonet in me, it could be twisting as I moved. Finally my fingers found the spot, but no blade, no blood, no wound that I could find just by feeling around.

Bruised or cracked ribs, then.

I didn't try to explore the leg—couldn't bring myself to. If I'd lost it, I'd want to die. And here in Vietnam, wanting to die, I would.

Hoping to distract myself, I looked around, anywhere but at my own broken body. I could just see one of Poet's boots nearby. I tilted my head—and even that slight effort stirred the burning in my side—I saw him, lying still, the mud around him red. The smell of blood and death joined the decayed stink of earth. I couldn't tell how seriously he'd been hit, but he didn't move.

The jungle burned someplace nearby, and in the flickering light of the growing flames, I could see other men lying around me. One was Andy Tyler. Another I couldn't identify. Beyond them, two more bodies, just visible—no, not two, but two pieces of one. I shuddered, then gagged, but the throbbing from my ribs and leg provided sufficient distraction to still the reflex.

Then, from the corner of my eye, I saw movement.

Gingerly, I turned my head in that direction, but saw nothing. My imagination? I didn't think so, but I could be delirious from shock or loss of blood, or a fistful of other things. When I glanced away, the movement returned.

I fixed my gaze on a boot print in the mud of one of my fallen friends, then let my eyes unfocus, expanding my view beyond it. When I was a kid in the astronomy club, they called it "averted vision." Sometimes you can see more by not looking directly at an object.

What I saw washed me with a cold wave of fear. In the heat of the steaming jungle, I shivered.

A woman, Vietnamese, straight and proud, stood over the fallen shape of Poet Williams. A white robe hung from her shoulders, and light flowed from her as though she posed with her back to the bright illumination of a Fresnel lamp.

She knelt by my friend, knees together demurely in the slick ground, and leaned down very close to his lifeless face. Her lips seemed to brush his ear.

She ran her fingertips over his chest, and Poet Williams opened his eyes, an expression of surprise lighting his face. I'd assumed he was dead, like everyone else. I watched wide-eyed as he stood up and began to glow, radiating the same white light as the woman.

I opened my mouth to call out his name, but the two vanished, leaving me in the brightness of the flames and the heat of the jungle.


"HOW YOU DOING, soldier?"

I woke with a violent start, which induced fierce pain in my ribs and back. I turned to the voice, and saw an Asian woman, all in white.

The woman in the jungle!

No, I was mistaken. A nurse. She placed a soft hand on my chest and eased me back to the mattress. Only then did I realize I lay on a hospital bed, antiseptic smells and noises of nurses and moans and cries of the wounded all around me.

"What happened to me?" I managed. "How's my leg?"

"Shh. Don't talk." She smiled warmly. I knew it was her job, but it made me feel warm too, all the same. "You'll be fine. You stepped on a *punji* stick—you know," she went on, "one of those little bamboo spikes the North Vietnamese leave lying around. Just one of their nasty little tricks."

She took my chart from the end of the bed and made a notation. Then she produced a thermometer and moved toward me. I opened my mouth and she placed it under my tongue.

"You were lucky. Sometimes they coat them with animal poo, and that's why they're so hard to treat." She looked at her watch, counting seconds.

I knew what a *punji* stick was, but I let her talk. I liked the sound of her voice.

"After that, as near as we can figure, you fell on your gun or a rock and cracked three ribs."

The doctors told me about it in great detail in the days that followed. A good thing, they said. Probably saved my life, they said. Just damn lucky I hadn't found another spike when I fell. But I knew better; Poet Williams had saved my life, stepping into that machine-gun fire.

One afternoon some time later, a doctor with stubble shadow and a receding hairline came in, hands thrust in the pockets of his lab coat. He'd been around before, checking on me. "The bad news is that you're not going to be able to make it back to the front lines. I know you've got your heart set on it, but it's not happening."

I smiled in spite of myself. "Damn. And I really wanted to go back, too." *When pigs fly.* "Is there good news?"

"You're going to be okay. In a few months. Meantime, you're going home."

"Doc, could I ask you a favor before I go?"

He grinned. "Sure, you can *ask*."

"There was a guy in my unit, Williams. Lafayette, I think his first name was. We called him Poet."

"Hmm," he thought for a moment. "The only Williams that came in was a James Anton, but he wasn't in your unit. How about I make a call or two and see what I can find?"

"Thanks."

He gave me a nod, checked my foot and the bandages around my ribs, and wandered off to look at other patients.

Just before they shipped me home, he told me that Pierre Lafayette Williams hadn't been found and was listed officially as "missing in action."


DAYS LATER, IN a military hospital in Okinawa, Poet came to me.

I don't know whether I was asleep and dreaming or awake that night. It felt like I was drifting, somehow cut loose from myself, like a cloud of consciousness in the room. My thoughts wandered up and down the past several weeks, particularly those spent in the jungle.

I pictured that firefight in the mud, imagining dozens of variations on Poet's death, watching as fire from an automatic weapon sawed him nearly in half, while he sometimes whispered my name, sometimes shouted it.

"Jared." I came awake—at least I seemed awake—to a thin whisper like a breeze through a screen door. I should have jumped, but I didn't, almost as if I expected it.

"Poet," I said aloud, "I should have paid more attention to where you fell, so they could have taken you home to your family."

"I ain't dead, Jared. Least I don't think so. And there ain't no body to send home. Most of my family wouldn't care anyhow. Daddy kicked me out when I joined the Army."

There he stood, at the foot of my bed, looking very bright in the darkness. I could see every detail of his face, though the only light source was a dim forty-watt in the hallway.

"Why didn't you die, Poet?"

"Maybe I did, in a way. But in another way I didn't. Here I am, anyway."

"Here you are."

The apparition nodded its head.

"What are you, Poet?"

"Not sure yet. Still learning that."

A comfortable silence settled between us, as with old buddies hanging out together.

"I should be lying dead out there, Poet."

He shook his head. "Not your time, man. You got to stay." He smiled. "Me, I gotta go. You be seeing me again."

I closed my eyes and must have fallen asleep. When I woke, he was gone.


I DID SEE Poet again, but not for eleven years. By that time, I'd convinced myself that his visit had been a dream and the woman in the muddy jungle a nightmare.

I'd thought about him many times, even thought about returning to Vietnam to see if I could find any clues about him, but I never did. My business was just starting to take off, and I really couldn't afford any time away from it.

The night I saw him followed a very frightening and embarrassing time for me. I let an employee—a friend—die.

I'd rented some dingy cinderblock office space on the second floor of an old two-story strip mall, just off 270 northeast of St. Louis. I couldn't have picked a more remote place, neatly above a lawyer and next to a private investigator.

I'd stayed late doing the books. I hadn't yet hired anybody but the two salespeople, Steve and Amy, and for the moment, I was CEO, CFO, and COO all rolled into one.

The summer of '80 was a hot one, and that night was no exception. Despite the two fans near my desk, great drops of sweat rolled off my nose and plopped, leaving dark splotches on my papers. I'd noticed, I guess, on some level the rising temperature as the evening wore on, but when I do the books, I block out everything but the radio and the calculator. So when Steve came running back screaming, "Fire! Mother Mary, the whole building's on fire!" I just stared at him.

Then the smoke, hanging thick in the air finally sank into my lungs and I coughed, realized I'd been coughing on and off for some time. I closed my eyes during the fit and when it subsided, I opened them and saw only jungle and the smoke of an approaching firefight. Blood pounded in my ears like artillery and choppers, and I stood up and ran. It felt like I covered a lot of ground, but I wasn't getting anywhere, just running through wet, burning jungle that all looked the same and smelled like smoldering wood.

I ran without a weapon, without a pack, without a plan, without so much as boots to soften another bamboo spike. I passed pockets of gunfire and explosions, feeling the breeze of shrapnel and bullets over my head and past my cheeks.

And all so hot, so very hot. So difficult to breathe. Everything began to float, like I was seeing it underwater. So hard. So easy just to lie down.

When I came to, I was on a gurney in an ambulance, and a paramedic told me, "You're lucky to be alive, pal."

I managed to mumble the universal "Where am I?" at him, and he said, "You're on your way to County General. You inhaled a lot of smoke running around like that."

They'd found me on the first floor. I asked for Steve, but apparently he hadn't made it. He'd died on the second floor, in my office. I'd run right past him.

Right past him.

I woke again in the hospital, still in relative darkness, and had a quick memory of my bed in Okinawa. I heard the beep and buzz of machines, and felt the oxygen mask around my face and the dull ache where they'd put the IV in my hand.

"Yo. You finally awake now." The voice was warm, reassuring. And familiar.

I looked up. "Poet?" My voice sounded muffled through the oxygen equipment.

"The same, man. I ask how you been, but I can see for myself."

"Smoke inhalation." My throat felt like someone had scrubbed it with steel wool.

"I see that. Did everybody get out?" His tone suggested he already knew the answer.

"No."

"No. Steve stayed behind, didn't he?"

I looked away, but could still see him from the corner of my eye, gleaming in the dark. The moment stretched into awkwardness. Finally, I asked. I had to know. "Am I coming with you this time, Poet?"

The warm half-smile. "Not this time. Not ready yet. Maybe next time."

"How do you know that, man?"

"Just do. Got to go now."

After he disappeared, I slept.


IN THE SPRING of 1992, I visited New York with a friend named Helena. Her smile lingered in my head like her perfume lingered in my room and on my skin, and I wanted this thing with her to be permanent. I could see her growing old with me, making sons with me, sons who would take over my budding business.

Helena and I, we'd just come out of a Broadway matinee of "Phantom," and we were discussing a late afternoon snack.

After we'd walked for a bit amid mixed smells of bakeries, restaurants, garbage and hydrocarbons, something caught my attention. Under the taxi horns and street crowds came the sound of squealing tires.

An ordinary sound, but something was wrong with this particular squeal. The years I'd spent in the jungles of Vietnam had left me with a sixth sense for trouble. A heaviness hung in the air, a vague impression of wrongness that preceded a disaster.

In my mind's eye, I vividly saw the barrel of that AK levitating from its hiding place among the dripping leaves. I looked around, but couldn't find the source of the noise. Other people must have sensed it too, because they looked around, ready for something. All but one, a young boy of 12 or 13 on the sidewalk ahead of me, earphones plugged in, grooving to a sound only he could hear.

He couldn't hear the oncoming danger.

And I could do nothing. My feet were paralyzed. I felt helpless, just like that day many years ago when Poet had stepped in front of me. *Run,* my mind and heart shouted. *Go get him. Help him.*

The instant my feet finally moved, a car rounded the corner too fast, jumping up on the sidewalk to avoid hitting the press of traffic. I shoved Helena toward a storefront, shouting, "Get inside!" Then I ran hard, but the car must have been doing fifty or more around that turn. As it mounted the curb, the boy finally noticed something wrong and leaned to his right, preparing to jump out of the way. The bumper caught him and pulled him up and over it, spinning him off in a flailing half-gainer.

Too late.

The vehicle sped down the sidewalk and back into a break in traffic as the boy landed with a sound that made my stomach lurch. As the car brushed past me, I lost my balance and grabbed a lamppost to steady myself.

And it was gone. People all around me stared, stunned.

That night, I lay in my hotel room. Helena had fallen asleep after our lovemaking, and her head rested against my shoulder. She'd called me a hero for trying to save the boy, but I knew what had really happened: I'd frozen.

"Good try, my man."

I looked up and saw him, dressed in his stained but clean jungle fatigues in his usual spot at the foot of my bed, there in the dark.

"Poet."

"As always." He grinned. "Still watching."

"Watching me? What on earth for?"

"Surprise." He raised a finger to his lips and smiled that old smile that made me feel so at ease. Then he spread his hands. "Big plans for you, White boy, but you ain't quite there yet." He paused and looked off into the distance. "Getting close, though. Getting close. Go to sleep. Pretty lady you got there. She love you, make no mistake."


HELENA DID LOVE me. For all of three years. After that, she decided she needed her "space" and left me for a dental surgeon. But not before taking a good share of me with her in an ugly divorce proceeding that lasted nearly as long as the marriage.

I was back in New York, on business this time, in a very large, very nice hotel room. Unfortunately, I hadn't brought any kind of aspirin or pain reliever with me. My foot had started bothering me again, and only one kind of analgesic would work for me. Plain, regular old aspirin, which, of course, the hotel store didn't carry. So I limped down the street in search of some.

Cursing the developers that always put the best hotels alongside some of the most dangerous districts, I went in the first convenience store I found, one with bars on the door and windows, and grabbed what I needed.

And then, aspirin in hand, I felt it again. That sense of wrongness.

Unfortunately, my sixth sense was a little late. I saw a man in a jean jacket and a ski mask pointing a Glock 19 at an aging Asian cashier, probably the owner. Though much older, he reminded me of Vietnamese men who'd fought on both sides in that jungle I wanted so badly to forget.

I put the bottle back and dropped to a crouch behind one of the long racks.

"Empty the drawer, Chinaman!"

I shook my head. The guy was clearly from Southeast Asia, not China, as any vet could have told.

I moved as quietly as I could along the shelves. In my mind, I heard the *suck-thwock* sounds of the Vietnam jungle. It seemed to me that I made enough noise to bring Andy Tyler back to tell me to shut the hell up. I got to the end of the row and peered around.

Just the one guy. Me, I would have brought a partner to watch the door. The old man rummaged in the drawer for his cash, piling the crumpled notes on the counter. The gunman couldn't see me.

Gathering myself, I leapt for the assailant, chopping down at his gun hand. He must have heard me, because he turned and squeezed off several shots as he spun. He shot wildly, holding his weapon in a sideways grip. The counter exploded, spraying glass everywhere, and I heard several displays behind me crumble to the floor.

We went down together.

He dropped the gun when we hit the floor, and rolled to get his hands under him. That was his mistake. I pounded the back of his neck hard, and he collapsed, motionless.

I picked up the gun and looked back toward the counter, but I could see no sign of the old man. Had he been hit? Damn. I pushed myself to my feet, but pain stopped me cold, and I sat back down hard on the floor.

I hadn't felt the wound until I moved.

I looked down at my stomach and saw a red stain on my clean white shirt, and it was spreading like spilled wine. I tried to collect my thoughts when I saw a bright flash of light from the corner of my eye.

Poet Williams stood by the door.

"Don't worry about the owner, man. He just fainted."

I said nothing. Just looked at him in awe. He was beautiful. He smiled his one-sided self-deprecating smile, and said:

*"Upon his shield came the warrior home*
*His face, transformed by Death's unholy grasp,*
*Become a mask of calm serenity . . . "*

He took a few steps until he stood directly in front of me, and whispered, "This is it, man."

A long silence fell between us. My breath became a bit tight. This wound was more serious than I'd at first thought.

"Are you Death, Poet?" My voice came like a file on rusty metal.

"No, Jared, I'm not. But I can be life, if you want it. Do you want to live?"

I looked at the glass pane of the storefront with its bars. I hadn't noticed the name when I walked in.

Nguyen's Corner Convenience.

I looked back at Poet and felt my eyes start to well.

I nodded.

"You did a good thing today." He held his hand out to me. "Come on, friend. You ready."

---

**MARK W. WORTHEN** is a creature of the night. Whether he's undead or not remains to be seen, but his midnight hikes earned him the internet handle "nitewanderer," derived from an old Robert Frost poem. Naturally, his writings lean toward darkness and things that go bump in the night.

Mark's fiction has appeared in numerous anthologies, including *Washed by a Wave of Wind: Stories from the Corridor* from Signature Books, *Vicious Shivers* from Undaunted Press, *Thicker Than Water* from Tigress Press, and *Beneath the Stones*, for which he also served as editor, from Bones and Caskets Press. Additional stories can be found at www.wilywriters.com.

Worthen has been a big fan of science fiction ever since he was young. He cut his teeth on the commercial pulp stories of Edgar Rice Burroughs and Isaac Asimov, and later, the more thoughtful novels of Orson Scott Card and heroic novels of Stephen King. But he's also always enjoyed the more literary novels and stories of Ray Bradbury, and perhaps his favorite writer of all time, Roger Zelazny.

# I AM VISION, I AM DEATH

BY ERIK WILLIAMS

ON THE EAST SIDE OF DALLAS, ELIJAH PULLED INTO A Motel 6 and bought a single for the night. He paid in cash. He'd wanted to make Shreveport before stopping, but the caffeine and speed had lost their effectiveness. He needed to crash for a few hours.

The room was small but adequate. Elijah brought in his backpack and locked the door. He slid the curtains closed and flicked the A/C on full. After a quick shower, he crawled into bed and set the alarm for five in the morning.

He checked the date on his watch. Two days, he thought. Two days since he'd gotten the call that Mom was on death's door. She'd only last a few days, according to the doctor. A week, tops. Elijah frowned. It would be another whole day of driving to get to Jacksonville.

Elijah looked around the room at the sparse walls and small TV and plain art in faded frames. "I am Loneliness."

Then he took a few pulls off his flask and went to sleep.


AGAIN, HE DREAMED he was the stranger, trapped inside his skin and seeing through his eyes.

The dreams were always different. The settings and atmosphere changed each time. The stranger, though, always remained constant. The same cadence in his speech. The same controlled anger pulsing through his veins. He had never seen the man's face, since he was always looking out through it, nor had he heard his name, but Elijah knew *him* and knew what he was capable of.

This time he was lying naked on a motel bed, watching the local news, KROU-Channel 9, Baton Rouge, he recognized, but he was humming some song Elijah had never heard. The previous time he was in Houston, smoking a cigarette and drinking vodka out of a plastic motel room cup. He knew it was Houston because of the 214 area code stamped on the phone set. Other places, he could only guess at.

Always somewhere different, a nomad like Elijah, though the similarities ended there.

After a few minutes, he stood and stubbed out the cigarette. He kept humming as he walked into the bathroom. Inside, a woman lay in an empty tub. She was gagged and bound, her eyes wide, her skin pale except for bruises on her breasts and thighs.

The stranger knelt next to the tub, then stroked her cheek with the back of his left hand. She didn't blink.

"I am Death," Elijah heard himself say through the stranger's voice.


ELIJAH OPENED HIS eyes and breathed deep. Sitting up, he glanced at the clock. He'd only slept forty-five minutes.

Another woman. In every dream the guy killed women. Not always the same way, but always women.

Elijah sipped from the flask and rubbed his face. The dreams varied in length from time to time, just as his visions did. He thought about how long he'd been having the dreams and wondered if it counted as living two lives. It sure felt as if it should.

A few more sips and Elijah lay back down.


THE ALARM WOKE Elijah at five. His head ached and his eyeballs burned. He wanted to sleep for another day but forced himself out of bed. After he dressed, he grabbed his bag, headed to the main lobby and checked out.

As he walked to the car, he heard a woman whimper. He turned and looked around the parking lot. It was dead quiet with the exception of the buzz of streetlights. For a minute, he thought he had imagined the sobs, when he heard another.

Elijah slinked toward the side of the motel's main lobby. The whimpers grew louder and more frequent. Then he saw the movement of shadows on the asphalt. Elijah pressed his back against the wall and peeked around the corner.

A large man, well over six feet, had a young girl pinned against the wall, and both had their pants around their ankles. The man rammed her from behind holding the side of her face against the brick wall. Her hands were duct-taped together behind her back and a strip covered her mouth. Blood trickled from her nose and tears soaked her cheeks.

Elijah looked away. He peeked again and they were gone.

I am Vision, he thought.

His eyes scanned the parking lot, looking for the large man. Then he found him, leaning against the front bumper of a semi-truck, picking his teeth with his nails.

Elijah pushed off the wall and walked toward the trucker. As he did, the bell rang above the motel's entrance. He glanced over his shoulder and saw the girl walking out wearing a maid's uniform.

He turned back to the trucker. The man had stopped picking his teeth and was moving toward the girl.

Elijah walked faster and pulled a knife from his back pocket. He flipped out the four-inch blade and held it at his side. His pulse remained steady as he maneuvered around several cars and flanked the trucker from the right.

Crouching between two cars, Elijah lunged forward as soon as the trucker walked by, slicing the knife across the right Achilles tendon. The guy crumpled to the ground and started to scream but Elijah pounced on his chest and covered his mouth with his left hand.

Wide eyes stared at Elijah, saying more than words. Elijah swiftly slit the man's throat, and blood poured from the wound. The trucker gagged and choked.

Elijah wiped the blade on the man's shirt and put it away. Searching through pockets, he found a wad of tens and twenties. He stashed them in his jacket and stood.

The girl was in the maintenance room a few doors down from the lobby and was pulling out her cleaning cart. Elijah breathed easy and moved away from the dying man at his feet, careful not to step in the pooling blood.

He reached his car and took a quick glance around the parking lot. Quiet. The buzzing of the lights. Cicadas singing out in the brush. Elijah climbed in, started the engine, and headed back toward the highway.


A LIGHT MIST blanketed the highway just after sunset east of Pensacola. Elijah slowed, careful not to overdrive his headlights, travelling through a gray cocoon. Thankfully, hardly any cars were on the road.

Elijah saw the silhouette of a person emerging out of the mist. As he closed, the headlights illuminated a man with a thick beard standing on the shoulder, his right hand balled into a fist and stretched out toward Elijah, thumb up.

Elijah hesitated for a moment, not wanting to be bogged down with a tag-along. Time was his enemy right now and the fog had already slowed him. But he didn't feel right leaving someone out in this weather where a passing semi might just as easily hit the man as stop for him. He contemplated a moment longer, then pulled over a few feet past the stranger.

The man walked up and Elijah lowered the passenger window.

"Thanks for stopping."

"No problem," Elijah said. "I can take you as far as Jacksonville. After that, you're on your own again."

"Deal."

The man opened the door and climbed in. Elijah noticed a small beat-up backpack, the patches of a handful of heavy metal bands sewn to its surface.

"Got a name?" Elijah said.

"Call me Miguel."

"Elijah." The guy didn't look Hispanic but he let it go. "Where you coming from?"

"Does it matter?" Miguel was older, probably pushing fifty, and his voice sounded worn and recycled.

"No." Elijah shifted into drive and accelerated. "Do you always hitchhike?"

"Wouldn't travel any other way."

"To each their own." Elijah couldn't see Miguel's face in the darkness of the car but imagined a smirk planted there. "Been traveling long?"

"Since I left home. Never settled down. You?"

"The same."

"You a salesman?"

"Yep. What about you?"

Miguel chuckled. "Shit, I'm just a bum on a quest."

Elijah looked into the dark where he thought Miguel's face was then back to the road. "Quest, huh?"

"Mind if I smoke?"

"Nah, go ahead."

Miguel rustled in his jacket, and a moment later the front of the car lit up. Miguel's face materialized behind his flickering Zippo. Then he snapped it shut and the car plunged back into darkness. For a good while they travelled with the lone purr of the engine.

Miguel broke the silence. "You're a shitty liar, you know that?"

"How's that?"

"You're no salesman."

Elijah's hands tightened around the wheel. "I'm not?"

"Nope. You're a bum, just like me. Travel from place to place. Work odd jobs; probably steal when you have to."

"I'm not like you."

"How's that?"

"I have a car."

"That you do." Miguel laughed and patted the dashboard. "That you do."

Elijah reached down with his left hand to his side. He tried to move slow and not make noise on the seat. If he could get to his knife without drawing attention, he could slip it to his right if Miguel tried anything.

"So how long have you had the visions?"

Elijah's hand froze on his hip. The voice. "What?"

"The visions, man. How long?"

"I don't know—"

"Bullshit. You see the ghosts of people who aren't dead yet. That's what you told your momma when you were eleven, right? 'Momma, I see ghosts but the people aren't dead' or something like that. Visions, man. Things that are gonna happen."

Elijah's hands shook. The voice. "How do you know?"

"I dream about it."

Elijah looked at Miguel and saw only the glowing orange tip of his cigarette. The voice. He'd known as soon as he'd heard it, but just hadn't placed it. The stranger. The man from his recurring dream, right here next to him.

"I've been having dreams about you for a long time," Miguel said. "I go to sleep and see you choking some pimp in an alley in Seattle. Or see you cracking a mom's skull right before she tosses her infant in a dumpster in Sacramento. Last night, I saw you knife some trucker outside Dallas."

It was hard for Elijah to breathe. "Who are you?"

"Who are *you*?" Miguel chuckled and took a deep drag, the orange tip glowing brighter. "Figured there was a connection between us. Something deep, you know, because it was always you and there was something, I don't know, familiar. Took me a while to figure it out. When I did, it made all the sense in the world."

Elijah wiped sweat from his upper lip. "How'd you find me?"

"The date. I knew where to be because that's where I had been. Like I said, when I figured it out, it all made sense."

"So tell me what you figured out."

"You'll see soon enough." Miguel took another puff and blew smoke at Elijah. "First you got to see Mom. Don't have much time."

Vertigo swirled about Elijah's head, and he swerved toward the shoulder before righting the car. "You don't know shit about my mother."

"Oh, yes I do. I know all about dear Mom. How your daddy used to beat her, and you. How she cracked Dad's skull with a bat and watched him bleed out. How you got orphaned when she went to prison. Oh, I know quite a bit."

Elijah's lower lip trembled. There was silence between them for a few seconds.

"I see things, too, you know," Miguel said. "Visions, like you. But I also see things that have already happened. Past and future, I see it all. Best of both worlds, so to speak. You will, too."

"You're insane."

"We're the same, you know. You just don't see it yet."

"You're Death."

"And you're Loneliness." Another drag. "You're Vision."

"I dream about you, too," Elijah said. "Seen you kill women. Innocents. So don't compare me to you."

"Why'd you kill that trucker?"

"To save that girl."

"You didn't have to kill him, though. But you slit his throat without a second thought. Doesn't sound like the action of a good man to me. I think you like it. In fact, I know you do."

"I use my gift for good."

"You use it as an excuse to kill, and it's a curse, not a gift. I almost went insane when I was fifteen, hearing all their voices. How old were you when it became too much? When you realized you had to run away to silence them?"

Elijah didn't answer. He was instead plotting ways to get Miguel out of the car.

"I guess it doesn't really matter," Miguel said. "You ran away just like me. And then you started killing just like me. So you see, we are the same."

"I don't kill innocent people."

"You want a medal or something? We'll see how you do when you're completely alone with nothing else in your life. Because when you've got nothing, when you don't have an anchor for all that hate, you stop pretending to care about strangers. All you care about then is feeling alive, like you matter. I matter to those women because I decide if they live or die. You'll learn soon enough, wait and see. You're not special. And before I'm done with you, I'll show you how you die."

Elijah moved his left hand for his knife.

"Pull over," Miguel said. "I want to show you something."

Elijah pulled the knife from his back pocket. Switching hands on the wheel, he grabbed the knife from his lap with his right.

"I want you to see." A gun cocked in the dark. "Pull over and I'll show you." Miguel jammed the barrel into Elijah's ribs. "Now."

"Okay, okay." Elijah took his foot off the accelerator and pulled over onto the shoulder. "Just take it easy."

The barrel moved from his ribs but Elijah could still feel it pointing at him.

Miguel rifled through his backpack. Elijah tried to see better in the dark, staring, willing his night vision to sharpen so he could locate the gun.

"Turn on the map light," Miguel said.

"What?"

"Turn on the map light. I said I wanted to show you."

Elijah reached up to the rearview mirror and flicked on the map light.

Sitting across from him, Miguel held the gun in his left hand and the severed head of a woman in the other. Elijah jumped back and hit his spine on the driver's side door.

"I'm not alone," Miguel said.

Elijah closed his eyes, waiting for the gunshot.

Nothing happened.

Elijah opened his eyes a millimeter at a time until the passenger seat came into focus.

Empty. The only thing occupying it was the light from the rearview.

He turned and looked forward. The mist still hung heavy on the road. The car, still parked on the shoulder.

A ghost, Elijah thought and exhaled slow and long. It had felt more real than any other. And it had lasted longer than any of his previous experiences.

"Which means he's up the road." Elijah flicked the map light off. "I am Vision."

The accelerator pinned to the floor, the back wheels spun and then bit the asphalt. The car rocketed from zero to sixty in about seven seconds. The eight cylinders of the engine roared as the RPMs flirted with the red line. By the time he topped out in speed, the lights did little more than illuminate a gray wall.

The headlights reflected off something small.

Then Miguel was there, bathed in the glow of angry headlights, backpack slung over his shoulder. Elijah swerved and there was a sickening thud as Miguel was sucked under the right front tire and then the rear one. The car bounced almost out of control, but Elijah slammed on the brakes. The car skidded about fifteen feet. Breathing hard, he glanced in the rearview but saw only mist.

Just drive, Elijah thought. Get to Mom and wash the car off while it's still dark.

But he needed to know Miguel was dead. Then the dreams would end and maybe the part of him connected to Miguel would finally have peace.

Elijah shifted into reverse and backed slowly until a lump of twisted flesh appeared in the rearview, the brake lights blanketing the lump in red. He grabbed his knife, opened the door and approached the body slowly, just in case Miguel pulled the gun.

Something moved. Miguel rolled over, gurgled blood and wheezed for air. Elijah knelt next to him, the knife held to his chest, ready to stab.

Most of Miguel's body was crushed. The right side of his head was caved in and only his left eye remained. It stared at Elijah.

"Who are you?" Elijah said.

Miguel appeared to be grinning, a mouthful of broken and chipped teeth pointing out at Elijah. A long breath escaped his mouth. Elijah watched Miguel's life sputtering out in the red brake lights.

"This is how you die." Miguel gurgled blood.

Elijah blinked and found himself kneeling over the empty pavement. Miguel had vanished. He ran around and looked at the front end of the car. It was undamaged.

"What the hell?" He'd never experienced anything like it. A vision followed by a vision?

A semi raced by and honked. Snapping out of his disbelief, Elijah climbed back aboard and drove on, determined more than ever to get to Mom.


THE GUARDS WERE expecting him and called for an escort from the infirmary when Elijah arrived. A thin, gaunt man met him and took him to his mother.

She was a sack of bones with sunken eyes and birdlike arms. He walked over to her and kissed her on the forehead. Her skin was clammy. She smelled of wet-wipes and urine.

"I'm here, Mom." He leaned over her, and saw a glint of recognition in her milky eyes.

"Knowing you were alone and unloved here in prison has been the only comfort in my life. You murdered Dad, and left a broken kid to roam the broken world. My only hope is that you don't die. That you continue to rot away, alive and in misery, forever, and ever."

A single monotone sound emanated from the heart monitor. A flat line drifted across the screen. A doctor and a nurse raced in and pushed Elijah aside and started CPR. Rather than watch, he moved toward the door feeling empty and defeated. Ten minutes later, a doctor found him in the hallway and told him she was gone.

"I am Loneliness," he said when he was by himself.

Elijah stood there a long time, thinking about her, and his life. Thought about Miguel, the stranger of his dreams. Thought about the people he'd killed before they could do bad things, the images of them replaying in his head all at once like a surreal movie. And now the one thing he'd always had in his life, his focus of rage, the woman who had ruined him, was gone.

His hands trembled as he rubbed the back of his neck, thinking, wishing he could make sense of everything and feeling more alone now than he ever had.

Just get out of here, he thought. Find a motel, sleep, and then bury Mom tomorrow.

After signing out with the guard at the front, Elijah walked to his car and climbed in. When he tried to start it, nothing happened.

"Come on."

He turned the key again. Nothing. Not even a click.

Deal with it tomorrow, he thought and got out.

Elijah grabbed his backpack from the backseat. Looking at the solitary patch sewn on the front reminded him of when Mom had first given it to him. His favorite band for her favorite son.

Fuck her, he thought, shaking the memory off and slinging the pack over his shoulder. He slammed the door and walked from the car down the road away from the prison.

I am Loneliness, he thought as he pulled his jacket tighter against a chill wind. I am Vision.

The headlights of an approaching car rounded the bend up ahead. As it neared, Elijah stuck out his fist and cocked his thumb up.

The car slowed and pulled over just past him. "Need a ride?" a woman said.

Elijah stared at the car a moment before walking toward it. "Yes, I do."

"I can take you as far as town."

"Sounds good." Elijah climbed in the passenger seat and set his pack on the floor between his feet. "I appreciate it."

"Got a name?" Her accent was soft, maybe Georgia.

Elijah looked at her. He couldn't make out much but could tell she was thin. Her breasts were nice and round. Her hair, auburn and long. She looked like Mom when she had been younger.

"Miguel," he said.

I am Vision, he thought. I am Death.

---

ERIK WILLIAMS is pretty much a nobody in the world of fiction. But he's working real hard to change that. At least he says he is. Then again, he's only been writing since 2005 so he's not really doing too badly, right? At least don't tell him he is. He's a bit sensitive.

His short stories have appeared in *Apex Digest, Greatest Uncommon Denominator*, and *Necrotic Tissue* magazines as well as this here anthology. His novella "Blood Spring" is available from Bad Moon Books. His novelette "The Reverend's Powder" is available from Sideshow Press. His first novel, *Demon*, will be published in 2011 by Bad Moon Books.

See, he is working hard.

# SANTA MARIA

BY JEFF CERCONE

---

"CAN YOU BELIEVE THESE PEOPLE? WHAT THE HELL'S the matter with them?"

Rob ignored his friend and pushed his way through the crowd, bumping an elderly Hispanic woman in the shoulder. He started to apologize, but she was too preoccupied to notice.

"Santa María, Madre de Dios, ruega por nosotros pecadores ahora y en la hora de nuestra muerte . . . " She whispered the prayer, tears soaking her grizzled cheeks and her arms clutching what Rob assumed were her two grandchildren, who stared wide-eyed at the spectacle.

Dozens of people, the devout and the curious, had gathered at the underpass of the Kennedy freeway, positioning for a glimpse of the stain on the wall. A certain civility had taken hold despite the stifling Chicago heat and the decidedly unholy stench of exhaust fumes, sweat, and urine.

Most kept a respectful distance, queuing up and allowing a few at a time, usually a family or a group of friends, to move up to get a closer look. Rob noticed, then felt guilty for pushing his way to the front.

"They're nuts!" Mitch said, not caring who he offended. "It doesn't look anything like her. It's a freakin' stain!"

"I dunno, if you stare at it long enough, it could look like her," Rob answered.

Behind them, people held their camera phones up to capture the image on the wall.

"So how do you explain the one that appeared in rust on the water tower in Des Moines?" Rob asked. "And then there was the other one that was supposedly just a random case of brown patch on that football field in Texas . . . "

"I had a rash once that looked like Danny DeVito if you saw it in the right light, but nobody was asking me for autographs," Mitch said, shaking his head.

"You're all class, Mitch," Rob said, chuckling inappropriately loud.

It was Mitch's idea to come here, not because either of them was religious; he just thought it would be worth a laugh, and he suggested that Rob could get some footage for his film class. They had been friends all through high school and Mitch hadn't changed a bit, Rob thought. He wished he could say the same about himself. Iraq had done a number on him. But it was good to be home and among friends. And nice to be able to laugh again.

A small, middle-aged man in front of them turned and frowned.

"Show some respect, boys. The Virgin came to see us and all you can do is make jokes?" He shook his head, the brim of his fishing hat stained with sweat.

"Sorry, sir," Rob said sheepishly while Mitch rolled his eyes.

A young woman was hugging the stain on the wall as her three little girls watched, the youngest holding a beat-up plastic doll that was missing an arm and the oldest holding the leash of a large black lab that had plopped down in a mud puddle to cool off.

"Come up here and tell the Virgin your sins!" the woman barked at the girls, who approached the wall cautiously. "Ask for forgiveness."

They waited another twenty minutes for their turn, Rob only having to shush Mitch a few times. The man in the fishing hat was on his knees at the wall now, holding rosary beads in one hand, his other touching the stain. After a few moments, he struggled to his feet and put the beads in his pocket. He looked at Rob and Mitch and tipped his hat, then turned and walked toward the sidewalk.

As they moved closer, Rob took out his video camera and began filming the crowd, then swung around to follow their gaze. In front of the wall, an impromptu shrine had emerged, with a couple dozen or so glass candles, the kind they sold at the discount store on the corner, some with pictures of the Virgin, others with Jesus. People had left bouquets of flowers, cards, rosary beads, Bibles, and teddy bears. Rob noticed that the little girl had left behind the one-armed doll, probably at her mother's urging.

"Unbelievable," Mitch whispered. "Isn't it scary to think about how many desperate people live around you?"

"Come on, now. If they want to believe in something, who's it hurting?" Rob retorted, panning and tilting the camera on the stain. "It does look a little bit like her."

"You've been overseas too long, dude," Mitch said.

Rob zoomed in on it. If you stared at it long enough, it certainly looked like the outline of a woman wearing a robe, her head tilted slightly. He could sort of make out a feminine face at the top right and hands clasped in prayer above her chest. On the news, city officials were claiming salt runoff from the highway above caused the stain.

"Come on, dude. I gotta get back. I'm meeting Melissa for dinner," Mitch said, tapping Rob's shoulder.

"I think I'm gonna stay here and get some more footage."

"Whatever, Jesus freak. Call me later." Mitch said, then headed back to the car they had parked a few blocks away.

Rob waved the next group in line forward, then stepped back a little to give them some space, filming the whole time. The three old ladies didn't seem to notice him as they added to the pile of offerings against the wall and fell to their knees.

Rob was kneeling as well as he zoomed in on the women, panning from their feet and up over their hunched backs to the stain on the wall. He began to pan toward the shrine but doubled back to the stain. He was sure that he'd seen a pair of eyes open where the woman's face would be.

He focused again on the stain for a moment until he shrugged it off as his colorful imagination working and turned the camera back to the shrine.

He zoomed in to capture some detail of the gifts and felt drawn to the one-armed doll. He wondered if the little girl missed her doll or had already forgotten about it.

"It'd be nice if they can forget, wouldn't it?" a booming voice said behind his ear.

Rob jumped to his feet, almost dropping his camera, and spun around. There was no one within ten feet. He looked at the nearest person in the crowd, a bald man who was praying the Rosary.

"Did you say something?" Rob asked.

Annoyed at the interruption, the man shook his head, then returned his gaze to the wall.

Rob stepped around the group at the wall and resumed filming over their shoulders, zooming in on the stain.

This time there was no mistaking it. The eyes were open. And staring at him.

He lowered his camera and looked around, convinced Mitch was somehow playing a joke on him. He moved a few steps closer and stared at the stain with his naked eye and saw nothing staring back. He raised his camera and zoomed in.

Again, her face was alive. Soft and feminine and bathed in yellow light. Her open eyes followed him. Then she spoke.

"Your case will be heard tonight, Rob Tanziger. Be here at 3 a.m." she said, again in a deep, gravelly voice that reminded Rob of his drill sergeant.

He lowered his camera again and stared at the wall. Still nothing but a dark stain. But he heard the voice again, this time as if he were thinking it.

"Don't make us come find you."

Rob backed up, quickly making his way to the sidewalk, staring dumbfounded at the wall the whole time. Okay, he thought, that didn't just happen. You didn't just get threatened by a fucking stain on a fucking wall that looks like the fucking Virgin Mary. Maybe you should call the counselor tomorrow. Maybe you need to talk about what happened over there in the desert.

"Watch it, man!"

The man he ran into was solid as a wall. Rob groped around for his camera, then picked himself up.

"Sorry buddy, my bad," he said, gazing up at the tall, chiseled Black man in front of him.

"You heard it too, didn't you?"

"Heard what?" Rob said. "What are you talking about?"

"She spoke to you too, didn't she? I can tell the way you're high-tailing it out of here."

"I don't know what you mean. Excuse me," Rob said, scurrying around the man and heading toward the bus stop.

"She said something about 'a case', didn't she?" the man said, his voice cracking. "What does she want? How does she know?"

For once in Rob's life, the Fullerton bus came just when he needed it. He boarded, took a seat, and gazed back at the man, who had his face in his hands and was weeping on the sidewalk. He seemed much smaller now.


ROB GOT OFF the bus at California and headed home, jogging at first, then sprinting the five blocks to his studio apartment, passing by the El Ranchero, where he usually stopped for a burrito.

He tossed his backpack and keys on the kitchen table, then headed toward his desk, fumbling the video camera out of its case.

"Watch out, Cletus," he said.

The 14-year-old cat held its ground, pretending not to hear until Rob put the camera bag down on its tail. Cletus gave him a dirty look before hopping to the floor in search of another cool spot to sleep.

Rob took the disk from his camera and began downloading it to his computer.

He grabbed a beer from the fridge, and noticed his hands shaking as he opened the bottle. Harry Carey shouted, "Cubs win!" and it startled him. The voice was coming from the bottle opener his little sister had given him a few years ago, despite knowing he was a Sox fan.

He took two large swigs and settled down in front of the computer.

He watched as the scene he had witnessed earlier played back. The devoted followers. The gifts at the makeshift shrine. His lens focused lovingly on the one-armed doll. The footage was beautiful, he thought. Surely he could get an A on this project.

Especially if he caught the stain coming to life on film. *But that didn't really happen, did it?* And to his relief, there was nothing on the tape. No eyes opening. No Virgin Mary speaking to him. Just a dark stain on a freeway underpass wall that if you tried hard enough, you could see anything you wanted to in it. He'd done it plenty of times with little puffy clouds on clear days.

Okay, then you imagined it. Call Dr. Hammond on Monday and get your appointment moved up.

He'd almost convinced himself it never happened when he remembered the chiseled Black man he'd smacked into. He knew he hadn't imagined *that* guy. The bruised shoulder he could feel beginning to throb was proof of that.

There was only one thing to do. He packed some fresh batteries into his bag and slid a fresh disk into his camera, then laid down for a nap. It was going to be a late night.


HIS DREAMS WERE vivid and intense, and, as usual, made little sense. He could see the one-armed doll, its eyes open, its mouth moving, but nothing coming out. He saw Cletus standing on two feet opening the fridge and asking Rob where his food was. He saw his sister crying and running from him when he tried to talk to her. Like she was scared of him.

Then he was back in Iraq. This part of the dream made sense. This part was always too real. The Humvee exploding in front of him, one of the doors tumbling to a stop near his feet. His eyes burning from the brightness and the heat of the noxious flames. Pulling his buddies out of the wreckage, one by one. Two already dead and his friend, Ryan, on fire, his skin smoldering as he rolled in the dirt . . .

"It's almost time. You should prepare your defense."

The voice jolted him awake and Rob jumped from the couch, his sweaty chest still heavy from the nightmare. He scanned the room, not realizing he was still clutching a pillow. Cletus stirred at the foot of the sofa, looked up at Rob, then closed his eyes again. There was nobody else there.

It was just part of the dream. *Relax,* he told himself. The clock showed 2:15 a.m. He'd hoped to head out much earlier. He cursed himself for not setting an alarm, put on his T-shirt and shoes, grabbed his camera and dashed out the door.

At least he was able to catch the last bus. He settled in for the 15-minute ride. He had the bus to himself, except for the homeless guy who got on at California and headed to the back row for a nap, his pungent odor eating at Rob's nostrils as he passed.

The bus approached the underpass. Rob pulled the cord and headed to the back door. He looked over at the homeless guy, who opened his eyes as the lights above the door turned green.

"Good luck," the man said before rolling over to go back to sleep.

"What did you say?" Rob asked, hesitating at the bottom step. The man ignored him. Rob could hear him snoring already.

"Let's go, in or out?" the driver shouted. Rob stepped down, the doors creaking shut behind him.

After the bus passed he could see the shrine across the street, bathed in a soft glow from the candles people left behind. The crowds were gone, but Rob could make out one lone figure kneeling at the wall.

He approached quietly, not wanting to interrupt someone in mid-prayer, though he questioned why someone would be coming out in the middle of the night to pray to a stain on a wall, even if they were convinced it was the Virgin Mary. As he got closer, he realized that it was the large Black man he'd run into the morning before.

The man was not praying, just whimpering.

"Please stop. I'm sorry. Please stop. I'm sorry," he said over and over, staring at the stain.

Rob thought about leaving. He had lived in the city long enough to know that it was not smart to engage crazy people on the street, particularly late at night. But he felt a need to help, so he eased up beside the man, who turned and looked at him, wild-eyed.

"Help me . . . I can't stop. Help me," he whispered.

Rob looked down and noticed the blood pooling around the man's knees and a pile of what looked like strips of old leather.

He followed the trail of blood up to the man's hands. He was holding a knife in his right hand and was cutting into his left arm, working the blade down from his elbow to his fingers, like he was peeling a potato. Most of his arm and hand was a pulpy mess, his fingers stripped to the bone.

"Please help me," the man begged.

"Jesus Christ, man, what the fuck!" Rob cried, then instinctively grabbed for the man's shoulder and elbow, hoping he could grip them hard enough to make him drop the blade.

But the man turned and slashed at Rob instead, getting off three quick swings, the first of which sliced through Rob's right forearm, though not too deeply. Rob backed off.

"Dude, you asked me to help you."

"I'm sorry . . . it's not me. It's not me . . . " the man cried, still slashing the blade in Rob's direction.

Rob grabbed his camera bag, figuring he could use it to deflect the knife while he tried to get hold of the man, but then another voice spoke.

"Do not interfere. His sentence is being carried out."

Rob turned to the wall, and it suddenly lit like a movie screen. The dingy highway underpass, stain and all, disappeared as the wall gave off a blinding, golden hue. Centered on the screen was a large, robed figure that looked part man and part . . . something else. It was large enough to fill most of the height of the screen, and had long, flowing hair with thick strands, each moving independently, like wriggling worms. It gazed down at Rob.

"Your trial will begin once we've completed with him."

"Who the fuck are you? What do you want?" Rob asked, fumbling to get his camera out of his bag, hoping to capture this on film.

He did not answer. His face changed as the moments passed. He was an old man with a beard and mustache, then a young Black woman, then the Virgin Mary again. The face morphed every few seconds, but the eyes, glowing with hatred and anger, never changed.

"What do you want from me?" Rob asked, stepping back and turning his camera on.

He looked through the lens, but this time all he could see was the same, dingy old wall. He lowered the camera and looked up into the light, shielding his eyes with one hand.

"You are accused of grave sins and you must be tried before this court and the throne of the Lord!" the thing shouted.

Behind the creature, a primitive courtroom scene unfolded on the wall. There was a witness stand on one side, next to a large, ornate throne in the middle facing the street. Both sat empty.

There was one row after another of wooden benches, filled with spectators turning to their right to watch. Some appeared human, some had wings . . . some had horns. All were focused on the man who knelt on the ground, flaying away at what was left of his arm. They cheered each time a strip of flesh fell to the ground.

The man, having done all he could do to his arm, took off his shoe with his good hand and started rolling his pant leg up, his face contorted in agony.

Rob turned his camera off and backed away slowly. Then he started to run.

"You cannot hide!" he heard behind him as he sprinted down the street, his heart pounding in his throat.

He didn't stop for several blocks, until he was too tired to continue. He realized he didn't even know where he was going. He rested, his hands on his knees as he struggled to regain his breath and orient himself. He took out his cell phone and called Mitch, hoping he was still awake.

By the fifth ring, Mitch picked up, annoyed.

"Dude, this better be important. I've got company."

Rob realized he had no idea what to say. All he could do was cry into the phone.

"Hey bud, what's goin' on? Calm down," Mitch said.

"I think I'm losing my shit, man. I think I'm going crazy," Rob stammered.

"Okay, bro. Settle down. Where are you?"

"I'm not sure. I went the wrong way home," Rob said, looking around for a visual clue. "That looks like the Logan Square monument up there. I'm near Kedzie."

"Okay, can you make it over here? We'll talk it out and you can stay here. We'll call the doctor in the morning."

"Yeah, the Blue Line is right over there," he said, his voice calmer. Mitch always had that effect on him. "Can you meet me at the station?"

"Of course. I'll see you in a few, bro. It's going to be fine, Okay?"

"Okay. See you there."

He hung up and took a moment to calm himself. He hit rewind on his camera, his hands still shaking, and then hit play. There was still nothing on the wall. Just the same dark stain. In the background, he could hear the man crying as he cut himself.

Rob turned the power button off and headed toward the train station.

Rob walked in, swiped his transit card at the turnstile, then walked down the stairs to the train platform. Despite the hour, there were plenty of late-night revelers still out.

He passed a group of men and women in their early twenties, all with either tattoos or lip piercings, some with both. They stared at him indifferently as he passed.

In the middle of the platform, a skinny, long-haired man was playing "Hotel California" on his guitar, and doing a fairly decent job of it. Next to him, a Hispanic man sang along with him, pumping his fist as they harmonized about not being able to "kill the beast." The singer didn't seem to mind the stranger intruding on his performance. In front of them, a guitar case sat open with a few dollars and a couple dozen coins scattered inside.

Rob opened his cell phone as he passed them to check the time: 2:59. He began to check to see if he had any messages when the screen went blank. A familiar golden light began to shine from it, then a face appeared. It was the thing from the wall.

"You cannot hide from us. Your trial begins now," the image announced in a grave tone.

Rob snapped the phone shut and threw it to the ground. It bounced and skidded toward the group of teens nearby. They turned and looked after it hit a tall boy's shoe. The kid picked it up and tossed it back to him, and Rob caught it.

"Sorry about that," Rob said, then hurried farther down the platform, stuffing the phone into his pocket.

The phone rang.

*Impossible!* There was no cell service down here. He took the device from his pocket, opened it, and the golden light glared out at him. He tossed the phone into a nearby garbage can, then continued down the platform.

"Enough!" a voice boomed. Rob stopped in his tracks. The wall off his right shoulder lit up and the impossible scene from the underpass appeared. The creature emerged from the bottom of the wall, its wriggling hair crawling around its ever-changing face, and soon rose twelve feet above the rest of the courtroom spectators, who were staring to their left at the witness stand, where a young girl no more than five years old sat next to the still-empty throne. She appeared to be of Arabic ascent, and by her headdress and blouse, maybe Iraqi. She sat nervously, eyes down, clutching a one-armed doll in one hand.

"Your trial begins now," the thing said again before turning its attention to the girl. "Of what doth the witness accuse this man?"

The girl looked up. Her eyes turned vacant and she slumped forward in her seat without saying a word. Another screen appeared above her and a scene began to unfold.

It showed the inside of a small, modest house. There were eight people in the room, four adults, three teenagers and a little girl. It was a tranquil scene of a family going about their daily life. Then a door was kicked open, breaching the silence and awakening Rob's memory.

Three U.S. soldiers entered the dwelling, shouting orders and pointing guns. The women and children in the house were screaming. A young man who Rob guessed was the little girl's father turned to run upstairs, but one of the soldiers opened fire, cutting him down from behind. The women and children went into hysterics.

"Sit down! Shut the fuck up! Shut the fuck up!" one of the soldiers screamed and Rob shuddered as he recognized that soldier. It was him.

The soldiers corralled the rest of the family, dragging them into the center of the living room and shoving them to their knees. The elderly woman fell to the ground hard and a soldier yanked her back up by her hair.

"Who did it? Who set up that bomb? Tell us!" a soldier yelled. Rob recognized him as his friend, Lieutenant Anderson.

In broken English, the old man said, "It was not us. We are no fighters."

"He's lying, man. It was one of them. It's right in front of their house for Christ's sake!" the other soldier said. Rob couldn't remember his name, and in fact it was their first time out together. "You heard that witness out there. He saw someone run inside just before it went off. What else do you want?"

"Just do him, man. Those are your friends all charcoaled out there," the soldier urged.

Anderson hesitated, then took the butt of his rifle and cracked it into the old man's nose. His frail face caved in on impact and he slumped to the floor. Anderson delivered two more blows to the man's head.

The women and children screamed louder. Anderson moved over to the only remaining male, a young teen, maybe fifteen or so.

"Was it you, you little fucker?"

"Come on man, he's just a kid," Rob saw himself say.

"That don't mean shit, man," the other soldier retorted. "I seen children and women blow themselves up just to take a few of us out. You can't trust any of 'em!"

"He's right. We gotta do 'em all. It could have been any of them. I ain't doin' this myself. You gotta help me," Anderson said, staring at Rob.

After a moment, Rob nodded his approval.

The soldiers moved behind the family, who sat cowering and crying on the floor.

Anderson looked at Rob.

"You ready?"

"No."

"Enough talk. Just do it!" the other soldier boomed, and Rob now recognized the voice. He had not heard it before that day and had not heard it again until today. It was the thing from the wall. Its eyes brimmed with hate.

Rob watched as he and Anderson pumped the family full of bullets, except for the girl, who was shrieking now.

"You gotta shut her up, man. Do her too," the other soldier urged him.

Anderson started to point his gun at her, but Rob pushed it away.

"We're done here," he said. "Let's check out the house next door."

The soldiers made their way out the front door. Rob stopped and looked back, making eye contact with the girl. Watching it now, he recalled hoping that she would be able to forget what she saw.

The door closed but the scene still played behind the little girl on the stand.

She ran up to her mother, whose face was frozen in a mask of horror. The girl prodded her, but realizing her mother wasn't asleep, slumped to the ground and started screaming again. The sound was drowned out by the gunshots next door.

Then the screen faded to black and the girl on the stand suddenly awoke. The creature and the spectators turned to face Rob.

"How do we find the defendant?"

"Guilty! Guilty! Guilty!" the crowd shouted.

"What should be the sentence?"

Rob snapped out of his trance and ran down the platform before they answered.

"Help me, please. Help me!" he shouted to the other riders, who either stared at him or looked down at their shoes. It dawned on him that he now seemed like the crazy person that people should not engage in the middle of the night.

He slowed down and looked back. The spectators on the wall were still watching and shouting "Death!" but the people waiting for the train seemed oblivious.

Then he started running again, but he lost control of his motor functions, and his body turned back in the direction of the courtroom scene. He was running full speed down the platform, his legs churning forward despite his brain's orders to go the other way.

He heard a train approaching at the far end and saw its light appear in the tunnel. Passengers closed their books and gathered their belongings, some moving out of the way as Rob ran past.

He was picking up speed and was on a collision course with the train. The wall was dead ahead, and as he looked up, he could see the creature, its arms outstretched and its head turned skyward as it roared, the jury around it cheering. It looked down and locked eyes with Rob, as it morphed back into the Virgin Mary, its wild hair suddenly covered in white linen. It clasped its hands and bowed, as if in prayer, then grinned, two rows of sharp, black teeth stretching its mouth wide as its face began to morph again.

The train grew louder, its headlight burning his eyes, and Rob reached the edge of the platform, now nearly airborne, save one step. He closed his eyes as he leapt onto the tracks.


"WHAT DO YOU think it is?"

The woman rubbed her hands over the stain on the desk, then turned to the man next to her and took a sip of her coffee.

"I think it's exactly what it looks like."

He let out a nervous laugh.

"It does have some resemblance."

"Some?"

"Okay, maybe more than a little bit."

"Has he seen it yet?"

"No, he hasn't been in yet, and it wasn't there last night."

"Who found it?"

"The lady from the cleaning service. She almost fainted. I don't know how we're going to keep her from telling people about it."

"Maybe *we* should tell people about it. I mean . . . these have been showing up everywhere lately. This is proof, isn't it?"

"Proof of what?"

"That he was chosen for this job."

"How do you think that would go over?"

"Well, I . . . wait, here he comes."

Footsteps and voices echoed outside the room. The door flung open and a man entered the room, trailed by a small entourage.

The man and the woman by the desk straightened up. The woman hesitated, then covered the stain with a pile of folders left on the desk before turning to greet her boss.

"Good morning, Mr. President."

---

**JEFF CERCONE** is an editor and writer whose fiction has appeared in *The Late Late Show* webzine. He was the editor of the now-defunct webzine, *Down in the Cellar*, which may come back to life someday.

He lives in Chicago, where the actual Virgin Mary sighting that inspired this story still draws people to the highway underpass at Fullerton Avenue to leave their offerings. He hopes whatever it is has better intentions.

# THE HEALING HANDS OF REVEREND WAINWRIGHT

BY GEOFFREY L. MUDGE

A NOTHER NIGHT, ANOTHER SHOW, ANOTHER CHORUS of cheers and applause and unbridled joy that we will never hear. In the darkness and silence, only the rumble of the diesel engine roaring to life lets us know our part has been played for the evening. This night's showcase was relatively slow and tame. The only serious injury to come from the affair was a dislocated shoulder suffered by the blind kid, Augie. The sickening sound, somewhere between a pop and a crunch as muscle and bone tore apart, still echoes in my mind. There's not much to listen to in here, and the few sounds that aren't screams tend to linger a little longer than they should. The only other noise is the wet, hacking cough coming from Juliana's corner. I think she may have contracted emphysema or TB, but she won't live long enough to be bothered much by whichever.

However, experience, the harsh mistress that she is, has taught me that the good shows are tragedies in disguise. Having been here the longest, I've seen the patterns through a dozen of them. Through pure luck or divine intervention, I've survived longer than all those that were here when I joined. Most of the kids travelling with me now were picked up in Memphis and are generally unfamiliar with the ins and outs of the business. In my time with the Reverend I have found that slow nights are almost inevitably followed by horrendous ones. Those nights, the anguished cries reverberating in my skull make me long for the cavernous silence between one and another.

Joseph, chained closest to the heavy door, thinks he heard talk of moving to Wichita. Isn't that peachy? Kansas. The heart of the Dust Bowl. The land of polio and starvation. A visit to the festering wound spewing the misery that has been slowly eating America's soul may not end well for some of us. Frankly, I expect some deaths before we finish, and there are so few of us left. When I came in, there were a couple dozen of us, but now there are only six, and we all know the carnivorous tumor in Ralph's brain will soon finish him.

Though it's been quite a while since we picked anyone up, I couldn't say just how long. Time is extremely subjective with no way to track night and day. The occasional feeding and the never ending shows are the only ways we have to measure the passage of time. In those terms, it's been twelve shows since Memphis, how long that is in normal people time, there's no way to know.

To be honest, the anticipation is almost worse than the performance. Almost. It's just so damn hard to sit in the hot darkness, afraid to speak to the only people who could ever understand this ordeal. But what would we say to each other? Speak words of hope that ring false and hollow the moment they leave one's lips? Talk of escape when metal and leather and malnutrition make it impossible? No, there are no words left in any of us. All the pleadings and prayers are spent. There is nothing for us but the sweltering silence of this dark oven.

And the show.

The goddamn show, it must go on.


THE SMALL FIRE spewed hot sparks and ash into the night sky as Abel hurled a fresh log into its embers.

"Hey! Watch out, you stupid bastard!" Lot yelled, beans and pork juice dribbling down his chin. Abel replied only by hanging his head and stumbling sullenly out of the weakening ring of light. Lot wiped his grimy mouth on his leather gloves. "Aw, hell," he muttered, "I guess I better go apologize to the big lout."

"Leave him be, Lot. He'll find a pile of dirt or a dead animal and he'll forget all about it." Adam's soft but powerful voice drew a hushed burst of laughter from the small group of shabby-looking men.

"Well, you're the boss," Lot sighed as he sat back down. "If you think he'll be okay, I'll get back to dinner."

"He'll be fine. Now finish that grub up quick, boys. We got a lot of work in front of us and you know the Rev hates to get behind schedule." Adam inhaled a last mouthful of beans and tossed the can toward the newly invigorated fire. The rest of the tired men quickly did the same. After much groaning and consternation, they began to shamble toward the heavily loaded trucks.

"Where is the good Reverend this evening?" Jeremiah inquired as softly as he could without belying his utter dread of the holy man. "He didn't want to share in the vittles?"

"My sincere apologies for not joining in the sumptuous feast this evening. I acquired other accommodations and dined alone in the confines of my trailer." The reverend's deep, haunting voice and soft Southern drawl crawled through the cool, dusty night air from behind the group of men. "Although I must admit I am slightly miffed that my presence was not inquired into until after the 'vittles' were no more than memories and grease stains." The last few words oozed from Wainwright's lips like a foul sludge and sent chills through the spines of every man who heard.

"Reverend! I . . . uh . . . that is . . . I mean . . ." Jeremiah tried to stammer some sort of coherent response, but as he turned to face the Reverend, their gazes locked and all his words seemed to slip away. Wainwright's eyes were all white with the exception of the pitch black pupils that pulsed and pinwheeled like a kaleidoscope. His direct stare was enough to make even the most resolute of men whimper, and Jeremiah involuntarily stumbled back a few steps.

The Reverend smiled coldly at his flock of miscreants. "Come now, dear Jeremiah, I merely sought to have a little jest at your expense. I am, all joking aside, glad that you are all well fed and eager to move forward. There is still so much work to be done. So much work. How go the preparations? Can we expect the main edifice to be erected soon?"

"The main edifice?" Adam interjected. "If you mean the big tent, we should have that thing up in a couple hours. As for the rest, Jeremiah here and Lot are gonna head to town at first light to start handin' out flyers. Me and the rest of the boys'll get the stage set up, and Abel is gonna get the kids fed and cleaned up for the show."

Wainwright scowled up at the uncaring moon. "Abel, you say? You are aware we have several little girls amongst our family of flagellants, correct? We have traveled far and seen much together, Adam, but I swear to all that is holy in this world, if that half-witted pedophile touches even one hair on their sacred heads, I will castrate you both with my bare hands!"

Adam laughed nervously as he struck a match on his thick leather glove and carefully lit a cigarette dangling from the corner of his mouth. "Relax, Rev. Abel may be slow but even he isn't stupid enough to go after them girls." A casual glance passed amongst the huddle of men as the same shadow of doubt crossed each mind. Adam caught the look as it went around and sighed heavily. He dropped his smoke onto the hard earth. "Well, I gotta go, uh, check on some stuff. I'll be right back." Trying his best not to flat-out sprint, Adam strode away from the group in the direction of the children's trailer.

Wainwright watched him for a short moment before turning his withering gaze on the rest of the workers. "Well, gentlemen, let's get to it, shall we? I have preparations of my own which must be attended to." The Reverend turned petulantly and walked away, darkness wrapping his tall, gaunt frame until it disappeared.

Jeremiah scooped the still smoldering cigarette butt from the ground and inhaled deeply. "This job gets a little more entertaining every day. What the hell does 'castrate' mean, anyway?" The men laughed nervously and made their way into the night, casting cautious glances over their shoulders for whatever demons might be following.


"STEP ON UP, ladies and gents, and God-fearing children of all ages! For today, the just and holy Reverend Wainwright will hear all your pleas and grant God's mercy to even the most wretched amongst you! A nickel gets you in and a dime gets you a seat! Don't be shy now, folks! Claim your ticket now. They will go fast, and you've travelled so far, I'd hate to see you stuck out here with me when the service begins!"

Jeremiah's powerful voice rang through the crowd milling anxiously in the brown field. The blazing Kansas sun beat the life out of all below, and to most it was worth the nickel just to get in the shade of the tent. Of course, the Reverend's men had been diligent about spreading word of the healing service throughout downtown Wichita, and the assembled masses were almost all injured, sick, or carrying someone who was. Bleak times often call for desperate measures, and hope in any form was a welcome relief from the pulverizing daily desolation.

It took only half an hour for the available tickets to sell out. Being the kind-hearted doorman, Jeremiah let a few families slip in late with a wink and a grin. Lot came strolling out of the tent once they were in and secured the heavy leather flap.

"That's a hell of a crowd. How much did we get?" he asked as Jeremiah shook the box filled with silver and copper.

"*Hooee*, gotta be fifty bucks in there!" Jeremiah cooed. "Days like this make it all worthwhile." He put the heavy box on his shoulder and walked with Lot to the trailers behind the tent.

"So, did you get a look at the folks comin' through? There were some tasty looking dishes in there." Lot's eyes gleamed with a lunatic glare for half a second as the question fell out. Jeremiah licked his lips and tried not to think about it too much.

"Oh man, it's too early for that kind of talk. I'm starving as it is and I don't want to have to think about it all evening."

Lot laughed heavily, punching his friend on the shoulder playfully. "But isn't the anticipation half the fun?" Jeremiah frowned, staring at the sun as it crawled toward its tomb on the western horizon.

"For some, I reckon it is. Not for me, though. I like to stay focused on what's in front of me. Now let's get this loot counted up so we can have a smoke before the *real* show gets going. By the way, you seen Abel lately?" Lot shook his head and whistled a few bars of Toreador, clapping his gloved hands as the two stepped into the shade of the hulking trailers.

Inside the big white tent, Reverend Wainwright had whipped the crowd into a frenzy. "Times are troubled, my friends," he crowed from his pulpit. "I can see it in your eyes, I can see it in your faces, I can see it in your hearts." His frenetic gestures rippled his long white robe as the light from a hundred candles danced in his dark eyeglasses. "I know your pain, dear people, God knows your pain. We have felt it in a hundred cities all across this great land. We've heard the countless prayers begging for relief, begging for mercy, begging for a 'surcease of sorrow,' as a man wiser than I once put it."

Wainwright hopped down from the small stage and strode resolutely into the heart of the crowd. "But you know what? He hears you, and he shares with me all your prayers. All those cries that you think disappear unheard in the black of night do not go unheeded. I have come to this barren place for one reason today. I am here to take away your pain." With a heavy sigh, the Reverend raised his arms to the Heavens. "Almighty Father! Smile on your dour children this day. Let your love rain on us and take away all the hurt Satan heaps on your flock!"

It took only one cry from the crowd to ignite the wild fire. "My daddy's got cholera! Can you help him?" Afraid to be left out of any miraculous proceedings, the mob began to shout as one. The pleading filled the tent and cascaded on Wainwright's back as he walked to the stage. He turned and gestured for calm. The wailing slowly tapered off until silence gripped the group in an anxious grasp.

"Please, my children, there's no need to grovel. As I said, your prayers have been heard and I am the answer to them. I will be here amongst you for as long as it takes. On this day the love of God Almighty will be felt by all! A lucky few amongst you will even have your ailments remedied by our most Holy Maker!" The crowd cheered and cried and gnashed their teeth in bliss. "Now, I see back in the back there, a child lying on the floor. Bring him to me."

A somber looking man in dingy denim overalls scooped the boy from the floor with the infinite gentleness and promise of protection that only a father can give a child. He carried the boy slowly to the front as the crowd parted for him like the sea for Moses. Pain etched the boy's face, but he bit back the stinging tears, wanting to be strong like Daddy but knowing he would soon break.

The man laid his son at Wainwright's feet. He removed his cap and spoke gently to the Reverend. "Please, sir, my boy, he fell down a well, his back is broken. The Doc says he ain't gonna make it."

Wainwright smiled warmly on the man as he put a soft hand on his forehead. "Your faith brought you here today and that faith will be rewarded, my son. Please take a seat over there and let the Lord do his work." Wainwright shook his hands and knelt down next to the boy, his back to the crowd.

"What's your name, child?" He asked as his gentle hands caressed grimy cheeks.

The boy gritted his teeth and forced a reply through his lips. "Joseph, sir." It was all he could manage through the haze of agony. Wainwright nodded calmly, and with a deep breath he removed his dark glasses and set his gaze on the boy.

A look somewhere between terror and awe crawled across Joseph's young face as he stared deeply into those hypnotic, dancing eyes. Wainwright lowered himself until the two were face-to-face. "Look at me, Joseph." He purred quietly. "Look deep and pour your pain into me. Give me all the bad things inside. Take the misery you feel and give it to me. All you have to do is let it go and you will be healed. Give me your pain."

The Reverend leaned close and pressed his hands to the boy's temples. Joseph gasped as Wainwright increased the pressure on his head until it felt like it might burst. He could feel every finger and nail digging into his skin, pressing and grinding like a vise. He couldn't look away from those hideous eyes, he couldn't fight back or break free. Even if he could, he had to admit to himself he wouldn't.

"Give me your pain."

Hot, rancid breath and small droplets of spittle fell onto Joseph's face. He could feel the bones in his skull flexing and tensing under the relentless pressure, and then there was a spark. The pain in his head dissipated and a pulse of charged energy leapt from his temples to his back like a heated wire.

"Give me your pain."

Like a black sludge, Joseph felt the ball of anguish slowly drain from his shattered spine. The bones mended and the nerves reassembled as Wainwright pressed his fingers harder into his cranium. The boy wanted to scream in joy, to jump up and dance a jig right there in front of the astonished crowd, but he was held by the Reverend's crippling gaze. Soon, the pain which had been collecting for days was being pulled gently away from him.

"Give me your pain . . . "

Joseph wanted nothing more than to give away his pain, his hurt, his memories of the furious, withering torture he had suffered.

"Please, take it away, take it all away."

He pushed all his hurt to the Reverend's healing hands. Wainwright's eyes spun and twirled and he smiled as the boy gave in and let everything be taken. Joseph had never felt so good, so alive, but even after the pain was gone, the electricity continued to drain him.

Fatigue suddenly fell over him and small twinges of fear replaced the joyous celebrations in his heart.

"Give me your pain . . . "

Joseph tried to shake free of the Reverend's hands, recognizing that something was wrong. He tried to speak, tried to tell his healer that he was all better, but he could not. The fanatical grin on Wainwright's face grew bigger as the boy tried to fight against his hold. Joseph's eyes glazed over and his will drained away. The Reverend smiled still, and pulled everything remaining from his victim, but was not yet satisfied.

"Give me your pain . . . "


I FEEL A gentle pressure and slight heat twisting the small of my back. So the show has begun and it appears that I shall be the first supplicant of the evening. I let out a little gasp as the pressure turns into a sharp pain grinding my vertebrae together. In the darkness, I know the other kids are looking at me wide-eyed, seeing little, but understanding everything. They know they are momentarily spared, but fear what may be ahead.

"Give me your pain."

I hear the Reverend's words scything through my mind. He must be in full swing now, the conduit open and the prostrated parishioner marveling at the miracle he'd brought to Wichita.

The sharp crack as my backbone gives out rings through the darkness like a gunshot. I would scream, but my voice was taken from me ages ago. I bend backward as my spinal cord tears and all the sensation drains from my legs like fluid. An icy chill grips my lower body, complemented by the fiery agony ripping into the rest of me.

"Give me your pain."

I try to imagine who is lying in front of the Reverend, slowly feeling their life return and their body becoming healed. It could have been anybody, really. We would never know the people Wainwright set his healing hands to, marking their existence only by the signature of their affliction. He took their pain alright, but he didn't keep it. He gave it to us. *Suffer the little children*, indeed. It could have been a source of solace to know that through our sacrifice, someone else was freed of their burden, but we know what else the Reverend takes.

When the families see the hollow eyes and hear the melancholy voice of the healed, they must understand as well. We don't really know how or why this reaper does his deeds, but in the guise of a holy man he draws the submissive to him like moths to a flame. For some, I guess, the end of agonies is worth the price of a soul.

As the echoes of my breaking back cease ringing from the dark walls, silence falls on us. Only, it's not silent, I can hear a slight jangling and the soft click of a lock releasing. A burning sliver of light blinds us momentarily before the door is flung wide open. The dying red sun envelops the huge frame of the man the Reverend calls Abel standing before us.

"Hello, Juliana," he whispers softly, his voice dripping like bittersweet poison. The sounds from the big tent waft slowly toward us. The door has never been opened during a show before and it is amazing to hear the cheers and exultations of the crowd. Taking a large revolver from his pocket, Abel climbs into the trailer and kneels carefully next to little Juliana.

"You an' me are goin' for a walk, girl." His shaky voice imitates calm and caring, but seethes with hidden malice. As he waves the pistol in the girl's face, he asks, "Are you gonna be a good little girl?"

Juliana's expression doesn't change, but she nods her assent. Abel fumbles with her locks, his thick leather gloves making the process almost comical. With a grunt, he finally gets her bindings undone and the last chain falls away.

Even after it's too late, the imbecile doesn't understand his mistake. At this point, my compatriots and I are no better than wild animals, beaten and starved, and to remove the leash of such a creature is both foolish and dangerous. Juliana springs toward her tormentor with a feral growl that chills even my screaming blood. Despite her atrophied and hunger-deteriorated muscles, she is on the big man before he can react.

With a hoarse yell, Abel falls backward out of the trailer, waving his gun wildly in the air. He understands the power the pistol carries, but not the operation that imbues that power. Juliana sinks her few remaining teeth into his wide throat and crimson liquid sprays the thirsty earth. The pistol falls from his fingers and he tries to yell for help but can only produce a gurgling whimper. The little girl, drenched in ichors and hopeless ferocity, steps back and picks up the heavy gun. As she aims at him, the two lock eyes. Abel holds his arms in front of his face in a futile attempt to ward off a bullet.

The big pistol wavers in Juliana's shaky grip. She looks back at us, tears leaving burning tracks on her squalid face. Her sad blue eyes lock onto mine and she says the last words I will ever hear her utter. "I'm free."

Juliana smiles as she puts the gun to her head and pulls the trigger. The horrifying impact spins her in a full circle as her pale face disintegrates into fragments of bone and brain. Blubbering and bleeding, Abel crawls to her and gently wraps her lifeless body in his massive arms.

The exultant noise from the crowd dissipates as the gunshot works its way through them. About a dozen of the more stouthearted revelers exit the tent to investigate. They immediately move to surround Abel, assuming the worst as he cradles the dead girl. Their cries for the harshest of justice fade to silence however as their mutual attention is drawn across the dusty field to our open cell. Their wide eyes and gaping mouths tell the story of the horrors we have become. They don't understand why we are here. They see only the blood, the bruises, the broken children in chains.

The Reverend bursts from the tent with Adam following close behind. After surveying the scene he waves hurriedly to Jeremiah and Lot. "I need you two to tend to the flock while I sort out this nasty bit of business. Jeremiah, you use that silver tongue of yours to keep the people distracted. Lot, gather the men and secure the tent."

The pair nod solemnly and move to their tasks. As they retreat, the Reverend turns his attention to Abel and the late Juliana.

With Adam in tow, he pushes his way through the small knot of dumbfounded onlookers. Unleashing a vicious snarl, Wainwright plucks Abel from the ground. "You fool! You damned fool! Do you realize what you have done?" He hurls the big man into the dirt with ease, leaving him whimpering and cradling Juliana's decimated corpse.

The Reverend sighs heavily. "Malaco—sorry, Adam—I believe my work here is done. There will be no more miracles today." A look of pure disgust crawls across his craggy face as the band of men assails him with calls for Abel's scalp. "Clean this mess up, Adam. Let no word of what transpired today escape this plain." With barely subdued fury the Reverend takes Abel by the ragged throat and drags him, mewling and whimpering, away from the angry mob.

As Wainwright withdraws, Adam raises a gloved hand and waves at Lot. The large man waves back and motions to the entrance of the tent. A pair of men, one called Isaiah and one I do not know, hurry through to join Jeremiah. Lot secures the opening, tying it behind them with a thick strand of rope. The other hands move slowly around the circumference of the tent, similarly binding openings and weak spots. A murmur of worry and discontent begins to swell inside.

Satisfied with preparations, Adam grins, and for the first time I can recall, he bares what appear to be large fangs. His teeth are slender and razor sharp, like a mouthful of needles. The small group of men around him gasps and takes an involuntary step back.

Adam laughs, pulls off his leather gloves and reveals not hands but coiled tentacles hung with serrated hooks. They uncurl slowly, pulsing and twitching as they taste the violence in the air. Adam lifts his head and howls at the bloody sun, and from beyond my line of sight, his brethren howl back. In those shrieks the assembled crowd hears, whether consciously or not, the somber message. *All must die.*

The small crowd outside is strangely silent as Adam sprints into the heart of the throng. The black, pulsating tentacles hanging from his arms wrap around one unlucky throat and constrict, easily tearing through flesh and gristle. Adam roars and puts his teeth to his victim's face, ripping off a huge swath of nose and cheek. Blood sprays in a wide arc, drenching the closest of the stunned spectators. The torn man tries to scream in unison with his tormentor, but can force out only a thin whine and look of pleading desperation.

No one moves to help him, though; the huddled mass is frozen in shock and silence. Their minds still reeling from Wainwright's miraculous spectacle, the grotesque butchering paralyzes nearly all of them.

After a brief moment, a young man in a dark brown suit begins to shriek and babble. His fear spreads like a contagion, and the remnants of the mob scatter in a unified display of self-preservation. Adam instinctively leaps at the closest of them. Tearing a huge gash in the man's leg to prevent his flight, Adam quickly stalks to the next victim.

Foaming at the mouth like a rabid dog, Lot runs from his post at the entrance and smashes into the largest clump of fleeing parishioners, ripping and tearing everything in his reach. As he gnaws on a young man's skull, I see he has the same sickle dentistry as Adam, and the same barbed appendages shredding flesh and bone. Lost in a frenzied bloodlust, Lot drops the mutilated corpse and unleashes his fury. Blood and bodies whirl around him, chunks of gore and clotted hair hanging from his fangs and hooks.

The screams of those caught outside are soon echoed by those coming from within the tent. Jeremiah has apparently set to his task with the same vehemence and vigor as Adam and Lot. The tent's white walls are soon soaked through with muddy red stains and cries for mercy.

In the chaos, a few of the victims are able to escape the abattoir by wriggling under the hot, sticky canvas. As they scramble for whatever safety the baked earth has to offer, Lot and Adam give chase. Soon they are beyond where I can see and all I am left with are the sickening sounds of the hunt and the screams of the slaughter.

The waning sunlight is suddenly blocked as Wainwright steps into the doorway. "I am sorry you had to witness this, my children. Please do not allow this savagery to affect your work. When given the opportunity, we will again perform such great miracles." The Reverend sighs as he glances at the small girl with the massive exit wound in her head. "It is a great shame to lose Juliana. I quite liked her." He pauses to cast an accusatory glance at Abel, who stands behind him, head down and crying like a whipped dog. "Have no fear, though. We will find more friends for you before the next show."

We have no reply to give as Wainwright slowly closes the door. He smiles warmly, but his eyes speak the truth, they always have. He knows we will all take the same way out as Juliana, given the chance; he calls us his children, but we will never be anything but slaves. The heavy, metal door bangs shut, cutting us off from the atrocities of Reverend Wainwright and his acolytes. Once again we are left without any answers or hope of solace. Once again we are left with nothing but silence and dark.

And the show.

The goddamn show, it must go on.

---

GEOFFREY L. MUDGE is a writer of horror and dark fantasy. Being an air force brat and travel hound, he has visited and lived in various locales around the world. In his travels, he has consumed the cultural fears shared by our global community and he hopes to inflict these fears on the literate populace with extreme prejudice. Mudge and his black lab, Boomer, are currently residing in central Texas and when not writing they enjoy frightening local children and wildlife.

# CONTINUITY

BY LORNE DIXON

A SOUND FROM OVERHEAD LIKE HELICOPTER BLADES spinning: the sputtering of film running through an old projector, gears threading through sprocket holes, a blip, a skip, and the picture onscreen jumped, the framing thrown off, blurring, correcting. The image froze. On the wide aluminized screen, two children inside a runaway mining car screamed, their mouths trapped open by the freeze-frame. The image was rough and unfinished, the color uncorrected, their faces speckled with black grain. This was how the twelve jurors saw the film, over and over, watching with bleary eyes and wishing it was over and they could return to the courtroom, where they could easily turn their eyes away from the prosecutor's enlarged photos of the victims.

In the last row, cowering in an aisle seat, the film's director, Marius Spiegler, sat with his arms crossed, his defense lawyers seated around him in a failing attempt to block the jury's sight lines. The judge allowing the film to be screened was bad enough for their case, but an unintended facial expression—not horrified enough, or too much—might color the jury's perception of the director. Better they not see him at all.

Craning his neck to see over an attorney's head, Marius studied the profile of the jury foreman. A professional wearing a mid-range suit and Buddy Holly eyewear, he lifted the glasses and dabbed at his wet eyes with his fingertips. During jury selection, they'd learned that he was a father of three—but since they were all grown and out of the house his lawyers had waved it off. Only moments before the house lights dimmed, the judge had pleaded with the jury not to let it become personal, not to let the disturbing images burrow too deeply under their skin. Examining the expression of horror and disgust on the foreman's face, Marius could see that the judge's admonition was already forgotten.

The screen went dark, flickered, and the picture returned. Alex Carmichael and Nhu Toai finished their scream as the coal car raced down the ramshackle track. Marius could tell the difference in the long shots where they'd used midget stunt doubles. He doubted the audience could tell, but to his eyes it always looked wrong: he *knew* the difference, even outside his own films. Another close up, and Alex and Nhu returned, faces full of comic panic. They were damn good performers for their ages, better than some of the seasoned professionals that had appeared in his films over the last twenty years.

The sudden dip appeared on the track beyond the coal car. Marius felt his chest tighten. The wooden crossbeams overhead loomed. He knew what was coming and wasn't sure he could watch it . . . *again*. He couldn't imagine a worse torment in Hell. But no, he couldn't turn away. If any of the jurors saw him divert his eyes, they might see it as a signal of guilt. So he stared straight ahead and tried to unfocus his eyes.

"It's just like a roller coaster," Victor Ferguston, the cinematographer, had told the kids as he helped hoist them into the car. Nhu batted her long eyelashes and told him she's never been on a *roll-co-ster*, and the crew had all laughed.

"Don't worry, it's fun, it's all make-believe for the movie."

The car shook as it raced down the track, jostling the kids inside from side to side, the camera moving alongside, capturing the action. Racing up to the dip, Alex closed his eyes. On the set, Marius remembered grinding his teeth together. The boy's eyes needed to be open. They'd need to reshoot.

The film was silent. No optical effects or digital soundtrack had been added. But Marius remembered the hard metallic ping that echoed through Sound Stage Four. The front right wheel broke free of its axle and flattened to the track, derailing the car and jerking it off the ground. Instead of descending the decline, the vehicle rocketed straight forward, as if attempting to jump the chasm.

Nhu screamed again. This time, she was *not* acting.

The scream, silent on screen but still echoing in his memory, was cut short before it could reach its highest pitch. The car passed under the slanted support beams over the dip. At first, the crew stood in place, confused and unable to process what had just happened. It appeared as if the car had just missed colliding with the lowest beam, narrowly passing underneath. But when the car tumbled down the slope, fell back onto the track, and emptied onto the sound stage floor, the confusion turned to shock. Alex and Nhu's bodies spilled out of the coal car. Their severed heads rolled out a second later.

THE JURY DELIBERATED on a rainy Thursday afternoon. The gray sky outside the courtroom windows reminded Marius of the childhood afternoons he spent alone at matinee showings of cheap science fiction and horror pictures. If he closed his eyes he could see the old Stateline Theater: purple velvet curtains on the walls, dim dome lights illuminating the aisle like an airplane runway, the scent of buttered popcorn fighting with the stench of cigarette smoke drifting down from the smoking section. The Stateline was long gone, torn down and replaced by a strip mall, but it stayed alive in his memory, especially on overcast days like this.

Victor, former cameraman and current co-defendant, sat across a cheap folding table in one of the courtroom's meeting rooms. The lawyers were *conferring* elsewhere, probably somewhere a cab drive away with a wet bar. "You see their faces?"

"Who?" Marius asked.

"The jury," Victor answered. He was spinning his wedding ring on his ringer, a sure sign of nervousness. He'd lost fifty pounds since the accident, and the ring seemed two sizes too large. "They were enraptured by the film. You couldn't have pried their eyes away with a crowbar."

Marius imagined Victor handing out comment cards, treating the jurors like the audience of an advance screening.

*Between 1 and 5, how would you rate the motion picture you've just seen? (please circle)*

*1 (very poor) 2 (poor) 3 (average) 4 (good) 5 (very good)*

Shaking off the image, he asked, "Vic, you see anything different this time?"

Victor drew a question mark in the air with his pinky. He spoke with his hands often, sometimes pantomiming more than verbalizing. The joke was that in an earlier life he'd been Harold Lloyd. "Different?"

"Yeah, like more." He put a heavy accent on *more*, turning the little word into a euphemism. Victor's crinkled brow made it clear he had no idea what Marius meant, so he added, "More, like a higher angle or something. I swear I could see inside the cart. I saw . . . everything."

Victor shook his head. "I've seen the footage a dozen times. You can't see anything until the cart—"

"The cart overturns, yeah, that's what I always saw, too." His gut tightened. He felt foolish. "But this time, I saw more. I saw the wooden beam tear their heads off."

"Jesus, Marius." Victor turned his head. "You know how movies work, we don't ever put anything on screen, not really. We film just enough to get the audience's imagination to fill in *what's missing*. You're just tired. It's been a shit-storm of a year for you—the accident, Beth leaving with the kids, this goddamn trial. You got this prosecutor calling you a monster every day. Ain't no surprise you're seeing—"

"This isn't me feeling guilty. I saw it."

The cameraman tapped his fingers against the table. "People swear they can see a dead munchkin hanging from the trees on the trip to the Emerald City. But all that's there is an out-of-focus bird flapping its wings in the background. But people think it's a dead midget, so they see it, *really* see it."

Marius felt heat rising behind his face. He shook his head. "This wasn't like that. This wasn't a bird out of focus."

"Man, it's *always* a bird out of focus."


MARIUS SAT AT the crowded defense table and watched the jury return from deliberation. At the end of the table, co-defendant Bruce Dunn, soundman, stopped tapping a ballpoint pen against the table, frozen by the sight of the nine men and three women taking their seats. The courtroom was silent. Then Victor leaned in and whispered into his ear, "It's like watching a test audience leave the theater, right? Trying to figure out what they thought by the looks of their faces?"

Marius nodded. It *did* feel that way, exactly. Just as frustrating.

On impulse, he turned in his seat and surveyed the courthouse. They'd conducted a lottery for tickets to witness the celebrity trial. His eyes flickered between the jury and the rows of onlookers, and he wondered, *who's the real audience?*

At a separate table, the fourth defendant, producer Andre Ferronte whispered into his lawyer's ear and smiled. He must have seen something Marius had missed. It happened sometimes. That was why it was best to have fresh eyes in the editing room, even if he had a final cut provision in his contract.

The judge called the courtroom to order and asked the foreman if the jury had reached a verdict. They had. The judge asked him to read it into the record.

Silence for a long moment. Suspense worthy of Hitchcock.


THE REPORTERS WERE waiting outside, a wide crescent swarm of low-noise microphones and hi-def cameras. The defense team led the way, pushing through the first wave that came running up the courthouse's marble steps with their arms up in defensive little poses, the last nerdy kids remaining in a game of eighth-grade dodge-ball. Marius and Victor followed, so close that their toes nearly touched their lawyers' Italian leather heels.

A storm tide of questions hit them, the ocean of voices drowning out individual voices until only a few spare words made it to their ears like flotsam riding on the tide: "—acquitted—", "—regrets—", "—vindicated?"

They kept moving, trotting down the stairs, avoiding eye contact, until a young reporter's voice broke through the noise. The question had nothing to do with the outcome of the trial. It was simply this: "What's your favorite movie?"

Marius turned and scanned the crowd. He was unable to pinpoint the source of the question. A dozen microphones sparred for position under his chin, each with a different news organization's logo printed on the foam windscreens. He mumbled the answer, "Luis Buñuel's *Un Chien Andalou.*"


HE DIDN'T NEED groceries, he needed to get out of his house. The beachfront villa seemed empty and sterile, like an abandoned hospital, and it was no place to come after winning a court case. He'd called around, trying to find some company, but the phones just rang until answering services or machines picked up. He didn't leave a message. *Some* of them might have been out, he knew, but not *all* of them. How many were looking down at tiny LCD displays, reading his name, and deciding not to pick up?

The supermarket was sterile and cold as well, but at least there were people inside, employees and college kids and couples.

Turning down the personal hygiene aisle, he saw a family bickering over shampoo. Shampoo—that was their problem. Not manslaughter charges. Not a yoga instructor from the valley with eyes for married women. Not a Rolodex filled with names that wouldn't return a phone call. Shampoo.

A young girl and boy sat in the family's shopping cart, watching their parents argue. They turned and stared up at Marius as he passed. He froze, unable to take his eyes off them for a moment, gripped the handle of his own cart, and fought the urge to crumble onto the tile floor. They were so young and innocent, so fragile. Forcing his eyes shut, he pushed on, passing the family, and snatched a box of single-sided razor blades off the shelf.

He got the hell out of there.

NOT QUITE DRUNK but far from sober, Marius split his attention between the forty-two-inch plasma screen on the far wall and the tabloid on the leather ottoman at his feet. Open to the article advertised on the lurid cover, he skimmed the text, ignoring all but the most important words and phrases: *manslaughter, acquittal, judge furious, tainted jury, rumored bribery.* He wondered if the paper had the article already written, or if tabloid writers were just that much faster than screenwriters.

On screen, Maureen O'Hara cowered against John Wayne's chest in *The Quiet Man.* She broke away and ran under a stone arch as thunder crashed and rain began to fall. Joining her, Wayne removed his coat and wrapped it around her.

Outside, the real rain had been pouring down for hours. Marius swept up the bottle of Ladybank Single Malt, pressed it to his lips, and sucked. He was sure a stomach full of whiskey would have kept Maureen O'Hara warmer than the Duke's coat.

Strings swelled. They kissed.

And then John Wayne began to cough.

Dropping the bottle onto the ottoman and not bothering to glance down to see if it spilled or not, he stared at the screen with more interest than he had all night. He'd watched *The Quiet Man* a dozen times since he'd first caught it as the bottom half of a double feature as a kid. He knew the graveyard sequence as well as any scene from any film. O'Hara and Wayne would kiss, and kiss again, and once more, until the inevitable fadeout. There was no coughing.

Except there he was, one of Hollywood's most treasured icons, clutching his chest and hacking, his face turning bright Technicolor red. O'Hara stepped away and disappeared into the dark blur at the edge of the screen. Holding his fists tight to his lips, his chest heaved and he bent forward, eyes squinting. The coughing fit continued as the fadeout finally came, later than it ever had, but Wayne remained on screen, surrounded by blackness, gasping for breath and convulsing.

Marius reached down and plucked the remote control from the sofa and hit the button marked info. A bar appeared on screen with the name of the channel, the film's title, and the time remaining. He hit the button again and half the screen was filled with a synopsis of the plot. He expected to see some notation about a special edition with restored footage but there was none.

*Then what the fuck was all this?*

John Wayne stiffened on screen as a massive shock hit his body. A moment later he went limp, arms and legs falling to his sides. The scene around him brightened, illuminating the hospital bed under his body. His eyes, still open, went hard and still, no more life in them than a pair of marbles.

Marius fumbled with the remote, juggling it in his hands, until he was able to gain enough control of his shaking hands to change the channel.

Then he sat down and finished the bottle of scotch.


VICTOR LOOKED BAD. Sitting across the booth, the cameraman was smoking again after ten years without a puff, the glowing tip of the European cigarette matching the color of his eyes. His skin was pale and drooping. It looked as if he hadn't slept in days.

"You okay?" Marius asked, though the answer was as obvious as the jitter of the cigarette in his hand. If he didn't know better, he would have taken him for a junkie on the sweat-and-piss-stain end of a two-week jones. "You look like hell."

Victor flicked the ashes, glanced over at the disapproving glower of a waitress leaning against a pie case, and stubbed out the smoke on the chrome napkin dispenser. "They'd ban *breathing* in restaurants if they could . . . I'm glad you called, man. Thought about ringing *you* up, but kept losing my nerve."

"What's going on?" he asked.

"Remember when you asked me if I saw anything different in the movie? I didn't lie to you. I wasn't watching it, didn't see a frame, had my eyes locked on the jury." He leaned across the table as he spoke, glassy eyes fixing on Marius. "But then afterward, maybe a couple days, things started to happen."

"Things?"

"Yeah, *things,* motherfucking *scary things.*" Victor tilted his head. His brow lowered. He fished inside a coat pocket and brought out a digital camera. Turning it on, he set it down next to Marius' coffee. "Tell me what you see."

His eyes flickered down to the LCD screen. "Your family?"

He nodded, and hit a button. "And this one?"

"Two kids? They the niece and nephew you always talk about?"

"And this?" he said as he brought up a third shot.

It was the waitress. From the looks of it, he'd snapped the picture moments before Marius arrived. "What's going on, Vic?"

"That's just it. To you, these are just pictures of people, right? My dad and mom, little Stephie and Ryan, a girl working at a greasy spoon. That's what you see. I see them, too. But when I look at these pictures, they're dead. Pale waxy skin. Sunken eyes. Except for Stephie . . . she . . . it looked like an accident . . . " Victor scrambled for the cigarette butt, not lighting it, sliding it between his lips and sucking on the filter. A moment later he'd regained enough composure to point at the camera and say, "Look at the next picture."

Marius hit the button. On the screen, Victor stood in the middle of his family and smiled.

He said, "When I look at it, I don't see anything out of the ordinary. My family's all alive in that one. Stephie's head . . . we're all okay. Do you know why? I do. Because I handed the camera off to my brother-in-law. I didn't take it."

The camera clinked as Marius set it down on the table.

"You don't believe me, do you?" Victor pressed a palm against his forehead as if fighting a massive migraine headache. "It's fucking insane, I know, tin foil hat stuff, but I swear to you—"

"Vic, stop." Marius raised both hands as if in surrender. "Do you know how I spent the weekend? I watched some of my favorite actors die. Marlon Brando, Gary Cooper, Roy Scheider. I saw Michael Redgrave die from Parkinson's. Richard Burton's brain hemorrhage. James Dean's car crash. If I watch a movie, any movie, there's always someone on screen who's died. And I have to watch it happen."

He waited for a reaction, a roll of the eyes or twitch or nod, but if anything, his words had calmed Victor. Exhaling, he reached for the camera and replaced it with a cell phone. "You need to talk with Bruce Dunn."

Bruce Dunn had been the soundman on all of Marius' features, including the last one. "Is he seeing these sort of things, too?"

"No," Victor said with a sad shake of his head. "He's hearing them."


AFTER BRANDON LEE stopped twitching, Marius got off the couch, kicked over a beer can, and loaded a DVD into his player. An FBI warning screen replaced the dead actor. Sitting down, he waited for the menu to come up, then pressed play on the remote control. *Un Chien Andalou* began, title flickering before surrendering to the silent film's first card: *Il était une fois.*

The next image was a barber sharpening his long-handled razor on a long strip of leather. Marius dropped the remote control. His hands rifled over a dinner tray on the couch next to him, digging under the plate of reheated Chinese takeout. He came up with the box of razors, opened it, and slid one between his fingers.

The barber smoked on the balcony. Marius thought of Victor. The barber stared up at the full moon, his face a blank slate, unreadable. How did Buñuel, both the director of the film and the actor portraying the barber, die? He supposed he could keep his eyes on the screen and find out.

Buñuel disappeared, replaced by a young woman's face, stark and pale, another emotionless ghost like the barber. Two fingers, one for the upper eyelid, one for the lower, forced her eye open. The barber leveled the razor blade.

Marius brought his own razor up to his face. He could feel fingers on his face and cool air drying his eye. But only for a moment.

The young woman's eye was replaced by the full moon, a single thin cloud, as narrow as a skeletal finger, crossed over. Then her face returned, eye pierced, sclera pulling back like elastic, a thick black bubble of vitreous humor bulging through the chasm, pushing past the edge of the lens sack.

Marius lost sight of the grisly image on screen as his own eyeball ruptured under his razor and the world exploded in a rush of psychedelic color.

It hurt worse than the movie let on.


DRIVING WITH ONE eye meant that half of Ventura Boulevard was a peripheral blur. To keep everything in sight, Marius had to swivel his head back and forth as if it were a pendulum, gesturing *no* to nothing and everything, and even then he found the car swerving from the yellow to the white lines. Worse, his destroyed eyeball pulsed with pain and tickled around the edges under his makeshift eye-patch, tempting him to jab at it with a finger. He imagined the outcome would be something like an already broken grape reduced to peel and wine.

He was thankful when the tall, arching studio gates appeared, and even more so when he was parked in the lot behind Sound Stage Four. He wobbled as he climbed out of the luxury sedan, stumbling in a half-circle as he fumbled with the remote control for the door lock button. Frustrated, he reopened the door and tossed the keys on the seat. He turned and staggered away, leaving the door still open and chiming.

Sound Stage Four was unlocked. He knew it would be the case—nothing had filmed there since the accident. He wasn't sure why, really. Maybe the insurance company still had an investigation open. Or maybe it was just superstition. He kept a hand on the cinderblock wall as he walked the main hallway. He passed a first aid kit side-by-side with an eyewash station. Normally, that sort of thing would have been worth remembering as a gag for a future movie. But he wasn't in the business anymore, all that was over.

As he turned the corner, he squinted with his remaining eye. Something was wrong. The house lights were off, but the diamond mine set was lit. He searched for lighting gear—quartz incandescent bulbs in shuttered lamp-houses, translucent umbrellas, and skirted lanterns—but all the equipment they'd used on that last day of shooting was gone, no doubt spirited away for another production. Only the prop torches fastened to the cavern walls remained.

"What are you doing here?" Bruce Dunn called. He was crouched down by the tracks in a dark alcove, a dark little nook that appeared to be another cave but went nowhere. He stood up, gripped the plaster rock wall, and nearly fell back down. Unshaven, his face resembled a well-worn hairbrush, thick wiry growth protruding from his face at random angles. He could have passed for homeless.

He had a bandage over his left ear, white linen at the top, a dripping red sieve at the bottom where blood pooled. Marius wondered if this was how Van Gough had looked. Then another thought: was it really the madness that cost the painter his ear, or was it the art?

"He's here for the same reason you are," Victor's voice echoed down from the other end of the set. He emerged from the darkness of the main tunnel, the one the set designers had actually built for all of the practical shots. He wore a pair of black driving gloves. The fingers were bound together with electrical tape. Marius wondered whether he'd taken off all of his fingers, or just the ones necessary to operate a camera. "We're here because there's nowhere else for us to be anymore."

It was true. When Marius had reached the point where he could no longer watch actors die—and after the alcohol ran out—the beach house began to feel alien and unreal, as if it were only there as an illusion, a device. Even while driving to the studio he'd felt as if the traffic he'd encountered was all planned and choreographed. He'd seen a road worker speaking into a two-way radio at a construction site and couldn't help but wonder whether the man was giving or receiving stage directions.

"Three out of four defendants," Bruce snorted. "A reunion."

From the doorway behind Marius, another voice boomed, vocal chords as dank and rumbling as a didgeridoo or Australian thunder. All three men turned. Andre Ferronte, the producer, waddled onto the set. "Four. All four defendants."

Unlike Victor and Bruce, Ferronte had no outward signs of damage.

The four men came together over the spot where the mining cart had toppled onto its side. The cart was gone, but fragments of the wooden sides remained on the tracks, splinters too small for the camera to pick up. Marius stared up the incline to the wooden beams that had decapitated them. There were no stains on the boards. They'd been cleaned up. Ready to go for another take.

Ferronte slid a tiny digital camcorder out of a pocket. "Do you know what a camera really is? It's an eye. The lens, the shutter, all these things you can find on your own face, flesh and tissue instead of plastic and metal, but still. So what does it mean when we look through the viewfinder or at a movie screen? How many sets of eyes do we see the world through? What does it do to us, seeing the world like two mirrors facing each other, reflecting forever into nothingness?"

Cool air wafted down the tunnel.

"So many old movies, so many people on film that have come and gone, but still we can see and hear them. We give life to ghosts." Ferronte turned on the camera and began recording, focusing on each of them for a moment before moving to the next. "Not just that, we worship them, return to them time and time again. The movies begin to mean something personal to us. Do you ever wonder why? Have you thought that maybe it's not the viewers connecting with the movie but the films reaching out to us?"

Marius wiped his cheek, preventing a sticky trickle of gelatin from reaching his chin. His eye-patch tickled.

Bruce reacted first, cocking his head toward the dark tunnel. His eyes widened. The sound of metal scraping metal hit Marius' ears a second later and his reaction mirrored the sound man's. Still recording with the camcorder, Ferronte stepped away and said, "And . . . action."

The mining cart shrieked as it rolled down the track and into the light. Its remaining three wheels rattled against the rails of the track as its broken axle turned, reminding Marius of a worn-down shopping cart straining to roll in a different direction. It slowed as it approached the drop, allowing them to stare up at it as it quivered on the edge.

They each stepped backward, off the tracks, leaving footprints where the children's bodies had spilled out, keeping their heads turned up at the tipping cart, holding their breath.

The cart rocked and began its descent. This time, however, it did not come off the track. It rocked back and forth and shook with the force of a violent epileptic attack, but it stayed on the rails and rolled down the drop, coming to rest between the men.

Marius ignored the waterfall of liquid eye rolling down his face.

Over the lip of the cart's top board a curl of black hair came into view. Then the top of a head. And by its side, a second, blonde. Rising, Alex and Nhu's faces came up, smiling, eyes full of play and mischief. They giggled.

There was no air to breathe. Either that, or Marius' lungs had forgotten how to function. He stepped toward the cart, astonished and bewildered, his thoughts clouding over in a dreamy trance.

"Test audiences prefer a happy ending," Ferronte whispered from somewhere in the darkness beyond the lights.

As his hands fell on the edge of the cart, his heart lurched in his chest and his throat seized as his eye flickered inside. The children knelt, still decapitated, each holding the other's head up like a hand puppet. Their impossibly alive mouths opened and broke into uncontrollable laughter.

It sounded like a laugh track.

Leaping back, Marius lost his balance and collapsed back on the heels of his hands. He screamed but it wasn't his voice that came out, instead the sound was replaced by a stronger set of vocal chords, trained for performance, more satisfying to an audience's ears.

Head reeling, he rolled onto his stomach and scampered on the floor into the shadows. He found Ferronte there, camera recording, and he reached up to the producer's hand. "—Give me the camera. I need the fucking camera—"

There was a clot of dried blood on his wrists, as dark and thick as mud. Strange that he hadn't seen it earlier. He ran his hands over them, fingernails digging down, uncovering the jagged lines buried underneath.

"How many razors were in that box, Mr. Director?" Ferronte asked.

The producer kicked his hands away.

The camera's lens stared down like a giant, consuming eye.

Victor and Bruce extended their hands to help him up. Behind them, in the blurry edge of his vision, the children climbed out of the mining car.

"Don't worry, in the end we're all just birds out of focus."

---

LORNE DIXON enters into a unique fraternity that currently exists of exactly one individual; the only author to have two stories appear in the same *Cutting Block Press* publication. For more on Dixon, we urge you to read his work and/or visit www.lornedixon.com.

# TESTAVILLE, OHIO

BY M. ALAN FORD

---

ROLAND GAVE TWO DOLLARS AND THIRTY-EIGHT cents to the gas station attendant, who then asked where Roland was heading. "Testaville," Roland said.

The attendant seemed unable to decide between a laugh and a frown. "Testaville? Lots of weird people in Testaville. We get truck drivers all the time who don't want to go in, and they're happy when they get out."

Roland smiled. "I know. I grew up there."

"Never been there myself. How long you been gone?"

"Five years."

"Well, maybe it's worn off by now."

Roland didn't laugh. He looked the attendant over quickly before pulling out onto the highway. The attendant was young, in his mid-twenties, about the same age as Roland. His shirt was cleanly pressed, his hat spotless and sharp, his attitude relaxed and easy to talk with. This was different from what Roland was used to, and he wasn't thinking of the big city.

He turned on the radio and listened to music for a while, though this far out, reception was intermittent and static-filled. He was not paying attention, in any case. It was background noise, something to distract him from the way his hands tightly gripped the steering wheel. Traffic was sparse. He nearly missed the exit, which was nothing more than a small lane abruptly branching off from the highway. He followed it around in a loop that plunged behind a hill and under the highway, and found himself on the familiar two lane road rolling in lazy twists and turns through low hills and stands of trees.

He found the spot he had come to know as "the border" and pulled off to the shoulder. There was nothing special about the border. No boundary markings, no billboard, no "Welcome to Testaville" sign. It was simply an ordinary pattern of trees and hillsides he had come to recognize. He left the motor running. He got out and walked a few feet up the shoulder and stood for a moment looking at the road twisting off into the hills. Then he turned back.

He reached in through the open door, turned off the engine and removed the key, and went to the back of the car. He looked up and down the empty road, then opened the trunk. Inside was a large suitcase along with all the other things usually found in a car trunk. Spare tire, jack, socket wrench, a few tools, can of oil, spare gallon of gas. He pushed the suitcase aside and pulled back the blanket behind it. Hidden under the blanket was a small trinket box made of pale blond wood darkened by age. It was unlocked but held closed by a brass latch, and the lid was painted with the image of a winged woman in a robe setting foot on the prow of a boat, as if descending from the sky only a moment before. He tipped the box back and forth. Inside, something rolled about.

He covered it with the blanket again and pushed the suitcase up against it. Then he got back in the car and started the engine. He did not return to the road immediately, but only after a pause to take a deep breath, and then he moved the car at such a slow pace that a sauntering man could easily have walked past it.

The pattern of hills and trees slid by like a scrolling painted panorama. The border, as best he could judge it, came abreast of the car. Then it was behind him. Then he felt it, that first stab of unease. It came like a hand gripping his heart, a sudden pressure in the chest and a flush of heat to his face, and his fingernails dug painfully into the steering wheel while his breath caught in his throat. He nearly turned the car around. Instead, he came to a stop again and breathed shallowly until the fear subsided, never completely, but to a point where he could continue on despite himself.

It stayed with him when the road straightened as it came out from the hills and he saw Testaville just ahead. It was a small town, only about ten thousand people, one of many that had sprung up in the building boom just after the war. He drove past house after house, in tract after tract, looking at the neat small lots, each with a stretch of lawn and a driveway. At one point he passed a gas station. The attendant, staring at the sky as he leaned against one of the pumps, wore a dirty shirt pulled half out of his belt, and his hat was held twisted in his tight fists.

Roland found his own house among the others. He slowed as if to stop, then sped up and drove past. He went around the block twice. Then he turned onto the main street and drove to the park. It was just as he remembered it, a field of grass and trees one block square, with benches and picnic tables, and a small playground with swings and a jungle gym about which children clambered. He parked, stepped to the sidewalk, and stared into the park for a long time.

A woman wearing a pink dress with a matching pillbox hat passed in front of him. She stumbled and fell. Roland helped her up. "Are you all right?"

She dusted off her dress. The heels of her hands were scraped where she had broken her fall. "I'm fine, sure." She gave him a faint smile. "Just accident prone, I guess."

Roland said nothing. The woman walked off. He crossed the street to a store where he pulled a soft drink from the refrigerated section. His hands shook so badly that they rattled the bottles.

*So soon?* he thought. *It can't be happening so soon.*

Keeping his hand steady, he took the bottle to the counter where a young girl, about sixteen years old, was arguing with the store manager.

"But I didn't touch it!" she said.

"This isn't the first time, Shelly. There was a twenty in here."

Roland looked at the cash register. The drawer was open, and a few ones, fives, and tens were neatly stacked in their respective bins, but the next bin was empty.

"I don't know!" she said. "The door was open. Someone must have come in."

"And they got into the till without you hearing it? Do you really expect me to believe that, Shelly?"

Chastised, she said nothing. They noticed Roland for the first time. He counted out the exact change for the drink, handed it to the girl, and popped the top with a bottle opener that was attached to the register with a tattered string. He went back outside, crossed the street again, and found an unoccupied bench to sit on. The day was cool, but he wiped the cold bottle across his forehead anyway before taking a long drink.

His hand was still shaking. He couldn't stop it. His heart beat so wildly he felt like it might explode. But it didn't, and nothing happened, and he took another long drink.

Then he walked around the park until he thought he could go home.


HIS MOTHER ANSWERED the door. She looked startled to see him even though he had called ahead. She hugged him and welcomed him in, and he carried his suitcase into the living room where he found his father just standing up from the couch. They shook hands, and his father said, "Good to see you, Roland. Welcome home. Are you going to see Julia?"

"Not yet," Roland said. "Maybe tomorrow."

"You should see her," said his mother. "They don't know what's wrong with her. She could die tomorrow and then you'd have missed her."

She seemed offended. Roland smiled and said, "I'll go to see her. Maybe tomorrow."

"She's been in the hospital twice now. You're a doctor, maybe you can help."

"I'm not a doctor, Mom. I'm pre-med. I wouldn't know what to do for something like this."

She led him up to his room. It was pretty much as he had left it, with the bed neatly made and some old clothes in the closet. The air was stuffy, as if they hadn't opened it since he'd left. He slid the window open, letting in fresh air and sunlight, and unpacked his things. He lay on the bed for a while, staring at the ceiling while his parents moved about in the other room. They had distracted him. He'd felt the crushing pressure build in his chest from the moment he had knocked on the door, and only now, forcing himself to relax, was he able to think clearly and hush the pounding of his heart.

It came back when they ate dinner that evening. They talked about how abruptly he had left town and whether Julia's family would let him see her. They had not liked his "crazy talk." People in town had not liked his crazy talk. Even his parents had not liked his crazy talk, and his father, always the blunt one, said without intending harm that things had been better since he had left. Quieter. Less stressful.

His mother, always the peacemaker, said, "Oh, leave him be . . . "

She looked tired. She always looked tired. She had darkened, deep-set eyes and a lock of hair that dangled out of place across her ear, and she rubbed her head as if it pained her. His father stared at his plate while he talked. Roland talked little, only nodding in agreement with whatever they said, because he no longer wanted to be accused of "crazy talk." And through it all, the fist tightened about his heart and sweat broke out on his forehead, and his fork rattled against the plate every time he tried to net a piece of food with it.

Finally he could take no more. He excused himself from the table, went to his room, and closed the door. He lay on top of the covers until darkness fell, then changed into pajamas and tried to sleep, but what he got was scarce. He woke often during the night, convinced that someone had been standing over the bed, looking down at him. But no one was ever there.

Exhausted by morning, he lay in bed for some time, listening to his father move about the house. Then came the slam of the door, followed by the sound of the car starting in the driveway, and moving off down the street. He got out of bed and looked in the bathroom mirror. His skin was pale and his eyes were as sunken as his mother's. Tense anxiety clutched at his throat, making his heart pound and his breath struggle coarsely through his lungs. Even wiping his face with a cold rag did not help.

He knew it would happen today. He was sure of it.

His mother fixed him breakfast. When she asked once again if he would please go visit Julia today, he said, "Probably." Instead, he returned to the park. By the time he got there, his hands were gripping the steering wheel so tightly that it hurt to let go.

It was a work day, so the park was empty except for a few children in the playground and a few housewives pushing strollers along the sidewalk. He sat on the same bench as the day before. The sun floated bright in the sky, the morning air was cool and clear, and the sounds of the children playing not too far away came sharp to his ears. He rubbed his eyes, then set his hands in his lap and twisted his fingers together. The sense that it was coming overwhelmed him. He felt ready to run or lash out. But there was no one to lash out at, and the only place to run was the road out of town, which he knew he would not do. So he waited, fighting against the urge to stand up, until *it* sat on the bench beside him and he recognized it as his own.

Long ago he had named it "Boris," after Boris Karloff. He did not look at it. He only twisted his fingers tighter and looked out across the park. He could see them all, now. One was following that woman, who strolled along and talked obliviously to her friend. Another sat at the bottom of the jungle gym, watching the children play as if waiting for one of them to fall. Another stood by a young boy on the swing. Every time the pendulum motion brought the boy swishing by, it reached out and shoved him aside, sending him into a crazy trajectory. The boy did nothing but right himself and swing higher.

That was what they did. The more you saw them, the more frightened you became. So Roland did not look at Boris.

Eventually, Boris spoke. It was a harsh voice, dripping, as if it spoke through a mouth full of phlegm. "Been a long time," it said.

Roland almost lurched from the bench. He swallowed hard to quell the panicked beating of his heart.

"Been five years," it said.

Roland swallowed again. Still looking away, he stuttered, "Hello, Boris."

"That's not my name. I don't have a name." Roland didn't reply. After a moment, Boris shifted its weight on the bench and said, "I went to your house as soon as I heard, but you weren't there. I figured you'd be in the park."

"That's why I came here."

"I'm surprised you didn't try to lose me."

"I wanted to get it over with."

"Is that why you didn't go to see her? You wanted to see us first?" Roland nodded slowly. Boris said, "I've been waiting for you. Five long years. Do you know how bad you made me look?"

Roland slowly shook his head. He had pushed himself down into the bench with his chin pressed almost to his chest. "I've had time to think," he said. "When I was four years old, I spent six months in a coma. You should remember that, you're the one who threw me off the roof."

"Good times, Roland. Good times."

Roland rubbed his eyes again. "I've been reading. That's just about the age that children are becoming aware of their surroundings. I think that had something to do with it. I think it affected whatever magic it is you work on us. I never learned to be quite scared enough. So it was your own fault."

"Well, what are you now, a fucking psychiatrist?"

"Just pre-med."

"Well, don't be too happy about it. I found someone to replace you. He's eight now, lives on the other side of town. He's thin, weak. Scared. Like you."

"Well, that's good. If he's like me, he'll probably get away, too."

Boris slugged him. It was a full-on roundhouse, a solid blow that caught Roland on the cheek and sent him off the bench. He hadn't been expecting it, even though he should have. Boris stood over him, blotting out the sunlight. "I got time for two," he said. "I'm glad you're back, Roland. We're going to have a great time together."

Suddenly Roland was looking directly into the sun. He shut his eyes in pain. When he opened them again, Boris was gone.

He raised himself slowly and returned to the bench. His cheek throbbed and felt moist. When he wiped it, his hand came away wet with something that was not blood.

He drove home. Coming into the living room, he found his mother vacuuming with intense concentration while her own thing stood beside her, pulling her hair upward with one hand. It lifted her so high that she danced nearly on tip toe, yet still she pushed the vacuum across floor as if that chore and nothing else deserved attention.

Roland deliberately slammed the door. The thing dropped her. It must have been there all morning, because when she shut the vacuum cleaner off and turned to face him, her eyes were so moist that she seemed about to burst into tears.

"Roland!" she said. "My poor baby, what happened?"

The thing ignored him. It kept pulling on a fistful of hair, causing her head to bob back and forth. "Nothing," he said. "I slipped and fell down, that's all."

"That's just like you. Always so accident prone."

He was about to reply, but the thing tugged so viciously that it yanked her head back. He pressed his lips together, then went to his bathroom and looked in the mirror. His cheek had a colorful bruise. He washed his face, then came back down the hall. She had turned on the vacuum cleaner again. "Did you see Julia this morning?" she asked over the din.

"I'm going there right now."

"Don't you want to call ahead?"

"I don't think that would be a good idea."

He went outside. The last he saw before closing the door was his mother bent over the vacuum cleaner with one hand vainly trying to wrest her hair from the thing's grasp.


HER PARENTS WERE startled by his visit and they didn't want to let him in the house. Only out of courtesy did they relent. "How did you know?" her mother asked.

"My parents called me in Athens. I got here as soon as I could."

"You can't go up," said her father. "She's not seeing anyone."

That started an argument. Julia's mother wanted to allow it, her father did not. It was settled only when she went up and asked Julia, and the answer came back that she would. All the same, they accompanied him up the stairs and down the hall as if they were his chaperones.

Her room had changed. Gone were the Elvis and Buddy Holly posters, the pink walls, the oversized stuffed teddy bear on the bed. The room had been painted crème, and in place of the flowery girl's dresser against the wall was a businesslike desk covered with papers. He had heard she studied stenography and now worked part time in a lawyer's office, though she had not been to work since falling ill. She sat at the desk now, a willowy young blonde woman with bright blue eyes. She turned in the chair as they entered, but she did not stand up. Her eyes brightened further when she saw him. They did not embrace because her parents were in the room.

Across her pale neck was a dark bruise. He knew then that he had made the correct decision.

"Hello, Roland," she said.

For a brief moment he was not frightened. He took a step forward, and she stood. Her cool hand held his, and he completely forgot Boris, and the others, and their families, and the unbearable tension in his chest. "What happened?" he said.

Her other hand floated to her neck. "Oh, they don't know what it is. They think it's a rash of some kind."

"You're a big city doctor," her father said. "Maybe you can talk some sense into them."

"Just pre-med," Roland said.

Julia dropped his hand and looked at her parents. "Daddy, could I talk to Roland alone?"

That started another argument. They didn't want him alone with her, the assumed concern being his crazy talk. But they finally relented. Before leaving, her father leaned close to Roland and said, "We'll be right outside the door. Don't try anything."

Roland nodded. They left and the door closed. She smiled and took his hand again, and pulled him to a chair beside the bed. He sat on it while she sat on the bed, still with his hand folded into both of hers. So broad was her grin that she seemed unable to speak.

"You never married," he said.

"And you?"

"No."

She laughed lightly. "Do you remember in high school, we nailed blocks to the wall and hid them behind the ivy vines so you could sneak into my room?"

"I remember."

"They're still there. Daddy never found them and I never took them down." Tears grew in her eyes, but she didn't cry. "I couldn't leave, Roland. Even though you begged me. I couldn't get married, even though you left."

"You still can."

She closed her eyes. Because of that, a tear leaked out.

"Come with me," he said. "I'm going to medical school. We'll live cheaply, I'll take care of you, you'll have a good life. All you have to do is leave."

"I can't, Roland. I'm too sick."

"You're not sick."

She yanked her hands away. "Don't talk like that. They'll hear you!"

They had reached their old impasse. He twisted his fingers together as the tension returned. He tried to think of something to say, something new that would change her mind, but he could only press his lips together in frustration.

She glanced up in fear at the walls. He wondered why, until at that moment a thing came into the room. He recognized it. He had seen it many times, hovering around her, pushing her into car doors, stealing her things, cutting her with its sharp nails so her parents could call her a clumsy child. Apparently it had tired of her after so many years. It came over, wrapped its strong fingers around her neck, and began to strangle her.

It overtook him as well. For a moment, sitting there in numbed shock, he could not move or speak as she gasped for breath, faltered, and fell back onto the pillows. She beat her heels on the mattress. She gagged and struggled. What she did not do was try to remove its hands from around her neck.

He did what everyone else seemed unable to do. He took a deep breath, and swallowed, and found his voice. "Julia!" he hissed, fearful that those outside the door might hear his crazy talk. "I know you can see it!"

"Shut up!" the thing said in its dripping voice, so loudly that they should have heard it outside. But the door remained closed.

Julia could not breathe. In rising terror, Roland did something even he thought he could never do. He stood and leaped to the bed. He wrapped one arm around the thing from behind and with the other hand tried to pry it loose. It was big and strong. It shrugged him off, and he stumbled to the floor and against the chair, which banged into the wall.

The door flew open. "What the hell!" her father said. He lunged past Roland and sat on the bed. As the thing continued strangling the life out of her, he brushed the hair from her brow and looked with concern at her grimacing face. Then he stood again. He was a large man and levered himself up by setting one hand on the thing's shoulder.

"Call the doctor," he said to his wife, who stood in the doorway. As she went running off, he aimed a finger at Roland. "And you! Get out of here!"

Roland gained his feet. He took a step and said, "Julia . . ."

"Get out!"

He came at Roland and shoved him to the door. Roland went downstairs where her mother was talking on the phone. From the stairwell came the sounds of Julia choking and struggling on the bed. Her mother hung up the phone. Roland paced back and forth, and neither of them spoke. The thing was playing with Julia, letting her breathe for a moment and then choking her again, while her mother sat miserably on the couch and Roland twisted his fingers together. When her father came down to ask about the doctor, he saw Roland in the living room and demanded that he leave.

Roland walked out to the driveway. He stood there for a moment, then went to sit in his car. When another car pulled up and a doctor rushed into the house, Roland started the engine and drove away. He went to the park and sat on the bench, twisting his fingers together and wondering how long it would let her live.

Boris appeared. This time it did not sit down, but stood over Roland, who tried to press himself into the bench. He fully expected to get hit again, but Boris only said, "I came to tell you she's dead. We killed her."

Looking at his hands, Roland said, "No, she's not."

"You think I'd lie about something like that? It's the best day of my life."

"I know you would."

"You're so smart, don't take my word for it. She's dead. Find out for yourself."

Then it was gone again, leaving two moist stains on the grass where its feet had been. Roland sat looking at the marks. His back was stiff, his neck sore. His fingers had twisted so tightly about each other that they hurt. Suddenly he pulled himself up from the bench. He hurried across the street to a phone booth beside the store, dropped in a coin, and dialed her number.

Her father answered, and Roland identified himself.

"You again," her father said.

"Can I speak to her?"

"No."

"What did the doctor say?"

"She's worse. We may have to move her to the hospital permanently. And Roland, you're not welcome back."

The buzz of a dial tone pierced Roland's ear. He hung up and leaned his sweating forehead against the cool metal of the phone. In a sense, Boris had not lied. Roland knew with a clear certainty that if she went into the hospital, she would never come out again.


AT TWO IN the morning, he quietly packed his suitcase and left the house. He feared his parents would discover him. He feared her parents and her thing. But mostly, he feared Boris would show up.

He opened the trunk and put the suitcase inside, then he dug out the trinket box with the winged woman painted on the lid. He tipped it back and forth to hear the rolling inside. This time he did not return it to the trunk. He carried it to the front seat and pulled away from the curb with the headlights off so they would not shine into the house.

He turned them on for the drive over, and turned them off again as he parked around the corner from her house. With the trinket box in his hand, he walked up and around the block. The night was chilly. The stars shone in a bright spattering across the sky and his breath misted in front of his face, but he did not shiver. He stepped across the lawn, careful not to trip in the darkness over the hose snaking out from the bushes, or step on the dry branch hiding in the ivy bed that would have snapped loudly. He found the vines beneath her window and pushed them aside. As she had promised, the little blocks of wood still formed a ladder up the wall. Climbing it was difficult. He had to shove the box under his arm and push the vines aside, worrying all the while that someone in the house might hear him, or that Boris might appear and push him to the ground.

At the top, he tapped on her window. It was a code she would remember, three and two like a full house in a poker hand. She was asleep and it took a few tries. Finally a light came on and a moment later the window slid open.

"Roland!" she whispered, then giggled.

"Step back," he said.

She did so. He rolled over the sill and into the bedroom. The bruise across her neck had grown and darkened. Seeing him looking at it, she touched it lightly with her fingertips.

"I'm getting worse. They're taking me to the hospital in the morning."

"I'll ask you once more, Julia. Come away with me."

Fear flashed across her eyes, then she giggled again. "No."

"You'll die."

"You're talking crazy, Roland. This is exactly why our parents got between us."

"Do you trust me, Julia?"

She looked at him, not so much fearfully as somberly, and she nodded.

"Then turn around," he said.

She grinned at him, as if he was playing a game. He was not. She looked somber again. She gathered the nightclothes tight about her neck, and turned. Roland opened the box. Inside was a small amber bottle and a clean rag. He set the box on the floor, opened the bottle, and poured out a clear liquid onto the rag. With this, he reached around and covered her mouth.

She struggled at first and he had to fight against her flailing arms. But he managed to put her to sleep. He wanted to take the bottle with him, but found he could not get the box and her body down at the same time. So he settled for her alone. He struggled with her, nearly dropped her for one horrific moment halfway down, and finally reached the bed of ivy. He did not have the will to go back for the ether.

He stuffed her into the trunk. When he had driven far enough from the house, he turned the lights on. There were no other cars on the streets. Lights in the houses were out, doors were closed, and people slept. He came to a stoplight at the corner of the park. He wanted to get out of town quickly, but worried what would happen if a policeman should stop him, so he waited patiently. He looked at the darkened park, at the benches and the trees and the playground, setting it in his mind because he knew this would be the last time he would ever see it.

He had become calm. Thinking about Julia, he had for a time overcome the simmering apprehension of Testaville. But then the light turned green. At that moment the hand gripped his heart again, his breath came short in his lungs, and Boris appeared on the seat beside him.

"Kidnapping, Roland? That's no way to start a new life!"

Something splattered as Boris stomped on his foot. The engine surged and the car shot forward. Roland lost control of the wheel. He tried to turn and went too far, and the car slewed through the intersection and onto the sidewalk and slammed into a telephone pole. The engine died.

Blinking, Roland looked around. Boris was gone. The right fender and headlight were smashed and the car was tilted at a mad angle half into the street. Roland closed his eyes and took a deep breath. Then he turned the key, chanting, "Please start. Please, just start . . . "

It did. He carefully pulled off the curb. He wanted to open the trunk and check on Julia, but he was too frightened. Instead, he kept driving.

This time Boris let him get to the edge of town. It was part of the game, the same as throwing him off the roof but not high enough to kill him, or telling him Julia was dead when she wasn't. Just as houses fell away on either side and gave way to open starlit fields, Boris was suddenly in the seat beside him again, laughing as it said, "Let's try that again!"

Roland was trying to watch the trees and hills, but Boris' foot slid toward the pedal again. Roland let go of the wheel with one hand and hit Boris in the face. Boris looked shocked. It reached out and smashed Roland's head into the window. The glass didn't break, but it dazed him, and once again, Boris stomped on his foot.

They skewed onto the shoulder and back to the road as Boris clamped its hands onto the wheel. "You'll die!" it said, laughing wildly. "You and the girl. I'll just come back, you know that!"

Roland thought he had recognized a tree flashing by in the single headlight. He stopped fighting. He wriggled his foot out from under its foot, and took his hands off the wheel.

"You win. Just kill me."

"About time you learned that. Maybe I will. Maybe I'll kill you both right now."

Boris wrenched the wheel again. The car slid over the shoulder with such force that Roland bounced in the seat. But this time, as the headlight swept across a field beside the road, he was certain he recognized it and knew exactly where they were.

"Idiot!" Boris said. "Did you think I'd take you all the way out?"

The car slowed almost to a crawl. Boris began turning the wheel about. They crossed the line separating the two lanes. Roland had crammed himself as far as he could into the seat and still would not look at Boris.

"No," he said. "But you keep thinking I won't fight you."

He jammed his foot onto Boris' foot. The car lunged forward again and Boris yanked on the wheel with both hands, causing the car to veer completely off the road.

"I'm the only one who ever would!" Roland said.

He fought for the wheel. They bounced back over the shoulder and Boris slammed Roland's head twice more into the window, the second time shattering it. The third time, Boris' hand went cleanly through Roland's head as if it wasn't there.

Roland felt his foot drop all the way to the accelerator. He turned his head just in time to see Boris fade completely away.

He kept driving. The fear flowed from him like water pouring down off a hill. He had almost made it to the next curve when he suddenly remembered Julia. He slammed the brakes and came to a screeching stop. He ran around to the trunk and opened it. Julia lay inside, unconscious, with her face bruised where she had banged it. But she was breathing normally and her pulse was strong. Roland lifted her out and set her gently in the back seat. He didn't want her waking up alone and frightened in the trunk.

He started the engine again, then looked in the mirror. His face was bloody and battered. He wiped the blood away with his sleeve until he could see well enough to drive. Then he put the car into gear and started off again, thinking he could not go back to his apartment in Athens. He would have to clean out his bank account, get far ahead of the police, hide her until he could explain what he had done and help her understand. He was thinking he would need a map of Canada when he glanced into the mirror again.

It stood in the road, in the shadows and moonlight, stopped at the border. The farther he drove the smaller it became, until he rounded a curve and it disappeared completely from sight.

---

**M. ALAN FORD** lives and works in the Valley, dude. He's fifty years old and spends his time working, reading, writing, and engaging in various other studious pursuits. His interests are category fiction of all kinds and academic subjects of all kinds. He has a B.A. in Psychology and stays in school as much as he can. It's a hobby. Some people build model planes, M. Alan Ford attends school.

# STONE

by Catherine MacLeod

SOMETIMES THE LAST PERSON YOU EXPECT TO SEE shows up in the last place you imagined finding her. And here she is now.

(A six letter-word for *encounter*: impact.)

She used to call herself Stone. I have to look twice, but no, she's not a figment of my imagination. She's dressed just well enough to go unnoticed. Long sleeves, high collar, no surprise there. She's brunette now, wearing gold-rimmed glasses she probably doesn't need. A gym bag and a coat over her arm. It's strange to see her shifting her own luggage; her assigned bodyguard usually did it for her. I remember him, vaguely. How she killed him is anyone's guess.

She never told her clients her real name. I wanted to know, but most of the others didn't. Her pimp said the alias came from the old saying, *You can't get blood from a stone.*

Don't believe it: she bled like nobody's business.

The ticket clerk wakes up as she says, "Hello?" A whiskey alto, never pitched higher than necessary, and always the first thing I recall about her. "I'd like a place on the next bus, please."

"How far?"

"End of the line."

I could have guessed—Stone's heading for Andu. Where else? Me too. There'll be a few stops before we get there, but most people headed that way tend to keep going. It's the end of the line in more ways than one: a good place for people who want to disappear. Not good for the faint-hearted, though—what gets you arrested here barely raises eyebrows in Andu.

The only crime there is getting caught.

Stone is the most frightening woman I've ever known. She'll do well, I'm sure. She always had a way about her: gracefully feral, treacherously kind. She left as many scars as she got, but deeper. I can still feel them all.

They say you never forget your first love.

I TRY NOT to stare, but fail. After all this time she's still horribly beautiful. But when she goes to the ladies' room I glance around.

I like people-watching. A bus station is a good place for it any time. This late at night it's perfect. The wind's picking up; there's rain on the way. It's a fit night for leaving this life, one way or another. We won't all take the same route, of course.

On the bench across from me a young woman shakes a half-dozen capsules from a bread bag and washes them down with Styrofoam-flavored coffee. She casts one cautious glance at the security guard, who's maybe the only unarmed person here, and ignores the rest of us. The businessman beside her is more modest. He opens his briefcase for cover, but a little coke still blows off his hand and dusts his leather shoes. Nobody cares.

Or almost nobody. The young mother beside me hoists her baby closer and takes a firmer grip on her purse. The child is nursing. A carefully-arranged fold of blanket hides the act. I don't find it offensive, but for whatever reasons, some do. My mother once said she stopped nursing me because I wouldn't stop biting, but this woman doesn't have that problem. She seems content, if watchful. The baby's quiet.

I've heard it said that a woman's breasts are the hardest pillow.

They're not.

A middle-aged man carries his bag-wrapped bottle off to a dim corner. I could be wrong about the middle-aged part, but the young aren't usually so discreet about indulging their appetites. Certainly not the boy at the snack machine, eating his fifth candy bar.

I enjoy seeing people feed their cravings. The only one I indulge in public is a penchant for crossword puzzles. I love learning new words.

Only one person knows what I hunger for in private. And Stone doesn't care.


(A SIX-LETTER word meaning *common occurrence:* cliché.)

Uninitiated young man, experienced older woman. How much older I don't know; to me, Stone seemed timeless. But naked she looked ancient.

Her clothes rustle softly as she sits beside me now. I remember every seam of the body under them. I was far from her first. She had scars the first time I met her. She wore them like gold leaf.

They were actually that expensive.

I slide down the bench to make room. "Excuse me, you probably shouldn't leave your bag on the floor. Sometimes things go missing."

She sets it between us. "All right. Thank you." There's no recognition in her brief smile. I didn't expect it. I was nothing to her but another serrated blade. But even those few words take me back. Stone speaks as if she's waiting to tell you a secret or trying to hold back laughter. She was always more courtesan than hustler.

I've met other women who sold their bodies, but none with Stone's verve. Her clients sliced and sawed. They stapled and stitched. They ornamented her with teeth marks. Once I saw a woman take a bite out of her upper arm, chew, swallow, and smile.

"Another satisfied consumer," Stone quipped as her surgeon patched the wound, and even he chuckled. Her indifference was charming.

She had a patron skilled in trapunto, a craft usually practiced on fabric. Objects are inserted under folds of cloth to make patterns. Most tailors use cotton batting. This one used screws and roofing nails.

"Lovely," Stone breathed. "Will I scar like that when you remove them?"

She did. This refined creature beside me is adorned with puckers like white orchids.

So many kinds of sex, and she accommodated them all. My favorite memory is of the night a client came in with a gang rape fantasy. Stone didn't have enough holes for everyone, so they cut a couple of new ones. She was blonde at the time. Redhead when they were done.

(*Whore* is an active verb.)

Stone in a bus station. I'd laugh, but I don't want to be noticed any more than she does. I can't resist a grin, though: a private joke between Stone and me. Very private, in fact, since she doesn't know I'm in on it. At one time kings sent private jets to fetch her. She plied her trade on yachts. Nobody would think to look for her here.

But someone is looking. The police, maybe. Business associates. Her pimp would never release a money-maker like Stone unless she cut her way loose. Probably with a straight-razor; she always did like those. She'd have to vanish now even if she didn't want to.

People with Stone's malady have a short life expectancy. For her, paranoia would be both habit and virtue.

Somewhere she has money stashed. Cash, maybe; diamonds, certainly. We gave her hundreds of them. It would have been an insult to give her mere roses. She could live well on blackmail for the rest of what's left of her life; but you can't commit blackmail and go unseen. She has her escape planned too well for such risks to be necessary.

The bus pulls in and a slow flutter of movement curls through the waiting room. Stone nods her thanks as I hold the door for her. As she passes I catch a whiff of mild soap, probably antibacterial.

When the last passenger gets off, we board to find seats. And a terrible wonder occurs, a reminder of Stone's particular grace. She packs her bag in the overhead compartment while stepping out of the young mother's way, and doesn't notice when the door slips and drops hard on her fingers.

She starts as I cover her hand with mine. "Please, sit down. You're hurt."

"Oh, it's just a scratch."

"May I sit here?"

"Of course."

I wrap my handkerchief around her hand as the bus fills. "You're going to have a bruise."

"I'll be fine. It won't bother me."

It would be rude of me to say, *I know.*

Stone feels no pain. Her pimp once tried to explain the syndrome that afflicts her. An insensibility to hot and cold, an inability to cry. I brushed him off. It was better not to know. We paid for the mystery.

But a woman who'll sell her breasts to the highest bidder is a magnificent rarity.

I still have them.


BEFORE TONIGHT I was a highly visible man. Vice-president of a company that makes nutritional supplements. I know something about appetites.

And about dropping out of sight when necessary.

This is the last time I'll go missing. I'm ready for it—just weathered enough to look ordinary; gray enough to look proper; dressed well enough to go unnoticed. Anonymity has its privileges. The unnamed can dine at their leisure. They have a whole world of experience at their fingertips.

I glance down at Stone's. They're starting to swell. It was really her hands I wanted back then, but they weren't for sale. Her hands and face were never touched during sex, allowing her to pass in the outside world. Intimacy was always followed by surgery, but even that had its appeal.

(Seven-letter word for *sex*: variety.)

Stone's breasts are as smooth now as the day I took them. Her only reaction to their loss was a slight wince at the sound of the electric carving knife.

It was erotic as hell.

You never forget your first time—the sighs, the anticipation, those first delicate drops of blood. I wanted it to last. I licked every crease and ridge, memorizing her ruined skin. My hands were actually trembling as I held her breasts, warm, soft.

Oh, soft. The others could tell it was my first cut, but I didn't care.

Stone didn't do private service, was never without a doctor and a bodyguard. It would have been like leaving the Star of India unprotected. Public sex isn't usually one of my kinks, but I was as indifferent to it then as Stone is to pain. And, it depends on the circumstances. I had a public persona to protect. That didn't stop me because no one in that particular audience could afford to talk.

I've often felt the need for discretion since then.

"I'm okay," she murmurs. She's caught me looking at her hands. "They don't hurt."

"Good."

"Are you meeting someone in Andu?" she asks politely. She knows. The last stop was an hour ago.

"Yes. You?"

"No, I'm just passing through."

I've heard there are places on the other side of Andu, but you won't find them on any map and you'd have to be mad to go. Could be. I believe there's always something beyond the end of the line—and I've always known Stone was insane. But it's an elegant madness.

I wasn't lying to her about meeting someone. I'm sure I will eventually. I'd hoped for a blonde at first, but now, after seeing Stone again, I believe I'd prefer wavy dark hair.

No other woman has ever quite measured up to her. Some have lasted longer than others, but I've never found in another woman what I found in her. I've left quite a trail of broken hearts in the search, I admit. But still, a first love is just that: your first.

THE RAIN SILVERS the windows, turning them into mirrors. Everyone finds something to do; no one wants to look at themselves too closely.

I start my second crossword. (Ten letters for *witch*: seductress.)

(Five letters, *to punish a sorceress:* stone.)

I saw her burned with cigarettes, hot steel, dripping wax. I watched needles pierce silky anatomy; soldering irons crinkle flesh like ugly snowflakes; pliers extract uncommon souvenirs. And not a cry from Stone, not a whimper or a sigh. Once, an exquisite, unrehearsed yawn. Her "Excuse me" drew applause.

The man pulling her toenails was thrilled.

Her pimp had rules, but not many, and none of them unreasonable—no extraction of internal organs, no marring of hands and face. They left us leeway. Only once did a client step out of line. He wanted her tongue, and drew his razor too quickly for the guard to react.

His own tongue was flopping in Stone's fist before he could scream. He screamed afterward, of course, as her guard threw him out. I remember it was raining that night, too. I don't think I ever loved her more.

He was stupid, trying to take more when Stone already allowed us so much. Some people never know when to quit.

I know.

I've traveled; I've indulged my cravings. I've collected enough treasures to create a physically perfect woman, if my talents included needlework. I've collected enough words to teach several languages. Perhaps in Andu I'll try both.

Stone knows when to quit. Behind those new glasses her eyes live up to her name. If they're the windows of the soul, hers look in on a place I don't care to revisit.

But there's no need. I've learned almost everything I ever wanted to know about her. No one asks a whore why she whores, but I don't need to.

There's so little of her body left to identify her as human, much less female. She sold it for exorbitant sums. I'll bet the price of her breasts she got out of the life because she ran out of saleable parts. No one goes through that for new shoes.

Stone's craving for money was born of hunger. Not long ago, curious, wondering if she *could* feel hunger—isn't it a kind of pain?—I did a few minutes' research. Yes, Stone can feel it—and I'm sure she did. She simply refused to give in.

When faced with starvation, the body will consume itself rather than succumb. I believe at some time in her youth Stone went mad with hunger.

But, I could say that of so many people.


THE DRIVER SAYS, "Andu in ten minutes."

There's one more word I've always wanted to learn.

I unwrap her hand. My handkerchief is flawlessly stained. "Not too bad. Maybe the bruise will fade quickly."

"I'll be careful." I take down her gym bag as the bus pulls in. "Thanks for your help." She moves as if to shake hands, and stops in mid-reach. It's the only time I recall seeing her flustered. I'm enchanted.

Boldly, I bow and brush my lips across her fingers, kissing them better. "It was a pleasure meeting you." I look her in the eye, and lie. "My name is Thomas."

"My name is Jade."

I let her exit first, out of courtesy and the urge not to be caught grinning. How could I not appreciate such a play on words? She vanishes into the rain like a ghost, this woman who taught me to love. This mystery who craves security more than affection.

Who still didn't tell me her real name.

(A four-letter word for *whore:* jade.)

But it's still a beautiful stone.

---

Nova Scotian writer **CATHERINE MACLEOD** has published short fiction in *On Spec*, *TaleBones*, *Black Static*, and several anthologies, including *The Living Dead 2* and the upcoming *Tesseracts Fourteen*. She shares a birthday with Bram Stoker, a fact which delights her to no end.

She's always loved jade.

# CAMPBELL'S POND

BY BRIAN KNIGHT

---

LESTER WAS A FAT, PALE, PIMPLY BOY. SIXTEEN YEARS old, and he had made only a few friends in his life.

Girlfriends? None.

As bad as things were for him at his old home in Missoula, city living had its advantages. He could always trade the hostile faces at his school or neighborhood for the merely indifferent ones a few blocks away where no one knew him.

Then came Uncle Frank.

Uncle, right.

Uncle Frank was an Indian of no tribe in particular, at least none he'd admit to, and fancied himself a Medicine Man. His medicine was meth, and after Lester's mom was thoroughly hooked on the shit Frank cooked, their house had become his house.

The arrangement had started with Frank crashing and eating there and Lester's Mom would get free product. But it wasn't long before Frank was living there full time, cooking his product, and treating Lester's mom like a fuck doll.

Then came the bust, which was good because it meant no more Uncle Frank, but bad because it meant no more Mom.

Now Lester lived with his real uncle in Pierce, and his already troubled social life had taken a definite turn from bad to worse.

Pierce was a speck of a town in the mountains of northern Idaho, and had nothing to interest him. No arcades, no music stores, no bookstores . . . even the closest Wal-Mart was almost a hundred miles away.

What Pierce *did* have was a small grocery store, a bar, a single convenience store/gas station, another bar, a lodge with two dozen new cabins built in anticipation of Lewis & Clark Centennial tourists who never came, a sports shop (for hunting and fishing supplies) next to a third bar, and a small, rickety hotel, with a bar in the lobby.

Pierce also had approximately five hundred residents, almost half of them unemployed since the local plywood mill closed down, all of whom spent the bulk of their time drinking and getting into each other's business.

His real uncle, not a Frank but a Larry, didn't have cable TV, so Lester spent most of his time in his room reading and re-reading the same dog-eared books he'd brought with him.

Lester had no friends in Pierce, which was nothing new, but in a small town there was no place to hide from the local kids, who had taken an instant dislike to him. Their favorite new sport was pounding Lester whenever they caught him outside, so he only went out at night if he could help it. His uncle was usually gone at night, his preferred haunt was The Flame Bar and Grill, and he slept through most of the day, so Lester didn't have to spend much time with him.

Sunday nights were the exception. By state law the bars stayed closed on Sunday, so after waking some time in the early afternoon, Lester's uncle spent the rest of the day sulking around the small house, yelling at anyone who called on the telephone, yelling at the evening news, and yelling at Lester to walk to the Mini-Mart and pick him up his beer.

Uncle Larry had a special relationship with the woman at the Mini-Mart, one that prohibited him from going within a hundred yards of her. She was happy to break the 'no beer to minors' rule to keep Uncle Larry safely away from the Mini-Mart.

These trips usually happened at twilight, so Lester would take a long route through cluttered, dusty alleys to avoid the town boys, and once at the little store he hurried to get out before one of them happened to stop by. This approach had been largely successful, much to his relief. He didn't want to know how Uncle Larry would react if someone stole his beer on the return trip.

It was on one of these Sunday trips that Lester got the surprise of his life from a girlfriend of one of his most enthusiastic tormentors.


"HAVING A PARTY?" She stepped from behind the chip rack as Lester heaved a case of Keystone from the cooler.

Lester closed his eyes and prepared for the worst. He knew that voice, everyone knew it. Every penis-equipped person in Pierce wondered what it would be like to hear it moan into their ear or shout his name in the height of ecstasy. It belonged to the hottest girl in town. The girl, Samantha Zenner, belonged to Rick Durham, the person Lester least liked to hear saying his name.

*Might as well get it over with*, Lester thought, and turned.

Rick was not there. Samantha was alone.

Lester blinked, scanned the aisles on either side of her, but Rick's grinning face was nowhere in sight. Finally remembering to breathe, Lester hitched in a deep one.

She stood in front of him, arms crossed under her plump and perky breasts, her bright blue eyes moving from his face to the case hanging from his hand, then back again.

"Is it a private party or do I get an invite?" Her impatient foot tapping caused her already short denim skirt to ride up a few inches.

"It's for my uncle." He searched the mostly empty store again. "Where's Rick?"

Her narrow smile vanished. She raised an eyebrow. "You that anxious to run into him?"

"No," he said quickly. Too quickly. He felt his cheeks glowing with embarrassment. "I just thought . . . "

She stepped closer to him, and words failed. He couldn't honestly verbalize what he was thinking.

"If I know Rick, he's off at The Log Yard fucking some hillbilly skank."

The Log Yard was an actual log yard. Durham Logging, owned by Rick's dad, put to use most nights by Rick and his friends as a place to get drunk and fuck girls.

Samantha took another step toward him, and Lester had to fight an urge to retreat. She poked him in the chest with a long, pink fingernail.

"Do you want to party with me or do I need to go find someone else?" She gripped his arm high up and pulled him close, her breasts pushing against him, and whispered in his ear. "This could be your lucky night. I want to get drunk and I want to fuck. If you want some of this, then make a fucking move or I'll find someone else to party with."

*She's only doing this to get even with Rick*, he thought.

*Rick will kick my ass*, he thought.

*Uncle Larry will kick my ass worse*, he thought.

*It's fucking worth it*, he thought.

"Where do you want to go?"


SAMANTHA DROVE HER father's pickup out of town and down the narrow, twisted highway as twilight sank into night. Lester couldn't help but notice the way she absentmindedly stroked the gear shifter's knob with her right hand.

"You ever fuck before?" She gave him a quick, speculative glance before facing forward again to negotiate a sharp twist in the road. She shifted down, and Lester watched her skirt ride up her thighs as she worked the pedals. She did not attempt to pull it back down. "Lester?"

*Answer her, dumb ass.*

It was his big brother, Charlie's voice. Charlie always came to him at awkward moments to coach or berate him.

Lester thought he should lie and say yes. Tonight appeared to be a sure thing, but he didn't want to look like a total loser.

"No," he said.

*Shit.*

Samantha giggled, and drove on.

"Where are we going?" Lester had never been this way before. The road had taken a decisive downward slant, and Lester wondered if she was taking him to the bottom of the mountain. He knew there was a river in the valley below. Maybe they were going skinny-dipping first.

Lester imagined a look of disgust on Samantha's face at seeing him naked, and felt sick to his stomach.

*Good thing you brought a whole case, little bro. You'd better get her shit-faced before you show her your man-tits.*

"Have you heard of Campbell's Pond?"

"Uh, no," Lester said, though the name did sound familiar to him. He liked the sound of her voice, and if he could keep her talking, there would be fewer uncomfortable questions about him.

"It's an old campground down the highway a little ways." A car passed coming the other way and honked. Samantha waved out the window and honked twice in return. "It has about twenty camping spots with fire-pits, tables, bathrooms, and it's all around a big pond. It used to be popular, but a few years ago a boy from town got lost there. He never turned up, and when a reporter came to do a story about it she disappeared too."

"Sounds creepy," Lester said, then wished he hadn't.

*God, you sound like a wimp.*

"A little," Samantha said, and winked at him. "Not too creepy, I hope."

Lester laughed nervously and shook his head.

"After the reporter disappeared, another boy fell in the pond and drowned. They never found him either."

A long, straight stretch opened up before them, and Samantha shifted up again, putting on speed. Her skirt rode a little higher; Lester could see the color of her panties.

*Pink!*

His dick, which had spent the last half hour in a state of semi-hard anticipation, pushed at the crotch of his pants. He crossed his hands over his lap.

"So no one goes there anymore," she continued. "Someone blocked the road that leads to it with trees. The Forest Service won't even maintain it. I mean, why bother? No one uses it."

"Oh," Lester said. He tried to think of something better to say. "Have you ever been there?"

"Only once, during the day. There it is," Samantha said, slowing and pointing to a faded sign in the truck's headlights.

*Campbell's Pond—5 miles.*

A newer neon orange sign below it read, *Closed To The Public*.

A narrow dirt road forked off the main road, swallowed by the trees.

"Wow," Lester said. "It's a long way in there."

"Uh-huh," Samantha said. "And since no one comes here, we can do anything we want without getting caught."

Lester suddenly found it hard to breathe. He tried to say something witty but only managed a weak croak.

Samantha leaned close to him as she slowed and turned onto the dirt road. "You've got almost five miles to think about how you want to do me," she said, and placed a hand on his thigh.

"Oh Jesus," he said, panting, almost hyperventilating.

This was just too good to be real.

As if reading that thought, Samantha slid her hand along his leg and squeezed, reminding Lester that she was real.


LESTER WATCHED THE odometer turn and almost groaned when Samantha stopped the truck a half-mile shy of their destination. The road was still blocked. Two old logs lay crisscrossed in their path. A sign, fixed at the crux of the decomposing logs read *God Damned This Place*.

"I guess we're going back now," he said, not able to keep the pouting tone from his voice.

"Uh . . . no," Samantha said, and giggled. "You can walk, can't you?"

She tore open his uncle's case of beer and opened one, tipping it back and guzzling the whole can. After an unladylike belch, she tossed the can out of her open window and snatched another as she stepped from the cab.

Lester grabbed the case and followed. When he tried to pull a beer out for himself, she slapped his hand.

"Not for you, big boy. I want you focused."

She straddled the logs briefly as she climbed over them, pausing to throw a sly glance back at Lester. Then she slid her leg over, showing more panty, and waited for him.

He set the beer down and worked his first leg carefully over the logs. He was much heavier than Samantha, and not nearly as limber. He heaved and strained for a moment, and almost fell over the other side.

When he was finished he found Samantha holding the beer in the crook of her left arm. Her pink panties hung from the index finger of her tilted right hand. She flipped them at him, but his clumsy swipe was too slow. They hit his face, hanging for a moment from his nose before he snatched them off.

She ran down the road ahead of him, looking back once to smile as she flipped the backside of her skirt up, exposing herself. He saw her ass for just a moment; it was perfect, shining pale pink in the moonlight.

"Come and get some, Lester."

Then the dark swallowed her, and Lester ran to catch up.


WHEN LESTER FOUND the lake minutes later he was out of breath. He stumbled to a stop and fell to his knees next to a cast-off sign that read *Closed For The Season* in faded letters. For a moment he thought he was going to puke, and he fought his gorge. He couldn't see Samantha, but he knew she was there somewhere, watching, waiting for him to find her.

He thought his chances of actually getting laid would suffer if she saw him puking his guts up in the dirt.

When his trembling legs would support him again, he rose and scanned the area. There was the pond, its water dark and still, and a few nearby camp spaces, littered with what might have been years of old trash.

No Samantha.

He walked the remaining distance to the lake.

Closer, Lester saw the outline of a dock that was poking into the dark water from the shore of a pond-side camp spot. Tied to a post at the end of it, a dilapidated raft rocked lazily. He spotted his beer at the foot of the dock, and smiled.

He jogged the remaining distance and paused before reaching the dock. The case of beer was a few cans emptier. A discarded T-shirt, bra, and denim mini-skirt lay in the dust next to it.

A hand slid by his cheek, coming from behind, and Lester screeched as it closed over his eyes, blinding him.

"You're excitable," Samantha said, slapping the back of his head as he tried to face her.

"Hey," he said, reaching up to rub his smarting head.

"No you don't," Samantha said, giggling again, a sound Lester now associated with lust and the perfumed smell of her panties, which now slipped from his grasp and dropped next to her pile of clothes. "We're going to do this my way, to start."

"Okay," Lester said, trembling.

"Keep your eyes closed," she said, and he felt her hand slide away. "Now take your clothes off."

This was the moment Lester dreaded. He'd hoped it would be too dark for her to see him, but he knew she could see him perfectly well in the moonlight cast against the lake. He did it with only the slightest hesitation though, starting with his shirt. He shook so badly he almost tripped stepping out of his pants.

"Wow! Nice package," Samantha said from behind him, and he felt himself blush, his face burning with embarrassment, and a little pride.

He kicked off his underwear, hoping she didn't notice the skid-marks that inevitably decorated every pair he'd ever owned, and waited.

"Keep your eyes closed," she said, grabbing his arms from behind and guiding him onto the dock. It rocked beneath him, water splashing up between the worn and slimy boards to drench his feet. For just the barest moment he felt flesh press against his back, and thought, *it's a nipple*!

*Hold your wad, bro*, the voice of his brother spoke in his head. *You don't want to blow it over a nipple do you*?

Finally she stopped, and he stopped with her, ready to take whatever direction she gave. "Just one last step," she said. "You don't want to miss the raft, so make it a big one."

But they did not take the last step. She held him in place. He felt her press against his back again, and her breath tickled the hair on the nape of his neck.

"Have you ever been fucked in a cemetery?"

"Uh . . . " he said, but she cut him off with another giggle.

"Of course you haven't. You've never been fucked at all. You're going to be fucked in a cemetery tonight."

"What?" Unease stabbed at his excitement.

"We're standing over one right now," she said. "Beneath the water. Some crazy preacher dammed up a creek and flooded it, but it's still down there. They found headstones when they were looking for that boy."

She urged Lester forward, and he took the last step reluctantly.

A cemetery under the pond?

"Lay down, I'll be right there."

Lester lay down, his lust cooling a little when water lapped at his backside from between damp, warped boards.

The raft rocked and whispered through the dark water.

He waited, the night air blowing cool kisses on his naked skin.

The giggle came again, this time from farther away.

Lester opened his eyes and groaned when he saw her standing on the dock. Her skirt hung crooked on her hips as she tugged her shirt back into place.

Standing behind her was Rick Dunham, and what remained of Lester's case of beer was hanging from his meat-hook hand. Lester's clothes were bundled under Rick's other arm. His laughter boomed across the pond. He raised an open can in mock-salute.

"Now you've been fucked in a cemetery, Lester," Samantha said, and her giggle dissolved into shrieking laughter.

*She's got a point, bro. You certainly are fucked.*

Samantha waved goodbye before following Rick onto the dark path that led away from Campbell's Pond.


LESTER JUST LAY there for a while, gazing into the sky at a fat, pale moon, trying not to cry; a fat, pale slug of a boy, stranded and naked on a wet old raft. Pondweed and water washed up between the warped boards and slapped his backside. His arms spread wide, his fingers brushed the dark water.

"Ouch!"

He jerked his right arm up, shaking his hand. Something had bitten him. He pulled his other hand from the water and sat up, examining the stinging middle finger of the injured hand.

A spot of blood welled from a tiny cut on the tip, just below the fingernail.

Even the fish had it in for him tonight.

*You plan to stick around here forever, bro?*

Lester sighed and scanned the shore. He didn't see Samantha or Rick, not that he'd thought they would stick around, but he wanted to make sure before going back to shore. His long trip back to town would be embarrassing enough without an audience, but he didn't know what he'd do if he had to face them again.

He would have to face them again, though. In a town as small as Pierce there was no getting around it.

He rolled onto his belly and slid closer to the edge of the raft so he could paddle back to the dock. His "package" had flopped into a crack between two boards, and he felt water splash up against it. He arched his back and slid to the side. He could imagine the fish down there, gazing up at what might look like a fat pink worm, trying to take a bite out of it as they had his finger.

Samantha had complimented him on his "package" earlier, but he imagined her driving back to town, or wherever they were headed with his uncle's beer, laughing to Rick about it.

The story would be all over town within hours. Everyone would know.

Lester cursed his mother for what might have been the millionth time. The selfish old junkie cunt. It was her fault he was stuck here in this redneck-infested shithole.

His mom had assured him the move was not permanent. A few months, a year at most, and she'd be out of jail with her shit all together again. But he had a feeling when she did get out, she'd pull a quick fade and resume her life as a junkie whore in a new place.

*When you get a job and make enough money to go out on your own?*

Lester had thought about trying to reach Charles, he had the number for the institution he stayed in, but Uncle Larry wouldn't allow it.

"Someone puts themselves in the boobie hatch is even crazier than the ones that get put there," Larry said, then told Lester to shut up so he could watch NASCAR.

*Fuck 'em,* Charles said in Lester's head. *Fuck 'em all. Just because everyone else in our family is screwed up doesn't mean you have to suffer.*

"Fuck 'em," Lester said, dipping his hands into the water and paddling, beginning his humiliating trip out of Campbell's Pond. "I'm out of here."

It would be a long walk back to Pierce, but if he didn't stop to rest he might make it back before daylight, so he might not be seen waddling naked into town. There were clotheslines aplenty, so he'd pick out some clothes, maybe sneak into his uncle's house for a bite to eat, then he would be out of there. He'd hitchhike back to Missoula, or walk the whole way if he couldn't find a ride. Even if he didn't have any friends willing to take him in, Charles was there. Charles could leave the institution anytime he wanted to. He would help him.

Lester let anger fuel him as he paddled back, but his throbbing finger reminded him to not let his hands linger. He didn't want another bite.

As he neared shore, he felt something like the pounding of a drum vibrating his belly through the water. He looked around for the source, but he was alone. The thumping smoothed to a steady thrum. The water seemed to vibrate.

A fish jumped in front of him, and another one to his left.

Lester paddled faster. He was nearly to the dock.

Only feet away, Lester pulled his hands in and let the raft coast, steadying himself to grab it.

A cry from shore shattered the nervous silence and made Lester jump. Samantha?

She ran toward the lake, from the direction where she and Rick had disappeared. Her shirt was off, her breasts bouncing with each stride.

*Rick got drunk and raped her*, Lester thought. A savage voice in his head, not his brother's this time, said, *she deserved it*!

He waited for Rick to come from the darkness behind her, but Rick didn't follow. A sleek tan figure flew from the narrow, tree-lined road and landed on the moonlit ground. It chased her, and before she made another dozen steps, launched itself onto her back, taking her down.

The mountain lion swiped at her back, and Samantha twisted under it, shrieking in pain. The giant cat screeched in return, a strangely unnatural sound, and lunged, fixing its jaws over the back of her head.

Lester heard the crunch of bone, and Samantha's struggle ended.

The mountain lion gave her a shake for good measure, then released her. It did not feed. It abandoned her body and turned toward Lester.

Lester found his voice and screamed as his raft bumped the dock.

The cat let loose another strange cry and streaked toward the pond.

Lester screamed again and pushed himself away from the dock, paddling at the water furiously. The pond around him boiled with jumping fish, but he ignored them. Fish bites seemed much less intimidating now.

The giant cat leapt onto the dock, but skidded to a stop before reaching the end. It growled, watching Lester as he put more distance between them. It didn't follow him out, the cat's natural fear of water outweighed its desire to kill, and as it paced at the end of the dock, Lester saw the mountain lion was in bad shape. One glowing feline eye watched him as he moved farther away from shore, but the other was gone.

The mountain lion stopped pacing and settled at the end of the dock, still watching him. There was a great bloody hole in the beast's chest where its ribs showed through the fur, as if it hadn't eaten in a very long time.

At last, Lester quit paddling and rolled onto his back, panting. His arms ached, his chest hurt, and he was more frightened than he had ever been. Despite what Samantha had done to him, being raped was one thing, but this . . . he felt horrible about how she'd died. He glanced over to where she lay, the mountain lion's final, brutal shake had flipped her onto her back. Her skirt was bunched up at her waist, and her front was dirty from her tumble in the dirt, but untouched by the mountain lion's claws. Even dead, she was hot.

He felt the breeze against his prick again, and felt a twist of shame that didn't quite kill his lust.

He forced himself to look away, and found a fish flopping on the raft's warped wood, inches away.

The smell of the thing hit him as he faced it, making his gut clench. Its mouth gulped air, its gills hung in loose flaps. Pondweed hung from the empty sockets where its little fishy eyes should have been. Most of its flesh was gone, and Lester saw a knot of blackened, slimy guts behind exposed ribs.

It flopped again, landing a few inches closer to him.

Lester slapped it back into the water with a cry of disgust.

His bitten finger throbbed with fresh pain, and he brought it up to his face, resisting the urge to stick it in his mouth and suck it.

The finger had turned a light shade of blue to the first knuckle, and it was swelling. The skin around the bite was black, and pus trickled from it like yellow tears.

"Oh God, oh God, oh God," he said, holding the finger close to his face. "Oh God, oh God . . ."

Lester fainted.


HE AWOKE WITH a jerk as something jabbed him in the side, and he screamed when he saw what it was. He'd drifted close to the shore at the other side of Campbell's Pond, coming to rest against a tangle of exposed tree roots. They poked out of the water, scraping against the side of the raft. Collapsed against them was the half-exposed body of a long dead moose. Mostly bones, with scraps of hide draped over it in spots, the snout of its skull was wedged between two thick roots. Its wide antlers stuck out over the edge of the raft. A gentle wave pushed him closer, and they jabbed him again.

A single glowing green eye stared at him from the brush up the bank, and a growl made the hair on his neck stand.

He grabbed the protruding antlers and pushed himself back into the open water.

The green eye disappeared, and Lester heard the brush rustling as the mountain lion moved from its spot, prowling the shore of the pond.

Waiting for him.

Lester wondered how patient a mountain lion could be.

It looked half dead already, maybe more than half dead. Lester certainly had enough fat on his bones to sustain him, and when he got thirsty enough, he was surrounded by water.

He looked around at the weed-choked, muddy water.

The fish had given up trying to board his raft. They'd quit jumping around him too.

He paddled farther out, stopping only when his bitten hand began to throb with greater pain. He brought it to his face; the dark blue hue had spread past his wrist, and the swelling had moved to his other fingers. The black spot had also grown, and his middle fingernail had fallen off. He grimaced and lowered it.

The night air had grown very hot and humid. Lester wiped sweat from his brow with his good hand and stared at the water. It was cool, inviting. He stuck his feet in and sighed with relief. He thought of letting himself slip in, just for a moment, just to cool himself off before the fish came back, but Samantha's words returned to him.

*They found headstones when they were looking for that boy*, she'd said, and though that might have been bullshit, he wouldn't dare to go down there to see.

Lester brought his legs back onto the raft in a near panic and brought his knees to his chest, hugging them.

Thinking about Samantha again, remembering her body, stunning even in death, he couldn't help taking another look. When he looked though, she was gone.

The mountain lion had finally dragged her off. Maybe it was eating her now.

Maybe now was his chance to get away, the only chance he'd get until the beast had finished with her.

In his mind's eye, he saw Samantha's dead body, face in the dirt, perfect ass pointing up in the air, while the emaciated one-eyed cat humped it.

*You are a fucking pervert*, Charles informed him.

Lester blushed.

It was now or never, he decided. If it turned out he was wrong, well, he wouldn't have much time to regret his decision. He wasn't going to last long if he didn't get out. The strange blue infection had moved down past his wrist and his swelled area was going numb. The middle finger had split, but he couldn't feel that at all anymore.

Some kind of weird infection, maybe blood poisoning. It would kill him long before he had a chance to starve.

He scanned the shore in the light of the awakening dawn, and the mountain lion did not show itself.

Steeling himself, Lester paddled toward shore.

He heard it before he saw it. A loud purring sound announced the return of the mountain lion. Then it appeared from the woods, stalked lazily down the dock and settled itself at the end. It growled once, but the growl sounded more like a human voice. Not English, but something older. Something forgotten.

"No!" Lester shouted. Somewhere close by a bird squawked and exploded into flight.

"Yes," the giant cat growled, and its cleft upper lip curved into an eerie caricature of a human smile.

"Lester," Samantha said, coming from the trees behind the dock. "Have you ever been fucked in a cemetery?"

She stepped onto the dock, giggling, patted the now docile mountain lion's head, then approached the water. She unbuttoned her torn mini-skirt and pushed it down her tattered, but luscious hips, letting it fall over her blood-and-dirt-crusted feet, then dove into the water.

As she surfaced and swam toward him, conflicting emotions sped Lester's heart; fear, revulsion, and lust. Her breasts bobbed above the water for a moment, and she slid beneath the surface again.

He fell back onto his elbows, panting, on the verge of passing out again, and saw her hands break the water. They grasped the edge of the raft, and she lifted herself out.

Lust won out as she slid onto the raft, crawling toward him. He sighed as her cold, wet flesh glided over his, shuddered as she pressed into him.

The mountain lion purred, lapped at a bloody paw. Around the raft, the frenzied fish breached the water, splashing them.

"Have you ever been fucked by the dead?" Her cold hand found his dick, guided it, and with a hungry groan, she impaled herself on him.


AWAKE AGAIN, WATCHFUL, Lester hid under cover of pondweed and muddy water. The open grave was like a bed. Partially filled over the years by silt, it was still deep enough to admit his bulk.

He watched the surface of Campbell's Pond.

People had quit coming to this place, but they always forgot. They always came back eventually.

Lester, Samantha, and the others would wait until then, and if their bodies rotted away before other people came, the thing that had resurrected them would find another way.

It always had.

---

BRIAN KNIGHT lives in Washington State with his family. His published works include *Sex, Death & Honey*, *Reservoir Gods*, *Broken Angel*, *Feral*, and *Dragonfly*. His short fiction has appeared in *Flesh & Blood Magazine*, *Best of Horrorfind*, and *Cemetery Dance*.

# ALL DEAD

BY JG FAHERTY

---

"COME FEEL ME, CHARLIE." KELLI BRUSHED HER hands over her breasts. The silk teddy just barely held its place, clinging to the edge of her nipples, exposing the roundness of the perfect breasts I remembered so well.

Then I snapped out of the trance.

"Get the fuck away from me!" I swatted my hand at her. It passed right through her face, leaving me unsatisfied and even angrier, but not surprised. I was long past being surprised. She'd usually go away if I was rude enough, although it didn't work as well with her as the others. Probably because she was used to me swearing.

Kelli giggled that cute little-girl laugh that had always worked on me when she was alive. "Same old Charlie. You're so stubborn. Like the time we went to Disneyland, and you were afraid to ride Space Mountain. Remember that day?"

I stayed silent, trying not to stare at the delicate pink nipple peeking out from under the silk.

"I'll take that as a yes," she said, her voice low and husky. Her bedroom voice. She took a slinky step toward me. "We ended up riding it again and again. You had a great time. And this will be the same, only *I* can ride *you*, again and again. And afterward we can hold each other. An endless embrace. You and me, together forever."

God help me, I wanted it. I wanted *her*.

Then I remembered what she was really asking.

"No, you're not real!"

She leaned in close to me, stroking her hand sensually through the air over my crotch. "If I'm not real, then why are you so hard?"

I slid back in my chair, turned my head away. I didn't trust myself to speak. I couldn't even look at her.

"Have I ever steered you wrong?" She was so close. I wanted to feel her breath on my face, but I knew that was impossible. "You just need to trust me." Her voice sent shivers down my back.

"How can I trust you after what you did to me?" I finally asked. "You left me here, alone."

Kelli shook her head, put a sad look on her face and pulled away. "Fine. Sit here and pout, then. I'll come back when you're in a better mood."

Tears ran down my cheeks and I closed my eyes, unwilling to believe she'd give up that easily. When she didn't speak for several seconds, I glanced over just in time to see her fading away, her body shimmering slightly as it went transparent and then disappeared.

"Thank you, God," I whispered to the now-empty room. Once more I was alone with the only earthly things that mattered to me anymore: my radio, my books, and my bed. All three served the same purpose.

They helped me escape from the real world, and the unreal one.


AFTER KELLI DIED—I still have trouble believing it's been three years since she killed herself—I kind of lost it. I know I did. Hell, I welcomed it, pretty much let the madness take me over. She'd been my last link to sanity to begin with, my partner in my never-ending struggle. No matter how great the temptation got to just give in, each of us was there for the other, a rock to lean on, a giver of strength. I always told her I thought she was the stronger one, because she bore the pressure with a smile while I was the one who would scream and shout and cry.

Turns out it was all an act; she put on a brave face for me but inside her defenses were crumbling. In the end, she knew she was going to give in, was even looking forward to it, but kept it a secret from me.

I know all this because the first night after they took her body away, she came to me and told me so.

*I did it for you, Charlie. I knew it was the only way to get you to join us. You want us to be together, don't you?*

She knew me too well. We'd been married almost fifteen years; when you live with someone for that long, you don't have many secrets. Each facial expression, each twitch of the hand or quiet sigh, tells your partner exactly what you're thinking, what you're feeling.

Truth was, I *did* want to be with her. More than anything. At that moment, I'd have gladly done what she asked. In fact, I'd already gotten out of bed and was heading for the garage when the phone rang.

*Saved by the bell*, I told myself later.

It was Reynolds from work. He'd heard what had happened, and was calling to tell me to take as much time off as I needed, but he begged me to please just stop by the office and drop off the Zymanski file, otherwise the whole project would be late.

"Sure," I told him. And then I went crazy.

I threw the phone across the room. I kicked over a table. I smashed every bottle in the liquor cabinet. I threw something—a figurine, maybe, or a vase—through the front window. When the police came, they found me with a knife in my hand, slashing the sofa cushions. They pegged me for suicidal and brought me here.

My first six weeks they kept me heavily sedated; those were the best six weeks in the last three years. Oh, sure, Kelli came and visited; so did the others. But I was too doped up to understand them, too stoned to care. Most of the time I just laughed at them.

Then the doctors weaned me off the good shit, and reality came crashing down on me.

I was alone, but never truly alone.

That's when I decided I liked my little white room; that it might be nice to stay awhile.

I've never left.


WHEN KELLI AND the others get to be too much for me, I throw a fit and get a few days back on the hard stuff, the drugs that make me sleep through the night and laugh all day. Kelli hates it when I do that.

"She's not the only one who hates it."

A stern, disapproving voice behind me. I turned and saw my mother standing there, her arms crossed, a scowl on her face. The same look she always gave me when I'd do something she didn't think was in my best interest, like waste money on a new book or spend all day watching TV. When I got older, the supposed infractions changed—a new car, or working on a Saturday instead of coming to see her—but the look remained the same.

"This is no kind of life for you," she said now. "Sitting in this place. We both know you're not crazy. How long do you think you can fool the doctors?"

I smiled. It was always easiest to talk to my mother. I didn't know why they would even send her—she never could get me to do anything I didn't want to do. "As long as I have to, Mom. I'll stay here forever. Better than the alternative."

"Better than . . . ?" Her eyes grew wide and insulted. "You'd rather be locked up and hooked on drugs than spend time with your family, your wife? What kind of son did I raise?"

"A smart one," I said with a shrug.

"A smart aleck, more like it," she countered. "We'll see what your father has to say about this."

Before I could respond, she vanished, leaving me blissfully alone again. But the respite didn't last long; it never did. Things were just getting started for me.

Flickering movement caught my eye, and I swung around in time to see my father take form.

"Hey, Dad." It was hard to get the words out. My relationship with my father had been a lot better than the one I'd had with my mother. We'd done all the father-and-son things growing up: playing catch, going fishing, watching ballgames together. He'd taught me how to ride a bike and how to tune up a car. When I moved out to be on my own, he'd helped me buy my first house, walking through it with me and pointing out what needed to be repaired.

The day he'd put the gun in his mouth and decorated the living room walls had been the worst day of my life.

Until Kelli.

For a moment, he didn't say anything, just looked at me and shook his head. When he finally spoke, his words dripped disappointment.

"Why do you treat your mother like that, Charlie? All she wants is what's best for you. For all of us. You know how important family is to her."

"You should have all thought of that while you were alive," I said. "We were already together."

"Not all of us," he reminded me.

I closed my eyes. I knew what he was referring to. The extended family, the grandparents and great-grandparents. The aunts and uncles. The cousins and second cousins. The whole goddamn family tree. Two trees, actually, if you count both sides of the family. Hell, go back far enough and you had a freakin' forest of relatives. Hundreds of them. All dead by their own hands.

All waiting for me to join them.

"It's not going to happen," I said, opening my eyes.

Dad was gone.

Something like a knife stabbed through my guts. I'd never had the chance to say my farewells to him ten years ago, and he still preferred to sneak off when my eyes were closed or I was looking in the other direction.

"You're a fucking coward!" I shouted at the ceiling. "You hear me? A coward! You couldn't say goodbye then, and you still can't! You're all cowards and I'm not gonna join you!" I threw my pillow at the wall, just as the door to my room opened and two orderlies came in.

One of them held a needle.

"You seein' your family again, Charlie?" one of them asked.

I just smiled and held out my arm.

Two minutes later, I was lying on my bed, the world already growing fuzzy around me. Just before things went dark, I thought I saw my brother Jim, but I couldn't be sure. I hadn't seen him in twenty years, since he ran away and joined the Army.

*Jim can't be here,* I told myself. *He's still alive.*

Then I was gone, far from everyone's reach.


*CHARLIE. WAKE UP. I have to talk to you. Charlie?*

*Charlie!*

Kelli's shout brought me awake. I sat up, rubbed my eyes, and looked at her. She was sitting at the end of the bed, her legs crossed Indian-style, right by my feet. It was how she'd always arranged herself when she had something serious she wanted to discuss.

"What's the matter?" I asked.

"It's time." Her voice was solemn, her usual smile missing.

"Time? Time for what?" Still confused from my abrupt awakening, I tried to remember if there was something we were supposed to be doing.

"Time to come home. You've been here long enough."

I shook my head. "No, I'm not going anywhere. There's no home to return to, not with you gone."

Her lips tightened until they almost disappeared. "I'm not gone, Charlie. You have to listen to me. There are no ghosts talking to you. I'm not dead." She extended her arm toward me. "Touch my hand. Feel it. I'm real."

"You're not. You killed yourself, like all the others. You left me."

"No, Charlie, *you* left *me*. Right after your mother died. Your father and I tried to help you, but nothing worked. The doctors put you in here after you tried to burn the house down."

Burn the house down? I didn't remember that. But then, there were so many things I no longer remembered, so many things hidden behind the misty walls the drugs created in my head.

I looked at her hand. It trembled ever so slightly, just enough to cause her wedding ring to glitter in the dim light of the single bulb overhead.

"I'll prove that you're wrong," I said, and I reached out, expecting my hand to pass through hers.

It didn't.

Her skin felt cool and dry against mine, and her fingers tightened, gripping me tight.

"You're real. Oh my God, you're *real.*" I pulled her to me, wrapped my arms around her, clutched at her body. She sobbed against my shoulder, and I felt my own tears creating warm tracks down my cheeks.

Finally I pulled back, dried her tears with my fingers. "How long?"

Kelli gave me a half-smile. "Eight months, Charlie. Eight months I've been waiting for you to come back to me."

How could I have been so stupid? How could I have thrown away so much time . . . time I could have been with her? I leaned forward and kissed her, smashing my lips into hers, running my tongue into her mouth, tasting her sweet candy breath mixed with the saltiness of her tears.

I almost cried again when she broke the kiss.

"I can't stay, Charlie. Visiting hours are almost over. But if you show them you're better, we can be together again in the morning. For good, this time."

"Show them I'm better? How?" I was ready to do anything to be with her again, now that I knew my ghosts had been nothing but delusions.

"You have to prove to yourself that your delusions aren't real. You have to kill yourself."

"No! That's what the ghosts have been telling me to do."

Kelli cradled my face in her hands. So cool and soft against my skin, they calmed me the way water calms a fire. "Exactly. And since it's not real, nothing can actually happen to you. That's the only way you'll really believe it's all been a nightmare. You have to break the cycle."

It made sense. If everything around me had been an illusion, a figment of my own imagination, then committing suicide would end it, and I'd be left with reality.

I nodded. "I'll do it."

Kelli's smile burned any traces of fear out of me. I'd always loved her smile. "That's my boy." She gave me another kiss and then stood up. "I'll see you tomorrow."

I watched her open the door and leave. For once, the sound of the door shutting again didn't make me feel trapped or alone.

"Tomorrow," I whispered.

THE FIRST THING I felt when I woke up was pain. My throat ached with it; a burning, vicious red throbbing that caused me to gasp for air. It was like breathing smoke through a straw. I choked and gagged as my lungs strained to fill themselves. I tried to reach for my throat. I wanted to claw out whatever was obstructing the airflow.

My hands wouldn't move.

I could feel my eyes bulging from their sockets from the pressure in my throat, but I still managed to look down and see I was strapped to a table, bandages covering both wrists. I heaved my body, trying to break free. Each movement sent further jolts of pain down my neck, and caused me to wheeze even harder. My vision grew dim; spots twirled and danced before my eyes.

A figure came into view, fuzzy and indistinct. Something touched my arm. A second later, the pain went away and I was able to breathe easier. I drew in deep lungfuls of air, my panic receding as my body got the oxygen it craved.

"Is that better, Mr. Mason?" An unfamiliar voice, somewhere out of my range of vision.

"Yes," I said. It sounded more like a croak than anything.

Something touched my lips. "Drink this, it will help."

I sucked on the straw. Cool liquid poured across my tongue and down my throat, washing away the last of the pain with soothing wetness.

When I tried to speak again, my voice was almost normal. "Where am I?"

A man's face came into view. I knew him. Dr. Kray.

I was still in the hospital.

"You're in the infirmary, Mr. Mason. Do you know why?"

Kelli's face appeared in my mind's eye. Her visit. Last night? "I'm supposed to go home. My wife said that if I prove I'm better, I can go home."

One of Kray's eyebrows went up. "When did she tell you this?"

"The last time she came to visit. Yesterday."

The doctor's lips tightened, the kind of expression you see on people when they have to tell you bad news but don't want to.

"Mr. Mason, we've been over this before. Your wife is dead. You're in here because you've tried to commit suicide in the past. You tried again last night. Do you remember that?"

I didn't. "No."

"You tried to strangle yourself with your bedsheet. Your neck will be sore for a few days, and it will hurt to swallow, but you'll be fine. However, we're going to have to keep you sedated and restrained, at least for a while."

He jotted down some notes on a clipboard and gave me a professional smile that carried no real warmth. "I'll be back later to see how you're doing. Get some rest."

Kray left, the nurse who'd spoken to me following behind. I heard a door shut, and the room took on a feeling I knew too well. I was alone.

I closed my eyes and started counting.

I'd reached forty-five when she spoke.

"I can't believe you, Charlie. You screwed up again."

Opening my eyes brought the expected sight of Kelli standing by the bed. She looked as beautiful as she had the night before, and something inside me broke. My last traces of tenacity crumbled.

I remembered how she felt in my arms, and I knew the time had come for us to be together again. Even if I had to die to do it. I couldn't stand the thought of another day—another minute—without her.

Why had I ever bothered fighting it? What good was my life if Kelli wasn't in it?

"That's what I've been trying to tell you, silly," she said. "That's what we've *all* been trying to tell you."

Flashes of light glittered behind her, and the rest of them appeared: Mom and Dad, my grandparents, long-lost cousins.

"We've all been waiting for you," Dad said. He came forward and put a rough, calloused hand on my shoulder. "It's so wonderful. We can go fishing again, anytime you want."

My mother spoke up. "I'll be the kind of mother I should have been when I was alive, Charlie."

They gathered around me, my wife and family, telling me how much they loved me, missed me. They laughed and they cried. I cried, too, knowing that I'd be with them soon, that I'd never be alone again.

I don't know how long we stayed like that, but suddenly they all stepped aside. A moment later, the door opened, and I heard footsteps.

"Time for your medicine," the nurse said as she approached the bed.

She swabbed my arm, but before she could deliver the shot, I spoke up. "Nurse, my hand. It's all pins and needles. Can you loosen the strap? It really hurts."

"Sure." She undid the binding and started rubbing my hand. "Is the feeling coming back?"

Instead of answering, I pulled my hand away and grabbed her by the shirt, yanked her forward. Her head landed on my stomach and I shifted my grip, clenching her neck in the crook of my arm like a wrestler delivering a chokehold. I squeezed as hard as I could, but she managed to get out a brief scream before I cut off her air supply. I held on until she went limp, and then I let go, knowing I'd only have a minute or two, at best.

As fast as I could, I fumbled open the strap on my other arm and sat up. I didn't bother freeing my feet. The only thing I needed was right next to me on a metal tray—the needle the nurse had planned on using.

"Do it, Charlie!" Kelli whispered. "Hurry!"

The others cried out their urging as well. I grabbed the syringe and pulled the cap off. Without pause, I jammed it into my eye as far as it would go and pushed in the plunger.

Agony exploded in my head and face, and I howled, my cry of pain causing a second wave of torture to erupt from my already bruised throat.

I fell back on the table, my hands instinctively clawing at my eye, trying to end my suffering. Dim voices shouted, but I only heard pieces of what they said.

*Crash cart. Emergency. Code Blue.*

Then it all disappeared.


THERE WAS NO sensation of time passing, but at some point the black slowly brightened until I was surrounded by white. No walls, no floor, no sky. Just white.

"Hello, Charlie."

I turned around, and there she was. Kelli, in all her radiant glory. If anything, she looked more beautiful now than she had when she was alive.

My whole family stood behind her in a big, smiling group.

"Kelli." I started toward her, and she opened her arms, welcoming me.

She waited until I had my arms around her before she changed.

Her beautiful outer shell flaked off in cakey pieces, revealing green, scaly skin, a hole where her nose should have been, a giant mouth filled with jagged teeth. Red eyes that dripped pus-yellow fluids.

I tried to turn around, but her freshly-grown claws dug into my arms. Her head darted forward faster than a cobra and she bit a chunk of flesh from my shoulder. I screamed, but my cries were muffled by the rest of the family, all of them now hideous creatures, as they smothered me, joining Kelli for the feast. They tore at me, shredding my skin, pulling pieces of my flesh with their teeth and nails.

When they were done, there was nothing left of me except my bones and my horror.

"Welcome to Hell, Charlie," Kelli said, her voice clotted and phlegmy with my blood. Her human appearance had returned. "We're going to do this every day for eternity, unless . . ."

*Unless what?* I wondered.

"Unless you bring someone over," Dad finished.

*Bring someone . . . ?*

"The way I brought you." Kelli gave me an evil smile. "You've caused me a lot of pain. Three years I've been waiting for you to kill yourself. That's like a fucking eternity here. I've been gutted, tortured, and raped more times than you can count. I hope it takes you just as long to bring Jim to us. I hope it takes you for-fucking-*ever*."

*Jim? My brother?*

"That's the price, Charlie," my mother said.

"No!" I had my voice back. I looked down, saw my body had regenerated.

My family attacked again, only this time they all had fangs filled with poison.

"How long can you take it, Charlie?" Kelli asked, as I twitched and writhed from the acid in my veins.

Giving in is always easier when you truly know the stakes.

"Tell me how to find him."

---

**JG FAHERTY** has had a varied career, which provides a rich background for his writing. Currently the owner of www.a-perfect-resume.com, he has previously worked as a laboratory manager, R&D scientist, accident scene photographer, zoo keeper, salesman, and anatomy instructor.

An Active Member in the Horror Writers Association, JG's credits include more than two dozen short stories published in major genre magazines and anthologies. He also contributes columns, interviews, and book reviews to various newsletters and websites.

A life-long fan of horror and dark fiction, JG enjoys reading, watching movies, golfing, hiking with his wife and dogs, volunteering as an exotic animal caretaker, and playing the guitar. His favorite holiday is Halloween, and as a child, one of his local playgrounds was an 18th century cemetery.

If you see him at a horror convention, feel free to buy him a Guinness.

You can visit him at www.jgfaherty.com, www.twitter.com/jgfaherty, or www.facebook.com/jgfaherty.

# EXEGESIS OF THE INSECTA APOCRYPHA

## BY COLLEEN ANDERSON

---

*"In the beginning, it was a shift, a flutter of orange and black that caught her eye and held it, pulling her into a new paradigm before she knew there ever was one. The opening of the butterfly's wings fastened her two-year-old gaze forever."*

—Apocryphon[1]

*T*HE APOCRYPHA *FIRST APPEARED ON THE WORLD Wide Web in the early twenty-first century. Their legitimacy as sacred writing was not considered for two decades, with arguments reiterating that class Insecta could never evolve to the state of written language, let alone into a mindset able to formulate histories and concepts of time. In light of the documented case of the child with compound eyes being born last year, as well as several climatic shifts that haven increased insect populations, the* Insecta Apocrypha *are being analyzed for new interpretations. Whether they are indicators of a convergence of evolution and intelligence to a new level is not in the purview of this paper.*

*What draws the eye immediately is the symbolism. Butterflies and birds have long been seen as forms of the human soul. Just as the Bible opens with Genesis, so does the Apocrypha begin with a genesis of sorts, and at the awakening of a child's consciousness begins the search for the meaning of soul.[2]*

---

[1] Alice Rothwell, ed. *Sacred Writings of the Modern Cult Movements in North America* (New York: Random, 2014). *All subsequent Apocrypha quotes are from the same publication.*

[2] Rachel Urghart and Roy Hammerschmidt, eds. *Exegesis of the Insecta Apocrypha,* Rabbi Joel Shapiro, Chapt. 1 "Interpretations of the Soul" (Numinous Press, Toronto, 2032) 14

## APOCRYPHON I–DISCOVERY

EVER SINCE THAT first erratic flight, Libby's gaze followed minute forms of locomotion. Whether a larva wriggling, a beetle scuttling, a dragonfly flitting and hovering, or the leap of a grasshopper, she watched intently, tracing its path as long as possible. At the age of four, she squatted in the garden, staring intently at something that shivered the long grass. Inhaling noisily, she wrinkled her nose at the cloying smell but stayed put.

Her father's words were less than a fly's buzz and her chubby little fingers itched to pick up one of the writhing white maggots that worked its way in and out of what was once a mouse. The gray brown fur was nearly indistinguishable under the moving carpet that gently trembled.

In that instant Libby understood that life was cannibalistic, feeding on itself, but taking different forms. Life fed on death, death generated life—an intrinsic cycle.

Early on, she noticed that people shied from answering her questions about death and decay. It disturbed them, especially when insects were involved in the decomposition. There was something about the mindless infestation of life feeding voraciously on the dead. A need was deposited in her, a small egg incubating, maturing the more attention she gave it, until it could eat its way out of her. The larval thought was curiosity, but it was inherently tied to watching life and death.

Her father buried the mouse and its white pulsing attendants, digging a hole so deep that Libby never found the spot again.


ONE HUMID MORNING brought mosquitoes swarming from the creek in the back field. Libby had been walking with her mother, who had stopped to take a few pictures of plants. She listened to the whine of mosquitoes and held out her arm. They alighted, a half dozen or so, their needle thin proboscises piercing her flesh. They sucked and fattened on her blood. Although it itched slightly, Libby didn't interfere with their feeding until her mother turned and said, "Libby, what are you doing!"

Her mother frantically brushed the mosquitoes from her arm and dragged Libby out of the woods, swatting the whole time. At home Libby found her arm swathed in calamine. She watched it throughout the next day, fascinated by the reddish bumps that arose. If she scratched them long enough they enlarged and seeped a clear liquid before blood oozed like small volcanoes erupting. She licked her wounds, feeling the heat of her skin and the slight sourness of the scabs.

She never shied from any insect, letting red-backed ladybirds and butterflies alight on her, moving her feet into the path of shiny, black carapaced June bugs, or walking into a spider's web to induce the arachnid to crawl across her. Holding her mouth open, she would stick out her tongue, letting a few brave insects land so that she could feel the soft dance of their feet. Bites and stings often laced her skin and left her parents bewildered.

*Children have a natural curiosity and, like cats, they will watch anything that moves. They are sometimes considered cruel when, in their discoveries, they tear apart insects or hit another child with a stick. Libby's early experiences, when read without the fictional embellishments, are within the normal range of a child's development and expanding consciousness.*

*It is possible that this early infusion of insect venoms laid the tracery for Libby's later metamorphosis. Her next stage, in* Apocryphon II, *began at the age of six. Libby actively investigated the insect world and was ready to learn the depth of what they could do.*[3]

## APOCRYPHON II – EXPERIMENTATION

SHE FOUND AN orange striped kitten in the field behind her house. There was a small stand of alders near the creek and she stood under the fluttering leaves, holding the mewing kitten. Taking a string from her pocket, she tied one end around the cat's neck and the other end around a slender tree. Libby patted the kitten once, then walked away.

It took three days for the insect world and the mammalian one to intersect. Each day she strode quickly to the grove of trees and checked the kitten. The first day it struggled and mewed loudly when it saw her. She turned and left it. The second day, it lay on its side, panting, croaking out a feeble meow. Libby searched for insect activity and, on seeing none, left. The third day, she bent over, peering at the prone kitten. Its eyes were open and glassy. The slightly matted fur did not move.

Libby settled herself in the grass, cross-legged, her elbows on her knees, chin in hand. Eventually, she noticed a minuscule flicker. She bent closer

---

[3] *Exegesis* Shandra Radakrishnan, Chapter 3 "Psychoanalysis of the Messiah and Anti-Messiah in Relation to Major Religions" 39-46

and watched fleas, which fed on the living, abandoning the carcass, some leaping off, some disappearing underneath, and even a couple of them crossing the surface of the corpse's blind eyes.

Next, the flies descended, buzzing and settling upon the creature, especially around its eyes, ears, and nose. It had died with its mouth slightly open, the pink tongue showing swollen and dark. In crept a fly, glistening blue-black, and another, moving about, probing with insectile feet and mouth. The kitten's body crawled with insects, alighting and flying ellipsoid orbits. Libby removed the string from the cat's neck and returned home by dinnertime so as not to jeopardize her experiment.

Each day, she returned to sit and watch the insect activity. In just a few days, the orange and white fur began to move and ripple, like wind over grass. Glistening maggots tumbled from the mouth and eyes, feeding on necrotic tissue.

Eventually, ants and gnats and beetles crawled over the putrefying mass as the fur sloughed off, displaying the animal's liquefying organs. Libby held vigil through all of it, noting when flies grew bored with the carcass and when ants and spiders moved in to remove morsels. The kitten's body was a motel of activity. Only when the feeding slowed, with mostly bones and fur left, did Libby bury the corpse.

It was a couple of years later that she took a puppy into the same woods. This time she did not wait for death's slow claim but strangled the pup immediately, her hands choking off its whimpers as its black paws scrabbled in the air. When it stopped moving, she laid it on the ground, spreading out its silky ears.

Then she pulled a sharp kitchen knife from her pack. It glinted in the afternoon sun as she studied the black body of the pup. She placed the point against the soft, nearly furless area by the genitals and pushed in, sawing up through the skin to the ribcage. Only a small amount of blackish blood pooled out. Then she cut under the ribs in smaller strokes and across, forming a T. Pulling back the skin and opening the organs to the elements had already brought the flies. Her knife pricked the pink intestines that seeped a fetid black fluid.

Libby sat back as the flies settled upon her offering, humming their contentment. She twirled her wheaten hair, forgetting her hunger and almost missing the distant call of her mother. Scrambling up, Libby tucked away the knife and ran off.

Her diligence brought her each day to note earwigs and the black bowl of hister beetle backs moving in and out of the architecture of decomposing organs while maggots were born and grew fat on the meat. Within a few days the dog's black skin sloughed off the bloated body. Pupae from the flies eventually cracked their husks, emerging as a new generation.

Libby's interest only grew. Not far from her home was a two-story apartment building slated for demolition. The vacant shadows of the windows held only shards of glass. Plywood had been nailed up but vagrants and teenagers had pried them away. Libby had already explored the place, seeing what insects lived in dark and dank rooms.


WHEN SHE WAS twelve she found a little boy of about five wandering down the street. He seemed to not realize he'd strayed far from the familiar. Libby gave him a cellophane-wrapped candy and, as he popped it in his already sticky mouth, she said, "I've lost my puppy. Would you like to help me find him?" The boy nodded, pushing his stringy brown hair out of his eyes but not saying anything around the candy in his mouth. Gummy sweetness streaked his chin with brown and pink.

She took his hand and he followed complacently. It was easy enough to get him into the building and have him sit while she grabbed an old rag and some rope. She deftly tied him and before he could whimper, stuffed the gag in his mouth. He began to cry, soaking the rag with saliva and snot. Libby ignored him while she readied her tools: tweezers and scalpel. A few alert flies already circled the boy's face. From her pack, she withdrew several small jars, each holding a flickering, insectoid mass. In one she had scooped up beetles and earwigs and other ground insects. Another held the agitated buzzing of wasps, while a third showed the constant flutter of color from butterflies and moths. Two more jars contained flies and caterpillars respectively.

She ignored the boy's muffled shrieks, refusing to hurry.

After her experiments, Libby retied the gag on the unconscious boy, most of the insects having abandoned him, and threw a blanket over his body. He would be a better stew in the morning. She left and came back a day later, looking at his welted belly and peering at his crusting arms. Flies buzzed about the trickling snot on his face, landing and walking over his sweat-matted hair.

Libby continued for a couple of days, watching how the fly larva grew on living tissue. The boy stared vacantly, drooling, barely making a sound. When nothing more could be gained from her observations, she untied him and watched. He didn't move, just lay on his side. Maggots dropped off of his arms. There was no need to kill him. She packed up everything she had brought, removing jars, tweezers, scalpel, and rope, leaving nothing behind. Libby walked away from the building, never to return.

*Between the first* Apocryphon *and the second, there is a shift of personality. What could be considered normal behavior for a child diverges wildly by the second writing, indicating sociopathic tendencies. Although Libby exhibits the escalation of brutality from animal to human subjects, she doesn't seem to repeat these offenses, which is atypical for sociopaths. However, her behavior in detachment and lack of empathy is typical.*[4]

*Debate remains as to whether the Apocrypha only mark the first of each phase of Libby's experiments, or if indeed she only conducted one event at each stage. The first two Apocrypha remain nearly emotionless, whereas the third takes on a slightly different tone and it is believed that Apocrypha III and IV may have been written by Libby. Contention exists as to whether she wrote the first two, or if an unknown source fictionalized all of it.*[5]

## APOCRYPHON III—RESEARCH

SHE GRADUATED FROM high school at sixteen and gained her doctorate in entomology by twenty-two. She became a forensic expert in decomposition and the insects that populated the fleshy worlds of the dead. The microscopic realm of insect biology was as interesting as discovering that first maggot-ridden body.

Libby laid her groundwork well, knowing cell structures, the chemical interactions that drove ants, dragonflies, leafhoppers, moths, and the basis of different groups of social insects. Colonies and hives were fascinating in the caste structure of workers and drones. Not all ant colonies had only one queen and most workers were females, sometimes able to breed when necessary. Often drones lived only long enough to fertilize the queen before dying. In some species of wasps and bees, the queens mated with multiple drones and stored the sperm, releasing it over time to fertilize the continuous cycle of egg laying at their discretion.

Libby stored the information, then began to study communication of

---

[4] *Exegesis* Radakrishnan, 53-56
[5] *Exegesis* Carl Purdy, Chapter 5 "Interpretations of Voice" 76-78

hymenoptera; the bees, wasps, ants and their hives, colonies and social structure. She ordered yellow crazy ants from the Christmas Islands, Western honey bees and Buff-Tailed bumble bees, Asian giant hornets and German wasps. Besides hymenoptera, she brought in Kirby's Dropwing dragonflies from Namibia, Meadow Argus butterflies from Australia, ladybugs from Canada, and a host of other species. She concentrated on the pheromone trails of ants and tried to see if she could colonize species that were not hymenoptera. She tried to form messages from light, from chemicals, from Braille-like forms. Diligently, for five years Libby tested many types of command or communication and searched for any effect on hive activity, caste structures, or mating.

Her tests did not lead to any discernible change. Her research could have gone on forever. There were always many new paths to take in studying class Insecta. An estimated thirty million species were still unclassified, but Libby grew unsatisfied, feeling that she was not attaining her goal fast enough.

It dawned on her that though she had concentrated on hymenoptera for their social behavior that she herself was not social. How could she possibly understand such behavior unless she undertook the final phase?

First tidying her lab, Libby took two weeks off, leaving as many insects with the department as she took. After all, she worked alone and was known to keep to herself.

She went downtown and entered a department store. For the first time ever, Libby felt a bit displaced, as if she were an ant that had lost all pheromone signals to the colony. Bewildered, she stared at the array of cosmetics, jars and pomades, lotions, scents, eye and lip colors that surrounded her. Turning a slow circle, she could not pinpoint a place to begin until a clerk approached her.

"I want . . . " She made a motion around her face, struggling for what to say.

The clerk smiled and beckoned her to follow. "I know. You've not worn makeup before. Don't worry, I'll show you what you need. With your features, you don't need much but we can enhance and highlight what you have."

Libby sat through the experience, finding it alien, then proceeded to buy clothes that were more than utilitarian.

Always a good study, she had no problem in applying the makeup. She slipped on a slinky, red spaghetti strap dress that showed her long legs. Red stilettos added to her color, and then she made her way to where males swarmed. The lights and music throbbed around her, pulsating off her skin. She danced awkwardly but it seemed to matter little to the men that grabbed her about the waist and pulled her close.

The first man offered to take her somewhere else. Libby freely gave up her virginity in a car. But she did not stay, exiting for the next nightclub. The second man took her in the restroom, and a third in the back alley where they went to "share a joint". At the end of the night, Libby went with five men, finally finding herself in a threadbare hotel room with a naked flickering bulb. She pulled the closest one to her and kissed him, undoing his pants. When he tried to push her head down, she pulled back and sat on the table, pulling up her dress to take him in. It wasn't long before the others followed.

Libby repeated the swarming for a week, collecting as many men's semen as she could. When she felt she had accomplished that task, now holding enough sperm to release thousands of eggs, she shucked off the mating colors and set to work in her home, which bordered a large, state protected park.

She brought out the terrariums with the various insects and arrayed them about her. From bees, flies, dragonflies, beetles, grasshoppers, moths, weevils, wasps, and ants, Libby extracted eggs. She required special tools, often a microscope and careful incubation so that the eggs would not wither. Some she took from the hives about her place and others from the insects directly. When she had a good yield, Libby stripped off her clothing. Under a bright light, she made small incisions on her thighs, arms, and abdomen, and inserted a different species' eggs into each opening. Although she felt the pain, it was an abstraction from the task at hand and it only aided her concentration. Overshadowing the pain was a flush of excitement, warmth that spread through her in ways sex hadn't.

As she laid each egg beneath her epidermis, she took out a glass case crawling with army ants. Pressing each bleeding wound shut, she applied the ants along the fleshy rim. The ants in turn seized the edges of the cut in their lightning fast jaws and locked on. Libby felt sharp pricks and then cut off the glossy black bodies, leaving the head and mandibles as sutures. She stood with her stitching of ant heads, and opened all containers holding insects.

*A few variants of* Apocryphon III *indicate that Libby prayed or cried at this point. These have largely been dismissed as additions by unknown sources that wished to humanize her actions. There is no indication in any Apocrypha that she ever showed intense emotion.*

*It is argued that Libby was trying to become an insect and found the only way to communicate was to pass on her knowledge through her cells. Still others believe that she had in fact been imbued with the essence of Insecta from birth.*[6]

## APROCRYPHON IV-A—METAMORPHOSIS

NAKED, LIBBY WALKED out her door and into the park. In the white heat of the day she stood beneath the trees, her bare feet burrowing into leaf mold. Feeling the slight ripples in the air about her, she spread her arms. It may be that she knew the secret language of insects and called her disciples unto her with the release of a pheromone borne on her words. In a high voice, she trilled.

They came, great black clouds of pixilating Insecta. The air rippled and thrummed with movement. The green bottle flies with their metallic sheen, the beetles with their chitinous clatter, the buzzing drone of bees, wasps and hornets, the flutter of moths and butterflies, the gnats, mosquitoes, the walking sticks and praying mantises. They came from miles around. Still they were only representatives of the greater horde, but one came of every type, thirty million strong.

Onto each pore and hair the smallest insects landed, followed by others, coating her arms, her legs, her naked torso, her face and eyes and ears. When nothing could be seen but the pulsating cluster, it rose into the air, higher and higher, like an enormous runaway swarm. Lifting to the heavens like a gyrating, buzzing black host, it grew smaller and then... dispersed, scattering insects like seed pods.

## APOCRYPHON IV-B—METAMORPHOSIS

LIBBY WALKED NAKED amongst the trees under the moon's silvering light. Like Lilith in the Garden of Eden, she moved with confidence. The air seemed to blanket her as she raised her slim, bare arms to the heavens and she cried out in a voice like the chirrup of locusts. Into the skies, boiling from the ground, the myriad host arrived on the pheromone trail, the Insecta in their glory of gold and red, gunmetal black and blue, jarring green and earthy brown, a scintillating mass of color, of forms soft and furred, hard and chitinous. Sound rose like a roar, a thunder, an unearthly humming.

---

[6] *Exegesis* Purdy, 112-115

Those who heard the cacophony of wings and legs, and clatter of millions of mandibles thought the end was near. The insects came from all around, swarming up her legs, onto her head. Then they burrowed, chewed, and crawled within her. Some crept in her nostrils, others into her eyes, while flies and gnats filled her ears. Other vermin and plump larvae wriggled up her legs. All made their own way and she said, "I am of the hive. Eat of me and understand."

She did not scream nor run, but stood, her form limned in an odd moving pointillism. When an hour had come and gone, the insects pulled back as if one and departed. Where they had been, nothing remained; not bone, nor hair, nor flesh, nor sinew. It was as if she had never been.

*HER NAME COULD have easily been Deborah or Melissa or Mariposa, as would befit a benefactor of insects. Swarmings happen from time to time near urban centers yet no specific incident can be pinpointed in North America where a woman was consumed by insects. There is no extant evidence that she existed under any of these names; that she wasn't a myth generated for a troubled world of the new millennium.*

*Is this a metaphor in which Libby imparts her knowledge to the insect race, raising them up to the next level of evolution? Indeed, praying mantises have been known to lose wings and then regain them in a single generation—a startling discovery even before the* Apocrypha *were created.*

*More disturbing is a concept in which few scientists give credence (indeed, they refuse to even look at it), that Libby did indeed pass the mantle of a superior thinking race onto insects, and that homo sapiens' days are numbered. The aforementioned child with compound eyes supports this belief. She not only exhibits the ocular anatomy of Insecta, but displays disturbing digestive traits as well as the ability to communicate and direct insects in hive activities. However, this mutation also supports the argument that due to climatic and environmental changes the human race is evolving into something . . . else.*

*There are only four* Apocrypha *(Discovery, Experimentation, Research, and Metamorphosis), which coincidentally compare to the four stages of insect growth: egg, larva, pupa, and imago. Since the appearance of the first* Apocrypha, *global warming and pollution have seen the extinction of many amphibious species that kept insect populations in check. As well, entomologists have recorded a change in hymenoptera hive and colony organizations and structure, as well as the evolution of some other orders into new, highly organized social structures.*

*The question most debated about the* Insecta Apocrypha *is who wrote them? If Libby did exist and if she did not write them, then the only living beings that saw her deeds were the insects.*[7]

---

**COLLEEN ANDERSON** was once dubbed the Splatterqueen at Clarion West but believes that she has refined the horror since then. Her fiction and poetry have appeared in over 100 publications with newer works in *Alison's Wonderland, Shroud Magazine,* and *Evolve: Vampire Stories of the New Undead.* She is assistant poetry editor at *Chizine.* Other pieces will be coming out in *New Vampire Tales* and *I Do, I Do,* an erotic wedding anthology (and that's scary). Pieces of her mind can be found at www.colleenanderson.wordpress.com.

---

[7] *Exegesis* Shapiro, "Conclusion" 198-220

# EDITOR'S REQUEST

---

DEAR READER, FAN, OR SUPPORTER,
It's a dreadful commentary that the worth of indie publications is measured by online 5-star reviews, but such is the state of current commerce.

Should you have enjoyed this book, gratitude is most appreciated by posting a brief and honest online review at Amazon.com, Goodreads.com, and/or a highly-visible blog.

With sincerest thanks,

Eric J. Guignard
Series Editor, +*Horror Library*+ (vol. 6 onward)

# ALSO FROM ERIC J. GUIGNARD AND DARK MOON BOOKS:

## A WORLD OF HORROR

Every nation of the globe has unique tales to tell, whispers that settle in through the land, creatures or superstitions that enliven the night, but rarely do readers get to experience such a diversity of these voices in one place as in *A WORLD OF HORROR*, the latest anthology book created by award-winning editor Eric J. Guignard, and beautifully illustrated by artist Steve Lines.

Enclosed within its pages are twenty-two all-new dark and speculative fiction stories written by authors from around the world that explore the myths and monsters, fables and fears of their homelands.

Encounter the haunting things that stalk those radioactive forests outside Chernobyl in Ukraine; sample the curious dishes one may eat in Canada; beware the veldt monster that mirrors yourself in Uganda; or simply battle mountain trolls alongside Alfred Nobel in Sweden. These stories and more are found within *A World of Horror*: Enter and discover, truly, there's no place on the planet devoid of frights, thrills, and wondrous imagination.

"This breath of fresh air for horror readers shows the limitless possibilities of the genre."
—*Publishers Weekly* (starred review)

"This is the book we need right now!"
—*Becky Spratford; librarian, reviewer,* RA for All: Horror

"A fresh collection of horror authors exploring monsters and myths from their homelands."
—*Library Journal*

Order your copy at www.darkmoonbooks.com or www.amazon.com
ISBN-13: 978-0-9989383-1-8

# ALSO FROM ERIC J. GUIGNARD AND DARK MOON BOOKS:

## EXPLORING DARK SHORT FICTION #2: A PRIMER TO KAARON WARREN

Australian author Kaaron Warren is widely recognized as one of the leading writers today of speculative and dark short fiction. She's published four novels, multiple novellas, and well over one hundred heart-rending tales of horror, science fiction, and beautiful fantasy, and is the first author ever to simultaneously win all three of Australia's top speculative fiction writing awards (Ditmar, Shadows, and Aurealis awards for *The Grief Hole*).

Dark Moon Books and editor Eric J. Guignard bring you this introduction to her work, the second in a series of primers exploring modern masters of literary dark short fiction. Herein is a chance to discover—or learn more of—the distinct voice of Kaaron Warren, as beautifully illustrated by artist Michelle Prebich.

Included within these pages are:

- Six short stories, one written exclusively for this book
- Author interview
- Complete bibliography
- Academic commentary by Michael Arnzen, PhD (former humanities chair and professor of the year, Seton Hill University)
- . . . and more!

Enter this doorway to the vast and fantastic: Get to know Kaaron Warren.

Order your copy at www.darkmoonbooks.com or www.amazon.com
ISBN-13: 978-0-9989383-0-1

# ALSO FROM ERIC J. GUIGNARD AND DARK MOON BOOKS:

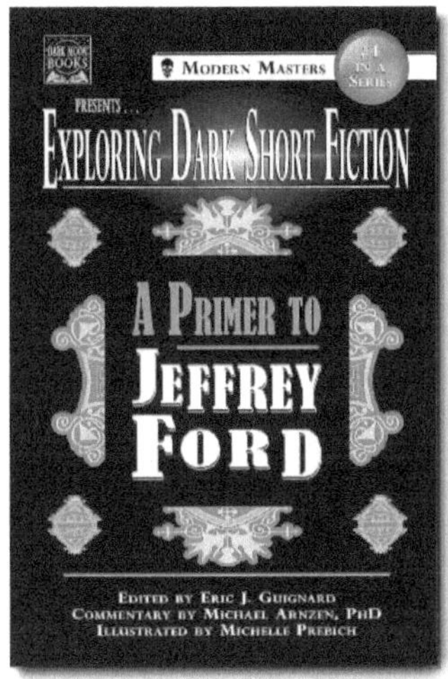

**EXPLORING DARK SHORT FICTION #4:**
**A PRIMER TO JEFFREY FORD**

Author of the fantastic and the bizarre, Jeffrey Ford's work has won awards and acclaim across the globe for his stories of humor, horror, and unconventional beauty. "Powerful and disturbing in the best possible way" (*Gawker*) and "Intensely engaging" (*Publishers Weekly*), Ford crosses speculative genres with literary ideals, which has earned him the World Fantasy Award (seven times), the Shirley Jackson Award (four times), the Edgar Allan Poe Award, and France's vaunted *Grand Prix de l'Imaginaire*.

Dark Moon Books and editor Eric J. Guignard bring you this introduction to his work, the fourth in a series of primers exploring modern masters of literary dark short fiction. Herein is a chance to discover—or learn more of—the extraordinary voice of Jeffrey Ford, as beautifully illustrated by artist Michelle Prebich.

Included within these pages are:

- Six short stories, one written exclusively for this book
- Author interview
- Complete bibliography
- Academic commentary by Michael Arnzen, PhD (former humanities chair and professor of the year, Seton Hill University)
- . . . and more!

Enter this doorway to the vast and fantastic: Get to know Jeffrey Ford.

# THE CRIME FILES OF KATY GREEN by GENE O'NEILL:

Discover why readers have been applauding this stark, fast-paced noir series by multiple-award-winning author, Gene O'Neill, and follow the dark murder mysteries of Sacramento homicide detectives Katy Green and Johnny Cato, dubbed by the press as Sacramento's "Green Hornet and Cato"!

### Book #1: DOUBLE JACK (a novella)

400-pound serial killer Jack Malenko has discovered the perfect cover: He dresses as a CalTrans worker and preys on female motorists in distress in full sight of passing traffic. How fast can Katy Green and Johnny Cato track him down before he strikes again?

**ISBN-13: 978-0-9988275-6-8**

### Book #2: SHADOW OF THE DARK ANGEL

Bullied misfit, Samuel Kubiak, is visited by a dark guardian angel who helps Samuel gain just vengeance. There hasn't been a case yet Katy and Johnny haven't solved, but now how can they track a psychopathic suspect that comes and goes in the shadows?

**ISBN-13: 978-0-9988275-8-2**

### Book #3: DEATHFLASH

Billy Williams can see the soul as it departs the body, and is "commanded to do the Lord's work," which he does fanatically, slaying drug addicts in San Francisco…Katy and Johnny investigate the case as junkies die all around, for Billy has his own addiction: the rush of viewing the *Deathflash*.

**ISBN-13: 978-0-9988275-9-9**

Order your copy at www.darkmoonbooks.com or www.amazon.com